IN ORBIT OFF THE WELL WORLD

The system didn't amount to much—just one lone planet orbiting a yellow G-type star in a perfect circle. But the planet was extraordinary beyond the perfection of its orbit. Not huge, not imposing, it glistened like a fantastic Christmas-tree bulb, perfectly round, with a dark band around its center. Its period of rotation was a little over 28 hours, standard, and it had no axial tilt.

The two hemispheres divided by that dark band were quite dissimilar although both north and south sparkled from the sunlight reflected by hundreds of hexagonal facets. The southern hemisphere was blue and white, home to seven hundred and eighty carbon-based races, each in its own hexagonal biosphere; the north, swirling with yellows, purples, and oranges, supported seven hundred and eighty races based on other substances and breathing esoteric gasses—if, in fact, they breathed at all.

By Jack L. Chalker
Published by Ballantine Books:

THE WEB OF THE CHOZEN

AND THE DEVIL WILL DRAG YOU UNDER

A JUNGLE OF STARS

DANCERS IN THE AFTERGLOW

THE SAGA OF THE WELL WORLD
Volume 1: *Midnight at the Well of Souls*
Volume 2: *Exiles at the Well of Souls*
Volume 3: *Quest for the Well of Souls*
Volume 4: *The Return of Nathan Brazil*
Volume 5: Twilight at the Well of Souls:
The Legacy of Nathan Brazil

THE FOUR LORDS OF THE DIAMOND
Book One: *Lilith: A Snake in the Grass*
Book Two: *Cerberus: A Wolf in the Fold*
Book Three: *Charon: A Dragon at the Gate*
Book Four: *Medusa: A Tiger by the Tail*

THE DANCING GODS
Book One: *The River of Dancing Gods*
Book Two: *Demons of the Dancing Gods*
Book Three: *Vengeance of the Dancing Gods*

THE RINGS OF THE MASTER
Book One: *Lords of the Middle Dark*

THE Return OF Nathan Brazil

Volume 4 of
THE SAGA OF THE WELL WORLD

Jack L. Chalker

A Del Rey Book

BALLANTINE BOOKS • NEW YORK

A Del Rey Book
Published by Ballantine Books

Library of Congress Catalog Card Number: 79-90103

ISBN 0-345-34105-8

Printed in Canada

First Edition: January 1980
Eighth Printing: February 1987

Cover art by Darrell K. Sweet

Contents

This one is for the old gang: Alan Mole, Harry Brashear, Mike Leib, John Yox, and Bernard Zerwitz, all of whom, including me, turned out a hell of a lot better than anybody would have had a right to expect. . . .

THE WELL
Section of

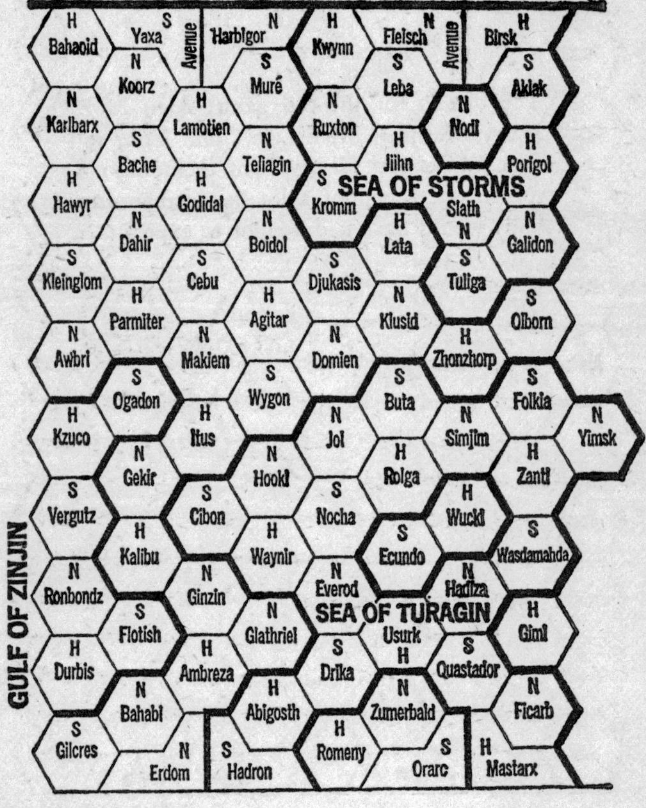

WORLD
Southern Hemisphere

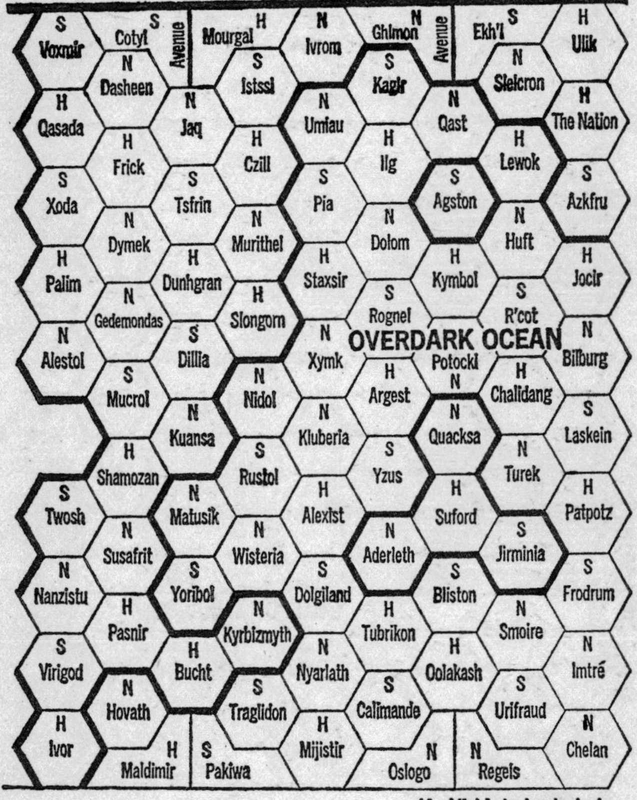

H—Highly technological
S—Semitechnological
N—Nontechnological

Parkatin, on the Frontier

IT WOULD HAVE BEEN FAR EASIER FOR HAR BATEEN to conquer the world if he had had a cold. Unfortunately, the Dreel automatically cleaned up the bodies they used; so this time conquest had to be the hard way.

Slabansport was a typical frontier capital; the spaceport was small but modern, mainly used by orbital shuttles ferrying imports from the huge freighters that called regularly. Near it, of course, were the bars and dives common to any port, as well as the warehouses, shipping centers, and local headquarters of the companies that fueled the opening of the frontier. The town itself, the largest on Parkatin, held barely twenty thousand. That would change, of course; already the burnt, brown deserts had bloomed for a thousand kilometers around Slabansport as imported soils and pipelines from distant water sources provided the moisture it craved. Parkatin was a hot, dry world, but it had water vapor and convection thunderstorms, and it would make a home for another billion humans in another generation or so.

Not, of course, for the benefit of humanity if the Dreel had anything to say about it. Colonies of them were there now, looking through Har Bateen's eyes at the seedy little bar just off the spaceport, so confident of success in breeding these animals and expanding to provide a massive new living spot on Parkatin for Dreel colonies which would inhabit and interact through the host animals in the same way that the Dreel were now using the body of Har Bateen.

The Dreel were incredibly complex organisms, yet the smallest organic life known to exist in the galaxy, perhaps the universe. They lived by the billions in the brain and blood and tissue of other organisms in a communal one-ness of self; all other organisms were mere animals to house more of them as far as they were concerned.

Har Bateen walked into the bar and took a stool at the wooden rail itself. There weren't too many customers yet. No ships were in port, but at least two were due over the next day or so, and that was really why he was there. Parkatin would be simple to overcome. It was here, through spaceterminals like Slabansport that travelers to other worlds—some in systems still unknown to the Dreel—passed. And one of those, sent home with the Dreel, meant a whole new planetary conquest operation.

Because ships *were* due, a full staff was on hand; prostitutes and gamblers and fast-buck artists were around, waiting, waiting for their "marks" which would include not only crew and passengers from the ships but also those who would arrive to unload and distribute the new goods.

Bateen ordered a drink and flashed a big roll as he paid for it, tipping much too generously. That drew some stares from the waiters, and a dozen minds were already mulling over the best approach to the well-heeled sucker.

Finally, it was Roza who made the first move: Roza, the queen of the local prosititutes, who still looked damned attractive despite her years and the hard life and who was so tough the others would stand back rather than challenge her right to the "mark." He had a big roll; there would be plenty left for other people. She slid silently up to him and sat, relaxed, on the stool next to his. "Buy me a drink?" she asked in a voice both low and sexy.

He smiled outwardly and inwardly, nodded, drained the last of his, and ordered for the two of them. The bar system was a standard one; the women, the men, the gamblers and whores, all worked for the place. The drinks arrived, his at least a dozen times more potent than normal and laced with an aphrodisiac. Hers was basically colored water.

They drank together and he went through the motions. Good scouting was essential to missions like this; some of the Dreel among his colony carried knowledge from the earliest takeovers to the latest tests on human subjects, and all such information was at Har's fingertips. As the Dreel divided to form new colonies the parent members imparted their information to the offspring. How, this Dreel colony mused with total confidence and satisfaction, could any mere animal compete with an organism like theirs? None ever had—and these would be no exception.

And so he went through all the motions, did the proper rituals, said and responded to the right code words, and within a short time the two were off to the back room of the bar. On the way the Dreel cleansed Har's internal system of the drugs and other contaminants, but slowly, through the pores. He would smell less than wonderful, but even if she were to notice she'd still go through with it.

They walked down a dungy corridor and he could see the occasional shapes of others, both male and female, resting, waiting in small rooms and cubicles, junior to Roza, but employees all the same. That was good, according to plan.

By getting there early, before the crowd, and flashing the roll, he'd been assured of getting the boss in such traffic. Take over the boss and then let the boss work on the underlings. Then, when the off-worlders came for their services they would actually pay to be taken over as new Dreel hosts. A perfect set-up.

The Dreel adapted quickly to any new host organism, but after that future generations would settle into the predetermined pattern. In the case of those inside Har Bateen they were most comfortable at thirty-seven degrees Celsius; too much lower, even a degree or two, would kill them. Something like kissing, though, was just perfect.

They reached a room, obviously hers because it was large and spacious and comfortable in comparison to the monastic cells of her underlings, and she quickly stripped and asked, coyly, "Okay, how do you want it?"

He smiled. "Let's just kiss for starters," he suggested.

He pulled her body to him, leaned down slightly and kissed her. She opened her mouth wide as did he, and tongues met, saliva was exchanged.

And with it went about ten thousand Dreel.

He kept at it a while, to make certain the transfer was complete, then continued in the normal manner she would expect, as the colony checked out its new host, found the right cells and nerves and message centers, and began a cycle of rapid reproduction to permit ease in takeover. Using the proteins in her body, they could duplicate themselves every thirty seconds, although to do so for very long would invite weakening her, perhaps even killing her. The mathematics loci of the Bateen colony had already done the calculations for exactly how much they could get away with.

In the meantime, Har Bateen continued the sexual play. They were several minutes into it before he detected an unnatural convulsion inside her. In the first ten minutes the Dreel had increased inside her to almost forty-one thousand in number.

Born with full knowledge, they wasted no time getting to their posts inside the body, riding the circulatory system around to where they were most needed, the brain and spinal column.

She suddenly released him and went limp, a puzzled expression on her face; she looked drawn, slightly worn and perspiring, as the Dreel used more and more of her own materials to duplicate themselves.

" 'Scuth me," she gasped, voice slurred, "I—I don' feel so good. Feel funny . . ."

He rolled away from her, off the bed, and stood, watching her with satisfaction. Her body was convulsing now, as nerves and muscles were placed under different control and tested. She jerked spasmodically on the bed, first as if in an epileptic fit, then, slower now, with more care, like a puppet on thousands of strings.

And then she was still, breathing hard but otherwise quiet. He went over to his clothes and took out a plain white box inside of which were a number of thick, chewy cakes. He brought them to her and offered them wordlessly.

She sat up unsteadily and reached out, took one of the cakes, and ate it greedily. In a very short time she'd consumed the whole box. There wouldn't always be time to replace the metabolized materials quickly, but the key transfer had to be in the best shape. The others—well, that was the risk of being a soldier.

Finally she finished and looked up at him. "We are in complete control," she assured him in language the woman Roza had never known much less heard before, a language so alien it seemed hardly possible to be coming out of a human throat.

"It is good," he responded in the same tongue, then turned and dressed. In a moment she did likewise. He watched her critically, trying to detect any flaws, any differences, but there were none to his eye. Her walk, her manner, all were down pat. Nor would she slip in more personal ways. The personality, the psyche, the spirit or whatever you call it of Roza was dead; but her memories, locked in the protein molecules of her brain, were still there. She knew everything that Roza had known, yet more, for the Dreel had ready access to all of the brain.

He started to leave but she stopped him. "Best to wait another ten minutes," she cautioned in her old, human tongue. Even the accent was perfect. "Podi and the others would get suspicious if we pulled that fast a 'quickie'."

He nodded understandingly. "You know best," he admitted and sat down on the side of the bed.

It was a deadly slow way to conquer a world, but it was most effective.

The hot sun beat down on the body of Har Bateen as he left the little bar. He was oblivious to heat, oblivious to anything that did not cause permanent harm to the host and habitat of the Dreel. He walked toward the spaceport, noting with satisfaction the large crowds of dockworkers gathering with their machines to unload as the first of the big ships came in. The large freighter shuttles sat humming on the pads, waiting for word that a mother ship was in orbit and ready to unload.

It was tempting to wade into the crowd, to get close, to try some air contact spreading, but it would be too obvious and the takeover itself would attract too much attention, even stop the unloading. The Dreel didn't want to do that, not at all.

The pattern had worked for a long, long time. Slowly, with deliberation and infinite patience, a world —world after world—could be taken over without anyone even knowing until it was too late, often without a single alarm being sounded. The Dreel were immortal through their inherited memories passed on to each new generation, but they were not physically immortal nor uncaring about life. If they had been, they would hardly have bothered to take over other places and races at all. Militarily, this was the most life-efficient method they'd ever developed in their nearly forty thousand years of glorious, unimpeded conquest. And yet each species was different, each race a new challenge. The Dreel loved the challenge of it all more than anything, and each victory was further proof of their superiority to all other lifeforms.

With time to kill, Har Bateen noticed a small crowd gathering curiously around a pair of creatures only one of whom was "human."

The man was tall and thin and looked as if he'd been through a pretty rough life; baggy trousers and well-worn shoes, a tattered vest over a thin, hairy bare chest; a long, almost triangular face that hadn't been shaved in a week. His thick, black hair was wrapped in a crude bandana of some sort, almost turban-like.

A true Gypsy, Har Bateen noted with surprise. It was there in the preliminary scouting reports that such a group existed, but just about no one had ever seen one. Not even any of those people gathering around him, Bateen felt sure.

As Bateen wandered closer, curiosity and boredom drawing him to the show just as it had drawn the human beings waiting for the freighters, the Gypsy took an odd sort of reed flute from his pocket and began to play an odd, almost hypnotic tune that caused the other with him to begin a dance.

His companion was strange indeed—about half the man's height, no more than a meter high, surely—

with shimmering blue-green scales along a reptilian body. Two thick legs ending in long, nasty claws supported the torso. He stood upright, although leaning slightly forward, and had two long, spindly arms that ended in tiny, clawed hands. The face was also lizard-like, although it held none of the rigidity of a reptilian head; it was as if a giant lizard had the muscular facial mobility of a human.

Perhaps most incongruously it was clothed in the same sort of baggy garments as the Gypsy, though shoeless, of course—no shoe made could fit those odd, oversized feet. It was as agile as a monkey, and it danced wildly to the haunting melody of the flute, faster, ever faster as the tempo picked up, its long tail acting almost as a third leg in a multi-limbed dance.

But this was only the beginning; it was moving so fast that the sunlight reflected from tens of thousands of scales giving it the appearance of sparkling with as many rhinestones; the effect was brilliant and added to the hypnotic power of the alien music. And now the crowd stood back, awed in spite of itself, appreciating the strange scene.

The lizard now formed an oval with his mouth, an incredible sight on such a serpentine face, and there was the sound of a great amount of air rumbling about somewhere inside. Now it came out in a steady *whoosh,* and the watchers gasped. Fire! He was exhaling fire and forming patterns with it! Circles, whirls, shapes odd and familiar appeared and vanished in split seconds while the lizard yet danced, a sparkling blur.

The Gypsy continued to play, but as he did his steel-gray eyes rested not on his lizard companion but on the crowd, looking at them one by one. Studying them, analyzing them.

Even the Dreel who were camouflaged inside the body and mind of Har Bateen were captivated. This was beyond their experience and they shared its alien grace and beauty with the others.

And now it was over suddenly, without fanfare, the last note and the last blazing sparkles faded into the hot, dry air so that only memory remained of the haunting, strange performance.

The crowd stood there, transfixed, still stunned by this performance, not saying a word, or acting in any way until, suddenly, one, then more snapped out of his trance and applauded. The applause quickly rose to a crescendo of cheers and whistles as well as clapping.

The Gypsy bowed slightly, acknowledging the tribute, and even the lizard-creature seemed to nod toward each one in the audience in turn. The strange man put his flute away and waited for the appreciation to subside. Finally he said, in a clear but oddly accented low tenor, "Citizens, we thank you, both my friend and I."

"Do it again!" somebody shouted, and there were nods and murmurs. "Yeah, more! More!" others called out, adding to the din.

The Gypsy smiled. "Thank you, my friends, we would be delighted to do so—but we must eat, and my friend here has a bigger appetite than do I. Some token of appreciation—Marquoz!—would be most gratifying."

At the name "Marquoz" the little dragon snorted, looked up at the man, and seemed to smile—a grotesque smile that revealed the nastiest set of teeth anybody there ever remembered—and then picked up a bag and advanced slowly on the crowd. They started moving nervously back.

The Gypsy laughed. "My friends, do not fear Marquoz! He will not eat you. He wishes only what I wish, money to purchase some more civilized food. Just a coin in his little bag, one coin, gentle citizens, and perhaps we shall have our eats and you another dance, hey?"

The braver ones in the crowd stopped retreating and when the lizard reached them and held out the bag, tossed one or two coins in. It became a torrent after a moment, quickly filling the bag.

"Enough! You are too kind!" the Gypsy called out. "Marquoz?"

The lizard snorted, startling the people closest to him because two puffs of white smoke exploded from his nostrils when he did. Then he turned and brought the bag back to the Gypsy. It was heavy now, and the man was thin, yet the bag somehow seemed to vanish, coins and all, into some hidden nether-space on his person. He smiled, bowed again, and produced the flute once more.

The second performance resembled the first yet was a totally different dance with totally different moves and strange fiery shapes to a different yet no less alien, and exotic, tune.

Har Bateen stood through the second performance, admiring it with the rest. Finally when the applause had died down and the Gypsy protested that Marquoz needed a rest, they started to break up and resume their milling around.

The Gypsy bent down, apparently to inspect the stoic Marquoz, and a large human hand slipped into that of the lizard. Small, spidery clawed fingers tapped idly at the man's palm. He nodded, then got back up and looked around.

Several people approached to talk to him, admire Marquoz, or ask questions about the strange lizard, but he laughed them away with the excuse that Marquoz had to get out of the hot sun and get a water rubdown. The reasoning seemed a little suspect—the lizard appeared not only comfortable but also more at home in Parkatin's heat than the humans but they accepted his explanation.

They started walking toward the strip of honkey-tonks and bars, away from the freight docks, two pair of eyes on Har Bateen.

The collective experience of the Dreel made few mistakes; getting tailed was not one of them. Bateen realized the odd pair was behind him—they were hardly inconspicuous in any event. That worried him—first, he'd obviously done something to arouse suspicion and hadn't the slightest idea what; second, a pair following so obviously meant that others were almost certainly about.

Well, so be it, the Dreel agent decided. Best to see what we're dealing with, anyway. He led them a merry path up and down streets and alleyways, always trying to spot the ones he *knew* must be following less obtrusively but never catching sight of them. The Gypsy was obviously Com Police. The Dreel admired the technique even as he was still confused to its method. A Gypsy went anywhere, out into the open, but into the worst places and the worst neighborhoods without attracting suspicion—and even if the man couldn't take care of himself, his big pet with its thousands of sharp teeth would certainly work against any surprise attacks.

And with that Har Bateen thought he guessed it. So obvious—yet no shadows. Why? Because they knew he wouldn't lead them anywhere, would only go up and down the dockfront streets. And one of those streets was a trap. They would wait. Wait for Har Bateen to panic and walk or run into the setup. He could try to lose them, of course—but that would be a betrayal of guilt. They could shoot him. He had important things to do; Har Bateen did not want to die at all, but particularly not right now.

He had about a fifteen-meter lead on them, although they were slowly closing on him. That was a lot of space. He chose his alley well, then turned into it quickly, as if making his break.

The Gypsy and the lizard speeded up; it was obvious that the little dragon could far outrun the man, but he stuck with him. They turned the corner into the alleyway on the run—and found themselves in a dead end, with tall buildings on all three sides.

The Gypsy whipped out a pistol with the same dexterity with which he'd pocketed the bag of coins and from the same apparent place. He looked up and around.

"Drop it *now!*" commanded the voice of Har Bateen not only from above but from *behind* them.

The Gypsy did not drop it immediately, but turned slowly, looking in the direction of the voice. Spotting the man, he sighed and dropped the pistol to the alley. He didn't know how Bateen had managed it but the Dreel now sat on a small ledge a good six meters up. He must climb like a monkey, the Gypsy thought. The walls were ribbed block, but *he* couldn't have made it up there in that length of time.

The Dreel stared uneasily at the dragon, who stared back at him with blazing eyes, catlike black ovals against a dark scarlet backdrop.

"Don't try siccing your big pet on me," Bateen warned. "Just keep him there."

The man nodded back and said out of the corner of his mouth, "Marquoz! Stay!"

The dragon snorted and seemed to grumble a little but sat back on his tail and relaxed slightly.

"All right, now, who are you and why are you following me?" the Dreel challenged.

The Gypsy grinned apologetically and spread his hands. "When we take the collection, you see, we often get to see who has the biggest bankroll. Marquoz, here, can be, ah, *very* persuasive for such a one to, ah, substantially increase his donation to us. We have been stuck in this god-forsaken hole of a planet for much too long. Business is not good—we were, ah, asked to leave the ship here, not our scheduled stop, and we have not yet been able to make our expenses and our fares out. And, to make it short, the local cops are wise to us."

The Dreel considered the explanation. It made sense—and the bankroll he had was more than apparent and was meant to be so. Still, there was something here that didn't ring true. For ones who'd been on this planet long enough to acquire a bad reputation why were they so obviously a novelty to the crowd? Bateen decided to take no chances.

"All right—that thing, there. What is it?" he demanded.

The Gypsy looked toward Marquoz, impassively sitting on his big tail. "I met him on a backwater frontier planet. He wasn't native to it; he belonged to a number of my fellow tribesmen who had been asked, shall we say, to stay a while by the local police. About three years, actually. I, of course, agreed to take him in a flash, and he took to me as well. I have no idea where they picked him up."

That didn't tell the Dreel much, but, then again, there were a lot odder lifeforms than Marquoz around not excluding the Dreel themselves. The story had the ring of truth—and the final clincher was the Gypsy's pistol. Not the supermodern type the Com Police would use, all gleaming and near-transparent with its ruby power source. Just a common tramp's pistol, a small laser driller, just like somebody of the Gypsy's type might carry.

"I'm coming down now," Bateen warned, "but as you can tell I am very good at athletics. My pistol won't stray from you even as I break my fall, and it's on wide kill."

"Look, all I want now is out of this. A mistake, that's all," the Gypsy alibied sincerely.

The Dreel nodded and jumped down. The Gypsy was amazed at the man's body and muscle control. He hadn't been kidding—the pistol stayed pointed directly at him. No human being he'd ever seen short of a professional gymnast could do that, and this character hardly looked the gymnastic type.

The Dreel approached the man slowly, one eye on Marquoz. "No funny business," he warned.

"What—what are you going to do?" the Gypsy asked uneasily, eyes only on the pistol.

Har Bateen allowed himself the very human gesture of a smile, a smile of one who knows what you do not. "Don't worry," he told the Gypsy. "I'm not going to kill you. If your pet stays calm and you don't try anything funny, then nothing will happen to you. But your life depends on your doing exactly what I say—*exactly!* Understand?"

The Gypsy nodded slowly, the fear in his eyes not lessened one bit by the assurances.

The Dreel walked cautiously in back of the man. "Take off your vest," he ordered.

The Gypsy looked confused. "This some kind of a sex thing?"

"In a way," his captor responded. "Don't worry—it won't hurt you in the least. Better than getting smeared all over the place, isn't it?"

Marquoz simply sat and watched. Bateen took a small blade from his pocket. "Just take it easy. A very small cut, nothing more." He saw the man flinch for the quick pricking, then watched with satisfaction as a small drop of blood formed at the puncture. He sliced a small hole in his thumb.

Instantly Dreel rushed to the opening, the capillaries of the hand and the edge of the thumb, then halted, waiting for contact. There had been plenty of time; a full team of ten thousand memory units had been assembled and waiting.

Har Bateen eagerly held the thumb toward the cut on the man's back. So confident was he now that he took his glance off the dragon sitting only a few meters away.

"Hold it! Freeze!" came a voice to his left, a voice incredibly deep and gravelly as if coming from a giant speaking through a hollow tube. "Drop the gun and stand away from him!"

Bateen was so startled he *did* freeze and his eyes looked over at the source of the sound.

The giant lizard was standing there, eyeing him coldly with those blazing scarlet eyes and in its hand was a Fuka machine pistol, made of an almost transparent material, with its red power center blazing; it would almost control the wielder, shoot the level and type of force its holder thought of. A pistol keyed to its individual owner; the kind of pistol only one authority possessed.

"Marquoz, of the Com Police," the dragon said unnecessarily. "I said drop it and stand away."

"But . . . but you *can't*—you're not *human,*" the Dreel protested. Intelligence said nothing about this!

"Neither are you, bub," the dragon responded. "I consider that your only redeeming social feature."

Hodukai, a Planet on the Frontier

THEY FILLED THE TEMPLE; IT WAS A GOOD SIGN, Mother Sukra thought to herself as she looked out from behind the stage curtain. The Acolytes had done a wonderful job of carrying the Word. Most were first-timers, she saw. Hesitating, nervous, unsure, but curious. That, too, was to be expected. The Fellowship of the Holy Well was still new here, and attractive mostly to the young, the most impressionable always, and the poor, the starving, the losers. The Holy Priestess, too, would know this and be pleased by the newcomers and the demonstrated effectiveness of Mother Sukra's organization after only a few months.

The High Priestess *was* pleased—and excited, although she betrayed none of this in her classically stoic manner. She had been in this position before, although not with so much of responsibility.

The lights were going down; stirring music, subtle, soothing subsonics, set the mood and soft lights caressed both audience and stage. She looked at Mother Sukra, now checking herself one last time in the mirror, smoothing her long saffron robes and touching up her long brown hair. Her timing was impeccable, though; she stopped at precisely the right moment and turned to walk on stage to the center spot. There was no dais, no podium tonight, no pulpit from on high; that would spoil the effect they wanted from the Holy Priestess.

Mother Sukra looked terribly alone on the barren stage.

Along the sides the robed men and women, the Acolytes, heads shaved and wearing only loose-fitting cloth robes, rose and bowed to her. A number of the audience took the cue and stood, and within a short period most of the hall was standing. Normal crowd reaction; the ones remaining seated were not those to whom they would be speaking. Later, she thought. Later all would come willingly.

"Be at peace!" Mother Sukra proclaimed, and raised her arms to the heavens.

"Peace be unto the creatures of the Universe, no matter what form they be," the Acolytes—and some in the audience—responded.

"This night we are honored to be graced with the presence of Her Holiness the Priestess Yua of the Mother Church," Sukra told them needlessly. Curiosity over Yua's appearance explained the large crowd at a service normally attended only by the few hundred devout. The audience was entirely human, which was to be expected, too. Although the Com now contained no fewer than seven races, only three or four were commonly seen in large cities on the human worlds and none in Temples, which they considered racially xenophobic. While the Temple was open to all races, its doctrine was not one to appeal to nonhuman types.

Unless, of course, you were an Olympian.

Everybody knew about the Olympians, but nobody knew much about them at one and the same time. Few had ever seen one; they were secretive and clannish. Their world was such that no one could live on it without a spacesuit, yet the Olympians could live comfortably on any of the human worlds. They ran their own shipping company and flew their own ships; sales were handled by an Olympian-owned but human-run trading company—no salesmen need apply to Olympus.

Such conditions breed an insatiable curiosity in people, but there was more. The Olympians were said to be stunningly beautiful women; no one had ever seen a male. Beautiful women with tails, like horse's tails, who all, it was said, looked exactly alike.

There was a full house on this frontier world waiting to see an Olympian for the simple reason that the Fellowship of the Well had arisen on Olympus; the Mother Temple was there; and, while humans were the congregation and humans ran the Temples, the Olympians alone could be the High Priestesses.

Oh, they were there, all right—the local press, the politicos, the just plain curious. They sat and shuffled and suffered through Mother Sukra's mummery and chants as they waited to see just what an Olympian was really like.

Finally Mother Sukra finished, and her voice assumed an awed tone.

"Tonight, my children, we are honored to present Her Holiness the High Priestess of our Fellowship, Yua of Olympus."

The audience sat up now, expectant, watching as first Mother Sukra walked off then eyeing the curtains on either side of the stage to catch the first glimpse of the priestess.

Yua paused, leaving the stage vacant for thirty seconds or so to heighten the suspense, then she strode purposefully out to the center. The lights dimmed and a spotlight illuminated an area dead center stage and almost to the extreme front, its stream of light forming a bright aura that seemed to make her even more supernatural.

She heard the whispers of "There she is!" and "So that's an Olympian"—the last said in many different ways—with satisfaction. She wore a cloak of the finest silk, or some synthetic close to it, embroidered with gold leaf. It concealed her form to the floor, but even those far back in the hall were struck by the classic beauty of her face and the long, auburn hair that swept down past her waist.

"Be at peace, my children," Yua opened, her voice low, incredibly soft, and sexy. "I am here to bless this Temple and its congregation, and to tell those of you here who came out of curiosity or interest of our beliefs and our way."

She could sense the mixture of awe at her presence —she knew well how stunning she appeared to the humans—and disappointment that they were seeing no more than this. She did not intend to disappoint the voyeurs, but not before the message was delivered, not until it would mean something.

"I come from a planet we call Olympus," she began,

and that got their attention again. Not only was she erotically charismatic, but this promised to be informative. "Our Founding Mothers discovered the world, which had been passed over by the Com as it was not a place where one could survive without prohibitively expensive modification or sealed domes, like the dead worlds of the Markovians. But *we* could survive there, build there, grow and prosper there, and we have."

She had them now; a cough was conspicuous in the big hall. They had come expecting the kind of cultism and mummery Mother Sukra had done. They had not expected to be addressed so practically on matters of common curiosity and therefore interest in such plain terms. They listened.

"We resemble you, and we are from your seed, but we are not like you. We were insensitive to many extremes of heat and cold, able to filter out poisons in alien waters and hostile atmospheres, and we need no special suits or equipment to help us. Listen well and I will tell you the story of our people, yours and mine, and of our beliefs."

She paused. Perfect. Nobody stirred.

"Yours is a frontier world," she reminded them. "Still rough, still raw. Most, perhaps all of you, were born of other stars. You are all, then, widely traveled in space. You know of the ruins of the Markovians on dead worlds, a mysterious race that left dead computers deep inside their planets and shells of cities without artifacts. You know that once this race inhabited most of the galaxy, and that it vanished long before humanity was born."

Some heads nodded. The Markovian puzzle was well known to everybody by now. Hundreds, perhaps thousands of dead worlds, had been found as humanity had spread ever outward. They were old, incredibly old, *impossibly* old since they appeared to date back almost to the formation of the universe.

"They were the first civilization. They grew and spread and reached godhood itself, their computers giving them everything they could ever desire merely for the wishing. And yet this was not enough; they grew stale, bored, unable to take joy in life. And so they decided to abandon their godhood, begin anew as new races of the Universe. They created a great computer, the Well of Souls, and they placed it at the center of the Universe, and on this computer world they created new races, all of the races of the Universe out of their very selves. Their old world grew silent while their creations, tested on the world of the Well, became the new masters of creation—our own people among them. At last all were gone; they were transformed into our ancestors, and the Markovians were us and we were the Markovians."

A number of the better educated nodded at this account. It was an old theory, one of thousands advanced to explain the Markovian mystery.

"But even as this is truth, for we all know of it, a puzzle remains, the eternal, ultimate question. The Markovians rose near the beginning of time; they were the first race, the parents of all who came after. And if this be so, then who created the Markovians?"

An interesting question in metaphysics. There were a number in the crowd who reflected that it didn't really follow even in her premise on the Markovians was correct that anybody had to create the Markovians, but they kept silent.

"Throughout history, humankind—and the other races with whom we have joined in partnership—have had many religions. They have many gods, a few have one god, but all have a single concept of the first creation. All have at their center a chief God, a prime mover, the one who created all else. He exists, my children! He exists and He is still here, still watching our own progress, evaluating us. Our First Mothers knew Him, and He took them to the Well of Souls where they were twice reborn. Through the principles of the Well these First Mothers were made greater than they had been, and they were returned here as a living sign, they and their children and their children's children, that God exists, that the Well exists, that we may attain states much higher than that to which we were born if we but seek Him out. For if we recognize the truth and His great and omnipotent power that is absolute, if we find Him and but ask, a paradise shall be born here, for us. And it is possible to do so, my children. It is possible to find Him if we look, and that is what we all do, all must do, until He is found. For God is among us, children!" Her voice was rising now, the emotional pitch was so effective, so sincere that it bore into even the most cynical in the audience. "He has chosen for some reason, a form like yours. He could be here, tonight, sitting beside one of you, waiting to be asked, to be recognized. We know His name. We have but to ask. To the First Mothers He called Himself Nathan Brazil!"

They were moved by the message and half-convinced, but for some it was a letdown. All the rationality had somehow quickly turned on a questionable point of logic to a matter of faith.

"Are you here, Lord? Is any of you Nathan Brazil?" she called out. No one spoke or made a move. That was better than some places where occasional wags had, in fact, own up to being God, causing a disruption in the service. Once in a while one would be a genuine loony who really believed it, and that was often worse. As much as High Priestess Yua truly wanted to find God, she was secretly glad when no response was made in situations like this.

The pause over, she continued. "Our First Mothers were human once, like you. Now, through the grace of Nathan Brazil and through the Well of Souls, they became something else: Olympians. We are immune to your diseases and have none of our own. We can stand comfortably unclothed at well below zero or near the boiling point of water. We see colors you see not, hear sounds you hear not, and our strength is that of ten ordinary women. If the atmosphere is mostly chlorine, we will breathe it. If it is mostly carbon monoxide, we will breathe it. If it is water, we will breathe it. Even in the vacuum of space we can survive, storing what we need for hours at temperatures that would freeze anyone else. Look upon the Olympian, true child of the Well, and join us in our holy crusade!"

With that the cloak swept back to reveal her full naked body and a collective gasp went up from the audience.

She was 160 centimeters high and looked about seventeen, the most perfect seventeen any had ever seen. Her body was absolute perfection, the combinations of very desirable physical attribute any adolescent male had ever thought of for his dream woman. It was almost impossible to gaze upon such perfection and remain sane, yet none, male or female, cult member or mere onlooker, could tear his or her eyes away. She was Eve still in Eden, and more, much more. She was impossible.

And even her movement was perfect, erotic, fluid, and catlike as only such an Eve could move. Looking straight on, it seemed as if her billowing auburn hair reached to the floor of the stage and beyond, yet now she turned, first to the left, then to the right, so all could see.

"Behold the sign of the truth of the message!" she proclaimed.

She *did* have a tail, equine, and yet, somehow, perfectly matched to her form and looking like it should be there. It was long and bushy and as silky soft as the hair which dropped down to it. She flexed the tail a couple of times, as if to eliminate any doubt as to its reality, although none who saw, doubted in the least.

"There is no other way to explain us, no other way to accept our existence, except through embracing the truth," she told them. "So come! Join us! Seek out God and find Him, and He will grant you Paradise! It is why we are here. We of Olympus are of human ancestry, but we are too few, too few. Nathan Brazil exists! Even our detractors and the Com admit this. He is by their records the oldest living man. You can verify this yourself. Join us! Join our way! Learn to recognize Him, to seek Him out, and a future of eternal bliss is yours!"

The cynics were recovering their wits now, even though they still could not take their eyes off such stunning beauty.

"I leave you now," she intoned. "Go in peace and join our holy cause." The Acolytes were fanning out, at the ready. Later the impressionable ones, the impulsive ones, with cool air in their faces and time to think it over, might hesitate. Grab those now. "See the Acolytes and join us now, this very night! You can only imagine the rewards!"

And she was gone, only her cloak remaining to mark where she had been. She didn't walk off, didn't move a muscle—she simply faded until she was no longer visible. Only her voice remained.

"Now, my children! Now! I bless you all this night!"

People started to move. A trickle at first, then a few more, and still more. The converts, the new blood, seeking the way to such perfection as they had witnessed. A number left, of course—but the bulk of the audience stayed seated, eyes still fixed where but a minute before perfection had stood, still seeing the sight in their mind's eye and afraid to turn away lest they lose it.

The spotlight dimmed, then was no more. The stage was dark for a moment, then soft lights came up as Mother Sukra returned to direct those who wished to join to the proper places. Of the High Priestess there was no sign.

Yua, offstage, peered out at the crowd, and a thrill went through her at the number approaching the Acolytes. She felt good inside, as if she had accomplished a great deal. There were times when it got discouraging, when few were swayed despite it all; but tonight the spirit was within her and the spirit moved them. It was good.

People, mostly Temple members, walked busily back and forth, their eyes glazed with renewed faith and zeal, ignoring her completely, which was understandable since they could not see her. Yet another attribute of the Olympians was in use, the ability to blend into just about any background. It was a good exit and a good way to avoid throngs of people, although, unlike invisibility, it betrayed you if you moved very rapidly. She waited until the coast was clear, then beat it for her downstairs apartment. She felt drained, as she always did after a rally.

That same look of dazed fanaticism was in the eyes of the young couple standing before the robed Acolyte. The Temple member, trained for this sort of thing, looked them over. No more than late teens themselves, he decided.

"You wish to join our holy cause?" he asked seriously. "It is not a step to be taken lightly, yet it is the first step to salvation."

"Oh, yes," they breathed. "We are ready."

"Have you family who is responsible for you?" he asked them. It was a required question and saved a lot of headaches later.

"We are married," the young woman assured him. "Just got a small farm outside Tabak."

"You wish to enter the Fellowship, freely and of your own will?" the Acolyte continued. Standard procedure. It was really a tough job, since the questions could easily break a mood if asked in the wrong tone.

The young couple looked at each other, then back to the Acolyte. "We do," they assured him as one.

The Acolyte was familiar with the type. Small farmers, probably given the land at marriage, both children of farmers who had looked forward to a certain but dull destiny. Now they saw a quick way out.

"Will we . . . travel?" the young man asked.

The Acolyte nodded. "You will see many places and experience many things."

"Will . . . will we see *her* again?" The woman almost sighed.

Again, the Acolyte nodded. "She, or her sisters, are with us as our teachers and our guides."

The couple was quickly accepted and passed on to the more formal processor, whose primary responsibility was to get their zeal on a piece of recorder paper along with their thumbprints in case of later legal challenge. Many times the Com Police and other religions had sent ringers to make sure that the laws were observed. They would be. Cops quickly tired and dropped out of the regimen; the ringers were often the best converts of all, since they were already involved in one faith.

The contract was not a simple one; almost nobody read it, including the ones who weren't for real —those who could read, that is—and none of the Acolytes could remember anyone taking advantage of the offer to have it completely read to them. Such procedures were recorded, of course, also for defense of later legal challenge.

And the contracts *would* be challenged, most of them, by family and friends outside the cult. In effect, they signed over everything they owned to the Mother Church, forever. Under Com law such a contract could be canceled even if not signed under fraud or duress within even days of signing; after that it was "sealed" and even if you later resigned, the Church kept all.

During the next seven days it was the job of expert indoctrinators to see that nobody canceled. It was a measure of effectiveness that few did.

There would be singing and dancing, hugging and kissing, praying and rejoicing in total communal fellowship, as individuality was worn down and the newcomers were kept in an emotionally high state. Recalcitrants during the mass period would see the Holy Priestess herself before they left. They usually didn't leave after that.

It was an easy cult to accept, too. Your bad habits, dietary and otherwise, were discouraged, and peer pressure usually got you into the mold, but they were not prohibited either. Nor, except for the indoctrination period, were they celibate.

They did good works, too. For every proselytizer stalking the streets and spaceports of the thousand human Com Worlds, there were five working in the poorest communities, feeding, clothing, sheltering those in need with no questions asked and displaying no prejudices of any sort. These good works were the more common, although slower, ways of gaining converts.

On the eighth day the young couple would undergo a sacred and solemn ceremony; their clothing and old possessions would be burned in a sacred fire said to have been carried from Olympus, and they would have their heads and bodies shaved and don the robes of the Acolyte. Then would come the full religious study, aided by hypnotics and all other means at the cult's command, until they were so immersed in the dogma and so dependent on the Mother Church for even the most basic things that they thought no other way. Then they would be ready to take to the streets, to ask every stranger if in fact he—or even she—was Nathan Brazil, and to carry out the good works of the Church.

It was spreading, yes, but discouragingly slowly from world to world, so slowly that none of the Olympians believed they would see it as a truly dominant force in their very long lifetimes. The nonhuman races paid no attention whatever; the concept that the one true God would choose to go around as a human was pretty insulting.

And through it all, government and press found nothing wrong in its behavior and didn't worry overmuch as it built because of its slow growth rate. Although they wondered about Olympus, about whether those strange superwomen whose world was off-limits to all were sincere in their religion or practicing a new and slow but effective form of conquest. If so, nobody would be alive to really see such a thing happen. It would be somebody else's problem unless something happened to cause a massive growth in church membership. Even the Olympians admitted that.

None of them had yet heard of the Dreel, let alone guessed their implications. Not yet, not yet.

Com Police Headquarters, Suba

THEY STARED WHEN MARQUOZ PLODDED DOWN A hallway. They always stared at a creature that looked mostly like a meter-high Tyrannosaurus rex wearing a vest and smoking a large cigar. He was used to it and ignored them.

The Com had expanded enormously in the past few centuries; it had also become far less totalitarian since the huge criminal-political drug syndicate had been broken centuries earlier. The old syndicate had carefully limited expansion so that frontier worlds were developed only at a pace which it could easily control and eventually take over. The discovery of a cure for their main hold on the leadership of those worlds—and the even greater shock at just how many worlds had been run by the power-mad hidden monarchs from their private little worlds of luxurious depravity—had caused a total reevaluation of the Com and the directions in which humanity had been going.

Hundreds of Com Worlds were seen to be totally stagnant; many were truly dying, their genetic breeding programs and mass mind-programming having bred populations resembling insect societies more than any past human ones, the billions toiling for the benefit of the ruling class and they for the syndicate. When the syndicate was broken so were most of the ruling classes, discovered simply because the drugs they needed were no longer available and they had to come to the Com or die.

Now there were new structures and new societies, some as bad or worse than those they replaced, but most at least slightly better and the attention of the Com spread outward toward more rapid expansion and the infusion of a new frontier spirit.

Over a thousand human worlds now spread over more than a tenth of the Milky Way galaxy. It was inevitable that they should finally meet others, and they had. The Com had by then encountered fourteen races, some so alien and incomprehensible that there could be little contact and no common ground; others, such as the centaurlike Rhone, with expanding cultures of their own. There had been some conflicts, a lot of misunderstanding, but growth had been positive, overall, and humanity had learned a lot about dealing with alien races. The Council of the Community of Worlds, or Com, had seven nonhuman members.

Of them all, however, the Chugach of Marquoz's own origin were probably the least well known. They had been found on the outer fringes of the Rhone empire by the Rhone, not humans. Their huge, hot desert world was at first thought to be uninhabited, a swirling, harsh sea of desert sands.

The Chugach lived far beneath those sands, where it was cool, near the bedrock and even in its cavities, where the water was, with great cities and grand castles lay. The Chugach swam in the sand like fish in water, and, since their lungs were not that different from those of humans and Rhone, it was still a mystery how they kept from suffocating. A non-spacefaring race that bred slowly would be virtually lost to most of the people of all races in the Com.

It had taken the semifeudal Chugach a while to get over the shock that they were not alone, nor even the lords of creation, but they'd made do. A collection of thousands of autonomous regions, that translated roughly as dukedoms yet seemed to have an almost Athenian democracy, they'd had no central government, no countries, nothing with which to deal.

But they had knowledge, talent, and skills the Com did not have. They produced intricate glass sculptures that were beautiful beyond belief; they had an almost supernatural way of transmuting substances without complex machinery, taking worthless sand and rock and providing pretty much what you wanted or needed. They had something to trade, and the Com had technology they lacked. Once a single dukedom had entered into a trade agreement with the Rhone, its neighbors had to follow or be left behind. The chain reaction permanently altered Marquoz's home world.

He didn't seem to care. He said he was a deposed duke, but it was well known that every Chugach who wasn't a duke claimed to be a deposed one. Nobody much understood him or his motives, and least of all was his almost total lack of concern for his home world. He'd roamed the Rhone empire as agent for a hundred small concerns, always seemed to have money and a knowledge of alien surroundings, and he got results. He seemed to have a sixth sense when something was wrong; he was drawn to trouble like a magnet, and he proved himself capable of handling what trouble he found.

So he was a natural for the Com Police, who recruited him to keep from being embarrassed by him. Marquoz was neither understood nor trusted by his human and nonhuman counterparts as the only Chugach in the Com Police. But he got results every time—and superiors up to the Council itself did not share prejudice against one so productive. He might not be understood, but there was no question that he was a capable friend.

He strode into the lab section with that air of confident authority he always wore, his cigar leaving a trail of blue-white puff-balls in the air behind him. He spotted a technician instantly as the boss of the section, and strode over to him.

The man was standing in front of a wall of transparent material more then twelve centimeters thick. Behind it were cells, cages really, in which sat, thoroughly bound, a middle-aged man, an elderly woman who looked like everybody's grandmother, and two fairly attractive young women, neither of whom looked to be much older than sixteen. All were naked; although securely bound, the cells contained nothing except the chairs to which they were bound—and even the chair was fashioned out of the material of the cell itself when it was molded.

Dr. Van Chu saw the dragon's reflection in the glass but didn't turn from observing the four people in the cells.

"Hello, Marquoz," he mumbled. "I figured you'd still be in debriefing."

"Oh, I took a break. You know how much respect I have for all that nonsense. I filed a report. I fail to see what repeating the story a few hundred times will add."

Van Chu chuckled. "Every little bit helps. You've dropped a nasty one in our laps this time. Worse than the last time. Can I persuade you to return home and have a mess of kids or whatever it is you people do and let us get some rest?"

Marquoz took the cigar in his long, thin fingers and snorted. The snort produced a small puff of smoke from his own mouth. Chugach did not need to carry cigar lighters.

"That'll be the day," the little dragon responded. "No, you're stuck with me, I'm afraid, as long as I'm having this much fun."

Now the lab man looked over and down at him, curiosity all over his face. "What makes you tick, Marquoz? How is shooting and getting shot at on alien worlds for alien races fun? Why not Chugach?"

That question had been asked many times, and he always gave the same answer. "You know that every race has its oddballs, Doc. The ones that don't fit, don't like the rules or things as they are. I'm the chief oddball Chugach. I'm a nut, I *know* I'm a nut, but I'm having fun and I'm useful so I stay a nut."

Van Chu let the matter drop. Suddenly dead serious, "You sure you got them all?" he asked, motioning toward the prisoners with his head.

Marquoz nodded. "Oh, yeah. On Parkatin, anyway. Who knows how many in other places? Our pigeon, Har Bateen, was dropped on a farm about twenty kilometers from town only the day before. We traced back his movements pretty easily. Apparently he just walked up to the nearest farmhouse—man, wife, one young kid—and pretended to be on his way from here to there. They were hospitable—and the first three he took over. We got none of them. Man, we did a drop on 'em and had that farmhouse surrounded in minutes, but they just wouldn't give up. We just about had to level it.

"He took their little roadster and drove into town the next day, checked into a small hotel in the sleazy section, near the spaceport. A busy lad: we found eight he'd gotten there including Grandma over there." He pointed with the cigar to the little old lady in the cell. "Then he went to the bar, took the madam there, then wandered out and over to us. These characters vary in their desire to live—Bateen himself was pretty meek and after we stunned him and put a vacuum suit on him he behaved real nice. The roomers tried to shoot it out; grandma just wasn't fleet of foot—tripped and knocked herself cold. The others we had to burn. Likewise the madam, although she'd infected the two girls, there, and they were still unsteady enough that we had 'em wrapped and ready to ship before they could do much."

"How'd you know they weren't what they appeared?" Van Chu pressed. "I mean, I'd never guess they were anything but what they seemed."

Marquoz chuckled. "They stink. Oh, not to you. Apparently not to anybody but a Chugach. Not an ordinary kind of stink; a really alien kind of thing, an odor like nobody's ever experienced before. I can't describe it to you—but I'm hoping you folks can figure it out and synthesize it so we can get detectors. This crap kind of gives you the creeps—you can't know who's who."

The lab chief shivered slightly and nodded agreement. "At least you can smell them. We can't even do that. The whole lab's paranoid now."

"Find out anything yet?"

Van Chu shrugged. "A great deal. A little. Nothing at all. When you are dealing with the previously unknown it all amounts to the same thing."

"I'm not one for philosophy, Doc. What do you know?" the dragon shot back impatiently.

Van Chu sighed. "Well, they are an entirely new form of intelligent life. You might call them an intelligent virus. They're rather amazing under the microscope. Come on over here."

They walked through to a research cubicle, and Van Chu made a few adjustments. The large screen in front of them flickered into life.

"That's the enemy, Marquoz," Van Chu said softly. "That's the Dreel."

The screen showed a honeycomb-like structure.

"Looks like every virus I've ever seen or been laid up with," the dragon commented.

"There is some resemblance," Van Chu admitted, "but look at them under closer magnification." He made a few adjustments on his console and the view closed in, blowing up to where they could just see one of the comb-like structures. "Notice the striations, the pattern of construction of the stalk?"

Marquoz just nodded.

Van Chu shifted the view to the next distinct entity. "You see? A different pattern. If I blow them up and compare them all the way to the atomic level, it will show that no two of them are exactly alike in a given organism. At least we believe so."

"You mean those things smaller than cells are all individuals?"

"No, not individuals like you or me. I believe it's a collective organism somehow intricately interconnected in a host, even if not physically attached. The collective acts as a single organism, not as a group. We believe that each individual viruslike organism contains some specific information. There are key members and subordinate ones, together they make up the sum total of what the Dreel in each host knows, and limit its capabilities. We suspect that if an individual Dreel needs information on a particular thing it doesn't have to look it up, merely inject or simply meet up with another Dreel who has that specific information."

Marquoz was fascinated. "You mean one knows all the math, another all the physics, and so forth?"

"Vastly oversimplified, I think, but you have the general idea," Van Chu replied. "Think of each Dreel organism as a book. Put a number of them together, each having specific bits of information and you have the knowledge a specialist would have in the field. Put a lot of those together—design your own, in fact —and you have a library. When all of the basics are added for full functioning, then somehow a librarian —a consciousness—simply appears. Then they breed themselves new units as necessary."

"Pretty nice. No education, no being born or growing up, just meet a host, duplicate the basics, get in, and there you are," the dragon noted. "Must eliminate a lot of hang-ups."

Van Chu chuckled. "I suppose. It's very different from anything we have ever seen. One wonders how they could have evolved, let alone progressed to a high enough state to be invading other areas of space."

"They wouldn't have to," Marquoz noted. "All they'd need would be, say, for one of our ships to land and get bit by a local animal. From what you say, within a few days they'd be the crew."

The scientist nodded agreement. "Yes, exactly. That fellow you captured over there—he is a Dreel. He is also Har Bateen, with a personal history going back to the day of his birth, and, most importantly, *he knows that history*. He knows everything Har Bateen ever knew. That's the most frightening thing. Were you not able to smell them out, there would be absolutely no way to tell them from the original. None."

"Tried talking to them?" the Chugach asked. "We had 'em so tightly wrapped on the way here that was impossible. We had no idea what we were dealing with, just that it had something to do with mixing blood. We couldn't afford to take chances."

"Oh, yes, we've talked to them. I can play the tapes if you like—or you can use the intercom and talk to them."

"Just a digest. I'm due back upstairs, remember. They'll have discovered that I'm missing by now and have an alarm out all over the place."

"How'd you manage it?"

Marquoz gave a throaty chuckle. "One advantage to being a strange alien organism. They don't know much about how or where I go to the bathroom, so they take my word for it."

Van Chu cleared his throat. "I see. Well, all I can tell you is that for quite a while they all insisted that they were ordinary humans and that they protested all the foul treatment. Bateen even claimed he thought the Gypsy was going to rob him and so just defended himself."

"Good story," the dragon admitted. "But no go."

The scientist shrugged. "He—they all—could talk their way out of anywhere but here. They didn't change their tune until we took the blood samples—remotely, of course—and started running the tests. Only then did Bateen admit—no, he *proclaimed*—himself a Dreel, as he called them. He's incredibly arrogant. We're just so many animals to him; all we're good for is being hosts for the Dreel. He claims that they aren't even from this galaxy, and that they have been at this takeover bit so long that nobody can remember when it didn't happen. Holy mission stuff, as fanatical as this Fellowship business at the spaceports."

Marquoz sighed. "I hope he's just bluffing. I don't like the implications."

Van Chu looked down at him worriedly. "What do you mean?"

"Well, if *I* can smell 'em out other races probably can, too. A fair percentage, anyway, if they're intergalactic. That brings up the point that what they can't take by stealth they take by force—and an intergalactic flight is beyond any technology of ours I ever heard of."

The scientist looked a little frightened now. "You mean a war? A *real* interstellar war?"

"To the death," Marquoz agreed, "with the other side holding the cards. I think we'd better shut these folks down, if we can, as quickly as possible—and then make a deal if we can, which I doubt. When you make those detectors of yours, which you will, the Dreel will know their cover is blown, know we're onto them. I think we better know what we're up against fast."

The Chugach turned to go, but Van Chu called after him. "Ah . . . Marquoz?"

The dragon stopped and his large head turned slightly, fixing a single reptilian eye on the scientist. "Yeah?"

"How'd you happen to stumble onto all this? I know, you smelled them out—but how'd you, the one person able to smell that stink, happen to be on that particular backwater planet, in just the right place, to smell it?"

"It's simple," Marquoz responded dryly, heading for the door. "I'm an accident-prone."

Kwangsi, the Council Chambers of the Com

THEY WERE THERE, ALL THE COUNCILLORS OF THE Community of Worlds except those indisposed by accident or illness. Still, counting the human and nonhuman worlds, it represented 2160 planets and 2144 Councillors were there, an unprecedented number.

A Council meeting was always impressive: there were the representatives of all the human worlds except those on the frontier too little developed for self-government, also the huge centauroid forms of the Rhone worlds, almost as numerous as mankind's; the dozen or so Kafski in a special amphibious section for comfort's sake, their starfish-like bodies undulating with tension, also the Tarak who resembled great beavers, the Milikud, forms who seemed like tiny whirlwinds; and all the others, even the one lone representative of the Chugach. They all knew why they were there; they just didn't like it.

The President was human this term, a giant of a man who looked the part with dark skin and snow-white hair. His equally gleaming white Councillor's robes gave him a commanding presence even in so large a hall. His name was Marijido Varga. His one failing was his thin, reedy voice, but this didn't matter in so great a chamber which spoke so many languages that all would be translated automatically by communications computers whose technicians tended to alter the voice to fit the position, anyway.

The opening ceremony was simple. Varga simply rose, hammered a symbolic gavel three times setting off a signal at each Councillor's seat, then proclaimed:

"The Council is in session." He paused a moment to allow late arrivals to settle down, then continued.

"This extraordinary session is called because of grave emergency. The Com, we believe all of us, is threatened by an external enemy who refuses all entreaty to peace and accommodation and whose only goal seems to be total physical and mental enslavement or extinction."

He went on to tell about the Dreel and how they were detected.

"Since we became aware of this threat, which I must refer to as an invasion, the High Council Presidium has met and unanimously ordered the following measures: One, the development of detection devices so that we can tell friend from foe. Thanks to the wholehearted cooperation of our brothers the Chugach, this has been accomplished, although you'll understand that it will take some time to manufacture such devices and distribute them in sufficient quantities to everyone. The resources of half a dozen races have been marshaled for this project. Two, a careful surveillance of frontier worlds beyond the Parkatin perimeter. The results showed extensive infiltration of those areas. At least one world, Madalin, had been entirely overrun. However, we did not locate their base, and we believe it to be a mother ship or ships. Good sense dictates that we assume the mother ship or ships to be accompanied by fighting craft of, say, at least fleet strength."

That assessment caused a stir. Penetration of the Com by an enemy fleet of unknown capabilities and uncertain location was potentially disastrous.

"Three, we ordered research into ways we might protect ourselves. So far we have learned that the Dreel organism is operative only on organisms with a bloodstream within temperature limits of ten below to about eighty-five above zero." The Milikud and several other races that either had no bloodstream or whose systems were outside the temperature limits seemed to relax a bit.

Varga didn't let that last long. "We have intercepted signals from beyond our frontiers that indicate the Dreel destroy all races that they cannot take over and use. This information was confirmed, indirectly, by our almost pathologically confident prisoners. The Dreel are engaged in a drive to make the Universe a Dreel Universe—and no one knows just how long it's been going on. They appear to find other forms of higher intelligence simply intolerable."

Again the tremendous stir, although the audience already knew most of this. One does not make life-or-death decisions on one speech or report. What Varga had said thus far was mostly for the record. The President shuffled his papers and continued. His speech, of course, was not his own but had been drafted by his civil service assistants and approved by the entire Presidium.

"On protection: The Dreel is a form of virus, and vaccines for those races who need them have already been developed by our excellent Com labs and medical computers. However, it will be weeks before the vaccines can be produced in quantity, and months or longer before everyone can be innoculated. You must believe we are proceeding on this as fast as possible. In the meantime, we are, alas, dependent on the detectors, which are not a perfect solution. The Dreel maintain a body but kill the intellect. We can destroy the Dreel in a body, but doing so leaves just that—a body that is alive, but little better than a blade of grass, mindless and incapable of caring for itself. As a result, except for victims used in research or interrogation, we have ordered that any Dreel discovered are to be killed at once, disintegrated or destroyed by fire."

There was general agreement to this though none of the delegates liked what they were hearing one bit.

"Finally we attempted contact and negotiation with them. We approached Madalin and called to them. The Dreel were aware we know of them, so we must assume their intelligence is at least as good as ours. I will now play an edited transcript of that discussion, if you will consult your viewers. It does not last very long. As our recording begins, the Com negotiator is hailing Madalin's capital."

Screens designed for the various races went on.

"Markatin, this is Com Presidium ship *Dworcas Bagby,*" came a voice. "We wish to confer with your leadership."

The screens, which had remained dark, suddenly lighted. The face was a stunner, that of a girl perhaps twelve or thirteen. She looked dirty, though, and her hair, worn in long braids, was matting from lack of attention. She was nude.

"I am Diri Smeel," she responded in a child's singsong. "I will speak with you."

The speaker on the *Bagby* was obviously taken aback, and there was a long pause before the voice of the Council negotiator was heard again.

"I wish to speak to someone in command," he said in an emotionless monotone, trying not to betray surprise or emotion.

"I am in command here," the girl said. "You wish our terms. All Com fleet and police vessels in space are to be evacuated within five standard days. Local forces are to disarm and place themselves at the disposal of the Dreel commanders when they arrive at each spaceport. All interworld commerce is to cease when ships reach their destinations."

A choking sound became audible as if the Com negotiator couldn't believe his ears. Finally he managed to continue. "We did not come to surrender, we came to reach an accommodation."

The girl appeared unfazed. "You have no alternative. We do not offer death, only peace and order. You will not die. We will simply enter your bodies and direct your thoughts and actions."

"But that is the same as death," the negotiator countered.

"It is not death," the Dreel girl insisted. "It is proper: Higher orders domesticate lower orders in nature; the horse, the cow, the romba, the worzeil—all serve you. We are a higher order, and therefore you must serve us." She stated it matter-of-factly, as if she'd been insisting that her sky was blue or people grew old.

"We seek only to live without conflict, but we cannot accept your view of us," the negotiator told her.

The girl showed some surprise. "It is natural," she insisted. "Order. You cannot struggle against the way things are. It would be like saying that minerals are vegetables or that space is filled with oxygen. It would be false to say such things. It is false to say that the higher should not own the lower. It is against nature."

Full circle. "We do not accept your view," the negotiator repeated. "We cannot allow you to conquer our worlds."

Still more surprise. "It is not something one accepts. Not something one allows. It *is*. It will be. It has been for more than a billion years and will continue to be. We became a galaxy. Not a world, not a system, not a sector or quadrant. A galaxy. Then we set off, more than two thousand years ago, for this galaxy. We are now here."

"Then we must fight."

She was undisturbed. "The mule may kick but he will still plow. We have attempted a peaceful and methodical domestication. We will not argue, however. Often animals must be trained to do what is proper and right for their masters. If you will not do so now, this discussion is pointless."

The negotiator had had just about enough. "What will happen," he snapped back, "when the Dreel meet a higher race?"

She looked puzzled, not comprehending the question. "That is not possible," she replied—and tuned them out.

"At almost the same point," President Varga told them, "the Presidium ship and its attendant naval escorts were attacked by ships of the Dreel. Fourteen ships were in the Com party, thirteen were as heavily armed as anything now in service. What you heard was recorded here, by our message relay. None of the ships has been heard from again."

Varga paused to let that sink in. That information had not been made public. Pandemonium took over the hall, and Varga needed several minutes to regain control. Finally he said, "Councillors, the Com was established by my race over a thousand years ago after a period of interplanetary war that was fought over ideologies now long dead. The awesome weapons that had exterminated life on nine worlds, including the world of my race's origin, were sealed. The Com Police, established to monitor future threats to interplanetary peace, was composed of people prepared to apply whatever tools were necessary to prevent such conflicts. Properly supervised, the Com Police interfere not at all with a planet's internal affairs, but they guarantee that planets shall harm only themselves, not others. Similar systems were established by the Rhone, the Tarak, the Milikud, and the Botesh, and these were integrated into a single structure when we merged. In fact, our races merged for the same reason that the Com system was established: not to influence one another but to keep harm from one another. The weapons were not, however, destroyed for no one knew what crises might arise—and, of course, the threat of their use has deterred many a would-be conqueror. Only a majority vote of all the members of this Council can unseal those weapons; only such a vote can direct the Com Police, who are trained in their use, to apply them. I think we must take that vote and I, speaking for myself and for the Presidium, must report to you a vote of twenty-six to five for so doing."

And there it was, the request they had been expect-until now. The mission to Madalin had shown the Com to be impotent against alien invaders who claimed to have subjugated an entire galaxy.

Maps distributed with the briefing materials before the meeting showed that action had to be taken immediately. The Com comprised about two-thirds of one arm of the Milky Way. Assuming the Dreel came from Andromeda, as some of the captives had boasted, they had reached the Com's arm near its outer tip and were proceeding inward. It was most likely that the first civilization the Dreel had encountered was the human one—so the Dreel campaign had just begun. Still, they had absorbed at least one human world and had commanding positions on several more; they had had ample time to plant agents unobserved on almost all the worlds.

Now the Dreel, would accelerate their operations because within a year mass innoculation would have denied these human, then Rhone bodies—in geographical order. The Dreel would need those bodies; otherwise their expansion would be limited by their host's gestation periods and by the time it would take for each new host to grow enough to be useful. From the Dreel point of view, most tragic of all would be loss of the knowledge they would have gained by subjugating established civilizations.

"Our military analysis is based on several assumptions," Varga told the Council. "First, the Dreel are technologically in advance of us, at least in the ways that would count in a conflict. Second, they are at least as smart as we are. Given the fact that the opportunity for a high-profit takeover is diminishing—and given that they now know that we are aware of them—we assume they will launch an all-out attack on worlds within striking distance of their main fleet. That they haven't done so yet indicates that though they are technologically superior, they are still numerically very much inferior to us. We caught them before they were ready; before their key agents were in place and set up to be fully effective; on all our worlds before they had secured enough resources to supply the fleets needed to beat us; before they had taken enough of our population to man those ships. We must hit them. Now. We must go after them with everything at our command. Now. We urge that you vote to open the weapons locker; that a general military and scientific mobilization be ordered throughout the Com; that we hit them first at Madalin, destroying the entire planet to draw their fleet into action before it is ready. I call for accelerated debate on this matter—and an immediate vote."

The presentation was over. It was time for the most momentous decision by any of the races since they had sequestered the weapons. The debate wore on long after the sun set. Late in the night, they voted. Each Councillor had a specific key to the impregnible machinery that guarded the weapons locker; 1081 delegates would have to use their keys to enable the military experts to use the weapons. Weapons activation had been attempted before, but never successfully. Centuries earlier, the sponge syndicate had tried for a majority by drug blackmail. Had they succeeded, they would have been the absolute commanders of the then all-human Com; the attempt failed narrowly when the syndicate chief mysteriously disappeared—atomized, it was believed, by the Com Police.

This time, after the delicate point about the composition of the military staff was resolved by placing in overall command a Tarak—a capable general of a minority race—they voted, by almost three to one, to go ahead.

Immediately, the keys were activated. The proper signal was received by the great computers who guarded the machines. The highly trained staff was already in place.

And throughout the human and nonhuman worlds of the Com the word spread faster than could have been thought possible—the news that struck fear into every individual who heard it:

The weapons locker is open.

In the Madalin System

ALTHOUGH AWARENESS OF THE WEAPONS LOCKER was almost universal—it was a nightmare employed to scare both children and adults—few knew what the phrase really meant. The majority of people seemed to think of it as some sort of giant safe that held all the terror weapons their superiors thought too monstrous to employ.

Actually, the weapons locker was a very small computer-run world that had been created long ago, programmed with the most formidible defenses known to that time, then towed to a spot by totally computerized ships and maneuvered to its final hiding place by a master computer that immediately erased all memory of the action. No one knew the whereabouts of the weapons locker, nor had anyone for more than a thousand years. All anybody knew was that it was one of the uncounted trillions of pieces of space junk somewhere in the Com "neighborhood." However, the Com *could* communicate with it—i.e., was able to receive a signal the directionality of which was so scrambled that not even the most evil of computer geniuses had been able to trace it.

Now that the proper signal had been sent, the weapons-locker computer did the only thing it was designed to do: It broadcast a complex set of instructions that was relayed by countless millions of communications computers.

The terror weapons were not packed away; they weren't even obsolescent, since as new devices were developed they were routinely programmed to obey only activating signals from the weapons locker.

Now those who manned the fearsome weapons and who had trained on them using computer simulations could use the real things. Deployment and actual commitment were completely computer controlled, of course, but people, human and nonhuman, decided if they were to be deployed, and where, and when.

The fleet that closed in on Madalin was unlike any fleet ever before seen inside the Com or, perhaps, anywhere else. The ships were huge, the ships were tiny; all bore little relationship to the standard naval vessels everyone knew. Security on the weapons had been absolute; the crews who rode and directed them lived apart in their own communities, and when they left the service all knowledge of the weapons was erased from their minds.

The nerve center of Task Force One was a relatively small object, a sphere with long, thin spikes protruding from its surface. Its battle computers would decide how best to employ the fleet. Yet it, too, was merely a convenience; aboard each of the other craft was a computer and a backup crew able to generate the proper instructions.

Madalin was on the screens and Task Force One was already implementing the proper attack when the Dreel moved. Sensors inside the spiked sphere detected ships approaching at velocities far greater than any manageable by the Com technology. It was obvious why the first force had failed. Their weapons computers had been geared to defense against attack by vessels of Com capability, but the enemy had been upon them before they could bring up the proper defenses.

The weapons-locker control was under no such handicaps; it had been created to face the impossible and counter it, if indeed it could be countered. Signals flashed in nanoseconds, screens went up, ships went into defensive postures, catching the Dreel by surprise. Their information could not know what lay inside the weapons locker, since even the Com was not sure.

There were only twenty Dreel ships—a squadron, basically. The task force had been expecting more, and they moved to defend, being too slow to go after the foe.

The spiked sphere served a double purpose in such

a situation. It had been designed to *look* and be deployed as if it were a command and nerve center. It would draw any attacker logical enough to make the most basic assumptions in military terms. The Dreel ships, moving at almost five times the best Com velocity, homed the command sphere just as it was hoped they would.

Computers on the defensive perimeter ships tracked the Dreel's twenty tiny needles and made way for them. The intent should have been obvious, but the Dreel were overconfident even though facing an alien military machine they had never tested. They did not determine the reasoning behind the formation. Rather, they approached the command sphere directly—and in so doing they ran a gauntlet.

Distances were huge and deployment perfect; all twenty ships cleared the outer perimeter before the trap was sprung. Defensive screens appeared all over, and small marblelike ships opened up on the attacking fleet. The Dreel's tremendous speed suddenly became their weak point. They were going far too fast to take much evasive action or undergo rapid course changes; the marble ships were so small that special equipment had to be invented to detect them. They were all automated, and none moved now. They just fired, fired all along the gauntlet, letting the Dreel ships run right into their energy beams.

Twelve of the Dreel ships took direct hits; the other eight somehow managed to alter course slightly and slide around the beams, but even so they weren't able to bring their own weapons into play. They were away and off the screens before any of the military computers could change aim.

At the speeds involved, defenses had to be totally automated and controlled by self-aware computers able to handle the reaction times involved. The initial attack had been detected, countered, and was over before the task force crews even had time to see on their screens that they'd almost had it.

The Dreel had been burned and burned badly. They would pause a bit before attacking again, particularly since only the eight ships remained. Surely, their own computers, alien and probably faster than the Com's, were analyzing what had gone wrong, seeing how they had been fooled, and devising counterattacks. But ships turn in a finite amount of space, and you don't brake easily at Dreel speeds.

The actual destruct signal had to be operator-given on the Com task force; it was given with little hesitation. The officers had all seen the film of the only post-Dreel contact with Madalin. Such a pretty world, really, in the screens, all blue and white, glistening in the reflected light of a yellow star less than one hundred and fifty million kilometers away. A frontier world, but there had been over a million human beings on that world, a million souls lost to the Dreel.

Small triangular-shaped ships deployed around the planet, each one in line of sight of the other. No one except the computers controlling the action really knew what was involved here. All the observers knew, however, that these were planet destroyers.

Position correct, charging correct, all ready—then a single flash, so quick it was hardly seen on the visual screens of the hundreds of watchers in the ships.

In the blink of an eye, that pretty blue and white world had turned a fiery orange, then faded to a dull yellow. Lifeless, barren, no seas, no air, no trace or sign that, but moments before, this had been a world of life and beauty. The atmosphere of the planet, and the top ten kilometers or so of crust, had simply ceased to exist.

The Task Force Commander, a huge Rhone who was the personification of the classical Greek centaur, remained grim-faced as the cheer went up from the technicians on the command bridge. He allowed them their moment of triumph—after all, some had trained for years for missions like this, but had never actually been able to use the equipment before—then reached over and switched on the intercom to all stations and ships.

"Well done. However, let us not forget that we have not won this skirmish. That wasn't an enemy planet down there—it was one of ours. Those were *our* people, that was *our* world. We can ill afford many victories like this one, for each one means we lose a little more of ourselves." He paused. All was suddenly very quiet in the command center. "Break off and return to station. This was the opening counter-attack, but we have not yet engaged the main force. Welcome to the war, citizens."

Dreel Central, about Five Thousand Light-years from the Com

THE RECORDER'S TINY SHIP DOCKED EASILY. THE mother ship was an entire world, more than ten thousand kilometers in diameter, but it was a world inside-out. It took the Recorder almost four hours by shuttle from the surface spaceport where he had landed to reach the chambers of the Set.

The chambers themselves were modest, for the Dreel were an austere people with little use for art or creature comforts. It came from inhabiting another's body—the Dreel, safe and secure inside a body, cared little for it beyond that it be in excellent health and remain undamaged.

Thus the seat of Dreel power was a chamber no more than thirty meters square, furnished only with hard plastic benches and enclosed only by undecorated steel bulkheads. The Recorder expected nothing else; he sat on one of the benches and waited patiently, if a little nervously. All Dreel shared a desire for long life, and Dreel leaderhip had more than once been known to kill the bearer of unhappy tidings.

Still, The Recorder's concern was strictly for its own self; that the Dreel were here, that the great mother ship had brought them across the intergalactic void over an impossibly long time, was reassuring. That the Dreel might lose never crossed The Recorder's mind.

"Recorder, give your report." The voice echoed from the walls. Its suddenness startled him, but he recovered quickly. They already knew what he had to say—this was, as his title implied, strictly for the record, and in case questions were necessary.

"Subjects have an effective defensive force not realized in the early scouting reports," he told the Set. "Their weapons, while slow, are of an extremely high order and in many ways inconsistent with their past history. Obviously, the relatively static culture that we found was atypical of the races involved. Such weapons as these, and the highly unorthodox methodology employed—much of which had obvious nonmilitary applications not reflected in their technological level are quite obviously a product of a savage evolution. Although apparently at Level One evolution—peaceful, highly developed, relatively static, as we have found elsewhere—they are not so. We depended too much on past models. These are at least Level Three cultures—barbarians, if you will, wild animals—with a convincing veneer of Level One."

"Such a finding is inconsistent," the Set objected. "A Level Three culture would continually war, continually fight among itself. We are faced with an affront to the laws of nature if your information is correct—a pack of ferocious animals who have reached a working compromise. We could accept that of one race perhaps, but there are fourteen totally different types of life-form. It is against the laws of historical evolution. Such a civilization as is represented by this 'Com' should be at the highest level, beyond wars or threats of wars; it should be as it observably is, in social stasis, at precisely the level where the only possible advancement is Dreel assumption of control."

"Nevertheless," The Recorder responded, "they have a stasis reality and yet did not destroy the weapons of their barbarian past—and, most incredibly, did not lose the knowledge or will to use them. This is a fact. More, it applies to all of them. Therefore the different races are cooperating with each other against us."

The Set remained silent for a moment. The Recorder waited, still patient, knowing that within the heart of the massive mother ship the Set—countless Dreel without body—were interacting, searching for answers, devising plans. It was a giant live, organic computer with billions of years of wisdom and experience accounted for among its myriad components.

One of the things the Dreel had learned in all those years was pragmatism; it was the last refuge of the puzzled, and it worked.

"Much work will be done to explain this anomaly," the Set announced at last. "It is possible that laws of historical evolution do not apply universally as they did to our birth-galaxy. Therefore, faced with a civilization technologically capable of detecting us, further passive infiltration is hereby ended. If it is a Level Three we are dealing with, then we must counter it as we would a Level Three culture anywhere, no matter its outward appearance."

"That is a dangerous road," The Recorder pointed out. "Although slower than we, they successfully destroyed twelve of our ships on the Madalin attack to no losses on their side. Our fleet numbers under forty thousand ships, our factory-ship capacity is limited, and we do not control sufficient worlds to use their own facilities."

The Set was actually shocked. "To suggest that the Dreel might lose to such evolutionary inferiors! . . ."

The Recorder became alarmed. "No, no! I mean nothing of the sort! Only that the most submissive pet might still bite, kick, or otherwise injure the master."

"We are aware of that," the Set replied coldly. "Know that superior numbers are not always the answer. *They* are on the defensive, not we. They must meet our threat. The twelve ships lost were lost because they had to face a preset gauntlet. The situation will be reversed. Be at ease, report to Medical. Go."

Even as The Recorder left, the Set was ordering that, while undergoing medical check, additional Dreel be added to his system to counterbalance the obvious alienation The Recorder had suffered while in the Com. The historical anomaly had obviously unhinged him. Recombination was needed. Never before had the Dreel faced this sort of society; never before had it been at such a disadvantage. The victory here would be all the greater for the difficulty the Com presented. A herd might trample a warder, but never the race of warders. Now was the time for the Dreel to show its true superiority, which was power.

On the Freighter *Hoahokim*

THEY CALLED HIM GYPSY, NOTHING MORE. A TALL, quiet man, dark-complected and without the almost universal Oriental cast of the human race, he had a strong Roman nose and dark, flashing eyes that were a hypnotic mask. Gypsy was not a Com Policeman; in fact, he seemed to hate all authority and authority figures. Marquoz had run into him some years before on a backwater planet where Gypsy was playing his pipe and passing the hat. That had been the first time Marquoz had performed the dance, impromptu, and they became fast friends. Even now, the Chugach knew little about his human companion and understood less. Deep down, though, each seemed to sense a kindred spark in their attitudes toward themselves and others.

They had hit upon the act almost at once, and it proved even more effective when they discovered that, on most planets, people took the little dragon for some sort of exotic animal—not so unusual when you consider that most Com citizens never left the planet of their birth and knew as little about elsewhere as ordinary people had since time immemorial.

Marquoz was snoozing in the stateroom while Gypsy strolled on the deck. The Chugach awoke with a snort and a tiny puff of smoke from his nostrils as the door opened and the man entered. There was no pretense at being a pet on ship; spacefarers generally recognized all the races.

One reptilian lid popped open and watched as the

man entered. "So? Find anything you didn't find on the last three thousand ships we've been on?"

Gypsy flopped on the bunk, sighed, and spat. "Naw. I got up to the passenger lounge and there was one of those superwomen there—the ones with tails, you know? —spoutin' all the religious guff. Maybe I should'a gone into the religion racket—lots of bucks and an easy life. I *did* do some faith healing once."

Both dragon eyes popped open. "You? A faith healer?" Again the smoky snort, this time of derisive amusement.

Gypsy's shaggy head nodded slightly. "Yeah. Great scam. Whip 'em all up, sing a lotta hymns, then summon the sick to be cured. Put a shill or two in the crowd so's you can have a couple of real cures to get things started. Bums'll do it for a fiver—good actors, too, if you don't pay 'em until after the scam. Who knows? If you actually cure anybody legit you make a fortune; if you don't, well, it's because they didn't have enough faith. Part of the secret of a good scam—always put the blame for the breakdown on the mark."

"Did you really cure anybody?" Marquoz asked, skeptical but interested.

"Oh, sure, one or two here and there," Gypsy responded matter-of-factly. "The mind can cure a lot of ills on its own if the person really believes. Hell, I can stop my bleeding at will and refuse to recognize pain—the needle scam, you remember."

The Chugach nodded. "I still don't know how you do that. Must be something different in our two races. Put a needle into me anywhere and it hurts like hell. I'm still feeling the Dreel immunization shot."

Gypsy chuckled. "Naw, I don't think it's anything racial. I think anybody with a good brain can do it. It's really willpower."

Marquoz shrugged. "Have it your way. No one of my race has come close to it. I think there's more to it than you believe—something humans can do, and perhaps some others, but not we, any more than you can snort fire and smoke."

"Have it your own way." Gypsy sighed, then changed the subject. "That Olympian is really a stunner. All the attributes of every dream woman anybody can imagine, but I can't get turned on by her. There's something about her—other than the horse tail, of course—that just isn't human. In some way I think she's a lot less human that you, Marq."

The Chugach chuckled at that. "Perhaps I should go up and see her." He stopped a moment, then snorted slightly. "I wonder if she'll ask *me* if I'm Nathan Brazil?"

"Probably," Gypsy responded lightly. "I dunno what she'd do if you admitted it, though. Crazy kinda religion. I wonder how Brazil stands it? He's probably gone far underground to keep the hounds off, poor guy."

Saurian eyelids rose. "You really think there is such a person?"

"Oh, sure," Gypsy replied. "Him and me we tied one on a couple years ago, before this cult thing became big and spread out. Hell of a nice guy, too. I wonder how these alien beauties ever got fixated on him."

Suddenly Marquoz was lost in thought. Finally he said, "Gypsy, are you *sure* there is such a person? I mean, he just wasn't putting you on? The cult's been going a good decade, after all."

"Nope, he was Brazil, all right. I was on his ship—freighter a lot like this one only a lot older and noisier." His brow furrowed. "Lemme see—the *Stepkin*—no, that's not right. The *Stehekin,* I think. No luxury, spartan cabins, old-style everything, but it carried a hell of a load and he kept it up. Brazil was the name on his pilot's license. We used to joke about it—according to the renewal stickers it looked like he'd been alive forever." He paused. "Hmmm . . . Maybe that's why they got stuck on him. Something of a legend, I think. Oldest pilot in service though he looked about twenty-five or thirty to me. Knew some spacers who said their father and their father's father had known him. Some folks are just born lucky—I guess he's got a greater tolerance for rejuves than most."

The dragon nodded but he was still thinking hard. Gypsy was a bundle of surprises; he would never tell anybody his age and it was almost impossible to tell, but he'd been around countless planets and ridden on equally countless ships. His experience was fantastic but never volunteered—you just had to ask the right question or be in the right conversation.

"What was he like, this Brazil?" Marquoz pressed.

Gypsy shrugged. "Little runt—couldn't 'a weighed more than sixty, sixty-five kilos, maybe a head shorter than me. Long black hair, scraggly beard. Liked to dress in loud but ratty clothes and smoked really stenchy cheroots. A tough guy on the surface but something of a softy deep down, you could sorta tell. I wouldn't want to have ta outfight or outdrink him, though. Always real full of life, didn't seem to take anything or anybody serious at all. But down there, buried with that soft spot, was a real serious sort—cold, calculating, pure mind and raw emotion. You'd never guess it to look at him, but in a fight I'd want him on my side."

Marquoz nodded attentively. Despite Gypsy's tendency to fractured purple prose he had an incredible knack for reading other people, human and nonhuman. Sometimes Marquoz thought his human companion had a supernatural or at least psychic power—an empath, perhaps. Marquoz had learned to trust the man's judgment of others. And why not? Gypsy was almost always right.

"I wonder what the Olympian would say if you told that to her?"

Gypsy sat straight up on the cot, looking stricken. "Jesus! I wouldn't dare! I'd be knocked on the head and smuggled off to one of their Temples for interrogation! I had some friends disappear like that around those broads!"

A small reptilian hand flashed palm out in mock defense. "All right, all right, I was only interested." Marquoz laughed. "Seriously, though, I think there should be a thorough Com Police check on him. If he's the free soul you say he is, he might be cashing in on this cult himself."

It was Gypsy's turn to give a derisive chuckle. "Not likely! No, if I know him at all I'd say he's gone and buried himself so far underground the best security force we have couldn't find him. Besides—I know a couple of Com biggies who've tried to get the records on him. No go."

"You mean there aren't any?"

"Of course not," Gypsy responded impatiently. "Everybody leaves a trail of records a kilometer long. Even *I* could be tracked down by a computer match of ticket and travel information with ship schedules throughout the Com. No, *that* kind of record hold they only give to people involved in something nobody should ever know about. What he could have been involved in I don't know, but he sure isn't the type to be a Com agent or anybody else's. Nonetheless, he paid for that ship somewhere."

"You've heard rumors, though?" Marquoz prompted.

The man nodded casually. "Yeah. Mostly that at one time he had blackmail on every Councillor who could make a decision. There's something awful shady about that Brazil. Lots of tales, too, about him showing up in trouble spots, working angles all over, like that. I think he's an operator."

To Gypsy, an operator was one of the movers and shakers, one of the men and women behind the government who *really* controlled things. Among other attributes, Gypsy was extremely paranoid.

Marquoz just nodded. "Anybody able to get a Com block on his entire past history would be able to hide real good, wouldn't he?"

"Why're you so interested in him, anyway?" the man pressed. "I don't know anybody who ever had a really bad word to say about him. Operator or not, these Olympians have him in a real bind. I feel sorry for the little guy."

The diminutive dragon shrugged. "I just wonder. The more I hear about him, the more I wonder. God or not, the man seems to have a lot to hide and a lot of clout to help the hiding. Such men interest me."

Gypsy was about to say something when the ship's intercom came to life.

"Attention! Attention!" The throaty soprano of the captain came through. "The Dreel are making forays into the sector just ahead of us and we have been ordered to heave to and stand by. Since it appears the wait may be a long one, I am preparing to put us in orbit around Cadabah, and for safety I must insist that all passengers debark there. When the danger is over we will reload and continue our journey. This decision is in the best interests of all concerned. Please be ready in the docking chamber in twenty minutes with enough luggage for an overnight stay. We apologize for the inconvenience."

That was all, but it was enough—standard procedure in a combat zone, of course. The passengers would be safer and more comfortable in a spaceport, customs and immigration aside, and the captain could make ready for a fast getaway.

Gypsy sighed and got up. "I didn't realize we were that close to the fighting." His voice was tinged with concern.

"We weren't," Marquoz responded. "This is bad. The war news wasn't that wonderul when we left, but if the front's shifting this far in we're in worse trouble than I thought."

The war was not going well. Shorn of their ability to take over worlds by stealth, the Dreel had closed on the weakest and most vulnerable systems with what looked like its whole fleet. The fleets and weapons-locker teams had gone to counter them and been drawn in. This time the Dreel were on the defensive; no longer could they be surprised by the Com weapons. The Dreel's were faster by far and more maneuverable than anything the Com had—and the weapons locker was as fully stuffed with terror weapons as legend had made it. That was the problem. The weapons-locker weaponry was built to destroy suns and reduce planets to cinders, but not for ship-to-ship fighting or wading into an enemy fleet. It was meeting the deadly fly with nothing less than an atomic bomb.

In ship-to-ship combat, the Dreel were far superior. They had the middle ground of weaponry and the fast ships for it, and much better generalship. They were winning, since their main fleet and combat control ships could not be touched. Only their lack of numbers had kept them from totally overrunning the Com in weeks. Now it had been years, of course, many years —but the Com was losing. The Dreel were overrunning more worlds than the Com could vaporize—and if you blew the worlds up, you didn't hurt the Dreel very much anyway.

As Gypsy and Marquoz made their way aft, the Chugach asked his companion, "What do you know about this Cadabah? Anything interesting there?"

"Cruddy kind of place," Gypsy almost spat. "One of the old Com Worlds when Com was a corruption of Conformist, not Community. A bunch of farmers, mostly, all looking alike, thinking alike, acting alike. One of those human insect hives."

Marquoz sighed. "Deadly dull, then. Well, there's no helping it."

The docking chamber was already filling with the other passengers.

The Olympian was there; she stood out, like true royalty in a pigsty, clad only in a great cloak.

"She looks pissed," Marquoz noted with some amusement.

"Ah, boy! She'll be a pain in the neck for us before long," Gypsy predicted. "Once she gets bored she'll start trying to convert the lot of us."

He was right. Even before the shuttle touched down at Cadabah spaceport she was at it with a fanatic's fervor. One thing Marquoz gave her, no matter how crazy her religion, *she* believed it utterly. The more of her total zeal and commitment he observed, the more he agreed with Gypsy. If Nathan Brazil was indeed a real person, he was to be pitied.

He wondered how long the most sacred of seals on Council and Com information would hold as the Dreel advanced.

Kwangsi

As it turned out, Marquoz was behind the times. The Council was composed of politicians, true, but neither great people nor fools. As the Dreel advanced, the Council members read the handwriting on the wall and their judgments were reinforced by their computers and military leaders.

The Com would lose. Worse, as the Dreel accelerated their advance they would build up a sizable reservoir of captive worlds whose resources would be theirs to use. With human populations under control—even immunized ones, the Dreel had a major advantage: they could breed whatever characteristics were required to render immunization worthless. If the Dreel continued at their present rate and were not countered within a year, they would not be withstood. They would be too many, wearing the bodies of their enemy and not only building the additional ships and armament the Dreel needed but using captured industries as modified by advanced Dreel technology. Humans would be flying those ships against the Com, too.

War may be the most efficient stimulus of innovation and technological advance, but there wasn't time for that sort of thing. It didn't matter if the ultimate weapon was developed if it could not be manufactured and deployed before the Dreel won. And so the only hope lay in past research, forbidden research, research and information classified by past generations as too dangerous to allow. Everybody knew that such things existed, somewhere, in the files—but no one knew what or why or how.

By a near unanimous vote of the Council the seals

came off. Eager researchers pored over the files, often discovering that even the tools needed to understand such interdicted projects were hidden behind yet another set of seals. Much of it was, therefore, useless —and much more was useless because it didn't bear even slightly on the problem. Some of the material was truly shocking. Ways had been developed to remake humanity, its society and culture, into something alien, and every kind of insanity was represented there. It was this "Mad Scientist Catalog" that most interested the weapons researchers, though; they strengthened their stomachs and kept at it, looking for a quick and easy way to beat the Dreel.

Tortoi Kai was not a scientist but a historian looking in the records for clues to events carefully culled from the open references and filed away to be forgotten. She was chilled to learn how much of the past had been doctored by the historical boards appointed by past Councils. The farther back one went, the worse it got—wholesale attempts to change history by simply rewriting it or editing it to suit one's purpose—but even as she worked, restoring the past, entire staffs were distorting the present.

Kai was a typical historian; though her world was collapsing around her, she followed minor threads, becoming fascinated by the major and minor people and events that, when suddenly revealed, changed what she had been taught. It started in a thread, a name, encountered from a past 762 years dead; it was during the days of the sponge merchants, a dark time for the Com, long before the discovery of the first nonhuman race. The farther back she looked in the "window" encompassing that period, the more times the name appeared.

Everyone knew that humanity had originally evolved on a beautiful blue-white world called Earth, third planet from a yellow G-type sun. It was a world of conflicting ideologies, a world of rapidly rising population and rapidly diminishing resources, one that pushed out, almost at the last minute, into space. The ancient name of Einstein had decreed that none could surpass the speed of light; his physics held even today, refined and honed to the ultimate degree. But there were ways to circumvent Einstein's physics by removing oneself from the four-dimensional universe in which they operated. Tell scientists something's impossible and show them the math and nine hundred and ninety-nine out of a thousand accept the declaration. The other one will devote his entire life to figuring out how to beat it. Add to this Earth's total acceptance of the necessity for outward expansion and you give that one man the funds and personnel and equipment to let him do it.

Human beings love to break laws, even natural ones.

And break Einstein's law they did—bent it, anyway—so objects could travel slower than light yet effectively progress at a rate thousands of times light-speed. Expansion was rapid. There were no Earth-type planets anywhere nearby, but within five years scouting expeditions located several toward the core that could be made habitable with some creative planetary engineering. Debris and space junk would provide the resources.

People carried their ideologies with them; utopians and dystopians all attempted to display their superior system on worlds where corrupting competition did not exist. Cloning, genetic engineering on a planetary scale, social engineering on scales even greater, all created a series of worlds—soon numbering in the hundreds—with the utopians dominating. Each was sure it had the perfect system; each was determined to bring perfection to the whole race.

Earth could not maintain control. Depleted, dependent on the colonies for her survival, she held power only through military dominance. But the new colonies developed their own industries using their own resources, then, in secret, created their own military machines and trained personnel. It was ultimately easy. Most of the colonies buried their ideological hatchets in a quest for colonial freedom and joined up first to attack Earth's forces and later Earth itself. The extent of the damage—whole worlds burned away—shocked even the toughest party leaders. But it appeared that in victory they were condemned to wage war against each other.

When fanatics moved to do just that, though, wiser heads prevailed and the Com—the Council of the Community of Worlds—was created. The great weapons were placed in the weapons locker; the Council alone controlled and guarded it—and any technology that might break that control was automatically broadcast to the automated factories of the weapons locker of every Com World's patent registration computer complex, or destroyed. Research applying to such stored weaponry was placed under an interdict so absolute that near unanimity of the Council was required to get at it. Each planet was free to develop its own social system; the Council had no power there. But a planet could not spread its ways by force to other worlds. There the Council, through its weapons locker and through the Com Police, prevailed. The only ideological battles possible were on the developing worlds of the frontier; the only individuality, the only free souls, left were those who plied the spaceways to maintain the trade between worlds, those who served them, and those on the frontiers.

In the course of interstellar exploration, a microorganism was encountered that interacted with some otherwise harmless synthetic foods to produce a horrible mutation within the brain; a person's ability to think would slowly be diminished, until he was reduced to a mindless vegetable unable even to feed himself. The only known antidote was a spongelike lifeform native to the home of the microorganism. It contained an arresting agent that the best computers and best medical minds had not been able to duplicate.

The world was interdicted, of course, guarded by automated sentinels so none could reach it. All cultures of the microorganism were destroyed, and it was thought the problem had been solved. However, some of the organism and the sponge from the early researches fell into the hands of the underworld elite on a number of the Com Worlds and quickly was adopted as a means of furthering the aims of their interplanetary organization. By introducing the disease to a planet's leadership, by letting some examples of deterioration be made and by possessing the only means of arresting that decay—the sponge they now grew in their own secret labs—the syndicate came to control more and more of the Com Worlds.

On the communal, genetically engineered world of New Harmony had lived the syndicate leader, a man not just born but engineered to rule. His name was Antor Trelig. Trelig was the perfect conqueror—a human being with a great intellect and in perfect physical condition, but one totally without morals, scruples, or other inconvenient inhibitions. As the Councillor for New Harmony, he knew who ran what everywhere. Gradually, he and his criminal syndicate had assumed control of world after world, their aim the eventual control of a majority of the Council. Com expansion was slowed, so that as each frontier world became "ripe," Trelig's sponge syndicate could wrest control. Furthermore, the slower the expansion the easier it was to attain a majority on the Council. Then from his luxurious and well-guarded planetoid, New Pompeii, the self-styled Emperor of a new Roman Empire had tried to gain control of literally everything.

Not a word of which, historian Tortoi Kai noted with increasing horror and fascination, could be found in the history books. The wars, the weapons locker, yes—but sponge was discussed only as an amok alien disease whose cure had been discovered about seven hundred and fifty years before, a cheap and easily distributed cure that had sent sponge the way of smallpox, polio, cancer, and other earlier ills.

Kai couldn't resist something like this. She burrowed further into the records. Trelig, she found, had discovered the researches of an obscure scientist named Gilgram Zinder, who worked for some long-gone science institute. Somehow this Dr. Zinder had made a mammoth discovery, one so powerful that Trelig believed it would give him absolute control of the Com in a matter of months. So he had kidnapped Zinder's young daughter, Nikki, and blackmailed Zinder into quitting the institute and moving to New Pompeii to continue his researches. Some recalcitrant Councillors had then been invited for a demonstration; a few had gone, the rest sent agents or representatives. Three days later not only they, but Trelig and the entire planetoid of New Pompeii, simply vanished. None ever returned. Ever.

This Tortoi Kai pieced together from thousands of bits of information. Obviously the experiment, the great demonstration, had somehow gone wrong—but how? And why? And what was the demonstration to have been? Trelig was no fool; Zinder had something, all right, somehow, somewhere. What was it?

Zinder was the best clue. His early lab research and theories were all filed, but they were technically beyond her. So she asked the computer for a basic statement of his theories in layman's terms.

Basically, the computer explained, Zinder didn't believe in the absolutes of *any* physical laws. All matter, all energy, he theorized, was an unnatural state whose existence was maintained by a set of mathematical equations. The natural state of the Universe was a thing at rest, a constant and evenly distributed "ether" or single type of energy. The matter and the energy that we know were caused by the transformation of this single, primal energy into the forms obeying the laws we know.

That the Universe had limits was well accepted in physics; it had been born of a massive explosion of a "white hole" that opened from an alternate Universe into ours for no known reason. Zinder believed that the matter and energy gushing through this white hole had somehow transmuted the rest-state primal energy, the ether of our own Universe, creating the seeds for the Universe as we know it. Generally, Zinder's theory was in agreement with those of most of his colleagues except on the nature of the ether, the primal energy, of which there was no evidence. Powerful telescopes looking beyond the edge of the Universe had registered literally nothing. Besides, the scientists argued, if this Universe was naturally at rest, as Zinder proposed, then now, almost fifteen billion years later, we should observe signs of a return to the rest state. Our Universe had been nothing, a blank, until the white hole had opened.

Oddly, Zinder agreed that there should be signs of a return to the rest state; the fact that there wasn't any didn't convince him that he was wrong. He was the one scientist in a thousand who refuses to believe. Once created, Zinder argued, the matter and energy in our Universe were frozen, somehow, by the imposition of physical laws from *outside*. These laws were *imposed* and *enforced*, preventing our Universe from "damping out" the white hole intrusion as it should have. What agency could impose and enforce the posited laws? his critics had asked derisively. Was he suggesting that there was an omnipotent god, who caused the breakthrough and imposed such laws? Metaphysics! they sneered.

In fact, Zinder believed in such a god and believed he might be the one to prove scientifically the existence of such an intelligence. Other white holes must have broken through from time to time; there was physical evidence that some still did. *They* were damped out. Why wasn't the big bang of the Creation damped?

Although a brilliant scientist, Zinder was somewhat practical, too. If science would not allow him to proceed, perhaps metaphysicians would. Endowed by a religious foundation he found personally distasteful, he had set up his lab on Makiva, a huge for-hire science complex, and built on entirely new principles he had developed a huge self-aware computer, with the sole aim of locating the primal energy, discovering why it couldn't be seen or measured, and then, if possible, divining the imposed equations for those things we think of as real—divining them and, ultimately, *rewriting* them.

Tortoi Kai did not need to be a scientist to understand the implications of all that. Suppose, just suppose, Zinder had been right? If a thing could be analyzed to the nth degree so that the whole of it could be reduced to the mathematics of its existence, and then sufficient force was applied to change that math ever so slightly . . .

You'd be a god yourself. You'd be able to tailor-make whatever and whoever you needed. With the transmutation of any matter and any energy into anything else, you could have anything you wanted just for the asking. Anything.

Suddenly Kai recalled the Markovians. A galaxy-wide race of beings who had arisen so long ago they must have been the first intelligence to develop after the Creation explosion. They left tantalizing structures on worlds billions of years dead, yet no minor artifacts of any sort. And beneath each of their planets was an artificial layer, up to two kilometers thick, a mysterious quasi-organic computer, purpose unknown.

If Zinder was right, then the Markovians may have had no need for artifacts of any kind—their food, their art, their furnishings, anything they wanted they had only to wish for. Perhaps the computer gave whatever they desired to them.

The records implied that Zinder believed that to be the answer to the Markovian riddle. He had even postulated that our own worlds were generated by a Markovian-created singularity, a singularity of a far different sort than that at the heart of black and white holes. The place where the rules were made—and enforced. A secondary singularity in imitation of the greater one that maintained *the Markovians*.

But the Markovians were long dead. Zinder believed that they had reached such a point that they were absorbed into the god who created their own Universe. They had become gods themselves, and had risen to join their father.

Right or not, Zinder's theories accounted for a lot. Even eliminating the metaphysics, Tortoi Kai thought, suppose he'd been right about the basics? Antor Trelig, the would-be emperor of the galaxy, had believed Zinder right, had believed him right enough to have kidnapped his daughter, moved his project to Trelig's own world, and been confident enough to arrange a show of power.

But something had gone wrong.

The science teams jumped on the problem within hours of Tortoi Kai's discoveries. Although tremendously skeptical of Zinder's metaphysical theories, they nonetheless admired his grasp of esoteric science, his evident massive genius, and they recognized, as did Kai, that Trelig had believed it would work and someone high up had been so convinced it *had* worked that

Zinder's unfortunately incomplete notes—even the fact of his existence—were sealed in the security computers.

The scientists alerted by Tortoi Kai had Zinder's theories and his math but not his computer—the concept for which he managed, somehow, to hide from everyone—or the results of any of his experiments. Trelig had seen to that, obviously.

What had happened on New Pompeii? Tortoi Kai worked at that problem while the science teams were hurriedly using their seven hundred years of subsequent know-how to learn if Dr. Gilgram Zinder really had something.

But Tortoi Kai wasn't satisfied. Despite the accolades falling her way, she went to her superior, Warn Billie, with her worries. Her supervisor, a kindly, balding little old man who fit perfectly the stereotype of the stuffy academic historian, listened attentively.

"I don't like the extent of the burial of this information, Supervisor Billie. It's far too deliberate, done by someone with a keen knowledge of how to fool even a researcher with a good computer."

Billie nodded then said, "But a man like Trelig would naturally take such pains."

"No, not Trelig," she responded. "From what I can see he had been so fanatic that, if this were his doing, there wouldn't be a trace of information in the files. Besides, it couldn't be Trelig since much of the information was recorded after his disappearance and that of New Pompeii—and he could hardly have mounted such a campaign after he, we must assume, died. No, the rest of the story's in there someplace—I *know* it. Somebody, somebody *big,* wanted the record preserved, thought it was important enough for that, yet so dangerous that this individual buried the information so completely that most researchers would reach a dead end. The computer refuses to correlate it with the rest. In order to dig the information out, someone must ask precisely the right questions."

In the age of paper you could have dug out the information with a large team of researchers. And Tortoi Kai could have had thousands of people poring over the written documentation, trying to correlate it with what they already had. Probably they would have found the key. But the idea never occurred to her. After all, that was what computers were for.

Supervisor Billie, to whom such a procedure also would not occur, and for the same reason, tried to think. Anything so well obscured probably implied the Presidium. He suggested it.

She shook her head. "No, that's a dead end, too. I considered a Com Police link but I've searched the files for ten years afterward with every name I had and could find nothing."

Billie was not a stupid man, nor an unimaginative one. "What about—*more* than ten years?" he mused slowly.

She shrugged. "What use is that?"

The supervisor was warming to the task. After years of attention to administrative detail, he felt he was once again taking part in the adventure of history.

"Let's try a given," he suggested, still speaking slowly, deep in thought. "From your work it is apparent that there are still loose ends to be traced, loose ends that could save the labs time and lives. But how can there be loose ends? We have the whole story, all that was entered in the files—*but only up to the experiment!* Hence, something must have happened afterward. Why cover up a public theory and a demonstrably fatal failure at all? Why do so *unless the experiment did not fail?*"

Kai gasped. "But . . . that's impossible! We know—"

"Only half the story," he corrected her. "Now, let's go to the console and see what factors we might use for data correlation."

Billie walked to his office and sat in a padded chair facing the console screen. Kai stood beside him. "Free association," he said. "Go!"

"Antor Trelig . . . sponge . . . New Pompeii . . . New Harmony . . . Gil Zinder . . . Nikki Zinder . . ." She continued, rattling off as many of the possible key words as she could recall. As she uttered them they appeared on the monitor. Then the supervisor called up the names of all Councillors and their representatives who were invited to Trelig's demonstration.

He asked for correlation with Presidium posts later and other jobs.

The correlations took seconds but the printout was still spewing minutes later. Together the two historians pored over the massive output. By the early morning of the next day, after a sleepless night, they had some interesting puzzles and some new trails.

"Look—this Councillor Alaina," he pointed to her. "She was Secretary of Com Police on the Presidium when Trelig held his demonstration—she didn't attend, though. Just sent her assistant. Good thing for her—later she became Council President! And see?" His eyes moved down eleven meters of print, paper flying. "Here! It was she who announced the sponge-cure formula to the world some thirteen years later. A sponge cure! The syndicate broken. And here was Trelig, with whom she was connected thirteen years before, head of the sponge syndicate—as she, as Secretary of Police, had to know. And what two posts are best for burying anything?" He paused but Tortoi Kai was already ahead of him, at the console.

"Correlation!" she demanded. "History of research on a cure or arresting agent for the drug 'sponge' later than 1237." The date would bar retrieval of the early research on the subject.

The computer came up with the answer after a surprising delay, but it confirmed their theories very well. In the thirteen years between Antor Trelig's disappearance and President Alaina's announcement of the sponge breakthrough, there was *no* research of any sort on the subject. The syndicate itself nipped that in the bud. A cure had been produced without work of any sort by a powerful individual connected with the earlier Trelig incident.

Supervisor Billie beamed, although now the investigator would probably get tough. They were down to the deliberately disguised material. Until they had everything just right it would be a guessing-game with the computer.

"Where was the sponge cure developed?" Kai asked, also excited.

UNKNOWN, the machine replied.

"Who developed it?"

COMPUTER

"Whose computer?" Tortoi asked.

ZINDER'S

Pursuing their leads was still like pulling teeth, though, until they had the information to ask the right question.

"What year was it developed?"

UNKNOWN

"What year did the computer give it to Councillor Alaina?"

1250

She heard the supervisor slowly exhale behind her. So there it was. Gil Zinder's computer had given the powerful woman the sponge cure some thirteen years *after* the computer was supposed to have been destroyed.

"What is the location of Zinder's computer today?" Kai asked.

DESTROYED BY COM POLICE ACTION, 1250 SEE COM POLICE RECORDS FOR 9-2-1250

"We got it!" the supervisor whooped.

The records were clear. One day thirteen years after its disappearance, Zinder's computer and the planetoid into which it had been built reappeared at their former coordinates. Com Police received a call for assistance from a New Harmony shuttle, and everything they learned went straight to then-President Alaina's desk. One look and she sped to the area.

The ship had contained three aliens of unknown type and eleven stunningly beautiful women. Except for hair and eye color, all of the women looked exactly alike. But nine of them had large, graceful horse tails.

"The Olympians!" Tortoi Kai exclaimed.

Of the aliens, one was a blue-skinned creature whose human torso was topped by a devil's horned head and who sat atop goatlike legs; another resembled two fried eggs sunny-side up and oozed around creating tentacles as needed from the orange sacs atop its body. The third, which was only dimly perceived, appeared to be an energy creature of pale red, resembling a hooded cloak in which nobody could be seen.

And President Alaina received answers. At the demonstration, Zinder double-crossed Trelig at the last minute by activating a field—based on his theories—that removed New Pompeii from reality. But unexpectedly the planetoid was drawn like a magnet to orbit a strange planet—the Well World—one composed of hexagonal biospheres, each containing its own unique, dominant lifeform. The world's computer transformed anyone reaching its surface into one of the dominant creatures—as the blue satyr said he had been changed—along with Trelig, Trelig's assistant Ben Yulin, the Zinders (father and daughter), and Mavra Chang, who had been Alaina's personal representative. After years trapped on the Well World's surface, Chang and the blue satyr Renard, Ben Yulin, Nikki Zinder, and a few others made it back to New Pompeii, whereupon Yulin took command of the computer. Yulin then remade most of the people on New Pompeii into what he considered to be beautiful love-slaves. At the cost of Chang's life, Chang's group managed to kill Yulin and break his hold on the transformed women, then flee to the Com. The sponge cure had been a last legacy of Zinder's computer.

"So Zinder was right all the time," the supervisor breathed. "There *was* a singularity somewhere, Markovian-built, that kept the rules! The Well World! A laboratory for the gods!"

Tortoi Kai nodded gravely. "He was *entirely* correct. The records indicate that the three aliens seized a ship, flew off, and vanished completely—the ship was eventually recovered. Somehow they had returned to their home world. The others—with Alaina's financial help—founded Olympus. Eleven superwomen. Incredible!" She halted for a minute. "I wonder? Eleven superwomen? How did they breed—cloning?"

Billie shrugged. "Or else Yulin impregnated them and some bore males. No wonder they call their founders the First Mothers!"

"This also explains their odd religion, at least partly," Kai pointed out. "They have a kernel of the truth—but they have it the way centuries of isolation and telling and retelling would distort it. All except this Nathan Brazil business, anyway, which is almost certainly a later addition."

The supervisor agreed. "Yes, if Zinder was proved right, and the Olympians seem to be living proof, you could accept a god easily—they just went shopping for one and found him. I'll bet if we key Nathan Brazil into the computers we'll find the connection." He suddenly stopped his enthusiastic babble and looked toward his assistant. She was frowning. "What's the matter?" he asked. "This is proof Zinder was right! It means, I suspect, the end of the Dreel threat."

She nodded dully. "Yes, it does. But then what? This kind of power—in full public view, in Com hands. What sort of thing are we unleashing on ourselves *after* the Dreel defeat? Remember—the Com Police destroyed New Pompeii and its computer, and all the files were thoroughly hidden. Back then they were scared of such power. Aren't you? According to the records on New Pompeii, Zinder designed a dish-shaped object to remake an entire planet in seconds—to specification! Doesn't that scare you?"

He nodded. "It does, but so do the Dreel. After . . . well, you and I will write the history of it and watch the next act unfold, as always. It's too late to forget our rediscovery. For better or worse, Gilgram Zinder's legacy is back. It is real, it is here, and it will not be buried again."

Com Police Laboratories, Suba

"STAND BY!"

The technicians ran for shields. To reinforce the controller's verbal warning a series of buzzers sounded, then anxious supervisors visually confirmed that all were out of the danger zone.

They watched the experimental chamber on large monitors, for they were dealing with something they did not understand in the slightest and were taking no chances. The shielding on the room was sufficient to contain a thermonuclear explosion; the command center even had its own heavily shielded self-contained life-support systems. Even if the rest of the planetoid was destroyed they might survive.

Inside the chamber was a large, slightly concave metal disk; a small rod protruded slightly from its center. The disk aimed down at another disk, one that had no protuberance but was flattened slightly in the center. In the exact center of the lower disk a single plastic cup contained exactly four-tenths of a liter of distilled water. Nothing more.

The men in the command center grew tense as the operators hovered over their consoles.

"Energize!" came the command of the project director. "On my mark . . . Mark!"

A switch was thrown. Inside the experimental chamber the upper disk shimmered slightly and projected an odd violet light onto the lower disk and the glass it held. Now they would learn if this attempt would succeed, unlike the thousands tried earlier. So far they hadn't even managed to boil the water.

The senior scientists of the project wondered why Zinder had been successful with essentially the same setup. They were using the plans and the math Zinder had described in his position papers; the computers of Suba and the Council had assured them that if Zinder's theories were correct the device would work. Historical record said he was right. Why wouldn't it work?

They were missing Zinder's computer, they finally concluded, and the plans for it had died with him on some Markovian world that possibly was not even in our Universe and the machine itself had been destroyed in a Com Police operation where chunks of anti-matter had been driven into collision with it.

Once understood, the problem was simply stated. To do as Zinder said could be done, what *had* been done, a computer would not only have to analyze a substance, but also discover its basic mathematical relationships, apply Zinder's own formula to correlate it to his greater Universe, and isolate just that set of equations that fully describe that substance—in this case water, and not all water, but *specific* water. You were dealing not only in basic chemistry and physics, but in time as well. Apply feedback to the signal and the substance should simply cease to exist except in the memory of the computer. Reapply the signal to the Zinder energy flux and the substance should be restored. Or, take the substance's equation and rewrite it to produce, say, H_2O_2—with a little ingenuity and a sufficiently sophisticated computer the alchemist's dreams were realizable.

And so, all the available computers of the Com area were soon linked to one network, supporting a single goal. And when Zinder's violet beam descended, the contents of the glass were noted, analyzed, and stored.

"Feedback on my mark!" the controller called. "Mark!"

A switch was thrown. The water in the glass became discolored, then seemed to wisk out of existence. Instruments indicated normal conditions in the chamber. The scientists wasted no time getting there.

The glass was, in fact, empty. Not a drop of water remained, yet the glass was cool to the touch.

"Okay, so now we've done what any good microwave generator could do," one glum technician commented. "Now let's see you put it back."

Again the procedures, again the signals, again the eerie photographic effect, and now, when they entered, the glass was full again. They measured it. Exactly four-tenths of a liter.

They had the solution then. They played with it. Over the next few days they became quite adept at transmutation, even removing or adding atomic material. Lead into gold, gold into iron, whatever. Nothing more complicated, though.

"We're limited by our computer capacity," the project chief explained. "Until we develop a better, faster, smaller computer designed specifically for this sort of work, as Zinder did, we'll be limited. Give us a year, maybe two, and we'll be able to conjure up anything at will, I believe—but not now."

The political and military leaders sighed and gnashed their teeth. "We don't have a year," one said for all of them. "We have months at best."

"We can't do it, then," the scientist told them. "It takes time to design such a piece of machinery—although theoretically it's within our capabilities—and even more time to build one."

"Playing god is for later," a politician snapped. "First we must *have* a later. Is there nothing you can do now to use this device as a weapon?"

"We could just build a huge disk, or set of disks, and use them for example, to project feedback along the entire atomic spectrum. Within the device's limits, which are governed by power source and disk size, we should be able to nullify the individual atoms, although we'd be unable to store them or put them back together again. Whatever is struck by such a field would cease to exist."

"I thought matter and energy could never be created or destroyed, just changed," somebody with a little on the ball objected.

"That's true, within our physical laws," the project chief admitted. "But Zinder's mathematical reality is outside of those. In a sense we don't create or destroy, we merely allow the Universe to transmute the atoms and energy back into a state of rest—his ethers or primal energy. In effect, the so-called laws of the Universe are turned off for anything within that field."

"Build it!" they ordered.

Zinder Nullifiers, they called them. They were built in under four months, months of costly gains by the Dreel, who were constantly growing in numbers, resourcefulness, and boldness. Little testing could be done; the Nullifiers would work or they would not. If they did not, the Com faced annihilation; if they did, the fleet of the Dreel faced oblivion.

Three Nullifiers were built and two were deployed almost immediately, guarded by the planet-wreckers of the weapons locker and the best automated defenses the Com had. They resembled giant radar antennas, over fifteen kilometers across, and were constructed of thin, metallic fabric. When folded for travel the devices were able to keep pace with the fastest Com ships.

True to form, the Dreel allowed the attacking Com fleet to approach unmolested; Com forces penetrated the perimeter with no opposition. Only when the corridor could be effectively closed behind them did the attack begin.

The umbrellalike dishes had been deployed long before. Suddenly the Com forces slowed, inviting attack. The location of the Dreel main force and its central command world was known because the Dreel believed in commanding from the forward edge of the battle area, to be seen but not to be reached, advancing with the forward units.

The incredibly fast needle shapes of the Dreel ships closed on the fleet from all sides in a flash; they were ready. The two Zinder Nullifiers were deployed back to back; each could sweep one hundred eighty degrees. The balance of the Com force floated between the two projectors.

The Com fleet waited. Hoped. At the speed of the Dreel fighters, human control was out of the question

—computers alone could manage the necessary nanosecond response time. The crews could only monitor their screens while the Dreel closed, then suffer the jolts and unexpected accelerations as the automated defenses took over; the projector crews experienced pulsed vibrations as very short bursts of Zinder feedback were used.

Then the Dreel just weren't there any more. Not only did they vanish suddenly, but so did all other matter within the disks' foci. Light, even gravity vanished, annihilated; briefly a great hole opened around the task force, one in which absolutely nothing, not even a hard vacuum, existed. A scientist checked his instruments, frowned. "That shouldn't have happened. The device was to annihilate matter, not energy."

Scientists fell to, trying to locate the flaw. The military didn't care; their forces were committed and the thing worked. The task force accelerated and headed for the known command center of the Dreel. Meanwhile Dreel counterattacks not only continued, their intensity increased. As yet the Dreel had no idea of the danger they faced, could not understand what was involved.

The unwanted total annihilation was observed dozens of times before the science monitors had doped the problem out: Their relatively puny computers were unable to discriminate properly between matter and energy, and the violet ray was not fully controlled. The device had been designed for transmutation and re-creation by Zinder, not as disintegration weapon. Without the supercomputer the carrier was wild; it nullified everything it struck. Everything.

"We're tearing a hole in the fabric of space–time itself!" one of the scientists exclaimed. "Thanks to the pulsed field we've been able to let things repair themselves—but sustained nullification on a huge scale might be beyond nature's ability to counteract!"

"The Markovian brain might not be able to handle such a huge gap," another agreed. "The rip might be impossible to close!"

They rushed to communicators to warn the military leaders who made the decisions, but the military's response was an unexpected one. "We have lost almost a third of the Com; we face certain destruction. This is the *only* effective, deployable weapon you have managed to produce. While it is true that we *might* condemn ourselves by using it, we most certainly will condemn ourselves by not using it. We go on!"

As its forces simply winked out of existence, the Dreel Set did what any intelligent beings would do. They started a retreat, withdrawing as quickly as possible. For the bulk of their forces this was simple because they were faster than anything the Com could muster. But for the mother ship, an artificial planetoid over ten thousand kilometers in diameter, such flight was not possible. While the mother ship could attain the speeds required, powering up and the preparations necessary to prevent killing all aboard would take perhaps three days. In its present shape the mother ship was not as fast as the Com ships pursuing it.

Due to the limitations of their power sources, the Zinder Nullifiers had an effective range of under one light-year; they had closed to within a parsec of their quarry when it started to move.

The Dreel knew they could not outdistance the Nullifiers, but those aboard the task force did not.

"Turn the forward disk on and keep it on, aimed at the Dreel mother ship, unless needed for defense," ordered the military men; the military computers agreed that it was the only thing to do.

A hole opened before the Com task force, a hole in space–time. Not having enough experience to appreciate the effect of the Nullifiers, the fleet officers suddenly discovered that they could no longer see their quarry on the other side of the hole. Even light was destroyed—*and they were moving into the very hole they had created!*

Scientists all over the task force held their breath.

Something winked, momentarily producing an effect like a photographic negative, then there was nothing, not even Nullifiers.

The hole, though, didn't stop; it expanded in all directions, devouring everything in its path. The Dreel mother ship was caught when the hole was barely a light-year wide; it devoured two stars and their attendant planetary systems within five days. And it kept growing. And at its center was nothing.

Gramanch, a Planet in the Galaxy M51

THE BLUE-WHITE EXPANSE OF GRAMANCH SPREAD below the shuttle as it rose toward a small and not very imposing moon. Gramanch had several moons, most no more than cratered rock and airless wastes and none larger than three thousand kilometers around. The shuttle's destination was smaller than that but different in that it was a private moon acclimatized for its owners and not very natural at all. It was said that they had snared an asteroid, refurbished it as one would an old spaceship, added a drive, and moved it into orbit. Certainly it had not been there even a year.

Approaching it one could easily see the differences. One hemisphere was protected by some kind of energy shield that gave it the appearance of slightly opaque plastic; there were signs of greenery beneath, and of clouds.

The other hemisphere was harder to make out but as the shuttle approached the surface could be seen. It was pitted but not as cratered as the other moons. Only a huge concave dish whose metal ribs gleamed in the sunlight indicated that this must be the area of the space drive.

The Gramanch were a spacefaring race; they were expanding and had managed to do so without conflict, although there were some uneasy moments with several of the nonhuman spacefaring races they had encountered. The people of Gramanch were small, barely a meter tall, swaddled in long sable fur from which faces like miniature lions or Pekinese dogs peered. They were unusual in that they walked on all fours but sat on hind legs when they wanted to use their thin, delicate, ape-like, fingers with opposable thumbs. They were like some sort of impossibly furry kangaroos balanced on thick thighs and curled yet muscular, furry tails.

The ship docked easily and the passengers felt slightly lighter than they had been. The difference was enough to put a spring in their step, but not enough to be uncomfortable.

Their hostess, a striking female whose flaming orange fur was tinged with gray and white, greeted them as they debarked: "Welcome, welcome to *Nautilus,*" she told them, apparently totally sincere. "I am Sri Khat, your hostess and the manager of this facility. Please do not worry about your luggage; it will be transferred to your rooms. If you will just follow me."

They trotted happily after her, thirty-four in all, taking in the strange little world beyond the tiny two-ship-terminal.

It was green and beautiful. Grass was everywhere, and they could see copses of alien trees off to the left. The buildings, too, were alien, but were somehow pleasing and not a little imposing. Strange birds flitted through air that was exceptionally invigorating and pleasant; flowers, familiar and alien, grew everywhere; here and there small animals scurried to and fro. They passed beautifully manicured gardens and fountains spurting crystal-clear water. Amid this bucolic wonder the hostess stopped, turned, sat up and faced the crowd.

"Welcome again to *Nautilus,*" she repeated in the pleasant, professional tones of an old-hand tour guide. "This world, the only known product of the cooperation among private interests of alien creatures, exists for your comfort and pleasure. It is a resort free from pressures and fears. Feel free to come and go as you like, to wander our fields and woods, to fish our streams—to jump into a fountain if that suits you."

They chuckled at the last, as they always did, and she continued.

"Shops and stores here are for your convenience; no tax collectors will spoil your leisure. We have fitness programs, sporting courts, restaurants, clubs and lounges, and even a gambling casino for your enjoyment. Everything on *Nautilus* is designed to help you enjoy the money you have spent and will spend here. Maps are to be found in every guest room."

A furry hand made as if it were pawing the air, the Gramanch version of raising a hand. She nodded, recognizing the man.

"What is 'Nautilus'?" he asked curiously. "It is not a word that I've ever heard."

Sri Khat's mouth formed a toothy Gramanchian grin. "Nautilus is an alien word, of course," she told them. "In the legends of a long-dead alien race it was the name of a fantastic pirate ship."

They laughed again at that, for there was a joke in it. Their bank accounts would be far lighter when they left this place.

Another pawing. "Yes?"

"We've heard rumors that you can do wonders—arrest aging, cure even the most severe illnesses. Is that true?"

"It is true that we have certain curative methods," the hostess acknowledged. "As you may know, we accept a large number of seriously ill people every day for treatment in our special wards, and we don't charge for it. Our success rate is quite good with terminally ill patients. Of course, *you* are helping pay for the service by spending your money on *Nautilus,* so if you drop a bundle in the casino you can at least console yourself that your loss helped save someone else's life."

They liked that touch. It was also good for business.

"May we see where this is done?" another asked.

A head signaled the negative. "I'm afraid not, for several reasons. First, our space is limited—the medical work is done inside this world, far from here. Second, we cannot maintain a sterile environment if people other than the staff and patients continually troop through. And, finally, how would you like to be terribly ill and find yourself a tourist attraction in your own hospital bed?"

They accepted that.

Soon they were off to their rooms, settled in, and had their first gourmet meal.

Sri Khat relaxed in her private office and looked over the passenger list. It was a good bunch. Three corporation presidents, two in heavy industry with important political connections, plus one Vice Premier. A good batch.

This was a delicate business, but a rewarding one. The Gramanch had expanded peacefully but that was ending now. They were breeding too fast, consuming too greedily, their nine colonies were getting crowded—and they had counted. Some of the alien races with whom they shared their region of space outnumbered them five or even ten to one. The Gramanch were technologically superior to any of the others, without doubt, but they were competing with other races for the same types of planets and finding very few. An expand-or-be-damned attitude, based only on the uneasy realization of who outnumbered whom, was spreading through the ruling circles. Paranoia had inspired a mind set that would lead inevitably to aggression and conquest. The Gramanch refused to limit their population because other races outnumbered theirs; yet they could not support the population explosion their paranoia was creating.

That was the mission of the *Nautilus* this time: an exclusive resort with a wonderful reputation gained through free miracle cures and word of mouth, attracted the wealthiest and most powerful. Change those minds, and, perhaps, a disastrous future could be prevented.

Sri Khat was still sitting, relaxed, when *Nautilus* seemed to shudder. A momentary loss of power caused lights to flicker and small objects to fall over. The effect was something like that of a mild earthquake; but no such thing could possibly happen here.

She was on the intercom in a second. "Attention all personnel! Calm guests as first priority. Damage Control, see to any problems Topside! All hands stand by!" She flipped a switch anxiously. "Obie! What the hell happened?"

"I—I don't quite know," a shaky tenor replied. "One moment all was going well, then, suddenly, I felt a stabbing pain, a real wrenching pain! It caused me momentarily to lose control!"

"You're a machine, damn it! You can't feel pain!"

"That's what *I* thought," the massive computer who was *Nautilus* replied, "but—it was horrible! I can still feel it!"

Khat was thinking fast. "Are you damaged? Did something blow?"

"No, no, nothing like that. I've already performed a complete maintenance check. The source is external." He was calming down, anyway. How many times had she gone through similar things with the computer, calming and soothing him—it was impossible to think of Obie as an "it"? The most sophisticated computer complex known save one, Obie often behaved like a child crying in the night.

That didn't mean, though, that the situation wasn't serious. Obie was frightened only because so great a computer normally so much in control now faced something outside his experience. To be reminded that you are neither totally in control nor omnipotent can shatter your confidence.

"Analysis, Obie. What caused it?"

"No way to tell," he responded, sounding more assured. "It was not a local disturbance. It was not, in fact, anywhere in this galaxy, I think. I—I'm very much afraid that something might have happened to the Well of Souls computer. I experienced a double impact, one much stronger than the other, but from two directions. One would indicate the Well, the other is from somewhere in the neighborhood of the Milky Way galaxy. I'm afraid something terrible has happened—first because the impact was instantaneous, despite the distances, which rules out anything except the fabric of space–time, our very reality; and second because I can still feel it. I think we'd better drop this project for now and investigate."

Sri Khat agreed. "We don't want to shock or disrupt anybody, though. We'll have to manufacture failures of our own, refund everybody's money and send the Gramanch home. Then we can announce to our agents planetside that we've had mechanical problems and will have to go off for a complete overhaul. That should take care of it."

"But that'll take several days!" Obie protested.

"Nevertheless, we have a responsibility," she reminded him. "And we want an orderly withdrawal or we'll fuel their paranoia as you've never imagined when we go."

Obie emitted a very human sigh. "Well, you're the captain."

"You bet your sweet metallic ass I am," Mavra Chang replied.

In Orbit Off the Well World

IT WAS A STRANGE AND SOLITARY SOLAR SYSTEM; even Obie was not very clear on where it was located. He simply allowed himself to be drawn there along the massive energy force fields radiating from it to all parts of the Universe.

The system itself didn't amount to much—a medium-yellow G-type star of no special attributes except that it should have burnt itself out billions of years earlier and burnt in fact at a precise, constant rate; some asteroids and planetoids of no consequence or interest; a few comets and other such natural debris; a lone planet circling the star at about one hundred and fifty million kilometers out in a perfect circle.

Beyond the perfection of its orbit, the planet itself was extraordinary. Not huge, not imposing, it shimmered and glistened like a fantastic Christmas-tree bulb, perfectly round, with a dark band around its center. Its period of rotation was a little over twenty-eight hours, standard, and it had no axial tilt.

The two hemispheres defined by that dark band were quite different, although both north and south reflected sunlight from hundreds of hexagonal facets. The blue and white South Hemisphere was home to seven hundred and eighty carbon-based races, each existing in its own hexagonal biosphere; the North, swirling with exotic colors, supported seven hundred and eighty noncarbon-based races that breathed esoteric gases if they breathed at all.

In the first few billion years after the creation of the Universe, a single race had evolved capable of expanding beyond its planetary bounds. Carbon-based but nonhuman, it had attained a demigodhood on planets throughout the galaxies, a state that eventually led to boredom and stagnation that the race, in its greatness, recognized. Something had gone wrong in the climb to the top; the creatures had reached godhood and found it wanting. Somewhere, somehow they had taken a wrong turn, a turn they could not divine, and they were frustrated. So frustrated, in fact, that they had decided to give it all up, to restage the creation under different rules and circumstances. This banded, honeycomb world, the Well World, was their laboratory, where new races and biospheres were created by the best engineers and artisans and allowed to develop—up to a point. Then, using the great computer that was the planet beneath the crust, they created and developed worlds where the great drama of evolution could be replayed with different rules and a different cast. Giving their own bodies and minds to the project, the masters became their new creations, surrendering immortality and godhood in the hope that their descendants, alien and ignorant of the past, would find the greatness their creators had missed.

Over seven hundred years before the arrival of the Dreel on Parkatin, Obie had double-crossed Antor Trelig at his demonstration on New Pompeii. The computer thought everyone present would die but, instead, the Well of Souls, the great Markovian computer that monitored and maintained reality, had drawn them to the Well World.

"It has been a long time." Obie's voice spoke to her from the monitor.

Mavra Chang nodded absently. "A long time," she echoed.

They paused for a few moments, thinking, remembering experiences from centuries past.

In her natural human form as she appeared now, Mavra Chang was tiny and thin, with the physique of a champion gymnast. Her face was exotic and quite Oriental. Long black hair trailed down her back. Although well over seven hundred and fifty years old, she looked about twenty—Obie's control over the equations of reality was complete, although localized. A great computer, he easily handled complexities that had baffled the Com, yet he was quantum jumps below the Well of Souls in capacity or sophistication.

"Can you see anything wrong?" she asked him at last, breaking the introspective silence.

"No, nothing," Obie responded. "There is evidence of a slight seismic disturbance but it did no lasting harm. I am monitoring communications between various high-tech races, but business seems to be going on as usual. The Well World is being maintained."

On the Well World, the creators had placed limits on the technological capabilities of the hexagonal ecospheres to simulate difficulties the races would eventually face on their "native" planets. Some could use all energy sources; some were limited to gunpowder and steam; in others no machines would work that were not powered by muscle or tension. This seemingly random system also served as a check on aggression. A high-tech civilization would be helpless in a nontech hex whose military had trained swordsmen and archers; similarly, a low-tech or no tech hex would find it impossible to invade one that had sophisticated weaponry.

"Obie—the Well World's maintenance isn't performed by the main computer, is it?"

"That's correct. After all, something has to power the big machine. From all evidence, it appears that the Well World Computer is in excellent shape. That means the main computer—the one that maintains you and me and everything else—is the problem. I feel the discontinuity, the wrongness now, but I dare not open contact with the Well, you understand."

She did. Long ago, when they had first come here, Obie had contacted the master computer and then found himself unable to disconnect.

"My analysis," the computer continued, "based just on what energy output I can monitor, is that something terrible has happened. As you know, the energy that enforces the natural laws of our Universe originates on the Well World and it's usually a one-way street. Not now, though. I detect massive feedback pouring *into* the Well Computer. The Well is trying to correct for it but doesn't seem quite able to do so."

That sounded ominous. "What do you think happened?"

"Hard to say. Looking at the situation, I'd guess that somebody else discovered the principles just as Zinder did, built a huge dish—which is stupid without understanding what you're dealing with—then misused it, causing this feedback, damaging the Well of Souls. And the energy level of the feedback is increasing."

Mavra had a queasy feeling in her stomach. "Obie, that computer is all that stands between us and total annihilation. Can it handle the problem or not?"

"I won't know that until we isolate the cause. From the slight increases I've been measuring, though, I'd say not. Mavra, the Well World Computer can snuff out a white hole! What could have happened that would be beyond its power to correct?"

"Let's find out," she suggested. "Trace the feedback back to its source, but don't get too close. We don't want to be killed by whatever it is."

"I'll be careful," Obie promised. As he did, the big dish on his underside glowed, a violet field enveloped the whole planetoid, and it vanished.

Dolgritu

"CULTS MAKE ME NERVOUS," GYPSY SAID UNEASILY.

Marquoz was silent, staring at the huge central city square now packed with what seemed to be millions of people. Only his odd form and fiery breath kept him from being tossed about by the mob.

"And to think that only a few months ago it was a little nut-cult with few followers," Gypsy continued. "Hard to believe."

"Desperate people manipulated by circumstances they can't control almost always turn to the supernatural," the little dragon growled back.

The Fellowship of the Well had indeed grown; it was now the premier religious group in the Com. The cult itself was hard-pressed to handle this sudden success and acceptance; it couldn't "process" its followers but found they were more than eager to join and stay joined anyway.

The Zinder Nullifiers had been too rushed. Neither they nor their origins could remain hidden long. When Tortoi Kai's presentation on the history of Zinder's discovery, the nature of the Markovians, the origins of the Olympians, and even of the Well of Souls name itself, was made public, the data seemed to confirm everything the cult had been saying. When, at the time, the people realized a hungry giant was growing in the void and that the Com was powerless to stop it, locating the god implied by Zinder's math to get him to save the Com provided a powerful new incentive to belief in the Olympian creed. Even the nonhuman races seemed interested, although they rejected the idea of a god in human form that the cult sought.

So an awful lot of people were now looking for Nathan Brazil. If in fact he were as real as Gypsy said he was, Marquoz hoped he was well hidden.

Marquoz and Gypsy weren't present to watch the ceremony or listen to the speeches, but to meet with the High Priestess, who would address the crowd. The Olympians had made overtures to the Council about use of the newly declassified computer files. Marquoz had come to talk about that point.

The Council was scared, too.

Gypsy was entranced by the size of the crowd. He looked at it unbelievingly, admiringly. "What a scam!" he breathed. "What a wonderful scam!"

The Chugach seemed amused. "Why are you surprised? Nothing has taken more money or killed more people in the history of your race than religion, and for all its mummery this one has more going for it than most. When the true nature of god is being seriously argued by two dozen hard-headed astrophysicists, this is indeed the line to be working in."

Gypsy laughed. "So how are we gonna get through this crowd? It's gonna take us a year to get *near* the State Hall."

"One of your people's religions has a tale of a fleeing people caught with their backs to the sea while a hostile army presses. At the proper moment the sea parts. You do it like *this*." The dragon removed a flask hanging from his belt, drained it, then replaced it. Then he formed an oval with his wide mouth, inhaled, and slowly blew. There was the smell of brimstone, and fire shot forth. Marquoz, with Gypsy close at his side, had absolutely no problem clearing a path through the crowd.

A greater obstacle was the horde of security Acolytes surrounding the entrances to the State Hall steps from which the High Priestess Yua was to address the multitudes. Their stun rods and stern expressions implied they would not be intimidated by a little hell-fire.

Gypsy looked nervously at the guards, chosen partially for their size and bulk, but Marquoz simply chose the biggest, toughest, nastiest-looking of the lot and walked right up to him. The stun rod rose slightly.

"None may pass!" the Acolyte intoned in the deepest voice Gypsy had ever heard. Gypsy believed him.

"Stand aside, man," Marquoz replied, his own foghorn voice not a little intimidating. "We represent the Com Council."

"None may pass," the guard repeated, and raised the stun rod a little higher for emphasis. Gypsy could tell by the man's manner that he was just itching to use it, perhaps even more painfully than its designers intended. There was no doubt the fellow could use it as a club to break heads.

"Didn't I say we were from the Com Council?" Marquoz repeated patiently. "I am Com Police, and any attempt to prevent me in the performance of my duty is punishable by death."

The big man was not impressed. "None may pass." This time he added, "Not even the Com is above the will of God."

Gypsy was somewhat relieved to learn that the man knew more than three words. If he knew several more he might still be reasoned with.

"Your mistress sent for *me,*" Marquoz told the guard. "Your group seeks our assistance in matters concerning your quest. We were nice enough to agree to talk about it, and your mistress set this as a convenient meeting place. Now, it's your people who want something of us, not the other way around. You can admit us, tell your mistress that we are here, or send us away. We will convey indirectly to her who prevented the meeting. Your choice. In ten seconds I'm leaving."

The little dragon had made a tactical mistake. The guard had been provided with three choices and that was one too many. He looked puzzled, trying to resolve a conflict that was beyond him. Finally he resolved it by falling back on orders. "I have been told to expect no one and admit no one," he responded.

"Not even Nathan Brazil?" Marquoz shot back.

The guard blinked. "But—of course, if the Lord God should—"

Marquoz wasn't even going to let him finish. "Ah,

but your orders said *none* shall pass, and surely you were not told to expect Nathan Brazil—yet you would admit him. Either you make exceptions or you don't. If you don't, you'd bar even Brazil; if you do, then please let us in to go about our business."

That was too much for the guard. He turned to a younger, slightly less imposing Acolyte. "Brother, tell the mistress that there's a giant lizard out here who says he's a cop and wants to see her."

The brother nodded, turned, and left. Marquoz reached into his jerkin and extracted a silver cigar case inlaid with a very odd coat of arms. He removed a cigar and lit it in his customary manner. The guard blinked in fascination. Marquoz composed a grin revealing numerous nasty teeth and held up the case. "Have a cigar?" he asked pleasantly.

The guard just continued to stare, and the Chugach shrugged and put the case away, settling back on his huge tail to wait. Gypsy rolled his eyes and turned to watch the crowd.

Eventually the other Acolyte returned and whispered to the big guard and several others. Finally he sauntered over to them.

"The High Priestess will see you," he told them, "but not until after the services, which are due to start any minute now. Please wait until then."

Marquoz sighed. "How long will these services take?"

"Usually two hours," the Acolyte replied. "They are quite inspiring, and with this crowd should prove an experience that will move mountains." His eyes shone. "I have been with them since the beginning, you know," he added proudly.

The dragon snorted, then turned to Gypsy. "I wonder if there's any place left in this dump to get a drink?"

Gypsy shrugged. "Probably not, but it's worth a try."

"We'll be back," Marquoz promised, "in two hours or so."

As it happened they *did* find a little bar open; the proprietor was a steadfast materialist who kept railing to his only two customers about how the cult was a plot by the ruling classes to further oppress the masses.

In spite of their distaste for the man's poorly reasoned polemics, the dragon cop and his strange human friend remained in the bar until almost a half-hour after they noted the first crowds departing the square. Finally Marquoz stood up and started for the door. "Well, time to go find out if somebody who asks for favors then cools the heels of the person she wants a favor from likes that treatment herself," he said cheerfully.

The bartender broke off his discourse. "Hey! Wait a minute, you two! You owe me for the drinks!"

Gypsy turned and smiled. "Why, I'm surprised at you, sir. Oppressing the masses like that by asking for something as common and distasteful as money. The root of all evil, you know."

"What're you? Some kinda anarchist creep?" the bartender sneered, reaching under the bar. "Pay up or I seal the door and we wait for the cops."

The Chugach stopped, reached into his jerkin, and pulled out a folding wallet. "But, dear sir, I *am* the police," he pointed out.

They were outside before the bartender could decide whether or not to risk it.

The High Priestess was royally pissed, enough so that her manner betrayed her inner rage even as she strove to keep her features properly impassive. "You were due here long ago," she accused, like a queen snubbed by commoners. She addressed Gypsy with her opening comments.

Marquoz let her ramble on for a bit, and the unfortunate Gypsy took it, while the little dragon studied her. It was almost impossible to tell if she were the same one he had encountered on the freighter—she had exactly the same coloration and was otherwise a perfect copy. He finally decided that they'd never met. The original would not have mistaken Gypsy for himself.

Finally, when she paused in her tirade, he stepped in. "Citizen Yua, if you are quite through berating my good friend, who otherwise has no connection with the government, I shall be happy to discuss the matter at hand with you."

The Olympian started, puzzled at first by the sudden turn, then embarrassed—not by her mistake but for being caught in it—and finally once again, this time at the proper target. "How dare you treat me like this?" she fumed, and it seemed as if Gypsy and Marquoz were to be favored with an instant replay of her first assault.

"Shut up and sit down," Marquoz responded quickly, cutting her off.

"What?"

"I said shut up and sit down. It is *you* who have to impress *me,* not the other way around. Priestess or whatever, I am *not* a humble Policeman or a citizen of the Com or a Chugach at this point—*I am the Council and the Com!* My time is valuable and has already been wasted too long in foolishness. You have ten seconds to yell, scream, and do whatever stupid and demeaning things you wish. After that, I will walk out this door unless we are discussing things rationally in another ten."

Four Acolytes would have their minds wiped of the day's activities for being so unfortunate as to have been within earshot. As for Yua, she had never been spoken to so rudely. Hers was a race born to command and securely in charge of its own destiny. Even outside, she had been drilled on her innate superiority to other humans and found that they were easy to stupefy and control—which, of course, had made Marquoz the perfect choice for this particular job.

The Chugach, observing her carefully while feigning disdain, dared to take a cigar out of his case and light it.

Gypsy, who was an empath, read the fury, rage, and confusion that churned inside the Olympian priestess and admired how she regained her composure. She swallowed hard and said without expression, "Very well, sir. We will talk as equals." For her, that was quite a compromise, but it didn't suit Marquoz.

"Oh, no madam, we are not equals. I represent fourteen races on over a thousand worlds; I represent the power that is, and the power that your people have spurned. Your Council seat is ever-vacant, or we wouldn't be having this meeting. Your own planet came from the Council and your seed money was given by its then President. Now, as with many planets, you wish government services although you appear to contribute nothing to the support of those services. I am the Com, madam—convince me. First tell me what you want, then why I should give it to you."

To Gypsy, the woman seemed on fire. Had it been within her power, he knew she'd have incinerated them with a glance. But what Marquoz said *was* true, and it was galling to her.

"Very well, *sir*. During the recent war the computer files and seals were opened. I know that the weapons locker has already been secured—but, while the seals on other files are still inactive we seek to use them to fulfill the aim of our faith and our life's work."

Marquoz nodded thoughtfully, dragged on his cigar, and blew a thick smoke ring in her direction. "Okay, you think you can find Nathan Brazil in there. Let's say you could—why should we allow it? He's a citizen of the Com, and if he chooses to bury himself it is none of our concern. *We* don't want him, and I'm certain I would not like hordes of people trying to find me if I didn't want to be found."

"Oh, but He *does* want to be found!" she protested, the fire of fanaticism replacing the anger. "For He is God, don't you see? It is the goal of all to find the true name of God, which we have, and then to find Him. If we do so, then shall Paradise be ours!"

Marquoz settled back on his tail and rocked slightly. "But, surely you must see our position. You are but one religion out of tens of thousands. More, you're a *human* religion that is racially biased. There are uncounted billions of solar systems, tens of thousands of galaxies, all containing an almost infinite number of planets inhabited by just about every type of race you can imagine and a lot neither of us could. The Com is not antireligious, but it *is* nonreligious. We have no way of choosing the right from the wrong, the real from the unreal, higher spirituality from superstition and fakers. We don't try. Consider the *prec-*

edent, madam! If we allow even one religious group to have access to classified files, why, then, why classify them at all?"

"But we wish to find only one thing!" she almost shouted.

The little dragon shrugged. "This fellow, Brazil, has the same rights as you. From the Com point of view he has stated, by his actions and his use of rather political leverage, that he does *not* wish to be found. Other than your religious beliefs, can you give me one reason why the Com should allow this?"

"Other than—" Yua spurted, then stopped. Here was quite a challenge, yet she understood it. To this creature her beliefs were as nothing, so what sort of practical reason could she give? She wished that she had been better prepared, that they had sent older or wiser heads, that she might have the chance to commune with Her Holiness. But, no, she'd been convenient and properly located, she'd been offered the chance to refuse, and she'd taken the challenge.

Suddenly Gypsy interrupted. "Someone else is here."

Thankful for the opportunity to stall, the Preistess responded with a wave of her hand. "The Acolytes are all about, taking down the sound system and such."

The strange, dark man shook his head. "No, not them. Somebody is listening in on us deliberately. Someone is in this very room with us."

Both Yua and Marquoz looked around. The room was small and barren of any obvious places to hide, nor were closets or trap doors in evidence. "You are mistaken," the Priestess said.

"He is rarely mistaken," Marquoz replied in a very low whisper.

They sat in total silence for a moment, trying to hear what Gypsy heard or sensed, but the only noises were the muffled pounding and calls of the Acolyte and State Hall crews outside.

Finally Marquoz shrugged. "What difference? We discuss no state secrets here." He turned again to the Priestess. "I ask again, is there any reason—other than your beliefs—why you should be allowed access to the files?"

Yua was about to answer when Gypsy said nervously, "More than one. Several creatures are here in this room with us, listening to us."

Marquoz and Yua looked at him with concern. Marquoz was afraid that the odd nomad was cracking up. He turned back to the Olympian. "Well?"

Yua had had some time to compose herself. "Your own researches have proved our beliefs—surely you must know that. Your own scientists state that a master computer exists somewhere, that Zinder was right —and we are Zinder's children, we Olympians. You have been dabbling in the forces that led to our creation so you know that's true. Then why not indulge us on this one additional thing? If we are wrong, then little is lost. None need ever know—you can bury this precedent as easily as any other fact you wish. If we are correct, then this is something the Com must know."

Marquoz considered the argument, but finally shook his large head. "No, sorry. As you say, we can bury the attempt, but there's simply nothing in it for us. Brazil could have our necks for violation of privacy."

Yua pounced. "Ah! Then you admit that such a one exists!"

The dragon nodded. "Oh, yes, there is—or was—someone named Nathan Brazil, all right, although preliminary evidence seems to indicate that, if he's god, he's not the god you'd want."

Yua looked at him strangely. "What do you mean by that?"

"I've researched him as far as I could," the Chugach told her. "He's something of a legend among freighter captains. The oldest alive by far, a loner, a hard drinker and brawler for fun. Not exactly your image of god, is it?"

She shrugged. "Who can pretend to know or understand God or what He does?"

Marquoz sighed. "I'll admit you've got a point, but, no, I'm afraid you haven't given me enough to present to the Presidium. Sorry." He turned and glanced up at his distracted companion. "Gypsy? You coming?"

"Perhaps *I* can give you a good enough reason," said a new voice, a woman's, deep and rich, without accent. Yua and Marquoz both started, and Gypsy almost jumped out of his skin.

"See? I *told* you!" he said, voice quivering.

Marquoz's large head took in the apparently empty room. "Who speaks?" he demanded. "Where are you?"

"Here," the voice said from just behind him. He turned and saw a young woman dressed completely in black, slight of build and not much taller than he, wearing leather boots and a belt whose buckle was the joining of two dragon's heads.

"Who the hell are you?" he asked. "And where were you hiding?"

The woman smiled and cocked her head toward Yua. "Ask her. She can do that trick as well. I am someone who knows the truth behind this silly religion and I have the reason you will find Nathan Brazil or allow us to."

"You propose force?" Marquoz almost laughed at that.

She shook her head. "No, not force. The reason you must find Nathan Brazil is that he's the only one who knows how to fix the Well Computer—and if it isn't fixed that gaping hole in space–time your blundering military opened will swallow the Com in less than a hundred and fifty years."

Yua was on her feet now, long hair blending into her magnificent tail. "Who are you?" she demanded. "Who can enter a place guarded like this and do the things only Olympians can do?"

"Answers later," the mysterious woman replied. "Okay, gang, time to come out now."

Suddenly, six more shapes materialized about the room. Three were male, three female. All were large and imposing, and all held pistols of unknown design and type.

Yua, to the surprise of Marquoz and Gypsy, suddenly seemed to fade to invisibility before their eyes. The newcomers, however, were not deceived. Looking straight at the spot where Yua had vanished the woman said, evenly but in a tone of command. "That will get you nowhere. We can see and track you despite that little vanishing act. We know all about it."

As if to emphasize that point one of the women moved close to where Yua was last seen and tracked her outline roughly with the pistol.

Yua admitted defeat, though she still didn't understand what was going on, and faded back in, glaring not at the strangers but at Marquoz. "This is some kind of trick! What are you trying to pull, anyway?"

Marquoz sighed. "I assure you, madam, that I have far less an idea of what is going on than you do. My only hunch is that we've just been captured by some new alien menace, a scenario that is becoming repetitious."

"Just don't make any moves," the woman in black warned. "We're about to take a little trip, all of us."

Marquoz looked around, then at Yua. "How many security guards and Acolytes you got around here, anyway?"

The small woman chuckled. "We won't meet any of them." She smiled sweetly at Yua. "What's the matter, honey? No respect for Nathan Brazil's great-granddaughter?"

Blackness suddenly swallowed them, and, briefly, they felt as if they were falling. Then there was light again, artificial light. They had materialized in a laboratory of some kind, in exactly the same positions they had occupied in Yua's chamber.

Marquoz stared at the strange surroundings; Gypsy allowed himself to breathe again; Yua just stared at the small woman in black.

"Welcome to the *Nautilus,* citizens," the woman said. "I am Mavra Chang."

Nautilus—Underside

It was some time before anyone spoke. Finally Gypsy asked, barely audibly, "You got patents for that transportation gadget?"

Mavra Chang laughed. "No, and I daresay nobody ever will." She looked over at Marquoz. "You can keep your energy pistol. It will not work on the *Nautilus*. Only our weapons work here."

Marquoz looked around him. Since he was an alien both in form and mind, and one schooled in human reactions, it was almost impossible to tell what really was going on in that mind of his. Even Gypsy was aware that much of the reptile's humanity came from feigned mannerisms, that, deep down, something was going on no human could quite understand. And that was more or less a bond they shared, for of all humanity, Gypsy was the one individual the Chugach had never figured out.

Until now. Until this mysterious woman appeared.

The truth was that Marquoz was scared, although he never betrayed the fact even to Gypsy. He was suddenly faced with a total unknown, something that had powers beyond any science of the Com or even the Dreel. He felt like a small child among the wisest of adults: totally helpless. And he didn't like it one bit.

"There's somebody else here," Gypsy announced suddenly. "Not that invisibility trick, either. Somebody's here, all around us, something really weird."

Marquoz and Yua felt it too—an almost supernatural presence, hanging in the air.

Mavra Chang gestured silently to her team, and

they immediately holstered their weapons and departed.

Mavra, Marquoz, Gypsy, and Yua were standing on a raised platform in the center of an oval room. A large parabolic dish hung overhead. The platform would have been beneath the antenna—or whatever it was—if it were swung out and fully extended. Several meters above a balcony circled the chamber; a metal stairway opposite them led up to it. Sliding doors might have provided exits from the balcony, but it was too hard to distinguish shapes and a solid safety fence and guardrail further blocked the view. All was silent, except for a slight thrumming, as if the entire room were located in the bowels of some gigantic machine.

"Are you really related to Nathan Brazil?" Yua asked at last.

Mavra Chang smiled slightly. "In a way, yes. Many, many years ago, of course. It's been a long time since we've been back to human areas."

"What *is* this place?" Marquoz wanted to know.

"You are on a planetoid well out into space, away from normal commercial channels and any habitation," she told him. "It is, in fact, a fully self-sufficient vessel. We are well into it at this point, and below the equator. The Northern Hemisphere, as you will soon see, has been Terraformed and is quite beautiful. My crew and I live there most of the time."

Marquoz looked around thoughtfully. "This is Zinder's computer, isn't it?"

It was Mavra's turn to look startled. "Hmmm . . . Yes, it is. I see we shouldn't underestimate you."

Marquoz was more at ease now. He looked up at the still-stunned Yua. "My dear, I suspect you are standing on holy ground here. I would bet that your ancestors were created on this very spot over seven hundred years ago."

Yua was awestruck. She glanced at each of the others as if seeking an answer.

"Come, I am neglecting my manners," Mavra Chang said. "Please step off the platform—here, just a meter or two away will be okay, if you don't lean in." They did as instructed, and, satisfied, she called out, "Obie, how about a table and chairs, and perhaps some fine food to fit?"

There was no reply. All they heard was a quiet whine above them as the little dish swung out over the platform. There was a purplish glow, the glow disappeared and the little dish swung back.

A banquet table had materialized, heaped with food of all sorts; plush, padded chairs were set around it, one apparently form-fit Yua, who had a tail to consider. One place had no chair; it was assumed, correctly, that Chugach sat on their tails.

Gypsy was first to the table; he had concluded he wasn't going to be killed, and, since he was hungry, he just accepted the situation. "Jesus! Look at all this stuff! A king's dinner!" he gushed, then suddenly looked a little fearfully at Mavra Chang. "It's all real?"

She smiled and nodded. "A hundred percent. Not even synthetics. You might not like all of it after the plastic food you've been used to all your life, but try it."

There wasn't anything else to do, so they all approached the table. Marquoz was surprised to find a large roast at his place. *"Takliss!"* he said, amazed. "Broiled *takliss!* You don't know how long it's been!"

As they ate, Mavra explained a few things to them.

"First of all, let me tell you how we came to be here," she began. "We've been doing projects elsewhere, most recently off in M-51, and, frankly, after checking in a few hundred years ago and seeing how the Com had come to terms with its nonhuman races and how smoothly everything seemed to be going—surprised hell out of us, I'll tell you—we decided to go where we were needed. We'd still be there if Obie hadn't sensed something wrong. You see, we actually had a small quake here—I think just about everyplace in the Universe did."

"Obie?" Marquoz broke in.

"Good evening, citizens." A pleasant tenor voice materialized out of thin air. "My name is actually an acronym but the words are so out of date they have lost their meaning. Mavra, I thought you were never going to introduce me!" he scolded.

She shrugged. "Sorry about that. I thought you might want to get a look at them before they knew you were here."

"*I* knew," Gypsy pointed out between bites.

"Yes, you did," Obie agreed. "There are some interesting things about you, sir."

Yua was just looking more and more dazed. Marquoz noted her confusion and said, reassuringly, "He's a computer, my dear. We are, essentially, inside of him right now." He grinned. "Of course, since I saw the tapes of the destruction of New Pompeii, I find this all rather surprising."

Mavra Chang nodded. "You know the story about Trelig, then?"

He nodded. "Most people do, now. Some historians have made quite a reputation on it." Briefly he told her of Tortoi Kai's research and the reason for the breaking of the security seals.

Mavra shook her head at the story of the Dreel and the Zinder Nullifiers. "We knew that a weapon had been used against an external enemy—we've picked up a lot of broadcasts and plugged into a lot of computer banks in the few days we've been back. We're filling in the rest of the pieces now, hopefully, with your aid."

"Glad to be of service," Marquoz responded pleasantly. "But, tell me, which were you and all those other people come from?"

"Obie feigned his own death, of course," Mavra explained. "The same explosions that freed him from Ben Yulin's control gave him total self-control. He is independent of anyone. When the others left, I decided to stay."

"Decided to die, you mean," Obie's voice came to them. "She had been deformed by the Well and had no future in the Com except as a freak, so she stayed behind, letting the others think her dead, knowing that the Com would blow me up before it would chance me going amok. I got us out, then we formed a partnership. The others—seventy-one at last count—are from various races that we've picked up in our travels. Outcasts with our sense of purpose, you might say."

"They looked pretty human to me," Yua put in.

Mavra smiled. "Remember that Obie said I was deformed? He fixed it. Made me as I was before—keeps me young and in perfect condition. Any of us can assume any form Obie knows or can imagine, with any powers or abilities we think we need."

Marquoz let that pass for the moment. "And to what do we owe the pleasure of this visit?" he asked. "And why are *we* here?"

"Mostly luck, as to why it's specifically you," Mavra replied. "Good luck from what I've seen of you so far. You see, when Obie felt that disruption in space–time, we first checked on the Well World to see if the master computer was damaged."

Yua gasped. "You have visited the Holy Well of Souls?"

"Holy or not, I've spent entirely too much time on that crazy world."

"And was the Well damaged?" Marquoz was trying to get her back on the subject.

She nodded. "Obie?"

"The Well Computer was damaged by the unrestricted and improperly shielded Nullifiers used," the computer told them. "It's not a great or gaping wound now, but the rip in the fabric of space–time is growing. As it grows, the damage becomes more severe, since it's the hole, not the Well, that is the natural state of things. The Well's doing a fine job of inhibiting the spread but cannot damp it out."

"When we traced the problem," Mavra continued, "we wound up here and quickly were able to establish the reason for it, although we couldn't get too close. Obie experiences real pain this close to the fault. That's why we've moved a bit farther out for now."

"But that doesn't explain us," Yua pointed out.

Mavra nodded quickly. "I'm coming to that. Well, I put down at a frontier world to get a feel for the place—the Com has really changed since my day—and the first thing that happens is some robed people ask me if I'm Nathan Brazil. Well, before too long I've been briefed on the Fellowship of the Well and on its leaders, the Olympians. I had no problem recognizing who the Olympians must be, although I was tremendously surprised. I hadn't expected them to be able to reproduce, particularly not true to type."

"Two males were born of the First Mothers," Yua put in. "From that beginning we have built our race."

Mavra nodded, then continued. "So, anyway, I figure that I have to know more about this Fellowship and fast because we need them."

"You see," Obie's voice came to them, "the rent in space–time is expanding at a great rate. If unchecked, it will swallow the entire Com in a hundred and fifty years, although it probably will have destroyed all life in about a hundred around here. The tear will continue after that—growing faster and faster. There is no way I can fix it; not only is it beyond my powers, but as it widens it is creating ripples throughout reality as we know it. That is, well, think of all reality, all space–time, as a bedsheet. Put a tear in the middle and start pulling from all sides. Not only does the gap widen, but waves are sent through the blanket. Space, time, reality itself is distorted, becoming less stable. Right now you barely notice the instabilities, but they'll get worse, much worse, before the end."

"So, you see, there's only one thing we can do," Mavra continued. "We have to find Nathan Brazil. He should have been called to the Well World to repair this damage as soon as it developed, but he has not. Either the mechanism's been damaged or, for some reason, he refuses to go. As far as we know he's the only one in the Universe who can fix the Well Computer. Either we find him, or our home ceases to exist. It's that simple."

Marquoz thought it over. For his part, he had no reason to believe this newcomer, but with all this advanced science about and at her command he had no reason to doubt her, either. Still, there were questions.

"I return to my original question," he said suspiciously. "Why is it that we three are here? Why not a Presidium member, or the Council President, or someone equally distinguished?"

Mavra Chang smiled. "It *was* partly luck, your role, that is. I was after Yua."

The Priestess grew more interested but remained silent.

"The thing we know the least about," Mavra explained, "is the history of the group after Obie and I left. That meant finding a real live Olympian, and there are few of those around. We debated going directly to Olympus, but I had no desire to walk in there cold. The rally had been well publicized, and Obie has been monitoring all communications channels. The reports emphasized that an Olympian High Priestess would address the crowd. So we staked out the dressing room where she'd be relaxing after the show—no sense in causing panic—and were prepared"—she smiled sweetly at Yua—"to put the snatch on her. But she came in all huffed up about being stood up by a Com representative, and in listening to her tirade I figured that they were asking you for help in finding Brazil. I decided that we'd wait for you and that was that."

Marquoz nodded. It made sense. The only reason for their meeting was the fact that so few Olympians ever left their home planet; coincidence was diminished to mere chance.

"I want to know more about you," he told Mavra, acting as if he were in charge. "I want to know just who you are and what you meant by being Brazil's great-granddaughter."

"That interests me, as well," Yua added.

Mavra sat back, relaxed, and looked at them. "I was once a professional, for hire. A freighter captain who did odd jobs on the side. Councillor Alaina hired me to attend Trelig's meeting. I did, and we all got zapped back to the Well World. I was more than twelve years getting out of there. As to being Brazil's great-granddaughter, it's mostly a matter of how you look at it. I was the grandchild of people who Brazil returned to the Com from the Well World; he gave them new lives in new bodies. When my parents' home world fell to totalitarian forces, Brazil got me out—my grandparents, having grown old, had by then returned to the Well World—and placed me with a freighter captain. Surgery altered me to resemble the captain." She saw Yua's eyes open at that, guessed her thoughts, and added, "I was only a small child at the time and that's the only time I ever saw him." She turned her gaze back to Marquoz.

"Well, back on the Well World I again met my grandparents, in new forms, and they were among the people who survived our battle with Ben Yulin. He changed the bunch into his dream women—the tails were an afterthought, part of his sense of humor—including my grandparents. They became the founders of Olympus, your First Mothers, I'll bet."

Yua was a bit unsettled by the casual way in which her faith and the revered First Mothers were being discussed, but said nothing. Gypsy, for his part, had finished his meal and was now working on parts of Yua's and Mavra's with total unconcern.

Marquoz sat silently for a moment, thinking. Her story hung together, of course, and he would be the last to say that the Zinder Nullifiers hadn't botched everything up. The hole was definitely growing and they were all powerless to stop it.

"Tell me, Yua," he said carefully, considering his words, "with a minimum of service and religion and all that, just how you know that god is Nathan Brazil."

The Olympian looked a bit surprised at suddenly being center stage. "Why, two of the First Mothers, blessed be they, said so. They said they had been with Nathan Brazil on the planet of the Well and that He had not only told them He was God but shown them by His works."

"Ah, my grandparents." Mavra nodded. "It figures."

The Chugach turned to the small woman, who seemed with each moment to be less a captor. "What about it?"

She shrugged. "Obie would be better at this than me. He has *their* memories up to the last leaving and mine better than I can remember. What about it, Obie?"

The computer did not answer, but they heard the whine of the little dish overhead. Marquoz started to shout and to jump from the table and platform, but it was too late. The violet beam caught them all.

They were in a strange place, a place unlike any they had ever seen before. There were walls of obvious controls, switches, levers, buttons, and what looked like a large screen before them. No, not a screen, they saw, but a tunnel long and dark, a great oval stretching back as far as the eye could see or perspective would allow. As they looked closer they could see that the blackness was caused by trillions of tiny jet-black dots, like buttons, so close together against the gray-black of the mounting surface that they looked to be the walls. Between the black spots electrical bolts shot in a frenzy of activity, trillions of blinking hair-fine arcs jumping from one little black dot to another apparently at random, although they knew, somehow, that it was planned.

They were not alone in the chamber. Three were human: a young, neutered woman from one of the insect-like commune worlds, another young woman, fully developed but looking weak and thin, and a young boy also from one of the clone and genetic-engineering factories. With them were what appeared to be a mermaid riding atop a great creature like some gigantic alien cockroach, a green plant-creature with a head like a curved pumpkin and spindly vinelike limbs, a huge creature that looked like a six-armed human torso and walruslike, mustachioed face set atop a coiled snake-like body—and the thing that made the others all seem somehow kin.

It was pulpy, and somewhat shapeless, a giant beating and pulsating heart supported by six long, powerful tentacles. It seemed to have no eyes, ears, or any other sensory organs.

"The alien creature is a Markovian," they heard Obie's voice explain. "That is Nathan Brazil in his true form. You are inside the Well of Souls, in a control room for one of the races, probably ours, as the two women—Vardia and Wu Julee, two of Yua's First Mothers and, not incidentally, Mavra's grandparents-to-be—remembered it."

They were aware now that the scene, three-dimensional and lifelike, was in fact a tableau, frozen in place. Now Obie selected his starting point and the scene went into playback. For the first time they saw that the six-armed walrus-snake, among others, was pointing a weapon at the creature Obie called Nathan Brazil.

"Nate! Stay away from there!" the snake-man warned *menacingly. "You can be killed, you know!"*

The pulsating mass bent slightly toward the snake creature. "No, Serge, I can't. That's the problem, you see. I told you I wasn't a Markovian but none of you listened. I came here because you might damage the panel, do harm to some race of people I might not even be aware of. I knew you couldn't use this place, but all of you are quite mad now, and one or more of you might destroy, might take the chance. But none of you, in your madness, has thought to ask the real question, the one unanswered question in the puzzle. Who stabilized the Markovian equation, the basic one for the Universe?"

There was a sudden, stunned silence except for an eerie thump, thump, thump *like the beating of a great heart. Finally Brazil spoke again.*

"I was formed out of the random primal energy of the cosmos. After countless billions of years I achieved self-awareness. I was the Universe, and everything in it. Over the eons I started experimenting, playing with the random forces around me. I formed matter and other types of energy. I created time and space. But soon I tired of even these toys. I formed the galaxies, the stars, and planets. An idea, and they were.

"I watched things grow, and form, according to the rules I set up. And yet, I tired of these, also. So I created the Markovians and watched them develop according to my plan. Yet, even then, the solution was not satisfactory, for they knew and feared me, and their equation was too perfect. I knew their total developmental line, so I changed it. I placed a random factor in the Markovian equation and then withdrew from direct contact.

"They grew, they developed, they evolved, they changed. They forgot me and spread outward on their own. But since they were spiritual reflections of myself, they contained my loneliness. I couldn't join with them as I was, for they would hold me in awe and fear. They, on the other hand, had forgotten me, and as they rose spiritually they died materially. They

failed to grow to be my equals, to end my loneliness. Their pride would not admit such a being as myself to fellowship nor could their own fear and selfishness allow fellowship even with each other.

"So I decided to become one of them. I fashioned a Markovian shell, and entered it."

The scene froze again, and Obie's voice returned to them. "A replay of the last time, over a thousand years ago, that the Well of Souls was entered and alterations made. Although the reality of what you have witnessed may be slightly different, since it was constructed from memories, I did have two accounts to work from so it is reasonably accurate."

They found themselves back on the platform again and the little dish was already returning to its rest position. Gypsy noted that Obie had taken the opportunity to clear the table.

"Hey! Computer! We could make a fortune if we could build that sort of thing for theaters," the dark con man called out hopefully. He was ignored.

Yua looked incredibly smug. "The final proof!" she breathed. "You see now that we are correct. You see now the problem and the urgency. Let us find Nathan Brazil so that we may worship Him and beseech His favors."

Marquoz was a little more cynical. "Obie? Did everybody buy that story of his?"

"Not Ortega—the Ulik, or six-armed snake you saw; nor the twin Vardia, the plant-creature, a Czillian, who agreed with Ortega that Brazil was a mad Markovian throwback who simply did not join the great experiment and was, perhaps, the operations manager of the Well Computer—the chief mechanic, if you will—left to see that all worked properly. Much of the Well World still thinks of him so."

"What do *you* think?" the Chugach pressed.

"That there was a First Creator, possibly the way he stated, is consistent with what we know of the dynamics of our Universe," the computer responded. "There is a great deal of inconsistency in Nathan Brazil's character. Some of it suggests that his story is true, some that he is far less than what he says. Ortega is an Entry. He was originally a Com freighter captain, who, like Brazil, was transformed into a member of the race you saw. Ortega knew Brazil personally and professionally, and even after this demonstration did not believe. I prefer, like Ortega and the Czillians, to reserve judgment. Ortega was a self-confessed liar, thief, and scoundrel; he characterized Brazil the same way.

"I would suggest, however, that it does not matter at all whether or not we believe Brazil is god. That is totally irrelevant, something we may never know. The only thing we know for sure is that he knows how to work the great machine called the Well of Souls. As such, he is the one and only entity known to us who might repair it. Since he set the Well to call him if there was any problem, we must assume it has done so—in fact, I have monitored the call. Hence, we must assume that, if Brazil is still alive, he has chosen not to answer the distress call. Why? In the earlier incident he had lost most of his memory. This or something equally debilitating could have happened to him now, in which case it is even more imperative that we find him. The last time he was in the Well he set it to open for no one but himself."

Marquoz sighed. "That's it, then. Let's do it."

The High Priestess looked surprised at this sudden and simple acquiescence, but was very pleased.

"We'll need a lot of help," Mavra Chang noted. "He'll have buried himself very well. Even if we manage to dig him up, he might catch on and rebury himself even deeper—if, indeed, his disappearance is deliberate and not a sign of something more ominous. We can't use the government—he's obviously got a lot of influence there. That means the Fellowship."

Yua was ecstatic. "Of course we will channel all our resources into the search. I will convey—"

"*I* will convey!" Mavra snapped, cutting her off. "I think I had better see just who and what we'll be partners with myself."

"But you can not go to Olympus!" Yua protested. "It is forbidden—and you could not survive there, anyway. You haven't the physical adaptability for it!"

Mavra smiled. "I will. Marquoz, will you and Gypsy

please get off the platform and stand about where we did when we were served dinner?"

"With pleasure!" Gypsy responded and moved well away; Marquoz, too, was not eager to subject himself to the computer's scrutiny any more than necessary.

Mavra seemed satisfied. "Obie, you know what to do."

"Right, Mavra," the computer answered pleasantly. The dish swung out. Yua got up and started to say something, perhaps to protest, but it was too late. The forms, the table, the chairs were all bathed in the violet glow, and disappeared. The platform was bare.

"Now what . . . ?" Gypsy mused aloud, but Marquoz held up a small green hand.

And they were. Two forms, minus the furniture, rematerialized.

Two Yuas, absolutely identical, stood there. Two High Priestesses.

"Yua, you will take me to the Temple. We shall go by conventional ship; I wish no suspicions raised," one said in the High Priestess's voice.

The second Yua turned and actually kneeled before the speaker.

"Oh, yes, my Lady," she responded softly, almost adoringly. "You have but to command and I must obey."

Marquoz turned to Gypsy. "Remind me," he said casually, "not to get back on that platform, won't you?"

Gypsy nodded absently. "That thing changes minds faster than a fickle shopper at a bargain bazaar," he commented dryly.

Olympus

OLYMPUS WAS WELL OFF THE MAIN SHIPPING LANES. It had actually been discovered fairly early in Earth exploration and might have wound up as a grand Terraforming experiment except that the same space drive that allowed man to reach the planet also made possible the almost simultaneous discovery of a number of more attractive and less expensive planets more or less in a row.

It was roughly thirty-two thousand kilometers around at the equator, a bit smaller than old Earth, and farther out so it was colder. In fact, normal air temperature would be about three degrees Celsius on a summer's day, minus eighteen in winter. Geologically Olympus was very active. Volcanoes larger than any seen on old Earth spewed hot gases and molten magma all over the place; earthquakes were an everyday occurrence on most of the world, although severe ones were rare. To top it all off, the atmosphere was loaded with oxygen and a lot of other gases. The air smelled something like that around a huge chemical plant no matter where you were, and though it rained frequently the chemical content of that rain was a mixture of weak acids stronger by far than those around industrial areas on more Earthlike worlds. The usual materials wore away quickly here; the rains stung and irritated exposed human flesh, and the additives in the air were severe enough to require an artificial air supply. The place had developed a lush plant life well adapted to it as well as some minor insects and sea creatures, but nothing very elaborate. The environment was still too hostile.

The First Mothers, bankrolled by Councillor Alaina, had bought Olympus cheap. Although Ben Yulin had wished for idealized love-slaves, he had made them into superwomen able to withstand enormous extremes. Obie had been the engineer, and he'd done a fine job. The First Mothers found they could live easily on Olympus; their metabolisms permitted them to consume just about anything organic.

Initially, living conditions on Olympus were primitive; houses hewn from solid rock by borrowed lasers were the first homes, and for a generation the population was just a small band of primitives living as naked hunter-gatherers in an almost stone-age culture. They had two advantages, though, a large interest-accruing account in the Com Bank and continuous contact with the Com and its resources.

After a few months, all the First Mothers discovered that they were pregnant. All of the children born were female save two. It was then that they realized they could, in fact, found a new race.

Off-world cloning was employed to guarantee a large, steady supply of females who would be of roughly the same age as the two males when they matured.

The girls were raised to believe that it was their duty to have children as long as they were able and as often as they were able, and the population grew rapidly, eventually allowing the Olympians to dispense with cloning and the outside interests the process necessitated. Now, over seven hundred years later, the population of Olympus was well over thirty million and still growing, although the birth rate had been slowed centuries earlier.

And all the women, except for hair and eye color, looked exactly alike with one additional difference. Of the First Mothers, Yulin had created two before adding the decorative tail. After seven centuries, ten percent of the population lacked the tail. They were the Athenes. The tailed majority were Aphrodites (the last two syllables pronounced as one). They called their race the Pallas, although everyone outside of their culture referred to them as Olympians after their planet. (One of their early books had contained information on human myths, legends, and ancient religions.)

Mavra Chang, disguised as a Pallas, along with Yua made subservient to her by Obie, approached Olympus in an Olympian ship after transferring from a commercial freighter. Realizing the naïveté and vulnerability of their early state, the First Mothers had severely restricted access to Olympus. Over the centuries the rules had been chiseled in stone and made absolute. Only Olympians were allowed on the planet. Even freighters had to be Olympian owned and operated.

Although the planet was now modern and civilized, it produced little that was marketable. The old bank funds had been invested in the freighting concern, though, which also did some work for Com worlds. Although it was little known, skilled Olympian females were available for hire, as couriers, as guards, as private ship captains. They were totally loyal to their employers, absolutely incorruptible, and, as superwomen, not easy to tangle with. Their attributes made them very useful as couriers of secret information of vital material. The Temple, too, invested heavily in Com businesses; its recent growth had made its wealth astronomical.

All this Obie extracted from Yua's mind; also the linguistic differences, cultural forms and attitudes. Mavra would make no outward slips. But Yua was not the biggest help. She'd been raised in the Fellowship with the sole purpose of becoming a Priestess, so she had little contact with the greater society of her home planet, no more than one born and raised in a nunnery. Even her education had been turned toward dealing with the humans of the Com.

For example, she'd never seen a male Olympian. She knew they existed, of course; she was not sexually ignorant, although her drives in that direction had been in some way suppressed. Even though she had not met one, she retained a very low opinion of the males. They were not capable of advanced reasoning, she'd been taught, certainly incapable of any responsibility. They were little better than smart animals, sex machines good for little else.

Both Mavra and Obie found this attitude curious, but they reserved judgment. There was no reason for the males to be that way. Considering how Yulin created this race and his own egomania, the men would in fact be powerful sex machines but they should also be at least Yulin's intellectual equal, and he was, for all his amorality and ambition, certainly close to genius. Obie certainly hadn't programmed poor reasoning into the biology of the Olympian males.

There were no customs and immigration formalities at the small, spartan spaceport; if you weren't an Olympian you wouldn't be there. There were also no dives, bars, or other such spaceport fixtures—just the shuttle landing bays, the barge docks, and a small lounge. Everything was modern, functional; it all looked prefab and lacked traces of imagination.

The capital city, Sparta, reflected its name—no frills, all function. Set as it was in a huge bowl-shaped valley surrounded by snow-capped mountains on three sides and an oddly disturbing deep-purple ocean on the other, it seemed shameful that it was not as beautiful as its setting. Blocky buildings, wide streets with concrete medians, all dull grays and browns. Trolleys carried the people most places, smoothly and silently; the hill sections were served by cable cars. There seemed to be no private vehicles, although there were many trucks whirring back and forth in their own lanes.

People walked a lot, too, and in about every state of dress and undress often with gaudy cosmetics, lots of jewelry, every possible hairstyle—and tailstyle—and tattooing seemed to be in. Some of the people looked like old circus exhibits.

Mavra understood that needless decoration at once. All Olympians looked alike once they reached fifteen; then stayed that way, aging internally but not externally until they died, normally at the age of two hundred or so. They were all the same height; had exactly the same tone of voice, everything the same except for hair and eye color, which could be modified by dyes or special lenses.

So making oneself a recognizable individual was a passion to these women—and that's all Mavra saw.

Hundreds, thousands of identical women going about the city. No males at all.

Most of the drudge work, including that of moving the newcomers' luggage, was performed by robots built to withstand the corrosive atmosphere. There were smart and dumb Olympians because there were smart and dumb First Mothers and, of course, other factors of environment intervened as well, but nobody had to do manual labor and nobody did—machines were built for that.

"Hotel Central," Yua told the machine crisply; it looked like a glorified animated hand-truck to Mavra.

"Yes, ma'am," a mechanical voice responded and the machine quickly scuttled off to collect and transfer the luggage through underground commercial roadways.

There were no taxis; an Olympian was expected to know her way around and which trolley to take. Yua chose one and they jumped on as it rumbled off. The new arrivals joined standing ranks of neatly identical Olympians. Apparently nobody sat down in Sparta, Mavra thought glumly.

The trip took about ten minutes and the tram never stopped. It just crept slowly along with people jumping on and jumping off. Nobody tried to collect a fare.

The Hotel Central was a square block near the city center; like all Spartan buildings it was low, five stories, built for an earthquake zone on a planet that was entirely an earthquake zone. Mavra studied the building before following Yua through the front door. Probably rent closets where you can sleep standing up against concrete, she guessed. She was not impressed with what her grandparents' descendants had wrought, although, she knew, they would probably not be too thrilled by present-day Olympus, either. It's sometimes a blessing that great historical figures don't live to see what people do to their visions.

The lobby was drab and depressing as expected, but they had no problem getting a room. Again no money or identification was required. The society was communal to the *n*th degree and simply assumed that, if you needed a hotel room, you had a good reason to need it. You did have to register, though; Mavra suspected that somewhere somebody inspected those registers to see who was doing what with whom.

She signed as Mavra A332-6; apparently Mavra was a common name on Olympus—which pleased her. Nikki Zinder, also one of the First Mothers, had had a daughter—one of the founders—by Renard, the bookish Agitar satyr when he was still in human form—and she had named the child after Mavra Chang. She suspected that names like Nikki and Vistaru and perhaps ten or so others were also very common.

Mavra was using Yua's codenumber, which indicated to the clerk that they were a "bonded" couple. Such associations were common on Olympus; at some point almost everyone chose to have a child, and there was an ingrained insistence on two-parent family structure. A "bonded" couple checking in generally meant only one thing to the locals: They were in Sparta to visit a Birth Temple, to be impregnated.

They quickly found themselves being treated like newlyweds. This was uncomfortable for Mavra, but it had been Obie's idea. The cover easily explained why the two were doing everything together, and Yua's fawning adulation of Mavra might be dismissed as the reaction of a lover.

Their room was a pleasant surprise; it contained a gigantic soft and fluffy bed, an entertainment console, a versatile portabar, and a dial-a-meal food service area. Located on the fifth floor, it had a large draped window through which part of the city could be seen.

Yua delighted in pointing out the sights to Mavra. "Up there, see, near the mountains, were the First Mothers' original homesites, now a national shrine. At the base of that mountain was the Mother Temple, seat of the now interplanetary religion and the Olympian theocracy, while over *there,* to the right, the big cubed building in the distance, was where I grew up."

In the morning they would take a tour of the city, then visit the Mother Temple itself. Mavra still wasn't sure what she would do once she got there, but she decided to sleep on the problem. She still wondered where the men were. Was it possible, she mused, that, just as the tailless Athenes were superior to the tailed

Aphrodites, perhaps the males, a far smaller portion of the population, might be at the heart of the Mother Temple?

But that didn't make much sense, considering how Yua was brought up to regard the men she'd never seen. There was a puzzle here, one she wanted to solve—and which Obie was also curious about—but perhaps the answer would be found in the Mother Temple. If not, it could wait. There were more pressing things to do, and *Nautilus,* with an impatient Obie—not to mention Marquoz and Gypsy—was waiting.

Yua dialed meals and drinks for them as the sun, a ghostly red-orange, vanished behind the mountains. Then they lay down on the bed, roomy enough for them despite their tails and the most comfortable thing Mavra had encountered on the journey. She felt odd in ways she couldn't quite put her finger on, ways she hadn't felt in so long she could hardly remember. *I'm horny as hell,* she suddenly realized. Something must have been in the food or drinks; some kind of aphrodisiac that really worked on the Olympian biochemistry. It took all her willpower to fend off Yua's advances and get to sleep.

They were awakened by a buzzer. It was loud and annoying, the kind one wants on alarm clocks when getting up is a necessity. Yua groaned, looked over at Mavra and smiled sweetly, then got up. "It's the door; I'll get it," she said softly.

Mavra was having problems. If anything the sexual craving was worse; if it grew any more powerful it would be impossible to control. On the other hand, who should know they were there—and why were they being awakened by that someone?

It turned out to be a room-service robot laden with an assortment of odd-looking but tremendously appetizing breakfast items as well as a bottle of the Olympian equivalent of champagne.

Mavra got up. "What? We didn't order this," she told the machine.

"Compliments of the hotel," the robot waiter piped. "All fresh, no synthetics. We have also taken the liberty of registering you with the Temple of Birth. Another service of the Hotel Central," he added, almost proudly. "It is oh-eight-hundred now; your appointment is at ten-hundred hours. Pick up the card at the desk, take tram one eighty-seven. Thank you." It detached itself from the serving table and rumbled out, the door closing automatically behind it.

Mavra was disturbed. "They certainly assume a lot, don't they?"

"What will you do about it?" Yua responded. "There will be much suspicion if we do not keep the appointment."

Mavra nodded. Damn, I'm horny! She was almost looking forward to it! Still, Yua was right—not to go might arouse suspicion and make it hard to operate. The procedure would probably be pretty clinical anyway, and over quickly; then they could get over to the Mother Temple.

Yua seemed excited at the prospect. Mavra sighed and surrendered, sitting down to eat. The stuff was probably loaded with aphrodisiacs, but what the hell, she thought. At least today I'll find out where the men are.

When a race is physiologically identical to the *n*th degree it is easy for trained biochemists to mass produce whatever physiological results are desired. The fact that so little modification had been done to the people of Olympus was something of a credit to their leadership, if there was a leadership as such. In the case of reproduction, however, little was left to chance. A combination of aphrodisiacs designed for the Olympian body had brought Mavra and Yua to exactly the correct physical and emotional state. By the time they reached the Temple of Birth the two women could hardly think of anything nonsexual, and the internal physical and mental pressure was almost unbearable.

They obviously were expected and were ushered in with little fanfare by crisp, professional technicians. A slight, still rational corner of Mavra's mind wondered at all the prepreparation; it seemed all too pat.

They were directed to separate elevators, each of which seemed able to hold just one person. As they each entered the door closed on them and they sank, although slowly. Mavra felt as if a tremendous cloud were being lifted from body and mind.

"Sorry, Mavra." Obie's voice intruded into her mind. *"I do not wish to force you into this against your will."*

Obie! she thought back fiercely. *What the hell? . . .*

"I'm wired into your brain and central nervous system, of course," the computer responded. *"I'm sorry. You have to understand, these are my children's children. I created them—I* have *to know."*

All this birth stuff—you arranged it! You ordered it, somehow!

Obie sounded very apologetic. *"It isn't wasting much time. I must see what the males are like. I didn't program anything to make them different."*

Well, unless they're artificially inseminating, which I doubt, I am going to face a sex-crazed male in a matter of seconds, thanks to you. Get me out of this!

Obie was still apologetic, but only slightly. *"I feel confident you can deal with such a situation."*

She was coldly furious. *Obie—don't you* ever *do anything like this without my knowledge or permission again, you hear me?*

There was a pause, then a little chastened, the far-off machine replied, *"All right, Mavra."*

She'd undergone such mind linkages many times before, but never under similar circumstances and never when she was not in full control of herself.

The door opened into a bedroom; the floor all of it, was the bed. Well decorated with soft, indirect lighting, subtle music playing, sweet smells in the air, and lots of pillows all around. Near the far side of the room, reclining, was an Olympian male.

He looked as she and Obie had expected—the very essence of masculinity, incredibly handsome and muscular to boot, just as Obie had designed to Ben Yulin's specifications so many centuries before.

She approached him cautiously, trying to figure a way out of the situation.

"Hi, there," he greeted, softly and sensually. "Please come on over and lie beside me."

"Your hypno works on Olympians," Obie assured her. They were immune to almost every toxin, thanks

to Obie; but because Obie had designed them he would naturally know exactly how to get around his own designs.

She flexed small muscles in her fingertips, feeling the toxin ooze from tiny glands into the needlelike tubes Obie had placed under her nails. It assured her; she was in control again.

Approaching nervously as if still under the influence of the aphrodisiacs, she lay down beside him and put her arms around him just as he expected. She inserted little needlelike projections into his back without his even feeling them. He was under in seconds. She released him and sat up, commanding him to do the same. He obeyed.

"What is your name?"

"Doney," he responded slowly, eyes shut.

Mavra nodded, satisfied. "How long have you been here, Doney?" she was trying to satisfy Obie's curiosity and her own.

"I don' know," he answered. "Long time."

"How old are you?"

He didn't know.

"Do you do anything except this?"

Despite the hypnotics, he was surprised. "What else do men do? It is what we are born to do."

The rest of the interrogation established fairly well the pattern for Olympian males. They were raised by the Temple, raised for one purpose only. They were totally ignorant of the outside world or even that there *was* an outside world. Theirs was a carefree if cloistered childhood, full of toys and games and play and not much else. They were not taught to read or write, nor even the most basic arithmetic. At puberty they were taught the skills necessary for their work. Otherwise they remained children, working out and playing childish games in a huge playground-gym. Even their vocabulary was carefully limited; their every waking moment was programmed by the Temple. The males were never in unmonitored groups or given the chance to think, to question. They questioned nothing, wondered about nothing. The superiority of women in all things was unquestioned; males existed to serve and service, nothing more.

Mavra found it revolting. Obie tried to analyze the situation.

"Remember," the computer noted, *"your grandfather was a woman who liked women, only to be remade a man by Nathan Brazil, then remade a Yaxa by the Well—one of a butterflylike race that was entirely female, the males mindless sex machines. The early culture here was entirely female, the dominant personalities extremely female-oriented thanks to the Well World. And, of course, the two males were important; they had to be protected. It's easy to see how such a system could arise."*

I think it's disgusting, Mavra responded. *It's no different from the party prostitution houses in which women were raised as whores.*

"Oh, certainly," Obie agreed. *"I wasn't approving, merely stating how such a system could logically arise given the circumstances of this planet's founding. Fascinating, though."*

We ought to do something about it! the woman thought vehemently.

"Nothing much we could do, unless you want me to swing in and alter the entire makeup of the planet," the computer responded. *"Besides, we are now dealing with the effective destruction of the entire Com and perhaps all reality. Let Olympus and its society go; what difference will it make?"*

There really wasn't a reply to that one, and Mavra let the matter drop. *How long should I stay here?* she wondered, more to herself than as a question to Obie.

The computer replied anyway. *"An hour, give or take—give this fellow a memory of a happy liaison and put him to sleep. I'll let you know when it's time to go."*

She did it, being particularly suggestive in the hypnotic memories she was implanting. Soon he was happily snoozing, clutching a pillow like a teddy bear, and smiling.

She spent the time plotting new moves with Obie.

"Get to the Mother Temple," he suggested. *"We need to talk to the top of the political ladder, whoever that is. Indications are that someone's in charge of*

everything. Find out who. Play it by ear. I'll be riding with you just in case."

The hour passed slowly.

Yua was positively radiant; she seemed to be in a daze for some time after they left the Temple of Birth. They caught a tram for the Mother Temple, whose spires could be seen in the distance.

"To whom do you report?" Mavra asked her.

"To the Priestess Superior," the woman responded. "She is an Athene," she added with some distaste. Athenes were the tailless.

"But who receives *her* report? I mean, who is in charge here?"

"The Holy Mother, eventually, I suppose," Yua answered. "I have never seen her."

"But she's in the Mother Temple?"

Yua nodded. "So I'm told."

The Mother Temple was imposing; although no higher than the surrounding buildings, it was designed like a medieval castle of gleaming metal, with towers and short spires abounding. At night it was bathed in colored lights, but even at midday it was very impressive.

One approached by an impossibly long flight of stone stairs; the building itself was anchored in and rested against the solid bedrock of the mountains encircling the city.

To the right Mavra and Yua could see the Pilgrimage Trail which lead to the site of the first settlement. It didn't look like too long a walk and Mavra suggested they visit it before entering the Temple proper. The Olympians may have been Obie's children, but the dominant First Mothers had been Mavra Chang's grandparents.

The well-kept trail was littered with signs, exhibits, and displays telling the story of the founding of Olympus, of how the First Mothers had fallen under the spell of the Evil One while on the mystical Well World, which was pictured as a heavenly paradise, then spirited back to the Com by the machinations of this otherwise undefined Evil One who was then defeated in a great battle, leaving the First Mothers victorious but cut off from Heaven, and how they decided to build their own new world here, on Olympus.

The early huts were indeed primitive; Mavra guessed that they need not have been so basic, that the simplicity was a deliberate attempt to force the building of a new race and culture from the ground up, with as little contamination from the Com as possible. The First Mothers had recognized from the beginning that they merely wore the form of beautiful human women; that inside, biologically and otherwise, they were an alien race and would have been treated as freaks in the then totally human Com. They had been wrong in one thing, though; mentally they had risen above humanity and they carried that with them.

Above, carved in rock and gilded, were the names of the eleven First Mothers. Most of them were not familiar to Mavra, as they'd been refugees from New Pompeii, but there, too, was Kally "Wuju" Tonge, and Vistaru, her grandparents, as well as Dr. Zinder's daughter, Nikki, and Nikki's daughter Mavra. And, after the eleven names there was one more, off by itself and bordered in thick gold.

MAVRA CHANG TONGE, it read.

"Well, I'll be damned," breathed Mavra Chang softly. "Damn me if I'm not feeling foolishly emotional." There was a sense of history here, and family, and continuity after all, which seemed suddenly to grab at her soul.

Yua looked surprised. "Why, that's *you,* isn't it?" she gasped. "Somehow I just never thought of it!"

Mavra broke the silence. Turning, she said, flatly, "Let's get this over with." She walked back down the pathway not looking back and Yua followed. Outwardly, Mavra Chang was all business again.

Obie? Where are you now?

"There's a lot of debris in the system," the computer responded instantly. *"I am well disguised but within range."*

You have a fix on me? She was climbing the long steps to the doors of the Mother Temple.

"I'm locked on," Obie assured her. *"Just let me know when and if you need something."*

Olympians were walking up and down the stairs

and in and out the massive Temple doors. Most were tailed Aphrodites but one or two were tailless Athenes garbed in Temple robes and intent on some business or the other. It was a busy place.

The interior of the Mother Temple looked more like a spaceport lounge than a religious center; an intricate model of the Well World hung from the center of a huge chamber and myriad creatures had been depicted in the mosaic tiles that covered the floor and the walls. Many doorways and corridors led from the chamber and before each was a reception desk staffed by a priestess. The place was well organized, Mavra had to admit that.

Yua walked almost the length of the chamber before approaching a particular desk to give a crossed-arm salute and bow to the Aphrodite sitting there.

"Yua of Mendat to see Her Holiness," she reported quickly.

The receptionist nodded slightly and checked a list, then looked back up at Yua. "You are back early, High Priestess. We had no word you were coming."

"I report on discussions with the Com government of concern only to Her Holiness," Yua responded a little icily. "She will see me."

The receptionist shrugged almost imperceptibly. It wasn't her problem. "I'll tell Her Holiness you're here," she said, then looked over at Mavra. "Yes?"

"The sister is with me," Yua covered quickly, "and bears on the report. I will take full responsibility."

Dark eyebrows rose slightly. The Priestess punched Yua's code. After a few seconds, a small green light glowed. "You may enter now," she told them. "Reception Room three, on the right."

They walked past the desk and down the hall. It was disappointingly mundane after the Temple facade and the grand hall—it looked like office-building corridors everywhere. The door to Reception Room 3 slid open as they approached. Inside were two backless stone benches almost in the center of the room and a small chair of some plastic material sculpted to hold the human form, slightly raised and facing the benches. It's construction would have prohibited an Aphrodite from sitting; clearly this was Athene territory. A small table alongside the chair was the room's only other furnishing.

Mavra and Yua had barely sat when the door opened behind them. They rose and turned as an Olympian in a scarlet robe walked in, up to the chair, and sat down, thus proving she had no tail. She had some files under her arm and placed them on the table.

"Hello, Yua," she opened, nodding toward the High Priestess. "And who is this with you?"

Yua started to answer but Mavra cut her off. "I'm a spy," she replied casually. "I am Mavra Chang."

The Athene looked a little startled. "What the hell is this all about?" she snapped. "Are you mad?"

Obie? You got her?

"No problem, Mavra."

A violet glow surrounded the Athene, her form seemed to sparkle. Then the glow died out suddenly.

The Athene stood, smiled at them, gave the crossed-arm salute, and asked softly, "How may I serve you?"

Yua was astonished, first at her superior and then again at Mavra Chang. Knowing nothing of Mavra's link to Obie, Yua took this as further evidence that she was in the presence of a goddess.

"Who is in charge of Olympus?" Mavra Chang wanted to know.

"The Holy Mother, of course," the Athene answered.

Mavra nodded. "She has the ultimate, absolute power here?"

"Why, yes, of course. We all obey the Holy Mother."

"She is here, in this Temple?"

"Always," the Athene assured her.

"I wish an audience as soon as possible. Can you arrange it?"

"Oh, yes, surely, although it is highly improper for her to do so. But—I shall need a reason to give her."

She had considered that. "Tell her that Mavra Chang Tonge returns from the dead to find Nathan Brazil!"

The Athene supervisor returned shortly. "Please, follow me," she requested.

They walked a short way to an elevator. Mavra saw from the buttons that there were ten floors—five above and five below ground, most likely. The Athene picked none of them; the door closed and the elevator descended of its own accord. Mavra watched as each floor button glowed when the elevator passed, until they reached the bottommost—and they descended another thirty meters or so, judging by the time that passed.

The door slid open revealing a dimly lit chamber. Mavra's eyes could operate well in the infrared as could the Olympians'. Their view was distinct. The chamber was circular, the walls artificial but hard and without trace of opening but for the elevator doors, which stood at four opposing points and seemed to provide the only entrance and exit.

Mavra Chang turned to the two Olympians who had accompanied her. "Return to the surface and await my instructions," she ordered in a whisper. They saluted and did as instructed. She was alone in that cold room.

Or was she? She wished she had Gypsy's ability to say for certain. Her instincts told her that she was being observed from somewhere, but her eyes could not locate the source.

Suddenly the room seemed to burst into light; it was just that, but the effect was disorienting for a moment.

Obie's voice came to her. *"They're projecting hypnotics at you. I'm neutralizing them."*

It figured, really. You couldn't be a truly awesome leader unless you gave an awe-inspiring show. Again she thought of Gypsy. He'd love all this.

And now came the voice, incredibly ancient, impossibly weary, and altogether nonhuman. It was a voice somehow powerful yet filled with infinite sadness, a voice unlike any she'd heard before, and it seemed to issue from nowhere and everywhere at one and the same time. "Who and what are you?" it asked.

"Computer-amplified thought waves, first order," Obie informed her. *"This isn't part of the show. It's too*

complex for that." He sounded puzzled, and Mavra didn't like that at all.

"I am Mavra Chang," she told the voice while straining to locate the source. If Obie was correct, the source could be in her own mind.

"Mavra Chang is dead," the voice responded. "Mavra Chang is more than seven centuries dead."

"Mavra Chang did not die," she told the unseen person, creature, whatever. "No one can kill Mavra Chang." Her own voice, she noted, echoed slightly; the other's did not.

"You are mad, my child. Receive the spirit of your Holy Mother."

Suddenly she felt pain, a massive headache and an attack along her entire central nervous system. Mavra dropped to the floor in agony. Slowly she could feel the other, the *presence,* creep in, invading her mind, starting to take control.

Obie, taken by surprise as well, was quick to react now. Through the link to the body he'd fashioned for Mavra he fought back, casting out the alien mental presence. It was not a battle; once Obie had analyzed the manner of mental attack he countered it instantly, leaving Mavra free but exhausted on the floor. She was in shock and would have liked to collapse but didn't dare; her survival depended on a different tack. Slowly, unsteadily, she got to her feet and looked around. With a bravado she didn't feel she shouted, "You see? Shall we talk or will *I* now come to *your* mind?" Anger was always a good tonic, and Mavra was mad as hell. "Who dares invade the mind of Mavra Chang?"

Obie approved. *"Atta girl, tiger-cat! Steady and I'll make you into you again! That'll put the fear of god into 'em!"*

She knew that Obie was reaching down to her, that her form was bathed in the violet glow, but the renewal was very quick and was not consciously apparent to her. She knew, though, that her lithe, black-clad human form was being seen by the unseen other or others. If they had any historical records they knew upon whose visage they now gazed.

She could sense the astonishment in that strange

alien voice-not-voice as it gasped, "You *are* Mavra Chang!"

"I am," she acknowledged, grateful also that Obie had eliminated the shock. She felt in complete command. "And who are you?"

The voice was silent for a moment, apparently still astonished and perhaps a bit troubled by the power it had just witnessed. Finally it said, "I am Nikki Zinder."

Once again it was Mavra's turn to be shocked. "Now wait a minute! I know how I'm still around—but that's not possible." A computer, she guessed. A computer programmed to think it's Nikki. That *has* to be it. Obie was strangely silent; built by Nikki's father, he had considered the girl his sister.

Mavra remembered the original Nikki. Fat, naïve, sheltered from reality by her father until they'd landed on the Well World. Nikki had been full of sponge. Mavra had battled to lead the girl and Renard, a servant who was also sinking fast because of the sponge, to a haven of sorts on the Well World. Renard had made love to the girl when they'd both thought they were dying; he, though, had been changed by the Well World into one of the satyrlike Agitar; Nikki had been grabbed by Obie and cared for by him in the minor control room. There she'd borne the daughter Renard had fathered, and named her Mavra. And it was there that both of them had been changed into the form now called Olympian or Pallas. They had been among the First Mothers.

But that had been seven centuries and more ago. A machine that thinks it's a long-dead person, Mavra thought glumly. How do you deal with a machine?

"New Pompeii was destroyed," the voice noted. "I saw it with my own eyes. Obie was destroyed. The history tapes bear me out. You cannot be Mavra Chang."

"Obie is alive. I remained. We only made it appear that we were destroyed. You know the power of Obie, you know that he could do this, know why I can still be alive and much as I was then. You have Nikki

Zinder's memories—you must know that this can be so."

There was a short pause. "You speak as if I were not who I say," the voice noted. "I tell you that I am Nikki Zinder. I have remained alive, now bound to this machine. But I am not a machine. My mind and soul live, are preserved and amplified by it."

Mavra considered this. "But why? Why you, Nikki? Why not the others?"

"The others, like me, grew old. When it was clear that they would die, when Touri *did* die, they gathered and made their decision. They would find a Markovian gate; they would return to the Well World and be reborn yet again. They all left and, as far as I know, succeeded, my daughter included."

"But not you?"

"Not I. We were barely two centuries started; the population was just approaching viability. The Pallas needed guidance to build the proper society, guidance only we of the First Mothers could give them. We had the proper technology. I proposed that we First Mothers be preserved, cybernetically linked to computers capable of sustaining us indefinitely, so that we could lead. The others refused, but they could not force me to accompany them. Since then I have remained; I have shaped the growth and development of my people and led them through the founding of the Fellowship. The greatness you see today is my work."

Obie?

"I'm afraid it's true, Mavra. I wish it weren't. This explains the aberrant culture. Brain and soul can *be preserved as she says, but brain cells do not regenerate. She's got to be senile, Mavra—senile, probably quite mad, and still in complete control of a people who don't know any better. Better play along."*

Mavra considered her words carefully. "Nikki, look. Your own people must have told you. The Com is doomed, perhaps everything is doomed, by stupid people who misused your father's research. We must stop it, and that can only be done by fixing the Well of Souls itself. Only Nathan Brazil can do so, so we have common cause, your people and us. We have brought together the Com government and ourselves for this; we need your people for the legwork. Will you cooperate with us? Will you order that cooperation?"

Nikki seemed lost in thought. Finally the voice said, "Yes, Mavra. You will have whatever you require. The only condition is that Olympians be present when Nathan Brazil is found."

"I think we can agree to that," Mavra replied. "We think he might have been spooked by the cul—Fellowship, though, so we'll have to be very careful when we find him that we don't lose him again. I give you my word, though, as the same person who brought you from New Pompeii and kept you alive on the Well World, that your people will have access to him. Will you accept that?"

"It is sufficient," the voice responded. "Go now. The orders have already been given." She hesitated. "You can survive in our atmosphere as you are now?"

Mavra nodded. "Oh, yes." An elevator door opened. She turned and walked toward it, then stopped and turned back to the empty chamber. "Good-bye, Nikki," she whispered, then got on. The door closed.

Another elevator opened across from Mavra's and two Athenes emerged in their cloaks of priestly scarlet. They entered the chamber, knelt, and awaited command.

"With a computer such as Obie, the Com records, and our own followers, Nathan Brazil will soon be found," Nikki Zinder told them. "But beware. You saw how both the High Priestess Yua and the Archpriestess Tala are bewitched?"

"We saw, Holy Mother," they responded in unison.

"From Obie our race issued, but it issued at the command of the Evil One," Nikki said. "We do not know what the Evil One did while in control of Obie, but we can be sure that he was the last one to control my father's creation. It is more than likely, then, that Obie is still doing the bidding of the Evil One, for, as a machine, he has no choice. Mavra Chang was deformed and died in the assault on the Evil One; this I know for I was present. The thing we just saw was but a construct made by Obie, and, if made by Obie, it too is under the spell of the Evil One. Remember at all times that we are dealing with the devil incarnate; make certain that no others are placed under the spell as our two sisters have been. We require them to find Nathan Brazil. We have a pact with the Evil One, but the devil will keep his word only as long as it suits his needs. There is no honor in him, no trust or goodness. Monitor the operation; do what is requested, but keep out of the Evil One's control, trust no one under it, and, when Nathan Brazil has been located, be certain that only we get to him. Is that clear?"

"Yes, Holy Mother," they responded in unison. They had been dismissed and knew it; they reboarded the elevator.

Nikki Zinder, locked into her computer, was alone once more. Nevertheless the eerie voice continued to issue, a horrible crackling laughter.

"Oh, Evil One!" she said to no one. "You think to imprison the Lord God so that you may destroy the Universe! But you will not, you'll see. As your visage haunts and torments me in the male child, now your very self comes to trick me! I'll not let you, I'll not, I'll not . . ."

Silence reigned briefly in the chamber, then the eerie voice spoke once more, this time in the forlorn, plaintive tones of a very small girl.

"Oh, Daddy! Daddy! I want you so . . ."

Kwangsi

MARQUOZ LIT A PIPE BY BREATHING ON THE BOWL, then sucked on it for a few moments, blowing billowing clouds of acrid smoke everywhere. Finally he said, "The problem, of course, is keeping the Com out of it. I'm having one hell of a time lying through my prodigious teeth just to get us this access."

Mavra Chang's sharp, black eyebrows rose slightly. She was getting to like the little dragon, not only for his cynical, self-confident personality but also for the streak of larceny in him. Obie thought that Mavra liked Marquoz because the Chugach was shorter, not counting tail, than Mavra although, in sheer bulk, he outweighed four of her.

"You think they're catching on?" she asked.

He nodded. "I think they are aware that there's more to it than we've told them. After all, they are *not* stupid. Their agents report a great deal of change in the cult and its operations and a businesslike transformation of its Temples. Right now, because of Olympus's economic clout, they are humoring an influential interest group at little cost, but they're getting worried at how suddenly un-nut culty everybody's acting. They know such a powerful group can be a severe threat."

Mavra sank back, stuck a cheroot in her mouth, declined the dragon's offer to light it, and brought things more to the point. "So how close are we? Obie is digesting enormous gulps of data but it's all secondhand. You know we don't dare bring him in this close to Suba and the Council itself."

A speaker barked into life. It was an ordinary intercom, but some modifications had been made. Obie might not be able to risk a direct link with the Com computer complex but he could risk a small private line.

"Hello, Mavra," the computer's pleasant and uncannily human voice broke in. "I couldn't help overhearing. Want an update?"

"Please," she invited and settled back. Obie could, of course, simply continue the link she'd had with him on Olympus, but she was paranoid about keeping that sort of state up for any length of time. To her Obie was another person, and she valued her privacy even as she knew she enjoyed it only at the computer's sufferance.

"He's well hidden, I can tell you that," Obie told her. "Nobody can be erased totally from the computers, you know that, but if anybody tells you that no individual can do anything without computers knowing and reporting it he is dead wrong."

"You've had problems finding data on Nathan Brazil?"

"Oh, no. Not really, Mavra. Despite a really good coverup it was fairly easy to sort out the facts of his life back a couple thousand years—back to Old Earth. He's been born in at least three dozen places and died more than that."

"How's that?" Marquoz put in.

Obie laughed. It was eerie to hear a machine be so damned human, particularly a machine as powerful and absolute as Obie.

"Oh, yes. After all, records *are* kept. If you don't have logical backgrounds, then somebody's bound to notice. I've had to trace a very good mind determined not to be traced, and if it wasn't for three factors I can tell you it would have been impossible."

"Three factors?" Mavra was interested.

"Oh, yes. First, he does not seem to be able to alter his appearance, even surgically, and make it stick. He's tried. Since he's not a part of the Markovian reality like us but of the pre-Markovian original state of the Universe, the one that created them, he's apparently impervious to change by anything maintained by the Well of Souls. Once, long ago, on the Well

World itself, he actually managed to change bodies when his was badly injured. He can regenerate anything, it appears, and cannot be killed although he can be injured, even very painfully. Yet, even then, when he got out of his old body he later turned up in the Com looking just like his old self. It is very curious —he is a mass of contradictions. One would say that his current form was his original form, which is why he keeps reverting to it, except that all the data indicate he predates humanity's origin."

Mavra considered it. "I have often wondered about some things. I don't see how a god can be hurt, lose his memory, or cling to one form, among other things. He seems awfully ordinary, Obie, to have power such as you've described."

"I agree. He is a mass of questions with no answers. I would love to learn those answers, Mavra."

"We're trying."

Marquoz stepped back into the conversation. "You said three factors. Constancy of form is only one."

"Oh, yes. Well, the second thing is that he is a sailor. Back on Old Earth he commanded at least one ship that sailed a watery ocean, and he's commanded such ships, however powered, on a number of worlds. The combination of the shape consistency and the vocation made it easier to hunt him down."

"And the third?" Mavra asked.

"His religion. It is very curious, you know, that he should have one, let alone observe one. It is an ancient Old-Earth religion that came out of a collection of tribal groups a few thousand years ago. They seem to have started as polytheists of the routine sort and then, very suddenly, became the first monotheistic religion in human history, and codified that religion with a series of laws and customs. A number of other huge religions sprang from it but the followers of the original have remained small in number and have survived the millennia holding to their beliefs. It is called 'Judaism,' followers usually called 'Jews,' and there are some around even today, still a handful. Very curious."

"And he follows this faith?" Marquoz put in.

"Yes, he seems to. Although he does not live in one of their communities and seems never to have, he is often in contact with them, particularly on their highest holy days, and has been known to look after them."

Marquoz was not the only one fascinated, but his thinking followed the same lines as Obie's while Mavra was acquiring a more romantic if equally enigmatic picture.

"You say he observes this religion and has a special interest in the welfare of its adherents," the little dragon mused aloud, "yet there is no evidence that he is more than a participant in their rituals? He is not regarded as especially holy or godlike?"

"Absolutely not," Obie replied strongly. "Their god is universal but not tangible, certainly not an ordinary man. In fact, once, when what appeared to be an ordinary man showed up in their homeland claiming to be their god's human son, they executed him. A much larger religion grew out of that, though."

"More and more contradictions," Marquoz mused. "Why would Nathan Brazil be interested in such a group? If he *is* god why would he follow it as an adherent? If he's not, then he's at least a Markovian holdover who knows damned well where humanity came from—including his little group. It makes no sense at all!"

"Even more," Obie said. "The religion that sprang from the execution of the man who claimed he was god's son? It's called 'Christianity,' and it is still very much around and generally rather well organized even though fragmented into subcults. Those people have a legend that there is one immortal man, a Jew, who cursed god's son on the way to the execution and was in turn cursed to live eternally until the executed one should return to establish the rule of Heaven. It is clear that, no matter what the true origin, Nathan Brazil *is* this Wandering Jew, the source of the story."

"Less and less sense," Marquoz snorted. "I guess we won't know the answers until we find him. I'm getting interested in that myself, now."

"Obie?" Mavra called. "Can you give us what you *do* know—in brief, of course. How far back have you been able to trace him?"

Obie was silent a moment. Then he said, "Well, the

dates will mean nothing to you. Let's just say that the first real record I have was back in the days of Old Earth, when space travel was still in its infancy. He was a freighter captain, of course, sailing from Mediterranean ports to North and South America. Those terms mean nothing to you, I know—sorry. I find a couple of things interesting about the period, though. He called himself Mark Kreisel back then, and he was a citizen of a tiny island country called Malta although the company he worked for was not Maltese but from a much larger country far away called Brazil."

"Aha!" Marquoz commented.

"It is also interesting that Malta is not very far from what was once the country of Israel, the only Jewish state in the industrial age and the birthplace of the religion I mentioned."

"How far back was this, Obie?"

"Roughly eighteen hundred years, Mavra—the dating systems have changed several times since then and many of the old records are either inexact or unclear on which they used. That would give you a rough idea, though."

Marquoz was fascinated anew. "As far back as that . . . And even then he was near those unusual people with the small religion. Even then. I wonder, though. I would think he'd have been a citizen of that group's country."

"No, that would have limited him," Obie said. "The Jewish people have been ill-treated in human history almost from the start. Much of the world did not recognize the country and would have destroyed it had it not had a strong military and a few powerful allies. The Jews were always persecuted for being different from the main culture of the places they lived because they would not fully adopt the majority's ways."

"I think I have an idea of being mistrusted because of being a bit different," Marquoz noted sardonically.

"Malta, on the other hand, was a tiny island country nobody ever heard of, a polyglot of races and cultures, and absolutely no political threat to anybody," Obie told them. "A perfect vantage point, a perfect base, a nationality that nobody gave a damn about."

"And then what?" Mavra prompted. "I mean, what happened?"

"It would seem," Obie responded, "that Captain Mark Kreisel ran into a bad storm and that his ship was abandoned. He remained aboard in the old tradition to secure against salvage—the laws are pretty much the same on that now as then—and, though the ship didn't sink, when rescue parties went to find him he was gone. No boats or rafts were missing, and on the high seas, hundreds of kilometers from land or safety, the authorities assumed that he'd been washed overboard in heavy seas and drowned. That was the first recorded death of the man we now look for as Nathan Brazil."

Mavra was fascinated by the story and begged for more. Obie told of the many lives and many identities of Nathan Brazil over the centuries. As an astronaut named David Katz he'd been one of the supervisors on the building of the first permanent orbiting space stations; he'd fought in a number of wars and surfaced in a number of countries. In several guises, he was something of a legend in humanity's far past. As Warren Kerman he'd been chief astrogator on the first human starship; as a Russian cosmonaut named Ivan Kraviski he'd been the third man to step onto the alien world they would name Gagarin, the first Earthtype world discovered in space. As man had spread, so had Nathan Brazil, not leading the pack but with the leaders all the same.

Mavra was entranced, but Marquoz commented, "Funny. I would have thought he'd have kept a low profile—yet here he is, constantly in the headlines."

"Not so odd," Obie replied. "Every man he was was a real person, who was born someplace, grew up someplace, worked his way up and eventually died —never of old age, I might add. He has a penchant for disappearances."

"You say they were all real people," Mavra cut in. "But they couldn't be—could they? I mean, it's all the same man . . ."

"It was, I feel sure," the computer told her. "Yet

they were real. I cannot see how he managed it—yet, somehow, he did. It is interesting that all of them came from orphaned families or small families with few living relatives. Also, they were picked for close physical resemblance. At some point Brazil moved in and replaced each individual, usually at a juncture when the man was far from home and fairly young. One thing's for sure—he knew them well enough that he was never tripped up, never once. Everyone, even the people from the man's real past, seemed to believe the impersonation."

"I wonder—did he murder them?" Marquoz asked worriedly. "And, if so, what power did he use to become them literally when he never changed his physical form? It worries me."

That seemed to upset Mavra. "He would never cold-bloodedly murder anyone!" she protested. "Everything we know about him says he wouldn't. As a small child I have memories—he spirited me out past the Harvich secret police during the takeover—the only strong memories from that period I have. There was kindness in him, a gentleness."

Marquoz shrugged. "Nevertheless, if he did *not* do them in, what happened to them?"

"That's the key," Obie said over the intercom. "That's the major thing. If we can learn *that* we might find him. For, you see, over thirteen hundred years ago he broke his pattern. He became Nathan Brazil, he purchased a freighter, he went into business. And he stayed Nathan Brazil until just over twelve years ago."

"Interesting," Marquoz muttered. "I wonder why?"

"Fairly simple," Obie responded. "First, that coincides with the development of the rejuve process, which, even then, was good for a century. As time passed the process got better, the possible lifespan longer. Of course, as you know, the brain cells eventually die even in rejuve, but by the time this would have happened to Brazil everyone who knew him and was likely to run into him was dead and he had a new batch of friends. Com bureaucracy being what it was, he had only to renew his pilot's license every four years and that would be that. He became a legend among the spacers—the oldest man still to be flying. He'd drank with them, gambled with them, fought with and beside them, helped them out when they needed it, and they owed him. The spacers thought that he was just the only person lucky enough to be able to take an infinite number of rejuves. With the Com expanding, times between meetings even of old friends was great. The relativity factor complicated matters, and, of course, he'd find little to like in the sameness of the hivelike communal that made up most of the Com."

"But he finally did give it up, huh?" Mavra queried.

Obie was philosophical about that. "Well, yes, of course. If a cult that said *you* were God started a campaign to find you—wouldn't you think it time to change identities? Somehow I think any of us would."

"You've learned this all from the computer files?" Mavra asked, amazed.

"Yes and no. It was there, but only in bits and pieces. It has taken not only the computer files but also the legwork of thousands of Fellowship members on a large number of worlds to correlate," Obie replied. "We could not have done it without them—but now we are stopped until we can unearth some clue as to where he was reborn."

"Did he just disappear again?"

"That's about it, Marquoz. He kept ships an awfully long time—two, three hundred years or more, until they wore out. They were all named the *Stehekin,* a word whose meaning eludes me. The last one was found, a huge hole blown through its midsection. It had been looted. There was blood on the bridge that matched Brazil's—quite a lot of it—but no trace of him or his valuable cargo. It was assumed that he'd been lured out of nullspace by a false distress signal, attacked by pirates, and murdered. There's actually a plaque to his memory in Spacer's Hall."

"You don't believe it, though," Mavra noted.

"Of course not. That sort of thing is his favorite way out. No, I think he found some real person, reached the point he had to reach with that person in order to assume his identity, and did so. He is somewhere else now, as someone else, waiting a decent amount of time before he can resume a normal life again."

A new voice said, "Well, I think he should be pretty easy to find." They whirled, saw that it was Gypsy.

Marquoz nodded but Mavra looked at him strangely, an odd thought passing through her mind. It was ridiculous, of course, but . . . No, he was a little too tall, a little too muscular, a little too dark. She wondered, though. When Obie had picked them all up from the Temple that first time, the computer had not done anything more than simple teleportation. He'd made no detailed analysis; he hadn't stored the mind and memory of Gypsy and Marquoz. Later, they'd refused to use Obie's teleportation system. Both Gypsy and Marquoz had insisted on using spaceships. Afterward Mavra and Obie had run a check on Gypsy, just out of curiosity, and found nothing. Absolutely nothing. When even Mavra Chang's early history could be found in the files and all travel and expenses required records, there was not even a travel document showing that he existed. His thumbprints, retinal and blood patterns had matched nowhere at all.

Finally she couldn't resist it. "Gypsy? Ever heard of Malta?"

He looked a little surprised but didn't bat an eyelash as he replied, "Sure. It's the capital city of Sorgos, I think."

Marquoz chortled lightly. "I know what you're thinking. I've sometimes thought it myself. But, no, he has the wrong physiology. Brazil has occasionally been able to alter thumbprints but never retinal and blood patterns. Forget it. He's another mystery."

Gypsy looked confused. "What's that all about?"

"The lady was just wondering if you were Nathan Brazil yourself, that's all."

He chuckled. "Oh, hell, no. Whoever heard of a Jewish Gypsy?"

They all had to laugh at that. Still, Mavra told herself, there was something extremely odd about the man. His strange powers went beyond empathy. In an age in which everyone showed the proper papers just to go to the bathroom and even Mavra's had had to be carefully faked, Gypsy, according to Marquoz, had never been asked for them. In a customs line he would simply be ignored; stiff-necked hotel clerks, even when robots, never thought to ask for his documentation. Even on New Pompeii he strolled into high-security areas without a challenge. Why? What strange power did he have? Where did he get it? Could he influence Obie? Was that why the computer had taken no readout?

Seemingly ignorant of this mental speculation, Gypsy plopped down in a chair, yawned, and rubbed his eyes.

Even as Mavra stared, her preoccupation passed; her mind turned to other channels. dismissing the mystery of Gypsy as unimportant to their present work. She turned to the intercom and Obie and never once even questioned why the problem of Gypsy had suddenly become something she shouldn't concern herself with.

Nautilus

The Com computers were, with the exception of Obie, the greatest and fastest gatherers, analyzers, and disseminators of knowledge in the Com sector of space. To this had been added Obie, a pleasantly human personality that masked the ability to do millions of different, complex projects all at the same time. The speed and rate of human conversation and the slowness of the human mind must have been agonizing to him, yet he never complained about it or seemed to think of himself as something apart from man. Obie thought of himself as a human being and acted accordingly.

Still, with all the speed and versatility at their command they had the problems of bureaucracy and interstellar distances. The information they needed would probably be available to Obie in fractions of a second—if he had all the data. Data, however, were gathered on a thousand planets over an immense area. The data were collected by millions of departments, eventually stored, eventually correlated, eventually—sometimes after years—sent on to higher authorities. The searchers couldn't wait for this information finally to reach the Com; they had to go out and get it.

And that, of course, was where the Fellowship of the Well came in. The Acolytes probed, sifted, stored, and passed on all they could. They were everywhere. If they could obtain the information freely, they did; if it took official sanction, they got it; if they couldn't obtain official sanction, then they begged, bribed, or stole what they wanted. Mavra Chang had once been an expert at computer thievery; Obie was an even better tutor.

Occasionally, Acolytes were caught with their hands in the informational till. In such cases, human and lower-government agencies were taken care of directly by Marquoz; if all else failed, Mavra and the *Nautilus* crew could break anybody out of anywhere. If a coverup was needed, Obie could be counted on to provide one.

Obie was working on the three common points in Brazil's history. Certainly he would try to disguise himself, but it would be a true disguise, not one of the new popular shape-changing techniques. He wouldn't risk exposing himself by resorting to an experimental device.

Only a small number of Jewish communities remained, and those were carefully monitored. Then there was his occupation—Brazil had always been a captain. It gave him mobility, peace and quiet, and anonymity, all of which he required. Mavra would check in with Obie daily on the *Nautilus* to keep up with events. Having just returned from bailing out two Fellowship adherents accused of stealing garbage disposal records on the largest city of an obscure frontier world, she was eager to hear of any progress.

"Progress is where you find it," Obie said philosophically. "So far I have amassed a lot of information on Jewish captains—there are a surprising number considering how tiny a minority they are—but very little that is specific. Material that came in this morning seems to add to what I need, yet it's not enough. I have a number of suspects, none of which might be Brazil. I need an additional correlation."

"Of what with what?"

"All the Jewish captains and Brazil's life and disappearance—that's the data still coming in. Check back in a couple of hours when I have the rest of it. I may be able to pinpoint it accurately."

So she went Topside and asked Marquoz and several of the Olympians to meet her later on. They would come running, although it could take a day or two to assemble everybody on the *Nautilus*.

By late afternoon, when Mavra contacted Obie again, he had the search narrowed down fairly well.

"First of all," he began, "do you know what a rabbi is?"

She admitted she didn't, so Obie continued.

"Well, he is a priest in the Jewish faith—except he has no mystical powers, real or imagined. Literally the term is 'teacher' and means that his education has specialized in Jewish law and culture so that he's an expert—just as any other profession is the product of education. Each Jewish temple has a rabbi selected by the congregation for his knowledge of the faith—but there are numerous rabbis who have no congregation, who have other jobs, even, but who are considered experts and can instruct others. Many of these specialize in fine points of the law and live the faith, yet make their money in secular occupations. It's really a fascinating thing. Do you know, for example, that there are *three* rabbis who are also freighter captains?"

She was surprised. "Captains? Religious teachers?"

"See what I mean? And yet it's a triply good living, since it's not only lucrative and provides a lot of time for study but also is the best way to reach the small congregations scattered across hundreds of worlds. Of the three, *all* have at one time or another worked jobs in which Brazil's ship, as a private contractor, was also involved, so they all have met him. Two of them seem to have had extensive contact with Brazil over the years—decades, in fact—and may be considered close friends. But only one of them owns his own ship; the others work for shipping companies. I had encountered this before but had rejected the man because he was Hassidic—the strictest of the sects, or degrees, of Judaism, whose members are bound to rigid laws of dress, of eating, of religious form and observance. The Hassidim function in a modern world without compromising, basically keeping the laws that are thousands of years old. I had not expected to find Brazil in such a role since, clearly, he has observed very few of those laws himself. Also, this particular rabbi, is old; he's already undergone two rejuves, and he's taller and stouter than Brazil, with a full white beard. But, then, data that came in today persuades me of the logic of it all."

Mavra frowned. "Well, I can see that it would be an easy disguise—some padding, a false beard, some lifts in the shoes like I use. Yes. But beyond that?"

"Well, I was able to reconstruct route descriptions of this man's ship and Brazil's *Stehekin* for a period of three decades. You would be shocked at how often their routes are congruent—and remember, they both owned their ships, so they weren't bound by a traffic manager. Their side trips particularly interested me—they touched practically every strict Jewish community at some point in a two- to -three-year period. During the twenty years prior to Brazil's disappearance, they had celebrated the highest of Jewish holy days together at one or another congregation. They knew each other *very* well over a *very* long time."

"Doesn't that rule him out, though? Wasn't it Brazil's M. O. to find a young man to replace?"

"This is just as good. An old man who has outlived all his contemporaries. A freighter captain of repute and reputation. But, more important, roughly six months before his disappearance Brazil and this man met on a small planet. Our man was old, he was having medical problems, his physical was coming up and he couldn't possibly pass it without a rejuve—but medical records indicated that he just couldn't stand another rejuve. Yet, some four months later, *with no rejuve,* he took and passed a complete examination with flying colors!"

Mavra looked puzzled. "But—*four* months? You said they met last *six* months before."

"Sure! Don't you see? They swapped identities way back then! Brazil used the time to get the last of whatever he needed to simulate his man properly and then became him, while the old rabbi went off in the *Stehekin* posing as Brazil, who'd just passed his own examination a year before and had three years before another."

"Wouldn't somebody notice that Brazil had turned into an old man?" she asked.

"Oh, sure. If they saw him. But if he served ports where he wasn't known, and if he stayed on his ship for that time, there'd be no mystery. The *Stehekin* took no passengers during the period but did haul some freight. Then, two months after the switch, an 'attack' is arranged. Brazil is killed and that's that."

"But what happened to the man he replaced? Did he die or what?"

"Perhaps. It depends. Consider what Brazil could offer him. An old man who'd been everywhere and seen it all and was having his livelihood and love—you have to love space to work at it for two centuries—taken from him, with death shortly to follow. What Brazil could offer him was a new life in a new body, a renewal, new experience and adventure."

Mavra cursed herself for a fool. "Of course! There are Markovian gates all around! Brazil could have told him how to use one, even brought him to one. He went to the Well World!"

Obie chuckled. "I wonder what sort of creature he is now? I should dearly love to see how he manages to keep kosher!"

"Huh?"

"Never mind. It's not important. I'm sure that Nathan Brazil is now Rabbi David Korf, captain of the freighter *Jerusalem.*"

Mavra was genuinely excited at the news. "Then all we have to do is find out where the *Jerusalem* will make planetfall next and be there to meet it!"

"So it would seem," Obie agreed. "Except for one thing. After the switch Korf totally changed his operational area—I suppose to minimize chances of running into people who knew the real Korf well. The trouble is, he's an independent. It might be years before the relevant documentation for an independent gets filed. I've checked everything I could, but after about six years ago I have no sign that the *Jerusalem* ever made a contract or hauled cargo anywhere in our little corner of space. Brazil has not only pulled his disappearing act, he seems to have taken his ship with him this time."

According to the licensing board, Rabbi Korf had in fact returned and renewed his license only a year before. This was more puzzling than a total disappearance. The last renewal indicated that both Korf and the *Jerusalem* were still very much in service and, in fact, required recertification. But where? And for whom? There were no records to show.

"Strictly private, maybe? Perhaps illegal?" Mavra suggested.

Marquoz, who had arrived just a step ahead of the rest of the crowd, Temple and otherwise, was skeptical. "If *that* illegal, then why bother to recertify and reestablish his identity at all? If not, then he needs the cover—and that would also mean legitimate business. No, I think he's still hauling cargo in the open and quite legally between Com worlds."

"Impossible," Obie responded. "As the Fellowship people will tell you, we have *all* worlds covered."

Marquoz cocked a large reptilian head and his smile widened slightly in mock surprise. "No, you don't. Not by a long shot. What your Fellowship covers is *human* worlds. The Acolytes are not very popular in the nonhuman sectors—which, it would seem to me, would be the very place to best avoid the cult."

Obie was silent for a moment. Then he said, "My cost was astronomical, my builder perhaps mankind's greatest genius. I can do any calculation in an amount of time so small that it is incomprehensible to the organic mind. So, tell me—why didn't I think of that?"

"Too simple," Mavra told him dryly. "Obie, your problem is that you think like a human being, only faster."

"All right," the computer retorted, trying to channel the argument away from his own failings. "So now what? There are a lot of nonhuman worlds out there in the Com and allied with it, and we don't have the proper records for them or the proper personnel to get them."

"I wouldn't be concerned with the allied and associated worlds," Marquoz said. "If he was dealing there exclusively, he wouldn't need to recharter. No, he's within the Com proper, which means one of a very few races. We can eliminate some right off—mine, for example, which is serviced entirely by a nationalized shipping company; the nonorganic boys, since their trade's of a far different type; the non-carbon based, too, I think, are out—he's avoided the human sector because he didn't want to be stuck in his ship all the time. He wants to socialize, and that means a place where we can breathe the air and drink the booze without artificial aid. That narrows it down pretty well, doesn't it?"

"I agree," Obie replied. "The pattern's consistent. In my files I find that he's always had rather an affinity for Rhone centaurs—the ones called Dillians on the Well World. They meet all the other specifications, too—although this, in itself, is a problem since the Rhone is a spacefaring and expanding race itself, almost as large as humanity, possibly older and certainly more spread out. Without the Fellowship to do the legwork, it's going to be hell to track him down. He's chosen well."

It was Mavra's turn now. "I don't think it ought to be that hard. I don't know a damned thing about them or their culture—the closest I've come is being briefly in Dillia, which hardly counts—but if the Rhone are highly advanced then they have their own bureaucracy and central controls. They keep files and records someplace and they're probably as efficient at that as humans are."

"They could hardly be any worse," Obie snorted.

She smiled and nodded. "So, let's find those records."

All eyes turned to Marquoz. He sighed and said, "All right, I'll see what I can do."

It took ten days and a minor burglary. The Rhone, far better organized than the Com proper, required ship listings at five central naval district offices so that ships could be traced if overdue. The human areas of the Com only required that the ship file a plan at two locations before embarking; in many cases even that wasn't done, and the human area didn't really care since the procedure was for the protection of the freighter anyway.

Disguised as Rhone, with nicely counterfeited orders, seven of the *Nautilus* crew were dispatched to each naval headquarters. They had to locate a middle-ranking naval officer, one with broad access to traffic files. The newer he was the better, although the operation's headquarters for such large areas were so big that few people would know everybody and a complete stranger could probably walk through without being seriously questioned on his rights—as long as he knew the codes and passwords and had the right ID tags.

It was on the latter that the Rhone depended most for security; among the things preserved on the tags was an actual tissue sample from the wearer. A Rhone's sample was unique, and an electronic comparison of it with living tissue—say, of the palm—would be an infallible method of making sure the wearer was who he or she claimed to be.

On the off-chance that there might be an energy-binding system not thoroughly detectable even by Obie's absolute analysis, it was decided that only original-issue tags would be used. The system was simple: Lure the target officers someplace, drug them, transport them to Obie, then run them through the dish. Just as Yua and her supervisor had been reprogrammed by this process, so were the young officers. At some point during the next three days or so they would look at the shipping information and their minds would be able to retain all the information no matter how many ships were involved or how complex the routing. Later they would call a number and repeat that information. At no time would they be aware of what they were doing; they would have no memory of their kidnapping, of Obie, or of anything else. Once the compulsion had been carried out, they would go on about their business never knowing they had been used.

As the information came in, Marquoz had Obie make a printout for the rest of them to use. The third district showed what they wanted clearly, as Obie could have told them instantly if they'd asked. But, he understood people well enough to allow them some minor victories.

"There it is," Marquoz said, pointing to a single line. "'*Jerusalem,* HC-23A768744, M Class Modified, arrival Meouit 27 HYR.' Must not be carrying anything valuable—no classification codes. Probably grain or beer or something like that."

Mavra smiled slightly. "From what I've been told, a cargo of beer or ale would appeal to Nathan Brazil."

"Me, too," the little dragon retorted. "The date 27 HYR corresponds, I think, to June 24. That's five days from now. Anybody know where this Meouit is?"

"Obie does," Mavra responded confidently. "I think we'll get there well ahead of him." She sighed. "Well, I guess it's time to call a war council. We now know where the man we think he is will be five days from now. We'll have to be pretty damned sure we don't blow it."

They came to the *Nautilus* once more, to its beautiful gardens and Greco-Roman buildings, then down the elevator for the long ride to the asteroid's core, down a twisting corridor and across a huge bridge that spanned the main shaft for the big dish—the giant projector that took up much of the underside of the asteroid and was capable not merely of destroying but of reshaping and redesigning whole planets.

On one side of the bridge was the almost never used main control room. Now Obie alone supervised himself and the vast machinery that was the *Nautilus*. On the other side of the bridge was the small chamber with the little dish and the heavily instrumented balcony. This had been Zinder's original lab, transplanted here by the evil Trelig. Through monitors Obie could have addressed them anywhere, but he preferred this place for gatherings. It was his "office," his true home.

Five Olympians assembled there in their great cloaks, three Aphrodites and two Athenes, plus Marquoz and Gypsy and Mavra. Of them all, only Mavra felt totally confident when in this place; it was her home, too, and she was Obie's partner, not his possession. The others feared her a bit for that; the psychological effect was just right. Except for Yua, the Olympians were trying their best not to look terrified; they knew this was the seat of power—the place where their race was born, not by the act of a benevolent god but by the whim of an evil maniac.

When all were seated except Marquoz, who never sat on anything except his tail, Obie opened the conference.

"First, let me state the obvious," he began. His voice, materializing from empty air, was unsettling. "We are about to head for Meouit by the most direct course. It would take weeks to get there by ship. I am awaiting word from the crew Topside that our other guests are properly secured for what we call the 'drop.' That is what it will feel like—as if you are falling down a deep shaft. Please do not be alarmed; the effect is temporary. Even I feel some discomfort, much more since that rip in space-time."

The Olympians in the chamber looked apprehensive, but there was little they could do. They were at the mercy of the machine and could only pray that he trusted them enough not to do anything funny with their minds. They didn't know, nor were they told, that Obie could not perform such tricks *on* or *in* the *Nautilus* unless you were under the little dish.

"First of all," Obie continued, "remember that, for all our long hard months of work, we only suspect that Rabbi Korf is Nathan Brazil. There is a possibility, although I consider it low, that Korf is Korf. We must be prepared for this just in case."

One of the Olympians spoke up. "You have powers—the power in some cases to pluck people here from wherever they may be. Why not simply do so with this Korf and avoid any problems? We could find out what we needed to know here, at little risk."

"What you say is true," Obie admitted, "but only to a degree. In order to pluck, as you say, individuals I must have a sensor down there actually focused on the object. Mavra has been that focus in the instances you know of, but we cannot be positive that we'll be able to get close enough long enough for that to happen. Also, please remember, if this man *is* Nathan Brazil, he will look human but he will be something we are not—he will be a part of a different universal plan than we. We are all—*all*—by-products of the Markovian equations. Our reality is held firm by the great computer the Markovians constructed, the Well of Souls. Nathan Brazil's is not. He is independent of that computer except that it aids him in retaining what form he chooses and protects him from death. It also might protect him from being snatched by me. It might severely damage me to attempt to transport him when he is not a part of the basic equations. We can't risk it, not until we know more, anyway. No, it's direct action that's called for. We must convince him to come to us."

"I foresee a great problem there, then," Marquoz put in. "He has gone to great lengths to avoid detection. If he knows we're on to him, he'll flee and we may never find him again in time. Our approach must be subtle, gentle—but all avenues of escape must be blocked."

"That is ridiculous!" one of the Athenes snorted. "If He is asked if He is in fact Nathan Brazil, His master plan will be fulfilled and He will show His true powers."

"But how can you be sure?" Mavra shot back. "Oh, everything's panned out as your beliefs say so far—but, ah, perhaps more is required. Remember that he went public and was aboveboard until a dozen or so years ago. He must have been asked a million times by customs agents alone if he was indeed Nathan Brazil. You see? I think you have a problem —I think that, even under your own beliefs, logic dictates that you are going to have to ask him by his true name for him to admit it—and we don't know his true name. If I'm right on that then you'll panic him just as Marquoz warned."

That concept seemed to disturb the Olympians slightly. It was a valid point within their faith—and one that simply had never occurred to them. Nathan Brazil was *not* his true name; it was a traditional first name coupled with the name of an Old-Earth country he'd once been associated with.

"You—you're just trying to confuse us," the Olympian accused. "It is the logic of the Evil One!" She made a sign and the others did the same, even Yua.

"Think of it logically," Obie argued. "If you are right, then nothing is lost by using our methods. You will get your chance to ask. If *we* are right, then you will have lost that chance, probably for good, by refusing to do it our way. You don't have a choice, really."

One of the Athenes, the obvious leader, looked at her sisters and then back at the others. Though a fanatic, she was not stupid. They were about to plunge into some sort of abyss to reach this distant planet more quickly; it would be easy for this computer simply to exclude Olympians, leaving them in empty space.

"Very well," she said at last. "Your way. But we will have full access to Him as soon as He is contacted?"

"As soon as we know he can't get away, yes," Obie assured them. "My word on that." *For all the good it'll do you,* he added silently, although he could tell from Mavra's expression that she was thinking the same thing.

"He'll have a spaceworthy ship," Marquoz pointed out. "An easy getaway. He'll have to be approached cautiously, taken by surprise but by subterfuge, as well, not by force. We want him as a friend. It worries me that, although you say he should have been immediately called back to the Well of Souls to repair the damage, he has not responded to those calls."

"Agreed," Obie responded. "Either his memory has deteriorated again or he has deliberately ignored the signals. If the former, we may be able to return him to his senses; if the latter, it may be something beyond our control. We *must* be careful. Any suggestions?"

Mavra nodded. "One, I think. You remember, Obie, when you replayed for me the memories of my grandparents' odyssey with Brazil on the Well World?"

"Yes?"

"I think he really loved Wu Julee. Certainly she loved him. The Well World had turned her into a Dillian—a centaur—and you said he had a liking for centaurs. I wonder . . . . Suppose you transformed me into an exact duplicate of her as a centaur? It would mean nothing to anyone but Nathan Brazil. Even if his memory's gone bad it should shake something loose. As far as everybody else on Meouit is concerned I'd be just another attractive Rhone. I've looked over the shipping records—he has no return cargo, so he's going to be deadheading someplace unless he picks something up here. He'll come down looking for cargo. Suppose I meet him as the representative of a cargo company? By his reactions to my appearance we'll get a good idea of whether Korf is Brazil. I think he'd find an appointment with me emotionally and financially irresistible."

"And we'd be waiting inside at the appointed spots," Marquoz put in. "I like it."

"Well, *I* don't," the Athene leader snapped. "By not asking the Holy Question immediately you risk him smelling a trap and not keeping the appointment."

"Oh, we'll have people on him the moment we spot him," Mavra assured her. "If he makes to bolt we'll move immediately. Remember, we can take him by force if he decides to go back to the *Jerusalem;* if he bolts in any other direction he's going to be awfully conspicuous on a Rhone world."

"And we're going to have to sneak you down as it is," Obie added. "The Rhone aren't too fond of the Fellowship or the Olympians. Come on, you said you'd go along with us."

The Olympian stood and seemed about to say something, then sat back down. "All right. You win."

Marquoz turned to Gypsy. "You should be down there with us. You've seen him before."

Gypsy shook his head. "Nope. Sorry. I don't want to be anything but what I am. But it sounds like a good scam; it should work. I'll follow it from here."

"Suit yourself," the Chugach replied with a shrug. He turned and faced the empty air. "I, for one, do not wish to be a Rhone, though."

"No need," the computer told him. "The Olympians won't, either. You can all wait together. We'll send some crew down to rent a warehouse and establish a dummy company—this can be done in a day or so. They'll also scout around. We'll use one of the spare ships to get you in; disguise you as cargo or something and get you to the warehouse. Then we all wait."

Marquoz sighed. "Yes, then we wait."

"Drop's coming!" Obie warned. Before anyone could react the world went out around them and they were engulfed in a blackness without end, dropping uncomfortably, dropping to a point far, far away.

Meouit

THE ADVANCE CREW OF THE *NAUTILUS* HAD DONE AN effective job. The warehouse was dingy and located in a poor neighborhood, but it was close to the spaceport and easily accessible even to someone who had never been there before. The small signboard said, in both the Com trading language and in Zhosa, the local tongue, *Durkh Shipping Corporation.* It seemed old and worn, not brand new as it actually was.

It was chilly and near dusk in Taiai, largest city on Meouit, and flakes of snow floated in the air here and there. A young Rhone woman clad in an expensive fur jacket studied the scene accompanied by several larger Rhone males.

She looked barely in her teens, not beautiful but pleasant, even a bit sexy, with long, brown hair. Her skin was a light brown, her pointed ears jutted up slightly on either side of her head and seemed to swivel independently of each other. At the waist, the near but not-quite-human torso faded into short-cropped light-brown fur that covered a perfect equine body. She needed only the jacket for warmth; below the torso she was well insulated by fur and subcutaneous fat.

"Not bad," she said admiringly, "not bad at all."

The male Rhone who stood closest to her, much taller and more obviously muscular than she, was pleased.

"Shall we go inside and greet the others?" she suggested, and he moved to slide one of the doors open for her. The lights inside created an illuminated wedge in the semi-darkness as the door slid back, admitted them, and then was closed by the last centaur.

The young female Rhone sniffed slightly, then looked toward a corner. "How have you been making out, Marquoz?" Mavra Chang called.

The small dragon stalked out of the shadows puffing on a fat cigar. "Pretty crappy, if you must know," he snorted. "How'd you like to be locked up in a barn on an alien world with only religious fanatics for company for two days?"

She looked sympathetic. "Sorry, but we had to sneak you all in when we could. You could have let Obie make you a Rhone," she reminded him, "and have spent the last couple of days out in the open and comfortable."

"Thank you, I like to remain me," he grumbled. "I can see Gypsy was the smart one, though. He's back on the *Nautilus* sleeping on feather beds and eating like a horse, I'll bet."

"Well, we'll be getting down to the spaceport shortly," Mavra told him. "The ordeal's almost over. Our man is in orbit now and due down to sign the customs forms and releases in about two hours."

An Olympian stepped from the shadows. "Remember your word!" she warned. "He is to be brought to us!"

"We'll keep our end of the bargain," Mavra promised. She turned to face two of the *Nautilus* crew. "Well, come on, bodyguards. I'd like to get down there as soon as possible. I don't want to miss him."

She bade the others farewell and turned. One of the crewmen slid the door open and then shut it behind them again. A blast of cold air was all that was left now besides the waiting.

The Olympians stepped back into the shadows, and the leader turned to the other three. "Two hours," she whispered. "Are you ready?"

One of the others turned and removed her cape, taking from the lining four small, very sophisticated pistols. She handed one to each of the others, keeping the fourth for herself.

This was yet another reason why the Olympians had not wanted to reach Meouit through Obie.

Marquoz was busy passing the time with the

Rhone-shaped crewmen; one had some dice. They paid no attention to the Olympians whatsoever; all of them had been trying to tune out the strange women for two full days as it was. Which was just the way the Olympians wanted it.

"Check your charges," the leader whispered. The small activating whine went unheard.

Mavra Chang lounged around the shipping office trying to look bored, but deep inside her she felt almost like a little girl expecting the arrival of a favorite uncle but afraid at the same time that the uncle might have forgotten her.

Nathan Brazil . . . . The name had been so small a part of her long existence that it shouldn't mean much at all, yet it had haunted her since childhood. As a freighter captain herself back in the old days, she had known of him, heard the legends of the hard-fighting, hard-drinking captain who never seemed to grow old. From her grandparents she'd heard fairy tales of the magical Well World and Brazil's name had been there, too, always in the hero's role. And Brazil had plucked her as a small child from the forces of totalitarian repression that had engulfed her relatives and her world, he had passed her into the hands of the colorful Makki Chang, who raised her on a great freighter. Later, on the Well World, Brazil's name was mentioned everywhere, sometimes with reverence, sometimes with fear. Then too, there was Obie's playback only a few months ago of her grandparents' memories of a hideous, throbbing six-limbed mass that proclaimed itself master of reality, of all space–time, as the creator of the Universe. All Brazil.

The tugs had already established the craft's orbit, now the pilot boat would descend with the in-system pilot and the captain to process the cargo through customs, then the wait while cargo ferries transferred that cargo from the massive bulk of the freighter, which never made planetfall.

Mavra watched and her heart seemed to skip a beat as the information board inside the port authority office flashed the name JERUSALEM, her registry numbers, and the words IN PORT.

Outside, lights locked on the small pilot boat as it drifted down and gently settled into the first of the eight cradles around the port authority building. Mavra turned expectantly, watching the far door, where the captain and the pilot would enter in a few moments. She held her breath. Time dragged, and after a while she grew afraid that the captain hadn't made planetfall, that he was deadheading somewhere.

One of her two crewmen, playing at filling out some forms, leaned over and whispered, "Why don't you relax? Right now you look like you expect your long-lost husband to come home any moment now."

Suddenly conscious of how obvious she must have seemed, Mavra turned and pretended to be looking through some cargo manifests stacked in the anteroom. That, she could do more natually. But if Brazil didn't come out shortly somebody in the port authority was going to wonder why it was taking her so long to choose the correct form.

Suddenly the door slid open with a pneumatic hiss. The pilot, his face lined and elderly, which seemed perfect for his spotted gray coloring, led the way, clipboard in hand, and, behind, she saw the massive loadmaster. Both were apparently talking, and it was a few seconds before she realized that they were talking not to one another but to a third party almost hidden between them.

Mavra's first thought was that Korf was too tall; almost 170 centimeters, wearing a curious porkpie hat from under which massive folds of gray-white hair drooped and mixed with a full beard of similar color. Only the eyes and the nose were visible, and the rabbi's general build was obscured by a heavy black coat that reached his knees. If appearances were worth anything, he was twenty kilos too heavy and a century too old.

The voice, too, was unpleasant; very high-pitched and nasal, quite unlike the low tenor Mavra remembered of Nathan Brazil. Her heart sank; this, certainly was not the man they were after. She glanced surreptitiously over her forms and tried to find any of the qualities of that funny little man she'd known as a child—some of the warmth, the gentleness, anything.

That's it, she decided, crestfallen. We've blown it. All that work and we've blown it. She looked over at her crewmen and saw the same emotions mirrored in their expressions. One gestured slightly with his head toward the door and she nodded almost imperceptibly. They walked toward the door, hooves clattering on the hard, smooth plastine surface, walking right past the two Rhone and Rabbi Korf as they wrangled over the bill of lading.

"The maize, then, is in two-hundred-ton containers ready for gripping?" the loadmaster's deep bass was asking.

Korf nodded and pointed. "Yes. Shouldn't take but two, three hours to get that section. It's the building supplies that—"

At that moment, her mind now far from this place, Mavra had not made allowances for bureaucracies that wax floors and she stumbled slightly. Korf and the two Rhone looked up.

The rabbi, seeing she was all right, turned back to the papers then did a double-take, head shooting back up to stare at her. Embarrassed, Mavra barely noticed the movement but something in the corner of her eye told her that she had attracted more than usual attention. She stopped, carefully, just short of the door and half-turned her human torso to look at the human; for an instant their eyes met, and something in those eyes and that expression caused a chill to go through her.

Her crewmen, oblivious to what was happening, were already outside before they noticed her absence.

Mavra's rational mind told her that the strange man was more likely Father Frost than Nathan Brazil, but something in his reaction and her gut feelings said otherwise. No human would look at a Rhone woman that way, no human except one who might not be.

"I'm sorry if I interrupted you with my clumsiness," she said smoothly, trying to control herself. "My associates and I had been waiting to see the captain of the ship that just came in, but you must be he and I see that you'll be tied up for some time." She looked shyly nervous. "I—I'm afraid I'm not used to business yet."

The captain recovered quickly, although he still kept staring at her with that odd look in his eye. "I am the captain, Madam Citizen. What did you wish of me?"

"My father is in the import-export business. He and his associates are attending a conference at Hsuir where they just completed a big transaction. They asked me to find out what ships were coming in and might be—is deadheading the correct term?—well, leaving empty. I'm not really involved in the business, you understand, but with everybody at the convention I'm the only one they could call." She sounded so sincere that she almost believed the lie herself. "But I see I've come too early."

The captain nodded. "I'm afraid so. This stuff will take hours, and I wish to have a real bath and sleep soft and long tonight to put myself on your time. I *am* empty at the moment, though—could we talk tomorrow afternoon?"

She smiled sweetly and nodded. "Of course. Where are you staying? I will call you there. I know your name and ship from the listings."

"At the Pioneer. The only place here with rooms that also have individual kitchens—I have special dietary requirements."

She nodded. "I'll call—not too early," she promised.

"What did you say your company's name was?" he came back. "And yours, in case things clear up earlier?"

"Tourifreet, in your pronunciation," she answered glibly. "It is the Durkh Shipping Corporation—the number is listed." Again the smile. "We'll talk tomorrow, then," she added and walked out, leaving him staring at the door closing behind her.

"You're sure it's him?" Marquoz grumbled. "The boys don't seem to think so."

Mavra nodded. "I'm as sure as I can be. Our little mimic trick worked. He knows who I look like, all right—there's nothing wrong with his memory. It was like he'd been hit with a stun bomb. You could see it in his eyes, the war between his mind, which told him that this just had to be an amazing coincidence, and that emotional backwash that was winning control."

One of the crewmen who had been there said, "I still think you're nuts. He's too tall, too broad—nothing at all like the descriptions of Brazil."

She smiled slightly. "He wore well-made thick boots, I noticed, very much like those I normally wear when I have feet instead of hooves. With that long coat he has on to further disguise things he could have been on stilts for all we know, certainly lifts high enough to give him a dozen centimeters of lift. He had the old man's walk, which would further discourage things—and he's had a long time to practice, too. The coat is padded, who knows with what, to make him broader. Even the dark gloves poking out of those oversize sleeves obviously came from arms too thin and too short for that body. The beard's good, but I've seen good false beards before. And the hat helps. No, it's him, all right. I'd bet my life on it."

"Don't you think it was a bit risky just to let him go like that?" the Olympian leader asked Mavra. "We have no idea that he wasn't put off by your appearance so he would suspect a trap."

"I seriously doubt he suspects a trap, but he'll check anyway. There really *is* a trading convention in Hsuir, which is about all he can check, since it's on the other side of the world. The next thing I'd expect him to do is punch in the company name and see if he gets a number—he will. Finally, he might sneak over here late this evening or in the morning to establish that there really is a company warehouse. He'll find us here, old sign in place."

"And if you've made a mistake somewhere?" the Olympian pressed.

Mavra chuckled, reached into her coat, and pulled out a small transceiver. She switched it on and a tiny red light glowed. "Halka? How's our man doing?" she asked into it.

"He cleared port about an hour ago, Mavra," came a tinny response. "Went immediately to the Pioneer with one large bag. Went straight to his room, four-oh-four A, and hasn't been out since, nor has anyone else gone in."

She composed a knowing smile to the Olympian, a smile caressed with confidence and frost. "Satisfied? We'll be on him every step of the way now. Borsa will even have his hotel line tapped in short order. We've got him."

The Olympian remained skeptical. "If he *is* in fact Nathan Brazil, I wonder? . . ."

"Well, *I'm* satisfied," Marquoz announced, yawning. "I would suggest that we all get some sleep. It looks to be quite a busy day tomorrow, and none of us knows how or when it'll turn out."

Room 404-A, the Hotel Pioneer

As soon as he entered his room and locked the door, the man who called himself Captain David Korf checked the room for bugs. Satisfied, he sat on the comfortable bed in the hotel room, one designed to resemble first-class accommodations in the human part of the Com, and tried to think.

Somebody was on to him, he knew that much. Somebody who knew a lot about him, somebody who had baited their trap so that it would be irresistible to him. They had only really slipped once, in the shadows, which was very, very good—but it's tough to trail a sophisticated alien through a city when you're four-footed and huge, particularly late in the evening when few others are about. Hooves clatter no matter how muffled, and five hundred or so kilos of bulk is not easily faded into the shadows.

Korf glanced at the phone beside the bed. There were several people he could call, even the cops. No, the cops would only arrest a few of the tails and wouldn't tell him who or how or why. People so well prepared wouldn't employ stooges who broke easily.

He had no local friends, although he had cultivated several on his regular stops. But this planet was new to him. There *were* a few humans about from other ships or on layovers who he knew, even one or two he might count on in a fight. They should be looked up, he decided, if his choice was to find out who these people were instead of running.

Running appealed to him despite his curiosity, but that would not be easy. A human could not help but be conspicuous on a world inhabited almost solely by centaurs. The lone spaceport would be covered, of course. Not impossible to get through, no, but it would mean sneaking in using cargo containers or, perhaps, stealing a ship—weight tolerances would betray a stowaway. He rejected the cargo route because it was likely the containers wouldn't be pressurized. He could steal a pilot boat or somesuch, of course, perhaps a tug—but then what? The cops would have the *Jerusalem* covered, and there wasn't anyplace in range at the slow speeds the tugs could manage. Drifting in space for eons appealed to him not at all.

He sighed. No, running held too many risks and too many ifs. He would have to face them. He rather preferred the idea of a confrontation; his curiosity was piqued.

He would walk into no trap unprepared, though. Again he glanced at the phone, thinking of the few humans he could call, and he'd almost made up his mind to call when he thought better of it. No, anyone so well organized would have bribed the hotel operator by now—he would have, in their place—and it wouldn't do to tip his hand just yet. He needed out—a public call box. One selected at random would be best. He also needed to watch the watchers a bit, to see what he was up against. The Pioneer was a transient spacer hotel, though small. Just a glance into the human lounge off to his left on the way in had revealed about two dozen men and women even at this late hour.

He started thinking about what the watchers would expect him to do, then turned, grabbed the phone, and punched for the Durkh Shipping Corporation. A number immediately appeared in the little readout screen, which surprised him not at all. Durkh might even be a real company. He didn't bother to check on the import-export convention; if they were thorough enough to establish a corporate cover there would be, even if they'd had to throw it themselves to get people out of the way.

But—who were *they*? Not the cult, certainly. Maybe mercenaries hired by the cult—but what mercenaries if that was the case! Frankly, he just didn't see the Fellowship of the Well as having enough smarts to pull something like that. But if not them, then who? Moreover, who would have the contacts not only to trace him but actually to trace him all the way to Meouit, to this little bit of nowhere, and be ready with Rhone agents—and the girl!

She disturbed him most. Plastic surgery? Neoform? No matter what, there was no way they could have done that to anybody in the time between when he had taken the contract and the time it'd taken him to make planetfall.

Worse, who could know what *she* had looked like? Only people on the Well World, so very long ago, would know that and they were all dead, all except, perhaps, that scoundrel Ortega—but even he would have no way of extending his influence beyond the Well. It didn't make sense. Only a very few people had ever returned from the Well World, and they were all accounted for—certainly all who might have known what she had looked like back then.

He kept thinking about it. There was something new here, something potentially quite dangerous. The rip in space–time those assholes had caused—might it have strange side effects? He had not been on the Well World in generations; had someone capitalized on the rip to come back or come through to this space? Was it possible that anything could live in there?

Nothing makes sense, he told himself. There was only one solution. He got up from the bed and heaved his suitcase onto it, opening it carefully. He took off his heavy coat and the false padding that filled him out, kicked off the uncomfortable lift boots, carefully removed the massive beard by applying a chemical from a tiny kit he carried with him. Slowly he removed Rabbi David Korf completely, the bushy white eyebrows, the lines around the eyes, everything. Next he went to the window and looked out. Not far up, certainly not impossible. A sheer drop, though; it would be tricky to get down. The descent could be managed, though. Worse would be getting the window open wide enough—and it was damned *cold* out there, snowing fairly steadily now.

But—once down, then what? The snow would help,

of course, but any group that knew Wuju's form would be familiar with every cell in his body. It would have to be a good disguise, one of his best, one that would foul up even the most expert shadow. He had one for that. He didn't like to use it, but it *was* effective; he'd even used it once or twice in staging deaths.

He returned to his suitcase. He always carried the disguises with him, both as insurance and because he occasionally wanted to get out on worlds without attracting undue attention. The last-gasp disguise, he'd named it; but it was effective.

Much of "Korf's" hair was also fake, of course, but Brazil wore a fair amount of his own, stringy black, underneath. He trimmed it short with a set of clippers, then carefully shaved a large part of his body. Now actor's cream to smooth his natural wrinkles and ruddy complexion, and to darken it. A professional actor's cosmetics case aided him as he worked methodically, transforming himself into someone who resembled him very little. He couldn't hide the Roman nose, of course, but he could smooth it out and flare the nostrils slightly so that it looked quite different. Finally the wig, which he'd paid a fortune for over two centuries before. More work, then the special clothing. He was a very small man, which aided this particular disguise. In his emergency kit he carried five identities. His actor's kit could produce variants.

All of his outfits were reversible to black; that made it handy, although a white coat would have been nice out there right now. Well, so be it.

After over an hour of painstaking work he stood and studied himself in the mirror. Perfect. But he had no matching heavy coat for the fierce wintry weather outside; he would be very cold and very uncomfortable for a while.

Although this was his best disguise he had never liked it; still, he *did* enjoy the challenge. When you've been around familiar places long enough you need a way to get away, to be other people, talk to people you don't dare be seen talking to—and duck people who want to see you, as now.

He had to make himself up to resemble his description in the fake ID papers he carried. On most planets they'd be good enough to get him in and out without a second glance but customs and immigration at the planet's only port of entry would have no record of his arrival. On a larger human world that would make little difference, but here it would provoke an inquisition.

He gave the disguise a last look, then walked to the window. God, it looked cold out there! He raised it, not without difficulty for he was trying to be quiet. Barely large enough to get through, but it would do, he decided. The blast of icy air stung him; he hated being so uncomfortable, but he loved the challenge. Almost as an afterthought he went over and programmed some Rhone music so that it would shut off in fifteen minutes, then put in a wake-up call for the next morning with the desk. Just so, he decided, just so.

Taking a clear gel from a small jar he rubbed it onto his hands, took a deep breath, went out the window, positioned himself, and, with the gel's aid, used his hands as suction cups to carry him down the thirty meters of brick wall to the alley below. Once on the ground he spotted the rear entrance, entered, allowed himself a few moments to thaw out and to roll up and discard the gel, then strolled openly down the corridor toward the lobby.

It was getting very late now, but, as he suspected, the human lounge was still filled with people, most relaxing with pleasure drugs or social drinking, a little dancing—all the things an alien lifeform might do for companionship on a winter's eve in a strange place.

There was a cloakroom, conveniently unguarded. Who'd bother to steal a human-fitted coat here? He went there, selected one that fit both the disguise and his body, coolly put it on, returned to the lobby and with a nod to the front desk walked through the front door into the wintry weather. When no alarms flashed, no yells arose behind him, and no noticeable shadows materialized, he relaxed a little and began to whistle a little tune. This was getting to be fun.

The sun was coming up; it had been a quiet if chilly night for the crewmen watching the warehouse and the Hotel Pioneer. All would swear that none of them had been observed and that, so far as they knew Korf had slept the night away.

One of the Rhone shadows down the hall from Room 404-A jumped at a distant sound and realized that he'd been dozing. He looked down the hall as the elevator, a huge cage built with centaurs in mind, came up to a stop and the door slid back. A single person got out and walked down the hall. It appeared to be a young and pretty woman, dressed fit to kill, her walk an open invitation on a hundred worlds. She brushed back long brown hair and took out a small pad, consulted it, then started checking the numbers on the rooms until she reached 404-A. That perked up the watch, both the man at the end of the hall and the others hiding in nearby rooms. She knocked and there seemed to be an answer from inside, then there was some fumbling and the door opened slightly. She pushed on it and strode in, closing the door quickly behind her.

"I'll be damned," snapped a tinny voice in the guard's ear. "I thought he was a holy man or somethin'."

"You never know," another cracked. "Now *that's* my kind o' religion!"

The men would have been startled to discover that room 404-A held but a single occupant. The woman kicked off shoes and removed her wig and some plastine body molding but did not bother to get rid of the entire disguise. It was already dawn and Nathan Brazil wanted some sleep before he had to become Rabbi Korf again; he flopped on the bed and drifted off almost instantly. A slight smile lingered on his face at the thought that, should his shadows check the room after he left tomorrow, they'd get a hell of a shock from the case of the disappearing woman.

At the Warehouse–Noon

"HE LEFT ABOUT AN HOUR AGO," THE RADIO TOLD them. "Tolga and Drur are on him. We still haven't figured out the girl, though."

Mavra looked grim. "I think I can guess," she said dryly and signed off.

"The girl was Brazil, then?"

She nodded. "Of course, Marquoz. Simple thing, really, particularly with all his experience."

"But how did he get out of that room?" the head Olympian wanted to know. "You said you had people watching it!"

Mavra shook her head, feeling a little stupid. "I've stolen millions from tougher places using any number of methods he could have used. Damn! My thinking's rusty! I've depended on Obie too much! And he actually thumbed his nose at us by walking straight up to the room with a little petty ventriloquism and an unlatched door!"

"You know what this means," Marquoz said apprehensively.

She nodded. "Yeah. He's on to us."

"And he hasn't called, which means he's going to try and make a break for it somehow," the Chugach added. "I think we're in big trouble unless we put the snatch on him now."

Mavra thought furiously for a moment. "I don't know. It's broad daylight and so far we've only seen him in places that are crowded. He could call the cops to complain he was being followed or something and they could escort him right back onto his ship!"

"And what if he does?" the Olympian leader demanded. "What can we do then?"

"Call in Obie and kidnap the whole goddamn two and a half kilometers of it," Mavra snapped angrily. She wasn't mad at Brazil—in fact, it restored her faith in him and his legend—but, rather, at herself for being taken in so. At one time she had been the greatest thief in the history of the Com, and it was galling to be taken in this way.

They were still debating the mess when the electronic buzzer echoed through the empty warehouse. As they were yelling at each other, it was a moment before the meaning of the sound penetrated, then all fell silent suddenly.

The phone was ringing.

Mavra glanced over at a female Rhone crewmember and nodded. The Rhone shrugged and walked to the phone, which lay on the floor where it'd been placed as the only real furnishing. No videophones on Meouit, at least.

On the fifth buzz the woman picked up the transceiver and said, "Durkh Shipping Corporation."

"I'm sorry, I don't speak the tongue," a pleasant high-pitched voice came back to her. "Do you speak standard?"

"Of course, sir," replied the agent in her best secretarial tones. "What may we do for you?"

"*We* may put me through to Madam Citizen Tourifreet, if you will," replied the caller. "David Korf calling."

"Ah—oh, yes, just a moment, sir." The Rhone turned to Mavra and raised her eyebrows questioningly, pushing the "hold call" button.

Mavra turned to the others. "Well? What do you make of this?"

"I'd say his curiosity has gotten the better of him," Marquoz replied. "Either that or his late-night sojourn was devoted to tipping the odds in his favor."

"What should I do, though—considering?"

The Chugach shrugged. "Go through with the original plan. After all, we only want to *talk* to him."

She nodded and walked over to the phone, then

pushed the button again, and said sweetly, "Tourifreet."

"And a good day to you, Madam Citizen," Korf's voice replied pleasantly. "You wished to discuss some business?"

"Just Tourifreet, please," she responded casually. "We use no titles. Yes, well, ah, I've been in touch with my father and I have all the particulars. Twenty standard containers, agricultural products."

"Not much of a load," he noted, sounding genuinely disappointed.

"I don't know about that," she replied coyly, "but we have no objection to your taking on other cargo than ours, I'm sure."

"Destination?"

It's amazing how he keeps up the fiction, she thought. He was the coolest operator she could remember, better, even than her long-dead thief of a husband. "Tugami—on the frontier. New routing, pretty far out, but it's in a fine location for going elsewhere, or so my father says."

She could hear voices behind him in the background. It sounded like a busy office or marketplace. She also heard the rustle of papers and then he said, "Oh, yes. I see. I don't have all the frontier stuff in my navigational log. Yes, all right. I think I can pick up some minor Rhone sector cargo for intermediate drops. There's no rush?"

"Not that I know of."

"Very well, then. Shall we settle terms and sign the papers today? I want to move tomorrow at six."

She resisted the impulse to suggest they meet for dinner. Rhone dining was quite different from human, for one thing; and, for another, if he was still playing Korf's part he'd have his own kosher meals. "Why not drop over here when you're free? Anytime this afternoon or early evening," she suggested. "I haven't much else to do."

"All right, if you'll give me directions," he said smoothly. "Shall we say in an hour? I assume you're near the port authority."

"Very close," she agreed and proceeded to give him detailed directions. They signed off with the usual pleasantries and she turned to the others. "What do you make of *that?*" she asked.

Marquoz gave a dry chuckle. "That was the most entertaining show in town. Imagine! *You're* a total fraud, *he's* a total fraud, both of you *know* the other's a fraud—and yet it was such a convincing conversation I almost believed the both of you myself! My, my, my!" He chuckled again.

"Do you think he'll come?" the Olympian asked nervously.

Marquoz nodded. "Oh, he'll come. Oh, yes indeed, he will. He's actually *enjoying* this, couldn't you tell?" His tone became suddenly more serious. "But he won't come blind. If he walks down that street over there and across the square right in the open you can be sure that he's armed and ready with a variety of tricks and that he also probably has friends already in place. This is a dangerous man—to walk so brazenly into a trap he knows about. We shouldn't underestimate him again."

They all agreed. Mavra walked over to the doorway and opened it slightly. There was some wet snow about and it was still a little chilly, but the clouds had broken and sunlight streamed all around, so bright against the snow it hurt the eyes. She pointed as they looked.

"Up on that roof is Talgur, armed with a stun rifle and scope. Over there is Galgan, same, and up on that steeple or whatever it is is Muklo. Plus us in here and Tarl and Kibbi shadowing him. Should be enough." She shut the door.

"Too much," an Olympian voice snapped from behind them. Stun beams shot through the warehouse as well-placed Olympians easily cut down the crewmen, Mavra, and Marquoz. The Olympian leader looked around, then, satisfied, turned to the others. "The three on the roofs. You know what to do."

They nodded and dashed to the second-floor exits they'd spent two days scouting and preparing. In less than ten minutes all had returned. "They'll sleep till dark," one of the Aphrodites assured her confidently.

"Their vantage points were well chosen," the leader noted. "Take the far roof and the steeple—those are best no matter what route he chooses. Use the crew's rifles to pick off the shadows and anybody else who gets in the way. Full stun."

"And if they have stun armor?" one of them asked.

"Then kill them."

"Where will you be?" another asked her.

"Right in the square," she replied. "I shall become a statue until he is close enough to touch. Then and only then will I ask the Holy Question." She smiled broadly and there was more than a hint of fanatical rapture in her eyes. "And this time the answer shall be the true one, sisters! Salvation and paradise are at hand!"

The leader looked across the square. All was ready, she saw; her sisters now held the high points and she blended herself to near invisibility in the shadow of a large statue. As long as she remained still, no one would be able to tell where she stood. She depended on the others for weaponry. The cold did not bother her at all; on Olympus Meouit's snow flurries would be considered high summer. She was satisfied to wait patiently, perfectly still. Her people had waited so very long for this that another forty minutes would be as a raindrop in a heavy storm. That stupid little lizard policeman and that arrogant bitch, spawn of the Evil One and their minions, were all silenced. Her word! As if one's word given to the Evil One was binding! The Holy Mother had been right, she'd planned it all carefully, and she and her sisters had carried it out. There had been no mistakes. All was perfect.

In fact she'd made two mistakes. One was understandable; her religion did not permit her to believe that Nathan Brazil would use others to prevent unpleasant surprises, yet even now three very nasty spacers he had contacted the previous evening were sitting on other rooftops watching the show. The apparent disappearance of the leader in the middle of the square had surprised them, but the others, although they, too, were blended with the rooftops, wielded weapons trained on the square and those were clearly visible. Even using the weapons as points of reference you could barely make out the outlines of the Olympians holding them.

The second mistake was in forgetting that the stun settings were established for human-average body-mass; Rhone, which Mavra and all of her crew were now, were much larger and required a more powerful shot. What would have kept humans—and Marquoz, despite his bulk—out for hours had started to wear off in thirty minutes on the stunned Rhone inside the warehouse Mavra included. It was kind of like waking up one cell at a time, but slowly awareness, pain, and mobility was flowing back into them.

The man who pretended to be David Korf stood two blocks away looking down the street. *I feel like Frontier Rabbi, two-gun sage of the Talmud,* he thought crazily. He had removed most of the padding from the coat and it was on now so that it could be discarded in an instant. He'd cut his pockets so that when his hands were in them they rested on two highly efficient Com Police machine pistols, the kind you didn't even have to aim to shoot.

The kind nobody but cops was supposed to have.

He spoke into the portacom he held in his right hand. "How's it going, Paddy? What've we got?"

"Well, no innocents if that's a bother," a thickly accented human voice said. Most old spacers were somewhat nuts; Paddy, whose hobby had been folk songs, had decided he was Irish long ago and acted it despite the fact he had one of the blackest African skins ever seen. "Looks like they really is a convention someplace."

"No other ships in, either," Brazil noted. "So? Your other boys as good as you?"

"You kin trust me to pick 'em, Nate," Paddy replied. "We got us some of the supergals, it looks like, on the rooftops."

Brazil was surprised. "Olympians? Here? Damn! So it's that crazy cult after all!" He was almost disappointed. He'd been hoping for something more interesting. Paddy's reply raised his hopes again.

"No, it looks like the babes moved in on your other folk. There's dead or knocked-out horsies all over the rooftops. Looks like ye got a lotta people after ye, Natty!"

That was better. "You got the Olympians?" he asked. "How many?"

"Three that we see on the rooftops; there may be more, but if so they ain't layin' for ye on high."

That was manageable. Any others would be in the warehouse. If he was lucky the Olympians had done the dirty work for him and he had only to deal with them and not with the unknown enemy—if the two were different, as it now appeared.

"Zap 'em, hard stun, as soon as you see me," he instructed. "They're not human and pretty tough, so give it all the juice you got."

"And if that still don't get 'em?" Paddy pressed eagerly.

"Do what you have to," Brazil responded. "Then take their positions and cover me in the square."

"Righto. Come ahead" was the reply.

Brazil put the portacom in an inside shirt pocket and started down the street. It's a kind of pretty day, he thought. Idiotic way to spend a pretty day like this.

Ahead he saw the opening into the small square with a monument of some kind in the center—a huge Rhone of age-greened bronze pulling some sort of wagon, the god of commerce or somesuch. The statue was the only impediment, but it would provide cover for somebody, he thought. No, Paddy's men would have seen anyone.

Or would they? He stopped just short of the square, just out of sight, and peered hard at the statue. How many Olympians could use it as a backdrop to fade into? he wondered idly. He put his hands through his pockets to the pistols. Well, superwomen or no superwomen they'd have to be unarmed. He swallowed hard, inhaled then exhaled, and stepped into the square.

At that moment Paddy and his men fired. The Olympian women on the rooftops quietly stiffened and rolled over. Nothing was heard or seen in the square, but Brazil knew that his ambush had been successful; if not, there'd have been yells, screams—even possibly explosions, knowing Paddy.

He glanced over the warehouses washed in the bright sunlight, spotted the Durkh Shipping Corporation sign on one, and headed toward it carefully, keeping half an eye on the statue. With the snow the green centaur looked like it had white mange.

Inside the warehouse Mavra was the first to rise groggily to her feet and recover her wits.

They'd been double-crossed by the Olympians, there was no doubt in her mind. That meant the women were laying for Brazil in the square! She reached the door, slid it open, and saw him approaching diagonally across from her. Quickly she reached for the transceiver and flipped it to all-call.

"Talgur! Galgan! Muklo!" she called. There was no answer. She tossed the thing aside in frustration. She had to warn him, she knew, had to get him out of there— But how to do it without getting shot?

It was cold, yes, but to hell with cold! She removed coat and long sweater so she was now unclothed. That would show him she had no weapons concealed or otherwise. Without thinking further of the risk she kicked off on her powerful equine hind legs and bounded full-speed into the square right toward the tiny black-clad bearded figure approaching casually.

"Go back!" she screamed at him, all the time charging. "It's a trap!"

He stopped dead, seemingly amazed by it all and taken slightly aback by her rush toward him.

The Olympian leader, cursing, broke from her place by the statue and started running for Brazil, screaming, "Shoot her, sisters! Shoot!" As she did so, her shrill plea echoed eerily off the buildings on the square.

Brazil saw the Olympian amazon rushing him to his left and the specter of Wuju charging across and was completely stumped. "Holy shit!" he managed.

Paddy was quicker. As soon as he saw the Olympian break from the statue he drew a bead and prepared to fire. The Olympian leader beat Mavra to Brazil and screamed, "Lord, are you Nathan Brazil?" At that moment Paddy fired and she was knocked to the ground and lay unmoving, an amazed expression on her face.

Mavra was taken by surprise by the shot but assumed that at least one of her people had managed to retain control of a rifle. Two Rhone crewmembers, Brazil's shadows, suddenly galloped into the square, guns drawn, from two different street openings. Mavra briefly felt reassured. She tried to stop but her momentum was carrying her past Brazil.

More pulse-rifles fired from the rooftops, felling the Rhone. Again caught off-guard, Mavra swerved to avoid Brazil but he'd already shed his coat to reveal a large double-holstered gunbelt. One of the machine pistols was in his left hand. He didn't try to avoid her; instead, as she swerved and slowed, he jumped on her back!

She almost buckled from the unexpected extra weight, but as she stopped and reared in an attempt to throw him, she felt the cold of a pistol in the small of her humanoid back.

"Just don't try anything," he warned sharply. She knew his voice well from Obie's files. She stopped dead.

"Head up the street toward the port authority building," he ordered. She calmed herself and started slowly in the indicated direction, completely confused about what had happened.

"Who's up there?" she managed, pointing at the rooftops.

Brazil laughed, enjoying his full control. "My people, of course! You should've covered the back alley and the window last night!"

She was sweating now, and felt the cold very bitterly all of a sudden. She shivered.

"Mind telling me where we're going? I'm freezing to death!"

He laughed again. "Tit for tat. I damn near froze going down that brick wall in the snowstorm last night. You won't die. Just get to the port authority."

She bent around a little and glanced at him. He was a ridiculous sight, a man in leather high-heeled boots, skin-tight smooth brown pants, a crazy thick gunbelt with two holsters. He wore a thin cotton shirt of red and white checks, a gigantic white beard, flowing white hair, and the porkpie hat.

"Okay. Stop here," he ordered, just short of the heavily trafficked main street across from the port authority. "Now I'm going to dismount, but don't you think I can't shoot you where you stand. The locals take offense at seeing a human ride a Rhone, but this little pistol has a mind and will of its own."

She'd caught a glimpse of the pistol and knew it to be true.

He slipped off and she felt as if she'd shed a ton of weight. The sensation felt so good it hurt, and she stiffened up slightly.

"Now, the boys in the port authority have been paid pretty good not to notice us," he told her, "but since you're a native and I'm not, racial loyalty might yet overcome greed—although I wouldn't count on it. So what I'm going to do is holster this thing and we're both going to walk over there, into the authority waiting room where we met yesterday, and out Gate Four to the shuttle boat. Since they haven't finished unloading my ship yet they'll probably see no evil. I can't break orbit now, anyway."

She nodded, knowing that he'd never be this confident unless his own people had them covered the whole way and everything was already set up. It didn't matter; all she wanted was a talk, anyway.

She wished, though, that she'd allowed Obie to do an implant in her the way he'd done on Olympus. But she was still so angry with him for that trick with the Temple of Birth that she had adamantly refused this time. Now she missed his presence. She knew Obie could deal with Nathan Brazil better than she.

They entered the building and, as he'd said, nobody paid the slightest attention, not even to her—and she thought she was reasonably attractive for a Rhone—bare as the day she would have been born if really a Rhone. And in the middle of winter!

The pilot boat was automated and took no time at all to lift. She was thankful for the warmth and the chance to catch her breath. Brazil sat back and regarded her with a mixture of amusement and fascination.

"So tell me, Tourifreet or whatever your real name is," he began, "are you the head of this conspiracy or just a hired hand? Who knew enough to make you look like that?"

She managed a smile although still slightly winded. "Not Tourifreet, no," she wheezed. "Mavra. Mavra Chang. I'm your great-granddaughter, Mr. Brazil."

He took out a cigar, lit it, and settled back against the bulkhead. "Well, well, well . . . Do tell. Anybody ever tell you you favor your great-grandfather?"

Aboard the Jerusalem

THEY'D SAID LITTLE AFTER THE INITIAL EXCHANGE. The pilot docked quickly and they moved through the set of airlocks into the center of the ship. There was a lot of banging and shuddering aft, as the sounds of the ship being dismantled into containers by tugs came to them. He gestured and she walked forward on the catwalks, he following, until they reached the lounge.

The place was a mess; used food tins were all over the place, wherever he'd finished with them; piles of papers; books in languages she didn't know, with covers suggesting a decidedly peculiar taste in reading materials.

"Sorry the place looks like a dump, but I just wasn't in the mood to clean it and I wasn't expecting guests," he said casually, dusting off a padded chair and plopping into it.

"Aren't you afraid I'll overpower you now that we're alone?" she asked. "After all, I'm a lot bigger and stronger than you are."

He chuckled. "Go ahead. The pilot's keyed to me, the aft section's in vacuum during unloading, and the ship's inoperable until the stevedores finish the job." To illustrate his unconcern he unbuckled his gun belt and tossed it on the floor.

She picked up a book and looked at the cover. "I've never seen real books like this in the Com sections of space," she commented, curious. "Tell me—is it really what the cover seems to say it is?"

He leered at her mockingly. "Of course it is, my dear. Although they're never as juicy inside as they promise." The leer faded. "That was how people got information in the old days—and entertainment, too, for a couple thousand years. All B.C., of course—before computers in every home and office. I still like 'em—and there are enough museums and libraries around to get 'em. Some of the stuff they saved, though! *Whew!*" He paused again, settled back, and looked at her seriously. "So you're Mavra Chang, huh?"

She nodded. "You don't seem all that surprised," she noted.

He smiled. "Oh, hell, I knew you were still around someplace on that cosmic golf ball of a computer."

She was genuinely amazed. "You *knew?* How?" Visions of an omnipotent god floated by her briefly.

He laughed again. "Oh, nothing mysterious. The computer blew your death scene, that's all. He waited three full milliseconds before his vanishing act—well within the detection range of other computers. He could have and should have done it a lot quicker—a nanosecond, maybe, is beyond detection with all that antimatter flashing about. Obie took it slow because though he could stand the stresses of quick acceleration, you might not."

"Three milliseconds is plenty fast for me," she noted dryly.

He shrugged. "It's all relative. At any rate, his gamble was good. Nobody subjected those records to the kind of analysis *I* did. They saw you go, looked at the tape, saw you go again, and that was that."

That only slightly decreased her awe. "You kept track of it all, then? We thought your memory . . ."

"My memory's decent," he told her. "There's just so much information the human brain will hold, and after that it starts throwing out some to make room for the new. I got to that point once—fixed it in the redesign last time I was in the Well. And, yes, I knew about it, about Trelig, anyway. Alaina came to me first with the proposition. I did some figuring, decided there was a slight chance everybody'd wind up on the Well World—which they did—and figured that the kind of reception I'd get there wouldn't be parades and brass bands. So I suggested you. I don't know why I didn't think of your being in *this* before, though. Damn! I must be slipping!"

"*You* suggested *me* for that?" Some anger flared up in her. "So that explains it!"

He shrugged. "You did the job. You're still here several hundred years after you'd otherwise have been dead. Why not?"

There wasn't any satisfactory answer to that so she let it pass.

"Now, then, great-granddaughter, what the hell is all this about?" he asked, settling back.

"The rip," she told him. "It must be fixed at the source. You know that. Why haven't you done so?"

He grew serious suddenly. "Because I choose not to," he said simply.

She was shocked. "Maybe you don't know what's happening! In less than a hundred years—"

"Humanity's done for," he finished. "And shortly after that the Rhone, the Chugach, and all the other Com races. I know."

She couldn't believe what she was hearing and tried to think of reasons why he might be taking such a cavalier attitude. She could not. "You mean you can't fix it?"

He shook his head sadly. "I mean nothing of the sort. The rip will continue to grow and spread and eventually destroy the Universe as we know and understand it. Not everything—the original Markovian Universe will remain, but most of those suns and all those worlds are pretty well spent now. Unless some random dynamic comes along, though, it'll be a dead Universe, a cemetery to the Markovians."

The silence could be cut with a knife. Finally she said, "And you refuse to stop it?"

He smiled. "I would if the price weren't too high —but it is. I just can't take the responsibility."

Her mouth dropped. "Responsibility? Price? What the hell are you talking about? What could be worse than a dead Universe?"

He looked at her thoughtfully. "I don't know what you've been doing of late, but I suspect that if I had something like Zinder's computer world I'd travel, see everyplace that could be seen. Other galaxies, other lifeforms."

She nodded. "Yes, that 's part of it."

"But you're jaded, you've lost perspective," he told her. "With the Markovian equations, Obie can instantly be anywhere he or you want. Do you really have any concept of interstellar distances, of just how far things are? Remember back when you were a captain and it still took weeks or months to go between stars, even with us cheating on relativity? Stars are, on the average, a hundred or more light-years apart around here. This galaxy is hundreds of thousands of light-years across. Our next nearest galaxy is much farther. It took the Dreel thousands of years to cross it. That thing out there—that tear—is moving barely sixty light-years a year. It'll take a century to engulf the Com, almost twenty thousand years to eat enough of our Milky Way galaxy to destabilize it. It'll be many millions more before it eats a really significant sector of space when you think on that scale. There are countless races out there among the stars, tremendous civilizations now on the rise. How can I deny them *their* chance at the future, *their* chance at the Markovian dream? To save a few who can't really be saved anyway?"

She didn't understand, couldn't. "You aren't being asked to sacrifice them, only fix the thing so it'll save us."

He looked up at her and smiled sadly. "No, you misunderstand. The Well of Souls is powered by a singularity, a discontinuity from another Universe. It has a massive power source, but only one. In order to fix the Well of Souls Computer, I would have to shut off the power. That would destroy everything the Markovians created with it. Everything. You're asking me to destroy the Universe in order to save it."

Shocked, she looked at him, then glanced around the room. So there it was—cold, impeccable logic declared that more than a dozen races must die.

"What will you do then?" she asked him. "You can't stay here."

He sighed. "I've always had the power to save or

alter myself to fit existing conditions. There's just never been any real reason to do so. I've lived in this area longer than any other person; I've been human longer than any other person—I *am* a human being. What I will do is survive—I always survive. Survive until somebody replaces me with the Markovian or a better ideal. Survive until—if nobody has done so very far in the future—that time when the rip becomes too great. Then I can then turn the power off and fix the problem." He smiled grimly. "At least I'll have some company, huh? You, and Obie, and whoever else you choose to save."

She looked up at him, suddenly filled with new hope. "Save! Now *that's* an idea! Obie can manage whole planets! Maybe we can relocate—"

"No, I can't, Mavra." Obie's sad voice came into her mind. She straightened up in surprise, startling Brazil, who couldn't know what was happening.

"Obie!" she exclaimed aloud. "You son of a bitch! You installed a relay anyway!"

Brazil sat up, interested. "I suddenly feel like an eavesdropper," he said dryly.

"I'm sorry, Mavra. It was too important. I had to have the link to keep myself informed. If everything had gone right I wouldn't have told you."

"I gather," Brazil put in, "that we are not alone. Damn!" he added a little sarcastically.

Mavra, angry despite Obie's logic, unleashed a mental tirade. He let it run its course on it, which was a while since she had quite an extensive vocabulary. Finally, when she ran down, the computer said, *"Now will you relay what I say?"*

She threw up her arms in frustration. "Okay, go ahead," she told him. To Brazil she added, "He wants to talk to you through me."

"Fire away," Brazil invited.

"First of all," Obie began through Mavra, "forget the idea of spiriting whole planets away. I can't do it. Transform them into something else, yes, but to move them requires more energy than anything possible to design or build short of the Well of Souls itself, not to mention a near-infinite storage capacity. I can't save them, Mavra. A few worlds, yes, by transferring just the population, but that's it. And it would do no good anyway."

"Sounds like it's worth a try," Brazil said. "After all, each of these races started on a single planet. We have millions of years—and a real head start in technology—to redevelop. And you said you could transform a planet. Should make finding perfect sites easy. For the first time I see a ray of hope in all this."

"It's no good," Obie retorted. "Oh, it would last for a while, yes, but we do not have the time to spare for such a project. You have no late option to make the necessary repairs. What the rip in space–time represents is not a reversion to the passive original state but a two-way energy flow. As it grows it is engulfing massive amounts of conventional matter and energy. The rip is not transforming the energy but transmitting it. *The rip is the other end of a short circuit.* The more that is sent back, the larger the energy bursts inside the Well of Souls. We don't really have that much time. If the rift transmits enough material, the damage will be beyond compensation by the Well's protective circuitry, and the Well will self-destruct beyond any hope of repair—leaving this a very, very dead Universe indeed."

Brazil considered that, then shook his head. "It's a pretty strong machine," he replied. "I don't see it reaching that point, not any time soon. No, I have to reject the argument. For a hypothetical danger that might not arise for millions of years I'm expected to wipe out countless trillions of people? The Well World holds only the descendants of the *last* batch of fifteen hundred and sixty races developed—the actual total is thousands of times that. Races. People who are born, have a right to grow up, to live, to experience. To cut them off forever because of the *possibility* of imminent danger—and a remote one, at that—no, no, thank you. I don't want *that* responsibility."

Mavra—don't relay this! Stand by! I'm going to lock on and bring you both to me!

But I thought he couldn't go through you without hurting you! she objected.

I have to take the chance. Stand by . . . Now!

The world went black, and there was the sensation of falling.

Nautilus—Underside

WITH FASCINATED CURIOSITY, NATHAN BRAZIL LOOKED at the small laboratory and original control room.

Mavra, still a Rhone, was more apprehensive than anything else. It had felt odd, somehow slightly *different* being transported to the *Nautilus* this time—and Obie had not returned her form to its original contours. That was bad.

"Obie?" she called hesitantly. "Obie? Are you all right?"

"I'm here, Mavra," the computer's familiar voice told her from its usual central position in thin air. "I—I'm hurt. That's the only way I can describe it."

"What happened?" she asked, genuinely concerned. "Was it? . . ." She glanced at Brazil, who casually stepped down from the pedestal and started to walk around, looking at everything.

"Only slightly," Obie told her. "I—I had him as a unitary structure and could have transported him without harm, but I tried to get a full breakdown and record. I couldn't, Mavra. It—well, it caused shorts in *my* circuitry. I couldn't handle it. Ordinarily I'd be able to shut it down, but it's that damned tear, Mavra! I'm not moving or thinking as quickly. As the gash widens I lose a little of myself."

"If you weren't acting so damned high and mighty I could have warned you about that," Brazil said, showing little sympathy. "Every time you break somebody down to file him on your little electronic slides you're essentially killing him and then reviving him according to the plans. The Well won't permit you to kill me, and the core of being that is me is not a part of the Markovian Universe, as I said. You have no key to handle the difference in the math."

Mavra was much more concerned. "Obie, how badly are you damaged? Can you still function?"

"Creakily," he told her. "I think I can contain the damage by just not using those sections—but that means I'm very limited in what I can do. I'm going to have to be very careful now as long as we're this close to the rip."

"Then why don't we move away? Why torture yourself like this?"

There was a moment's silence and then Obie said, simply, "Ask *him,* Mavra."

She turned and looked at Brazil, eyebrows raised. "Well?"

Brazil, who was now up on the balcony, touring, stopped and looked over the side at her. "He's got a martyr complex," he said. "After all, he figures he's going to talk me into it or else we're all going to die anyway, him included."

"I *will* convince you," Obie promised.

Brazil smiled and cocked his head at the empty air. "I doubt it." He looked around. "How do you get upstairs or whatever? I'm curious about this place."

A door behind him slid back, revealing the bridge across the great main shaft. He turned, nodded approval, and strolled through. The door closed behind him.

"He's not what I expected at all," Mavra Chang remarked.

"Don't be too hard on him," the computer said. "Inside he's being eaten alive. Don't be fooled. It's driving him mad. How would you like to have the choice of seeing the people you call your own destroyed or destroying every race in the Universe just to make repairs on a machine? I don't envy him—I wouldn't like that decision myself."

She sighed. "All right, I'll try to be kind—but he doesn't make it very easy. I liked him in the beginning, back on Meouit. He was really slick, a pro. Now, though—now he's so cold, so callous, so insufferably flip. It's as if he *wants* to put distance between himself and us."

"He does," Obie told her. "He's very human, you know. He can be hurt physically and emotionally. Can you imagine living since the dawn of time, most of it as a man, watching everything you love wither and die in front of you as you continued on? He's got to be hard, Mavra. It's the only way to contain the hurt. Your ancestor, one of whose forms you now wear, was someone he cared about a great deal. Someone I think he loved. Yet, long as her life was, it was a blink of the eye to Nathan Brazil. And, in the end, when his true nature was revealed—as I showed you—even she was so frightened and so repulsed that she fired on him. Pity him, Mavra. He is in Hell and he has no way out of it."

She smiled slightly. She'd been hurt pretty badly herself through most of her long life, the kind of wounds that never heal. She wondered whether or not she seemed to others the same way that Brazil seemed to her. It was not a thought to dwell on; it was too close to the truth.

"Speaking of my ancestor"—she changed subject quickly—"am I to continue to look like her?"

Obie paused a moment, as if thinking about something, then said, "Yes, for a little while. I think your appearance will be an anchor for him, an emotional crutch. Will you trust me on this one?"

"All right, I'll go along for a little while," she agreed. "But you better have somebody Topside refit my rooms and redesign me a bathroom."

Obie laughed. "All right, I will. I'm transmitting orders and specifications now. It won't be for long," he promised.

She laughed with him, then grew serious. "Obie? What if we can't talk him into it? What then? Will you run him through and force him to do it? Or can't you do that?"

"I could," the computer admitted. "I could do most things with him I could do with ordinary people. The trouble is that once he steps inside the Well of Souls control complex he will be outside the Markovian equations in which we all operate. He'll revert, as he did before, to his Markovian form—and be free of any compulsions. I can get him there, but, once inside, I can't force him to do anything. No, he'll come around. He has a sense of duty, I think, if I can convince him of the seriousness of the problem."

She started to walk toward the stairs, then stopped and turned.

"Obie?"

"Yes, Mavra?"

"Suppose he *does* do it? What happens to us?"

There was a long pause. Finally the computer said, "Our own people will be on the Well World when that happens—you included. It's going to be tough going and I want no slipups. Since unlike the rest of our Universe, the Well World is not on the main Well of Souls Computer but on its own minisystem, now undamaged, you and anybody else who's gone through the Well will survive."

Suddenly Brazil's comment on martyrs came back to her. "What about you, Obie? You can't go to the Well World."

"I was constructed in the Markovian Universe according to a historical pattern developed in Markovian space–time," Obie said carefully. "That means I exist because everything else exists. When it doesn't—well, when he shuts that thing off it won't be that our Universe will cease to exist. Our Universe and everyone in it, everyone who's ever lived, every intention, every event major and minor, every great idea and major villany—they'll be wiped out in *all* dimensions. They will not only cease to be, *they will never have been.* Only the Well World and the dying suns and dead planets of the ancient Markovians will remain. They will be the only reality."

"You'll die then."

"I will never even have been. I will not even exist, except in the minds of those who have known me who are on the Well World."

She felt tears coming unbidden to her eyes and she wiped them, embarrassed at showing emotion yet unable to regain full control.

"Oh, Obie . . ." she managed.

He said nothing, letting her feelings run their course, but he was curiously touched in a very human sort of way. Could computers cry, too?

Finally she regained her composure and started to mount the stairs. At the top she turned again. "Obie? What if he does it? Turns everything off, I mean, and fixes it. For what? There'll be nobody left to appreciate it."

"You misunderstand the depth of his responsibility," the computer told her. "The Well World exists as a laboratory, yes, but also as an operational device. Inside its memory is the power to use the Well World to restart the Universe again—no, to create a new one. Brazil is being asked not only to destroy everything we know but to start it all again as well."

There was something almost overwhelmingly frightening about that. Mavra reached the door, went outside and over the bridge, down the corridor and entered the elevator to Topside, one of the few places Obie didn't monitor on the *Nautilus*.

She cried most of the way to the top.

Nautilus—Topside

"MARQUOZ!"

The sight of the familiar, squat little dragon puffing on his ever-present cigar seemed to reassure her, bring her back to reality. Mavra had never felt so helpless, so alone, not even when she *was* alone, making her own way from orphaned beggar to streetwalker to space captain and master thief.

She felt like hugging the little monster, but refrained. Instead she just held up a hand in greeting and waited for him to come across the grassy lawn to her. He could move damned fast, she found.

"Well! Mavra, I hope?" the Chugach's foghorn voice boomed. "Still in harness, so to speak?"

She shrugged. "Obie said it would help if I kept this shape a little longer. He's running this show."

And that, of course, was part of the problem. As had happened on the Well World many years before when Mavra was a hopeless cripple, she felt like a pawn, an ornament, in a grand design being woven by others, uncertain of her future, even of whether she *had* a future, and unable to do a damned thing about it.

Marquoz seemed to understand. "Obie had us bugged, as you know," he told her. "When the Olympians moved, he dispatched more of the crew to get us. Man, was that Amazon leader mad!"

That was more like it. Real. Down-to-earth. "What have you done with the Olympians?" she asked.

"Ran 'em through Obie, of course," the little dragon replied. "Tame as kittens now."

She nodded. "And where's Brazil?"

"Eating—eating big, too, for such a little man. Says it's the first nonsynthetic stuff he's had in ages except grain products. One of the boys is going to take him on the grand tour later."

That returned her thoughts to reality, and she didn't want any more of that right at the moment. "Where's Gypsy?" she asked. "I could use a good card game or something right now. Bet he lorded it all over you that he stayed back here nice and comfortable while we were getting shot up!"

Marquoz's large head cocked itself slightly to one side. "That's the odd thing. He isn't here. Obie said he asked to borrow a ship to fix up some personal things before he got completely tied down and trapped in this business. Rather odd—I didn't even know he could fly one. Even odder that Obie would give it to him."

She nodded, a funny feeling in her stomach. "He's a very strange man," she said, "with very strange powers. I wonder where he went?"

"Stranger than that," the little dragon added. "He didn't go anyplace at all. We were in the Rhone sector, we're still in the Rhone sector, and his ship's on standby in deep space just a few light-years from here, or so Obie tells me."

That was even odder. "Has Obie given you any idea about what's going on? I mean, is Gypsy doing something for us that we're just not being told about?"

Marquoz shrugged. "Who knows? What on Earth would anybody use Gypsy for? No, I got the distinct impression that Obie is as bewildered as we are—but, just like with the customs men, security men, and the rest, Gypsy seems to have a power over even Obie."

She shivered slightly. "I hope he's on our side."

"Oh, I have no doubt he's on his own side and no other," the Chugach said. "But he's not *against* us, I'll stake my life on that. Have, in fact."

"I hope you're right" was all she could manage. "Still, I'd like to ask him a few questions when he gets back. Curious, too, that he should take off like that just when Brazil comes on. I wonder if he *will* be back? Doesn't he want to meet Nathan Brazil?"

"Perhaps not," the dragon admitted. "We'll see . . . Well, come on. Let's go up and relax a bit. I'm not as adept at gaming as Gypsy, but me and the boys would be delighted to have you join us in a little game of chance."

Olympus, the Chamber of the Holy Mother

THE ELEVATOR DOOR OPENED AND A MAN STEPPED out into the chamber. That was sacrilege—that he was not even an Olympian male was simply impossible.

Nikki Zinder was aware of his presence as soon as he stepped into the chamber; she would have been aware of him earlier but she alone controlled the elevators and they had not been operating. None of them had been. It was as if he had simply appeared in the elevator out of nowhere.

"Who dares enter the chamber of the Holy Mother so?" she thundered.

The man stopped, looked around, and nodded, a thoughtful pout on his face, like a tourist strolling through some dead shrine. He took out a cigarette, lit it, and stood dead center in the chamber looking at the far wall. "Hello, Nikki," he said casually.

Bells and alarms went off all over the Temple several stories above them and computer monitors struggled to bring her cybernetic juices back under control. The Holy Mother was blowing her top.

"Who are you that you dare to come here so?" she demanded.

"You know who I am, Nikki," he replied calmly, quietly. "You have only to look at me to know."

"You are the Evil One Himself!" she screeched through electronic voice centers. "You dare to come here, Evil One, particularly in that guise? How *dare* you!"

Bolts of lightning shot out from all over the chamber, arcing and aiming directly for the man who stood in the center, still puffing on his cigarette. Though hot enough to fry anything living and to disrupt the flow of even a creature of pure energy, he stood at the center of the furious storm as if protected by an impervious bubble. None of the strikes found their mark.

Realizing this, Nikki turned off the electricity while considering what else might have some effect on him. There was a smell of ozone in the air.

"It's time to go now, Nikki," he said, still, quietly, calmly.

"No, Evil One! You shall not take me!" she thundered.

He smiled. "It's your time, Nikki. It's *past* your time. Long past. Your world is ending. Parts of it should never have begun. Parts of it are needed elsewhere now." There seemed to be tears in his eyes. "I'm sorry, Nikki. Yours is not the life it should have been—but none of us can fully control our fate. You were born for an unhappy destiny. Perhaps you would have been better unborn. Perhaps, then, none of this would have happened, none of this would have been necessary. But it is, Nikki. It exists. Cheated of life, your time is still past. You must go now." He said it sadly, the sincerity so deep it almost penetrated her senile brain.

"You are the Enemy!" she persisted, but now she felt fear.

He smiled. "I am the Friend," he responded. "Look at me, Nikki. Tell me what I am."

"You're dead!" she shrieked. "Dead! Dead! Dead!"

There was a rumble and the dim lights in the chamber went out completely except for a glow that emanated not from the machines in the walls but from the man himself. He, too, underwent a transformation. Suddenly he was very tall, caped, and hooded, and inside the black garments his form could be seen, a ghostly, ghastly form.

A skeleton. A skeleton looking at her, peering deep through the walls and the machines with eyeless sockets into the reinforced cell where her brain and nervous system were imbedded in a semiorganic substance that nurtured her.

A skeleton with a cigarette gripped between fleshless jaws.

"You are death!" she screamed. "Away with you! Away! I am beyond death!"

"I am rest," he replied. "I have come for you, Nikki."

"No!" she screamed, panicked to the core of her soul. *"No! Away, I say! No!"*

Computers struggled to correct the imbalances, restore normalcy, but deep inside the ancient brain something welled up, beyond control, and vessels burst. Dials flickered, reflected the struggle briefly, then zeroed.

Terrified Olympian technicians, summoned by the alarms, knew even then that the Holy Mother was dead. Still they made for the elevators, tried to reach the chambers. Eventually somebody remembered the emergency bypass system and activated it. Elevators rose to the Temple levels and quickly filled with High Priestesses. Back down they rode, nervous, unsure of themselves, and then burst through the doors into the Holy Mother's chamber.

No one was there. No one. And yet, on the floor in the center of the oval room were the crushed remains of a still-smouldering cigarette.

Nautilus—Underside

MAVRA CHANG'S SUSPICIONS ABOUT GYPSY'S UNWILLingness to meet with Nathan Brazil proved unfounded. The strange, dark man returned within half a day after her return from Meouit, though he would say not a word about what he had been doing in space except to note that he "felt a need to be alone for a little while." Somehow he seemed much different; he still talked like an old con man and was outwardly unchanged, but there was something deep down, something that anyone who'd known him any length of time sensed but couldn't pin down. Until now there had been a touch of the child in Gypsy; he wasn't feared for his talents and was generally liked because of this puckish humor. All that seemed gone now; only the mannerisms and act remained.

They were all gathered in the control room waiting, for what they weren't quite sure. It had been Obie's show from the start and Obie was still very much in charge. He was telling as little as he could get away with. If he had questioned Gypsy about the strange trip, he hadn't told anyone his results.

Brazil hadn't remembered Gypsy but when reminded of a few incidents that had occurred many years earlier —neither could remember just how many—he vaguely recalled the strange man.

And now here they were, at Obie's bidding. Brazil, Gypsy, Marquoz, centauroid Mavra Chang, and, interestingly, Yua.

"Prepare for drop," Obie warned. Mavra always wondered why the computer bothered; there wasn't anything you could do to prepare for it. There was the blackness, the drawn-out sensation of falling, and then back to normal once again.

Obie had asked them to gather in the control room to monitor televisor screens of the big dish, the giant Zinder radiator that was a large part of the lower surface of the planetoid.

They were seeing a world mostly blue-green and white but with patches of red, yellow, and other colors. Yua recognized it at once and gasped. "That's Olympus!" she exclaimed.

The image of the planet shifted a bit, first this way and then that as Obie oriented the huge antenna so that the planet was in the center of the screen. He matched orbital velocity with the planet's rotation so that he stayed in the same position relative to it.

"We need the Olympians," Obie's voice told them. "They can be brought into line with a minimum of alteration. I propose to do so at this time. I have rarely used the big dish except to drop to various locations by reversing the field; however, time is pressing and I must use it now. I also selected Olympus because I know the pattern of its inhabitants without further study. After all, I designed the race. I—" He broke off in midsentence, pausing for almost a minute and a half. What the hell was going on? They wondered.

"Sorry," Obie's voice returned. "I just intercepted a mass of messages from Olympus. The only real problem I had has apparently been removed without me. Nikki Zinder is dead."

Yua gasped. "The Holy Mother? But that's impossible!"

"No, not really," the computer responded. "Brain cells wear out, malfunction, and die even in the best of setups—and this was the best, believe me. A massive stroke, it appears. No signs of foul play—the techs say she just blew a gasket for some reason—except they found a cigarette on the floor of her chamber. Extraordinary!"

Gypsy sat back and lit a cigarette, inhaling deeply.

"No sign of forced entry, no way for anybody to get in and out," the computer continued. Their medical people have fed the medical monitor data through and

I've analyzed it. Amazing. I would swear she was frightened to death!'

Mavra Chang sighed. "Poor Nikki. I feel so sorry for her. She never had a chance at a real life."

To her surprise, Nathan Brazil spoke. "She's better off now. Life's a tragedy anyway." He seemed genuinely sorry.

She turned and looked at him. Now, divested of his makeup, he looked quite ordinary. A small man, almost tiny, with fine-chiseled features and black hair and eyes. Though he was not handsome, except for his diminutive size and build there was something classic about him, like a Greek statue in the old records.

"You're supposed to be god," she muttered. "Is there an afterlife where she might find happiness?"

To her surprise he answered. "Truthfully, I don't know, since I can't escape this one," he said quietly. "The math allows for the possibility of such a thing, but—who knows? The evidence is ambiguous. It doesn't matter, anyway—even that would be wiped out when this sector goes."

That was depressing, so nobody pursued it.

"You won't see much on the screens," Obie told them. "I am reprogramming the Olympians. Nathan Brazil has been found and is in command, and he has new tasks for them to perform. They will follow his orders—they will do whatever we tell them, gladly. You others are taking on the role of saints. They'll worship you as they would him."

"You know, this has possibilities," Brazil murmured. "A whole planetful of superwomen who'll do anything I tell 'em to. The hell with porn."

All of a sudden they heard a tremendous hum; vibration filled the great shaft outside and shook the walls of the control room. Only the image of the planet on the screen remained steady. The great power of Gil Zinder's full creation was being employed.

And then a great shudder was felt all over the *Nautilus*. The planetoid started to move. The vibration was so great that they were aware of the movement only because the planet on the screen appeared to revolve slowly. It seemed to be bathed in a glow. The vibration continued for some minutes, until Obie had completely circled Olympus, then slowly died.

"It's done," Obie announced. "We have willing workers now—millions of them."

"There seems to be something vaguely immoral in all this," Brazil commented sourly. "One zap and instant racial slavery." He looked genuinely disturbed. "If I'd realized the full power of this thing, I'd have gone to that party at Trelig's."

Mavra gave him a dark look. "Now's a fine time to find it out," she snapped.

"Is it true?" Yua asked wonderingly. "Am I now a goddess among my people?"

"It's true," Obie assured her.

"But—how will anyone know me from the others?"

"No one left on the planet has a tail or any memory that anybody on Olympus save you ever had a tail," Obie told her. "Your tail is your sign of godhood."

Marquoz gave a low chuckle. "It seems our little liberated chick is taking all too well to a wider Universe than she was born to," he muttered. Gypsy chuckled.

"Please, now, everyone come into the old lab," Obie invited. "I have some things that must be done and some things that must be said. Watch yourselves as you round the small corner to the doorway; the main shaft is very hot."

It was. It was like an oven; those who could sweat were soaked in just the time necessary to cross the few meters from the control-room door to the lab entrance.

The old lab felt almost frigid after the steambath, and they all stood gasping for a few moments.

Mavra, coughing, looked around and noted a number of rifle-carrying crewmen lining the walk. She grew apprehensive; Obie had been acting strangely since the problem in space–time began and she didn't like the look of this development at all. She began to fear that the effect of the rip in space had somehow unhinged him.

"Please move down to the lower level," Obie ordered. They complied, all eyeing the armed guards and wondering what the hell was going on. Soon they were facing the dais on the lower level. They could see the little dish, the original Zinder creation that had started everything so many centuries before.

"Please pardon the strong-arm stuff," Obie said, "but I expect some resistance to what must be done and, as I expect to die today, I want no one able to change things."

"Obie! No!" Mavra screamed.

"I must, Mavra," he replied, almost pleading. "I don't want to do it. I don't want to die, Mavra. Nobody does. But . . . I *must,* I think. I . . . I don't know. Maybe I won't. We'll see. But I have to act as if I will."

Nathan Brazil didn't seem very upset by Obie's statements. "Why all the histrionics, Obie? I'm not going to do it and you know it—and you know you can't force me to."

"You speak with your heart, Brazil," the computer responded, "for which I envy you. I, too, have a heart in the poetic sense, but I am cursed by my realization as an enormous machine. Machines are designed to think logically, to cut through all the crap at impossible speed and with all the information needed. We machines can't ignore the facts or the logic. It's always there, always right at your metaphorical fingertips. I can do quintillions of different calculations at the same time. I have no subconscious mind—just an infinitely large conscious one. I can be sad, I can be happy. I can mourn the death of my poor sister, I can fear for my own self, I can feel love and hate and pity. But I can't use my emotions to run from the truth as the rest of you can. You all cope because of your ability to shuffle things in your brain, reinterpret them through your emotions—be a bit psychotic, if you will. I cannot. I was not designed to do it, much as I envy the trait. *I am always perfectly sane.* That is my curse. That is the factor that makes my thing different—not just faster—than yours."

They said nothing; it was clear that none knew where Obie was headed.

"I say that Nathan Brazil must reenter the Well of Souls," Obie continued. "He must disconnect the Well from the power source. This will undo the last, say . . . roughly the last ten billion years, at once. All that we know will cease to exist. Then Brazil must repair what is broken and allow the Well to repair itself, too. He must do this because, if he does it right now, or in the immediate future, he will most assuredly be able to use the Well World to recreate the Universe. It will start back at square one, of course, for the Markovian races and for the forces of evolution that produce new forms in response to their preset natural laws. If he waits, as he now wishes to, Brazil risks a twenty-one percent chance that the Well will short out within the next few decades. That means a seventy-nine percent chance that it won't, which is what he clings to. I submit that a one-in-five chance is too great a risk to play with.

"You see, if the Well shorts out it will then be damaged beyond repair. There can be no re-creation. There will be only darkness, and life of any sort will exist only upon the Well World itself. Forever."

Marquoz, Yua, Gypsy, and Mavra all looked at Brazil. "Is this true?" the little dragon asked.

"I'm willing to take the risk," Brazil replied calmly. "It's four to one that most of the races of the Universe will have the millions of years they deserve."

"But is there a one-in-five chance of what he says happening?" Marquoz pressed.

Brazil nodded. "Something like that. I think he's probably exaggerating for effect. Five to eight percent—one out of twelve at the outside—more likely, within the next one to three million years, anyway."

"Those are better odds," the Chugach said to Obie and the others. "At five to eight percent *I'd* take the risk."

"He refuses to face facts," Obie came back. "Twenty-one percent. Now. This minute. Thirty percent in another century or two. Fifty percent in another two to five thousand years. Any moment after that. A race can accomplish a great deal in five thousand years—but it cannot achieve greatness. It's too short a time to produce even a minor evolutionary change; it's time enough to lose wisdom, but not time enough to earn it. So Mr. Brazil asks us to give the races of the Universe a few thousand years—at the risk of total oblivion for the entire Universe beyond any hope of reconstruction. I submit that the potential to be gained by immediate inaction are outweighed by the greater risk we take allowing it. The Well must be repaired. Now."

"I know more about the Well than he does," Brazil pointed out. "I think he's wrong."

"I'm a far better and faster computer than you, Nathan Brazil," Obie retorted.

He chuckled. "If you know more about it than I do, then *you* turn it off and fix it."

It was a good point, but Obie was ready for it. "You know I can't. I know what has to be done, but I'm a part of the equations. The moment the power is turned off I, too, will cease to exist. The Well will not recognize a surrogate, since only one of the older Markovian equations can open the Well and get inside. I can tell you what to do—but only Brazil can do it. And he knows it."

They looked at the strange little man. His expression seemed anguished. "I couldn't do it, anyway," he said defensively. "My god! Do you realize how many people I'd be murdering? I will not accept that kind of responsibility! I won't!"

"Standoff," Gypsy muttered.

"Not quite," Obie responded. "As I said, Brazil has an advantage: Human in his thoughts and soul, he can continue to run from the truth. I cannot. Therefore, he must be made to see things as I do. He must be forced to face the truth. In a moment I will swing the little dish out, I will enfold him and we shall merge. He will see what I see. He will be forced to see what I am forced to see. *Then* let him refuse."

"But—Obie!" Mavra protested. "You can't! Just trying to analyze him damaged you!"

"I expect the experience might be fatal," the computer replied, a note of apprehension creeping into his all-too-human voice. "I am not sure. I *do* know that it is possible, and I *do* know that the Well will keep *him* from being killed by the experience. But he will be forced to recognize the truth."

Brazil chuckled nervously. "Now, wait a minute! Ain't no way I'm going to go through with this. If you think—"

"You have no choice," Obie cut in. "The men with rifles will see to that. You will either do what I say or we will shoot hell out of you and they will throw you on the platform."

Brazil looked genuinely upset. He disliked pain as much as the next man. "Okay! Okay! I'll *do* it!" he practically yelled. "You don't have to go on with this!"

"I'm sorry, Brazil, I truly am," Obie responded. "I wish you were telling the truth, but you and I know you are not sincere. The dish is the only way I can make sure. Do you think I would take this course if there were any other way? If you were me and I you—would *you* believe it, even if it were true?"

Brazil sighed and seemed to collapse a bit. He looked totally defeated. "You got me there."

"I would like to speak with each of you in turn, in private, before I deal with Brazil," the computer said gravely. "Mavra, will you please step onto the platform?"

Forcing back tears, Mavra somehow made it up to the platform.

With the violet glow enveloping her she had no conception of time. But she knew she had to talk Obie out of it.

"Mavra, don't say it," his voice came to her. "For one thing, I agree with you a hundred percent. I don't want to do it. But I *have* to. Try to understand."

"I'm trying, Obie—but I just can't accept it."

"Look, Mavra. It's not the way Brazil says. I have no desire to be a martyr. With the death of Nikki, I'm the last of the Zinders. I hadn't expected her to die, Mavra. I had hoped that she could be helped by me, given the fresh start she deserved."

"If it's any comfort to you, Obie, I don't think you could have done a thing unless you wanted to wipe her mind."

"I know, I know. Still—it's kind of strange, isn't it? Her going today, that is. The both of us . . ."

"It doesn't have to be, Obie! Come on! We're partners. Fifty-fifty. You don't have a majority to dissolve the company."

"It's dissolved in favor of a new one. You know that. It was dissolved the moment they used the Zinder

Nullifiers. I know—both of us thought it would go on forever. New challenges, new worlds. I guess the biggest mistake was in not checking back here regularly. If we had, we could have handled the Dreel and none of this would have happened."

"You don't know how many times I've thought about that," she admitted ruefully.

"But we didn't, Mavra. It's done. What hurts most is that we did a lot of good out there. No matter how fouled up they were going, we managed to turn them around, put them on the right track. It was surprising how similar we were to most of the rest—although I guess when you consider they all sprang from the same Markovian roots, it's not that odd. Still, we saved a lot of lives, a few planets, maybe a civilization or two."

She nodded and smiled. "It's a record to be proud of. And, most of all, it was fun, too."

"It was. But for what? When Brazil pulls the plug on the Well, Mavra, they'll all be gone. They will never have been. The space and time that have been superimposed on the Markovian Universe will vanish. Such a *waste*."

"You sound like Brazil, Obie. Why not give them a chance, then? As he wants to?"

"They don't have a chance, Mavra—and neither do I. Either we destroy it all, for all time, with no hope of restarting, or we restart now. Either way I shall die. It's better this way."

"But must you die?" she pressed. "Why now? We'll need you."

"You should never need me," he came back. "That's the trouble. All of you have been too dependent on my big and little dishes. You've grown rusty from playing god, Mavra. And, no, I need not die. Truthfully, I do not know what will happen. I might go mad, I might just injure myself. I will probably short out. There will be no danger; I have already disconnected life-support and maintenance from dependence on me, so it's like old times again there. *Nautilus* will survive and work—for a while. Who knows? I'm *not* god, although sometimes it was easy to think myself so. I don't know what will happen. I only know that while I do what I must,

I find I regret a surprisingly small amount of my own life. I regret none of our association, Mavra. The others—to them I am a machine, or a powerful, alien entity to be feared. Only you, Mavra, see me otherwise. Only you have been my confidant, my close, dear friend."

He paused for a moment. She was too choked up to say anything, and she had the oddest feeling that Obie was feeling the same very human way.

Finally he said, "I will tell you what needs to be done and everybody's role in it. It'll be a memory read-out; you are already strong enough to resist all the extraction methods known to me. In a sense I give you more than that, a little part of me, the most human part, that will rest back within the dark recesses of your mind, but when you need me I'll be there. Still partners, Mavra."

"Still partners, Obie," she managed.

She was suddenly back in the chamber and the others were staring at her. She stepped down.

"Marquoz, please," Obie summoned. The little dragon sighed, got up on the platform, and looked around at the empty air. "Mind if I continue to smoke?" he asked. The violet beam descended.

"Marquoz," Obie said, "you are not here by accident but by design. Not mine, though, I am not clear whose. Perhaps there is some power greater than we. Still, in my estimation you are the absolute best person for the job. A great deal of work is to be done, and you must bear part of the responsibility."

"You seem awfully certain that Brazil will do it," the little dragon pointed out. "You also seem awfully certain that *we'll* do it, whatever you have in mind for us, anyway. Suppose Brazil comes back and still says no? Suppose he doesn't come back?"

"He'll come back," Obie assured him. "You must understand that only his body is a part of the reality you and I know and accept. His spirit, his soul, that part of him that is his personality and memories—it's not part of our Universe at all. It is so alien that I cannot begin to understand it. It is as if he is made of antimatter. You see it—it looks real, acts real, is normal in every way. But touch it and you explode. I understand antimatter; I can even *become* antimatter. He is of a past Universe and an alien form that is beyond me, for I have no frame of reference, nothing against which to compare him."

"That's what's going to happen?" Marquoz asked worriedly. "You and he are going to combine and explode?"

"No, nothing like that. He is adapted to our Universe; he can accept ours. You might say, though, that we are just a part of his reality. He is a bucket and we are water. You can fill a bucket with water but not water with a bucket. He will receive my data and see that there is no course open to him but mine. Believe me. But I will also get *his* data, and it will be in a form and amount that I cannot handle. It shouldn't harm him, except perhaps to shake him up. It will harm me.

"Listen well. I will tell you your role in what is to come. Brazil will be in charge, but I already know the basic idea that must be used. Accept his leadership—but never think of him as a god. He's not—he is a very human being, something which puzzles me a great deal. Think of him as the only known repairman for a broken machine. Act accordingly. Your job is to get him to the Well. On the Well World yourself, you will survive. Receive the information."

Yua received much the same instruction, although when she emerged from the violet glow she seemed a different person, more knowledgeable, more worldly, more self-confident. Obie had given her what he thought she'd need.

Gypsy was next. He didn't want to go, but the riflemen gave him little choice. He sighed and let the glow take him.

"Hello, Obie," he said casually.

"Hello, Gypsy," the computer replied. "I am giving you the least instruction and the least well-defined role in the coming drama because I believe you are the most resourceful of the bunch." He hesitated. "You agree with what I am about to do and what I am forcing?"

All the playful pretense was gone now. "Yes, Obie. You *know*, don't you? How?"

"You couldn't hide it from me forever. Yes, I know—and I think I understand, in a way. I didn't ask you anything about your motives or your own 'how.' I only asked you if you agreed."

"This is very hard on me," Gypsy said hesitantly. "Academically, yes. I guess I'm more like Brazil than like you, Obie. I—I just couldn't do it. I couldn't insist somebody else do it, either."

"You did once," the computer said.

He nodded absently. "I guess I did at that. I suppose we know our own selves the least of anyone." He looked up, although there was no one to see. "Obie? Do you forgive me?"

"I forgive you," the computer replied softly. "There is little to forgive. Help them, though, won't you?"

"I'll do what I can," he promised. "Who would have thought it would have come down to me, eh?" The chuckle was without humor.

"Good-bye—Gypsy."

"Obie—there must be another—" he began, then stopped. "So long, Obie," he said at last. The glow was gone.

"It's time, Nathan Brazil."

Brazil looked around at the others, all staring intently at him. "You're all *crazy!*" he muttered. "Crazy!" He turned and faced the pedestal. "Obie—it means this much to you?"

"It does," the computer responded.

Brazil hesitated a moment. "Then I'll do it. Now. Get me to the Well World, shoot me down to an Avenue, and I'll do it."

The computer hesitated—Brazil could feel it—and his hopes rose. They were quickly dashed when Obie replied, "I would like to believe that. I really would. But, once in, you could simply wish me out of existence and do nothing else. You could turn us all into toads. Anything but what must be done. We've been through this discussion before, Nathan Brazil. Besides, what you ask is now impossible. I am injured. I am in great pain. I can no longer handle the type of drop necessary for the Well World with any certainty. The hard way, Brazil. Try not to kill me."

Nathan Brazil sighed. "Now, damn it, I'm not going to do this and that's that!"

"On the count of three those riflemen will shoot you," Obie said flatly. "It's set on needle stun. It will hurt—hurt a lot. And when you're disabled and in pain they will come down and throw you up here. This is the time for us both, Nathan Brazil. One . . . two . . ."

Brazil looked uneasily at the riflemen and jumped up on the podium. "What a bunch of melodramatic bullshit," he muttered defiantly; but he looked nervous.

The violet glow reached down and surrounded the little man and then he winked out.

"Obie! No!" Mavra Chang screamed, rushing to the podium. But it was too late. Brazil was already gone.

They waited. Mavra listened for explosions, vibrations, or other signs of terrible things happening to Obie, but she heard only the smooth, ever-present hum of a machine-world. Perhaps Obie would be all right.

Obie, who could remold a planet in an hour or two, spent four with Brazil locked into him with no visible sign of an end. It got hard on the observers' nerves; Yua paced, Marquoz and Gypsy played gin rummy but neither's mind was on the game, and Mavra finally became so irritated that she started berating the guards for their actions even though she realized they were under mental compulsion from Obie. They took her outburst patiently, then, when she'd run down, two of them went Topside for food and drinks for the rest.

More time passed. Yua suggested they try to rest, but the others, even Gypsy, refused. "I don't know about you," Marquoz told the rest of them, "but I'm staying here until Hell freezes over. I *have* to know the end of this." He looked idly at Mavra. "You know, if something *does* go wrong with Obie you're going to be a Rhone woman from now on."

She hadn't even considered that. "It doesn't matter," she decided at last. "If Obie can't get us to the Well World we'll have to go in through a Markovian gate anyway. That means going through the Well and being changed into another creature, anyway. And this time whatever it makes us we will be for the rest of our natural lives."

It was a sobering thought.

Gypsy chuckled. "Yeah, Marquoz. They'll change you into a human."

"Heaven forbid!" the little dragon sniffed. "The odds are one in seven hundred and eighty, I believe. Don't bet on it. Remember—you could become a Chugach."

"Oh, my god!" Gypsy responded, mock-stricken. "Still, it would give me an easy way to light cigarettes. Or don't they have cigarettes on this Well World?"

Yua got into the discussion turning to Mavra, whose equine body towered over them. "You've been there," she said. "What is it like?"

Mavra smiled wanly. "Like anyplace else, really. Just imagine a planet that was a lot of little planets—fifteen hundred and sixty of them, in fact, each roughly six hundred and fifteen kilometers wide at the Well World's equator—they get a little distorted as you go toward the poles. Each one is shaped like a hexagon—the Markovians were nutty about the number six. Each one with its own plants, insects, you name it, and all with different dominant races. All the carbon-based ones are south of the equator—seven hundred and eighty in all. The ones north of the equator are non-carbon based. They can be anything."

"And you can walk between them?" the Olympian pressed.

Mavra nodded. "It's like an invisible, intangible wall. It can be freezing on one side and hot as hell on the other. But things like rivers, mountain ranges, and whatnot run through them without regard to the borders. It sounds like a boxy place but it's not—the coastlines are irregular, erosion, deposition, and volcanic forces all work there as elsewhere. But each hex is an artificial area ecologically perfect for that form of life specified by the Markovians. Supposedly each was a little laboratory. Markovian technicians dreamed up the places, established them, watched them develop to see if they'd work. Weather, climate, atmospheric conditions, all optimized for a particular set of planetary conditions. There are handicaps, too—in some of them no machines will work that are not muscle-powered. In others, only limited machines, like steam engines, work—and in some everything works, like here. This ranking of technologies was supposed to compensate, I think, for resources—or the lack of them—the new races would find on the planets they'd be seeded on. Magic, too, in some instances—the ability to control some powers through the Well. Artificial magic, yes, but no less real because only the one race can use it. Other handicaps might have existed too, I guess."

"You'd think they'd fight like hell—or overpopulate," Marquoz commented.

"The Well controls population, maintains it at around a million or so per hex," Mavra explained. "If something comes up—war, plague, natural disaster—that decimates a batch, then they reproduce like bunnies until the loss is made up. As for wars—well, there have been minor skirmishes. The humans there developed a high technological civilization that finally ran out of resources so they attacked the nontechnological Ambreza next door. The Ambreza found a gas from a strange Northern Hemisphere race—although all the Northerners are strange, even by Well World standards—and gassed the humans back into the stone age, then swapped hexes with them. The humans are primitive and tribal—were the last time I was there, anyway—and are kept on that level by the Ambreza, who enjoy the resources of their former land and the technology of the human's past. One big export is tobacco, Gypsy. It's not common but it's known and prized there. It can be an expensive habit, though."

"But there must be bigger wars, too," Marquoz prodded. "I would think it'd be natural."

"Natural, maybe," Mavra admitted, "but there have been only two that I know of. There was a famous conqueror who had problems because his high-tech weapons wouldn't work in a majority of hexes—a nonworking laser pistol is a poor match against a well-trained crossbowman—and some hexes were uncomfortable enough that his supply lines became too long, impossible to maintain. That was the big lesson—you can't conquer the Well World. Then, when Obie and I were there last, a war broke out to get to the shuttle spacecraft that brought some of us down. The object was to reach and control Obie. Space travel simply won't work on the Well World if developed from scratch, but here was a ready-made vessel. The war was bloody and brutal but settled nothing because the spacecraft engines were destroyed by a hermit race who didn't believe anybody should have them."

Marquoz nodded. "I've read the Com records."

"You said you crashed there," Yua noted. "That means you have never been through the Well of Souls transformation yourself."

She nodded assent. "That's right. A very nasty race called the Olborn had stones that could change any other creature—or themselves—into beasts of burden, like tiny donkeys. I got half the treatment, so I spent many long years facing down, on four hooved feet, with no hands and no way even to look up." There was an angry gleam in her eyes. "They kept me on ice in case they needed a pilot. They couldn't afford to let me go through the Well since they had no control over what or where I'd come out."

"They?" Marquoz prompted.

She sniffed. "A bastard named Serge Ortega. A giant creature with a head like a walrus, six arms, and a long snakelike body. An ex-human, it's told, and a former freighter captain. Somehow he found a way to make himself virtually immortal as long as he stays in Zone, the normal entryway to the Well World and a sort of embassy. He practically ran the Well World. Probably still does." She chuckled dryly. "You know, if there's any man I still truly hate it is probably Ortega. I swore I'd kill him someday, as I killed the men who murdered my husband. He had no *right* to do what he did to me!"

The sudden violence of her tone alarmed them. It was Gypsy, heretofore silent, who said, "I'd have thought you'd have gone to the Well World and done him in long ago."

"Obie wouldn't permit it," she responded. "Obie had no power over the Well World and wasn't about to put me back on it just to settle an old score. I have the funny feeling he always liked Ortega for some reason. I don't know. Ortega and I were bound up together for years yet I never once met him. Strange."

Clearly old wounds were being reopened; half-forgotten experiences were creeping out from the dimly lit back halls of her brain.

"And we'll all be going there," Yua breathed. "It sounds incredible. Exciting. I can hardly wait."

"Enjoy it while you can," Mavra said sharply. "The Well World is anything but romantic. It's dangerous and deadly. I never missed it."

"Well, even so, I—" Yua started to respond, but at that moment there was a sharp crackling noise as if a great bolt of lightning had struck near them. They all jumped, startled, and turned.

White-faced and shaking Nathan Brazil stood on the pedestal. He stared straight ahead, looking at empty space. They didn't move for a moment, just watched him apprehensively.

He tottered slightly, still looking vacantly ahead. Finally he said, "I need a drink. No, check that. I need to get very, very drunk."

And then he collapsed into an unconscious heap.

Nautilus—Topside

THEY WAITED TWO DAYS FOR NATHAN BRAZIL TO come out of it. His pulse rate was very weak, at times dropping so low it could barely be detected; he ran serious fevers, but never lapsed into delirium. He just lay there, almost dead, making the medical people wonder if he'd ever rise again. They brought him Topside, placed him in a luxury suite under guard, and summoned the medical staff. The diagnosis was simple: He was suffering from extreme shock, and little could be done for him except to see that he was kept warm, regularly massaged, and fed intravenously.

In the meantime, to forestall half the planet coming to the *Nautilus,* Yua and Gypsy visited Olympus. They returned a day later to report that Obie had worked some major magic—including the removal of tails from all but Yua. Still, the change unsettled Yua a little since Olympian history now clearly showed that no one on Olympus *ever* had a tail; the now-tailless women were called Pallas. All sight that there had ever been two varieties, the Athene and the Aphrodite, had vanished. They never were.

There were men, too, on Olympus—out in the open. They ran nothing and were still regarded as sex objects, but they were part of the society—and always had been.

More, the Fellowship of the Well had changed course—in this case by simultaneous "divine revelation" to all High Priestesses so there would be no mistake. In order to create universal Paradise, they had been told, Nathan Brazil must first go to the Well World itself, pass into the Well, and eradicate the old

Universe. The forces of evil would try to stop him. For Olympus to share in the Heaven to come, they and their followers must form an army to help Brazil attain his goal. As reward they would be a part of the new, Holy Universe, for though the powers of evil held sway in this Universe they, too, would be swept away in the re-creation, leaving a Universe without evil. Even to die in this holy crusade would guarantee a place in the next, great Universe.

And Brazil's own disciples—Yua of Olympus, Marquoz of Chugach, Gypsy of the Place Between Stars, and Mavra Chang herself, the legend brought back from the dead by the hand of Brazil—would lead and instruct and command in the final battle to come. The Fellowship had a most holy mission, it was now clear, and it was already preparing for it.

After hearing the report, Marquoz marveled at Obie's skill. "It is so much easier to lead a holy crusade backed by divine intervention," he noted.

Mavra Chang just smiled and shrugged. "It's the same old story. You don't get something for nothing, ever. They were offered a Heaven we can't deliver and life beyond the destruction of the Universe which, in exchange for their services, we can perhaps, deliver to some. They're going to fight and die for a lie."

"As usual," Marquoz added.

Their conversation was interrupted by a buzz on Mavra's communicator. She removed it from her belt clip and said, "Yes?"

"I think he's coming out of it," a medic said.

They all rushed to Brazil's suite.

Nathan Brazil had been floating in a nice, dark, quiet place of his own. Thought hadn't been required; it was warm and comfortable and it felt so very good. The quiet place was slipping away now, and memories were flooding his conscious brain. At first he could make no sense of them, and didn't try; still they came, rushing into his mind like soldiers rushing to battle, struggling to assemble themselves into some sort of order.

A small grove of palm trees around a clear blue waterhole; dry, hot country even then, but green, not as it was to become. A slight breeze blew from the southeast, a dry, dreadful, hot caress that carried no relief. Two young women, one rather comely, two small children. The pretty one's? An older man, beard graying and face weatherbeaten and tough. Hard to tell. You didn't talk much or attempt to strike up new acquaintances in these troubled times.

Hoofbeats. Men on horses. Barely a chance to look up. Romans! Only five of them, but nasty types. Looking for trouble. He hid in the bush and lay still. Odd, though, a corner of his mind told him. Sounded like more horses than that. Different directions, perhaps? Were others cowering like him in the bushes?

The Romans have dismounted now. The two young children, both boys, wade naked at the edge of the pool, splashing and playing. The Romans look around at them, at the old man and the two women, critically with an air of complete command. One calls in Latin to the others and points critically to the two small boys. He catches a word, blown to him on the hot wind. "Circumcized." There will be trouble; Antiochus has outlawed the practice for now. One Rome, one set of beliefs, one set of customs. Cultural assimilation, they called it. The world under one and as one.

The old man is defiant. He yells at the centurion, who yells back, then laughs and grabs at the younger woman. The old man is upon him now, screaming and cursing. Two Romans run to assist the centurion, swords drawn, and hack the old man almost to pieces. The women are screaming now. The Romans are around them. The younger one is grabbed and is partially disrobed by two of the Romans. The older woman rushes them with a dagger in her hand, but a blow from the flat of a Roman sword crushes her skull; she falls and is still.

He is still in the bushes and he is angry and ashamed at himself. He has spear and sword and suddenly he finds himself leaping out at the men in a blind rage.

A Roman is slitting the throats of the two young boys; he turns, startled, then looks amazed as a spear is thrust through his armor and into his gut.

The two men now have the woman down; they turn

in surprise, but their comrades have already drawn their own weapons and are moving toward him.

He was good, particularly when so angry. He just about tore off the sword arm of the nearest Roman with a strong inside blow, but the other was not to be taken so easily. A good swordsman himself, the Roman forced the man into the arms of the other two Romans who had stopped messing with the girl and come up behind him.

"I'll kill the bastard now!" the swordsman snarled, advancing on the captive.

"No! Hold!" cried one of his captors. "The bitch means something to him, otherwise why would he fight so? Tie him to the tree. Let him watch us, and die before his death!"

"Ai! Let's cut off his limbs and leave him there alive, to bleed to death or live a limbless cripple!" snarled the man whose arm he'd cut to the bone, still lying in agony on the sand. They laughed at that, and bandaged the other as best they could.

And it was done. He was tied to a tree with ropes too strong to break and forced to watch the rape, after which they killed her, not mercifully swift but slowly.

He wept, as much for the way of the world as for these people who had been tortured and slain. He'd known good, brave, fair-minded men of the Legions, men who'd have acted as he had in the face of such barbarism. Not now. Rome was expanding, extending her influence to the edges of the world, and that expansion required men in great numbers, men whose only qualification was that they would kill and delight in killing. When such vicious animals were used to spread "civilization," how long would it be before that madness sped backward to its roots and reached the throne itself?

And they were around him now, facing him as he stood bound to the tree.

"So this is the greatness of mighty Rome," he sneered at them.

They laughed, although he could see in their faces that they were taken aback by such coolness in the face of torture and death.

They drew their swords and leered at him. One

gestured at the carnage. "Those were your people?"

He looked the man squarely in the eyes. "I never saw them before in my life," he told them in flawless Latin.

"Then why did you fight for them?" another asked, confused and a bit unnerved by their captive's total disregard for personal well-being.

"The children of the Lord God of Israel should not be abused by animals spawned in Hell."

"Enough of this! You are a brave man but a foolish one," the centurion told him. "We will kill you and be done with it."

"I really wish you could."

The Roman drew his sword and hesitated a second, looking into his eyes before striking the fatal blow.

Four sharp sounds echoed, followed by a *whap! whap! whap! whap!* The Romans stood for a moment, looking confused, then toppled over, arrows protruding from their backs.

Four men emerged from the bushes nearby. All Hebrews, he saw at once, all holding bows. One was an older man; by their looks the others were his sons. Two of the sons checked the bodies of the slain Hebrews while the third son, with a sword, made certain that the Romans would stay forever on the ground. The old man approached him, drew a small curved knife from his belt, and cut the binding straps. He almost collapsed as the flow of blood, which had been restricted by his bonds, returned fully to his limbs. The old man was strong and caught him, lowering him gently to the ground.

"You've had a terrible ordeal," the older man said kindly in Hebrew.

He nodded. "There were just too many," he responded in the same language.

The old man nodded. "We were just a bit too far off." He sighed. "We heard the screams but arrived too late and approached, perhaps, too cautiously." He looked at the dead Romans. "It is just revenge," he murmured, almost to himself, "but somehow it does not seem adequate." Then back to the freed man: "You have relatives to whom you can be taken?"

He shook his head. "All I had lies there," he muttered. "I am alone in the world once again."

"You are young, and brave, and skilled," the old man told him. "You deserve a new chance. Come! I am of substance. I am Mattathias the son of John, a priest of the sons of Joarib, now of Modin. These are my sons—Joannan Caddis, Simon Thassi, Eleazar Avaran, and Jonathan Apphus on the Roman rolls."

"My name and family are dead with them," he said sorrowfully. "I died with them."

"Then you shall be my son," Mattathias told him. "You shall become the son who was their eldest brother but died so long ago in the wilderness." He turned to his sons, now standing there. "What say you?"

"He is a brave man who has lost much," one said. "And his spirit and his faith are sorely needed in these trying times." The others nodded assent.

"Any warrior as small as you who could penetrate Roman armor has a passion inside and the Lord's annointment," another said.

"It is settled, then," Mattathias said, satisfied. "You are as another son to me and welcome to my tribe and house. And henceforth you shall be known as Judas Maccabeas, my lost son who returns to me in these days of trial."

And they knelt and prayed together that the Lord God of Israel accepted this and it was in fact His will. And when they were finished he looked up at them all and said, "Perhaps with your faith and your patriotism we may bring mighty Antiochus himself to heel!"

Nathan Brazil awoke.

His head felt as if it was bursting; he could only groan, and the medics came with painkillers to aid him. He got his eyes to focus, finally, and tried to sit up. With a low moan, he quickly collapsed back into the bed.

"Well, I see the gang's all here," he muttered.

"How do you feel?" Mavra asked. Her concern was evident.

He managed a low chuckle. "Oh, about like anybody would a day or so after being at the center of an explosion."

"What happened to you in . . . there?" Marquoz asked. "Do you remember any of it?"

Brazil winced, not from pain but from memory. "I wish to God I didn't! You know, Obie wasn't kidding—the human mind is a fantasy land operating to delude itself by assuming whatever point of view is easiest to live with. Can you imagine coming face to face with yourself—your *real* self—with no place to hide? Even Obie doesn't realize the kind of horror he perpetrated on me, the terrible torture he put me through. I don't think he could have done it if he'd known. You realize we—all us nonmachines—are crazy? Absolutely stark-raving mad? No *wonder* the Markovians felt they hadn't reached utopia—they hadn't. I wonder if this is the sort of thing that happened to them. I mean, linked mentally to their monster computers they must have undergone much of what I just did, been forced to face themselves with no place to run. What a terrible disillusionment it must have been! My God! No *wonder!* It explains everything! The Well, why they performed their great experiment, why they were so willing to commit suicide—and why they failed this time, too. We—all of us—created in their image, yes, but reflections of their darker sides as well. My god!"

"But weren't you there?" Mavra asked. She was bewildered by all Brazil's monologue. "You're a Markovian—aren't you?"

He gave a dry chuckle, then groaned a little as it hurt. "No, not a Markovian. Something . . . else. Don't worry. I can fix their pretty machine." Then, suddenly, he was off on his own again. "My god! No wonder the Well isn't self-aware. They couldn't have *stood* that . . ."

"Obie—is Obie dead?" Mavra pressed fearfully.

"I—I don't know. I don't think so. No, I'm sure he's not. But he's—well, he's of no help to us now, maybe not in the foreseeable future. You see, to Obie the whole Universe and everything in it is strictly logical and mathematical. That's what we are to him, strings of numbers, relationships that balance. *I don't balance.* I'm not a part of any math he understands and he doesn't have the key to understanding my 'formula', driven to assimilate me, and for that he needs the key. But he can't get the key unless he assimilates me. He must solve the problem, and he can't solve the problem until he solves it. He's stuck in a loop. In a way I guess you can say I drove him crazy."

"And what about you?" Marquoz broke in. "He thought you might drive him crazy, yet he threatened to drive you sane. Did he?"

Brazil chuckled again. "The mind is a resilient thing, Marquoz. I'm probably saner than any living being has ever been, possibly saner than the Markovians were after their mind-links to their computers, yet I'm still quite mad and slipping more into madness the more I think. When you face the unthinkable you retreat, you shove it away, back into corners of your mind that you can't reach."

"Unfortunately, I think I understand you," the Chugach responded. "Still, except to you, that bit of metaphysics is of little consequence. The question on the table is, simply, have you changed your attitude on fixing the Well of Souls?"

Nathan Brazil sighed. "A byproduct of the mind-link is that you remember things you never wanted to remember. The worst part is, the more of those memories you dredge up the more you realize how futile it all is. Rome rose to great heights, yet its own methods caused it to decay from within. I wonder if that isn't true of the Markovian experience as well. Will we just do it all over again, even reach this point once again? Is the whole business of life doomed to repeated failure because there is something wrong with the experimenters? I wonder . . ."

"But will you fix the Well?" the little dragon persisted.

Brazil nodded unhappily. "I'll go to the Well, if possible. I'll enter and stand there and analyze the problem. But I won't take the responsibility for murdering so many. I *can't* accept the responsibility any more." He turned slightly on his side, looking at them, and his eyes fixed on Mavra Chang. He pointed to her.

"*You* will take the responsibility," he told her. "When I stand inside the Well so will you. I'll ask you to give me the order. *You* will tell me to pull the plug on the Universe."

He sank down and lapsed into unconsciousness, but the instruments informed them that, this time, it was closer to normal sleep.

Nautilus—Topside, Later That Same Day

MAVRA CHANG PACED BACK AND FORTH IN THE LARGE reception chamber, where she had spent most of the afternoon and a good part of the evening, looking grim and somewhat unhappy.

Marquoz waddled around the corner, stopped, yawned, and stared at her for a few moments. "You know, you really ought to get some rest and eat something, too. You can't eat like a bird anymore. You're a Rhone now and you require a great amount of energy."

Mavra stopped and looked at him for a second. She was tired and wan; the strain showed on her face. She looked as if she had aged ten years in the past few days. "Perhaps you're right," she said hoarsely. "I don't know—that's all part of this, I guess. Everything has changed. Obie's gone, even as we sit here comfortably on him; the Universe is going—have you *really* considered that what we're trying to do is destroy all that we know? And me, well, I'm stuck in a reconstruction of my ancestor's old Well body, but I don't *feel* like a Rhone. Do you know what it's like to want a roast beef or something and realize that you can only digest leaves and grass?"

"You're just feeling sorry for yourself," the little dragon responded. "I know what that's like—but from what I've heard it's not like you. I heard that on the Well World you were transformed into a handless cripple yet managed to surmount that difficulty and beat Ortega and everyone else at their own game. What's changed you?"

She thought about it. "Oh, I don't know. Maybe I'm

getting old. Maybe I've just grown fat and complacent during my years with Obie."

Gypsy cleared his throat and they turned. Neither knew how long the strange, dark man had been listening. "You know what's wrong, if you just face it," he said.

Mavra just looked at him questioningly.

"You're not the boss this time," Gypsy said. "You're not in charge, not even in control. Being a Rhone didn't bother you one whit on the snatch operation because *you* were in charge. Not anymore, though. You're not even a full partner; with Obie you were a partner only when and because he allowed you to be. Now it's all in the hands of a little guy you don't even know. Even back on the Well World they left you alone; you were the mistress of your own destiny. Not now. That's what's eating you. You gotta be the general all the time, or at least *think* you are."

His speech was galling because she knew, deep down, that what he said was true. Gypsy had the uncanny ability to reach down inside your soul and see truths, and he wasn't at all diplomatic about telling you what they were. For a moment she understood what Brazil seemed to be saying about being inside Obie. There were things you didn't want to face, didn't want to even think about—and you certainly became uncomfortable when they were thrust under your nose.

"Who are you, Gypsy?" she asked. "Where do you come from?"

He smiled. "I could give you a long, drawn-out biography, but even then you'd have no way of knowing whether I told the truth. What difference does it make? None of us really knows the others anyway. Take Marquoz, there. Why would a man leave his people, live and work entirely cut off from the environment, and the culture that he was born to? I'm the guy who was around every dingy spaceport milking the marks with any sort of con, never taking a sucker who didn't really want to be taken but taking all those who did. I'm the guy who doesn't fit, the square peg who's found some way to survive and enjoy himself. Freighter captains are like that, too, I think—and thieves, and secret agents, and those kinds of folks. I'm not sure about Marquoz, but he's definitely a square peg, too. So are you. The staff of the *Nautilus*—all square pegs, more or less. That's why *we're* here and *they're* out there." His tone became grim and distant. "That's why we survive—and they don't."

A long silence ensued. Finally Mavra Chang said, "I guess I'll go out and munch the lawn or something. I think the time's approaching when we have to get to work."

She didn't have to go as far as the lawn; Obie had prepared for her hunger, as she well knew, with stores of grain pilfered from Brazil's old ship. It didn't taste great but it went down well, and the more she ate the more she wanted to eat. She didn't feel good, but at least she felt better.

When she returned to the main hall she found Nathan Brazil. The tailor shop had found a black pullover shirt and a pair of shorts that fit him, and a pair of plastine sandals as well. He'd taken time to remove all the rest of his makeup and looked, they guessed, pretty much as he always had. He certainly looked both casual and comfortable. He *was* a small man, barely 170 centimeters tall, slightly built and very thin despite strong shoulders and strong, sinewy arms. He was dark, almost as dark as Gypsy, and two bright, brown eyes flanked a conspicuous Roman nose that sat atop a mouth very wide, rubbery, and full of teeth. His hair was cropped short, the better to use disguises, and he was clean-shaven, for much the same reason.

He looked up at her, nodded, and smiled a bit. "So how are you, great-granddaughter?" he greeted lightly.

"Surviving," she responded coldly. Obie had been right on that score; they were too much alike to feel comfortable in each other's presence.

"Well, surviving is all we can do," he came back. "I've called a petit council meeting—no reflection, that term—shortly, so the rest will soon be here. I've been seriously hampered by lack of materials. Everything was in Obie. When were you on the Well World?"

"Over seven hundred years ago," she replied, fascinated by his sudden but easy transformation from world-weary sage to crisp businessman. "We looked in on it occasionally, but they were Obie's checkups, nothing more. It was pretty easy to do—just monitor transmissions, mostly. Ortega and Dr. Zinder both had transmitters capable of reaching us, but Obie never used them. We were supposed to have been destroyed by the Com Police. Obie felt he was better off dead to all parties. I certainly have no love for the place, barely knew Zinder, and never met Ortega—although I have less reason to love him than anyone."

Brazil smiled. "Still mad at the old bastard? I'd think by now you'd have faced the fact that, under similar circumstances, you'd have done to him exactly what he did to you. I'd never accuse the old boy of having a conscience, though."

She looked surprised. "You *know* Ortega?"

He nodded. "Oh, yes. Matched wits with him lord knows how long ago on a number of capers in the Com. He's a wily old scoundrel. I've always liked him despite the fact we're usually on opposite sides. He was on the Well World last time I was there—my welcoming committee, in fact, and later on, my adversary. He should have been dead then, but the Olympian record indicates that he's somehow managed to survive."

She nodded. "Some kind of magic spell, I was told. But he's a prisoner in Zone, even though he practically runs the place."

"Then he's likely still there and even more in control," Brazil noted. "That can be good or catastrophic, and I have no way of knowing which in advance. Damn! The worst thing about the loss of Obie is that we'll be flying blind in this. I won't know conditions on the Well World until I get there. A real-life *kriegspiel*. I've never liked the game."

"Kriegspiel?"

"Chess. You know the game? Only the opponents sit back to back with their own boards and a referee tells you that your opponent's made a legal move. You have to figure out from the illegal moves where your opponent's pieces are. And we don't have a referee in this one."

"You make it sound like we'll have to fight another war on the Well World," she said, slightly puzzled. "I'm not sure I'm clear on this yet."

"We probably will," he responded, then looked up. "Well, here come the other three now, so if everybody will relax I'll explain what this is all about."

"Let's first set our own situation properly," Brazil began. "First, I have to get from a hex near the south of the Southern Hemisphere to an Avenue, an opening to the Well of Souls at the equator. The best-case distance is over forty-nine hundred."

"Excuse me," Marquoz interrupted, "but why so far?"

"Fair question," he replied. "I keep forgetting that you're not up on this sort of thing. In fact, only Mavra and I have ever been there, so I'll return to the basics.

"The Well World is a construct. It was created a little over ten billion years ago by a race known to you as the Markovians. You know the story—we keep running into the remains of their dead planets as we expand outward. Cities, yes, but no artifacts of any kind. No machines, no ruined food stores, no art or pottery, even. Nothing. The reason is rather simple. The Markovians were the first race to develop out of the big bang that started the Universe. They evolved at the normal rate, or maybe a little faster than normal due to local conditions, and they went through most of the stages our peoples have. By the time the Universe was barely two and a half billion years old—I know that sounds long, but on a cosmic scale it's not—they'd spread out and reached virtually every place in their corner of the Universe. Having reached the limits of expansion, they turned inward, eventually developing a computer linked to each of their minds. They removed the entire crust of each of their planets and replaced it with a poured quasi-organic substance about two kilometers thick—the computer—then programmed it with just about everything they knew. They matched their minds to their local computers and, presto! A civilization without need of anything physical. They replaced the old crust atop the computer, of course, and built cities more to delineate the physical space, the property, of each than to serve any utilitarian purposes. Then they settled back and dreamed up their own houses—and the computer created the things by an energy-to-matter conversion. Hungry? Just think of what you wanted and the computer served it up to order. Art? Create anything you wanted in your mind and the computer realized it for you. No wants, no needs, the perfect materialist utopia."

"It sounds pretty wonderful to me, if a little like magic," Yua commented.

Brazil chuckled. "Magic? Magic is doing something the other guy can't do. We haven't learned how to do it yet, so it's magic. When we learn how and understand it, it's science. Obie could do it, of course. That's what his builder, Gilgram Zinder, discovered—the same principles that made the Markovian computers work. Of course, Obie was a tiny, primitive prototype when compared to the Markovian models, but he was able, within his design limits, to do those things. Zinder wasn't the first to stumble onto the Markovian history, only the first to be able to build a machine that could do the conversions."

"But the Markovians are all dead," Gypsy pointed out.

Brazil nodded. "Yes, all dead. They got bored, fat, lazy, and stagnant. My latest theory is that they spent too much time connected to their computers and tended to merge minds with parts of their devices, which forced them to face up to the fact that they'd gone as far as they could go, done everything they could do, reached the point all races strive for—and there wasn't anything there. No challenge. Nothing to look forward to. Since the idea seems to have spread and taken root among Markovians all over the Universe within a fairly short period of time, this computer concept becomes the most logical. They spent very little time playing god, it appears. A few generations, no more. And then, as one, they decided to scrap everything and try again."

"It sounds logical," Mavra agreed. "But why theorize? Weren't you *there?*"

Brazil coughed slightly. "Well, ah, yeah. But it—well, it's just so long ago that my memories of that time are pretty well nonexistent now. A lot of this stuff is rediscovery. Bear with me. I've lived an awfully long time."

They accepted that, although not without some reservations. Mavra, at least, thought that there was something decidedly phoney about Nathan Brazil, something she couldn't put her finger on. A mass of contradictions, Obie had called him. That was putting it mildly.

"Anyway, the Markovians decided that they'd made a wrong turn somewhere in evolution. They couldn't accept the idea that what they had was the be all and end all, because that made all striving, all progress, a joke in their minds. They couldn't handle that. So, they decided they'd blown it—and they'd have to start again.

"The means chosen was peculiar," Brazil continued. "They couldn't wipe out the whole Universe without wiping out themselves as well. So they created a monster computer, a computer as big as a planet, and one that had to be manually operated. They were large creatures that would be real monsters to any of us now—like big, throbbing leathery human hearts standing on six long, suckered tentacles. They were, however, our cousins in that they were a carbon-based lifeform whose atmosphere though different from ours, was close enough that we could breathe it. Now, they poured a crust over this planet-sized computer, this master brain, and then divided it into fifteen hundred and sixty hexagonal biospheres. Since you can't cover a sphere with hexagons, they divided large areas at the poles into mini-biospheres around the polar centers. These are North and South Zone, the two areas where the creatures they were going to invent could gather comfortably and talk, trade, or whatever."

"How'd they get in and out?" Marquoz asked.

"Zone gates," Brazil replied. "In the middle of each hex is a gate—a big, black hole it looks like, shaped like a hexagon. It'll take anybody in a hex to the appropriate Zone for him. There's a lot of little gates in Zone, that'll take an individual back home. But while they might be considered matter transmitters in the same sense that Obie was able to move this whole world from one spot to another instantaneously, they will only take you from your home to Zone and back to your home. As set up, they're no good for general transportation, although they can move inanimate objects and so are nice for trade. The Northern Hemisphere is a weird place, devoted to noncarbon-based life because it occurred to the Markovians that they might have evolved the wrong way. The south is carbon-based life. A special gate exists in each Zone to transport to the other so there can be some trade and contact between hemispheres."

"And these hexes? They are sealed?" Yua asked, fascinated.

"Oh, no," Brazil replied. "Their barriers are pure energy. But you've already been told a lot of this—about the technological limits and the like. I'm afraid I face a roughly forty-nine hundred kilometer walk through the Southern Hemisphere to the equator, where there is a physical barrier that keeps north and south divided. But it's also a transportation system used to get Markovian technicians in and out of the Well of Souls. There are Avenues there, broad streets if you will, that form the borders of equatorial 'hexes'—the only nonhexagons, since they have to stop at basically a straight line, they're somewhat wing-shaped—to the doors to the Well of Souls."

"The Well of Souls," Marquoz echoed. "An odd name."

Brazil shrugged. "Why the 'Well' I don't know. The 'Souls' part is real enough. There's something deep down in all sentient life that can't be quantified but takes it a half-step from the animals. We call it the soul; religions are founded on it, and I have evidence it exists. At one point on the Well World a group of mystics who were convinced I was dying transferred me into the body of a deer. So there's a soul that is you—it's what the Well uses to change you into something else once you get there. The Markovians had a problem with souls. They couldn't invent them. In order to start their prototype races they had to use people, if that's the proper term, and change them. The Markovian artisans and philosophers and theoreticians got together and each designed a hex. Then they redesigned Markovians into races best suited to each engineered biosphere. The Markovian volunteers thus gave up their form, but, more than that, they gave up their immortality. They were convinced that what they were doing was right and that they should become mortal and primitive once more. And they lived, and died, and tried to make their cultures work. If they did work out—and cultural development was handicapped by each hex's technological potential and the like—then the technicians went into the Well of Souls and made a few adjustments to newly developing planets in our expanding Universe so that they would develop into the reality being represented in the particular hex. At the proper evolutionary moment, the civilization in the hex would be transferred, seeding the planets with souls, so to speak. Then the old hex would be cleared away, scrubbed down, and turned over to a new designer."

"Interesting," Marquoz said. "But if that's the case, who are all those people there now? Shouldn't the place be bare as a billiard ball?"

"Well, there were always some who didn't want to go in any group," Brazil told them. "Since they were about to lose their home hexes, though, they had little choice. What you have now on the Well World are the last fifteen hundred and sixty races, successes and failures, that were created. The end of the line."

"I noticed on the Well World that many of the Southern Hemisphere races were at least vaguely familiar," Mavra put in. "Some—not all, of course. There were giant beaverlike creatures that seemed to have existed in human myth, according to my friend of the time, Renard, who was a classicist. Centaurs were in the old legends, he said, and winged horses, and even Agitar—goatlike devil creatures. I never was clear as to why."

Brazil shrugged. "Well, by the time you were down to the last of the race you were down to the bottom of the imaginative barrel in most cases. As a result, those of limited imagination, pressed to create a race, stole ideas from the animals and plants of other hexes. A lot of the subordinate stuff, the plants and animals, is also similar from one hex to another, again with variations. The Well made them just different enough that they can't breed outside their home hex. That included the vast majority of microorganisms, so you can't have a widespread plague, either. As to the myths, well, I told you that those today are the leftovers. Some didn't want to be leftovers, particularly the thinkers, those with something to contribute. They occasionally hitched rides when other groups were seeded, sometimes legitimately, when conditions warranted and you had a kindly supervisor, sometimes by crook. Our own Earth had a small colony of centaurs—brilliant men and women—and a number of other races both legit and problem oriented. They didn't last. The illegals the Markovians helped exterminate, finally; the good ones, like the centaurs, were mostly murdered by men because they were different."

He paused and suddenly seemed distant, as if his mind were off in another place. "The Spartans of ancient Greece hunted down the last of them like animals. They stuffed a pair for their big museum. I couldn't stop it—but I burned down that damned museum." He turned full attention back to them. "There were others, many others," he said, "but they were all wiped out. I suspect that that centaur business is the reason the Rhone haven't a real trust for humans. Who knows? Maybe a now-vanished Rhone civilization got to the stars earlier and discovered the facts. Hard to say. They *know*, though."

"The Well recognizes you," Mavra pointed out. "Why don't you just have it bring you to it? Why take such a big walk?"

Brazil paused a moment, thoughtful. "Mainly because I can't talk to it until I'm inside. It figures I am a technician, so it sends me where I'm supposed to be—the human hex. I have to start from there. Worse, those who are in power on the Well World, particularly those with access to good records, know this. They'll try and stop me from reaching the Well—and they know the hex where I've got to start. It puts me at something of a disadvantage."

"Why should they want to stop you?" Yua asked.

"Obie said that the Well World would survive your actions."

"It will," Brazil agreed. "Mostly because it's maintained by a separate computer. But, you see, my actions will wipe out the civilized Universe. Oh, I suppose one or two races—maybe more—will survive, the race or two that evolved naturally instead of through the Well. But the rest—gone. The Universe will be a pretty dead place. So, I pull the plug. I fix the big machine—or, rather, I let it fix itself and help where I can." He turned and looked them squarely in the eye. "Now, who do I use to reseed this Universe?"

They were silent. Understanding dawned on all, one by one, except for Yua, who looked a little confused. "You need the Well World to reseed them," Mavra almost whispered.

He nodded. "*They* know that, too. Better than we. To them it'll be a choice of their own survival or everybody else's. They're no different from anybody else. They'd rather survive and let the Universe go hang. But even if we figure a way around that—and there's a way, but not a sure one—there's the basic fear. Once I'm inside the Well they know I can make any changes I want, changes not only in the Universe but to the Well World itself. They'll be nervous. Even though I didn't do anything the last time, they don't know that I won't this time. They don't understand me or the machine, and what people don't understand they fear. Balance it out. You're a practical, logical leader. Would you take a *chance* on letting me get into the Well when by preventing me you could be sure of business as usual? I think not."

"But you're immortal," Mavra noted. "They should know that. They couldn't hold you forever."

"They don't have to, but they would be prepared to," he told them. "Remember what they did to you. They could do that to me. Turn me into an animal or some kind of vegetable. Keep me sedated in a cell with no way out. Oh, I might eventually break free but it'd take years—hundreds, thousands maybe. Too late to do our project any good. No, there was enough skulduggery last time, when they didn't know who I was, just knew we were going to get into the Well. It'll be hell this time."

"You mean that there will be no one to help us?" Yua gasped. "Everyone will be against us?"

He shook his head. "Some will help because they understand the problem or will trust us. Some will violently oppose us. The rest will stay on the sidelines but join those against us if we appear to be succeeding. The average being, of course, will be the most frightened of all. Now, obviously, this means an even longer run to an Avenue since I can hardly go in a straight line—and it means I'll need lots of muscle to get through."

Even Yua understood his meaning. "The Fellowship."

He nodded. "Exactly. If we require allies and fighters every step of the way, then we will have to make sure we have them where we need them. That'll be the Olympian holy crusade—with you four helping and, I hope, leading. But for these allies we will give up the element of surprise. Zone is going to see a veritable horde of people trooping through the Well and they're going to find out the story. They'll be laying for me, you can bet on it. The best thing we can do is keep them harried and off-balance. The Well tends to distribute newcomers evenly—Entries, they're called—around the hemisphere in which they enter. We'll all enter in the south since we're carbon-based. That means seven hundred and eighty hexes filled with sentient races—plants, animal variations, water creatures, insect creatures, and creatures that are none or all of the above. Although there are wide variations based on the size of the people and the capabilities of the hex, we can assume about a million whatevers in each hex. That's seven hundred and eighty million people, more or less, in the south." He gave a smug look to Yua. "Now, how many Olympians are there?"

Her mouth formed an oval shape. "Over a billion," she breathed.

He nodded. "And if we add just the committed Fellowship, those we can trust to do the job? None of this conditioned crap—they have to really believe it, since the Well will remove any artificial restraints."

She shrugged. "Another million, perhaps more."

"Okay, now add to that certain others whom I will invite and allow. I think we can put one and a half billion people on the Well World. That's a lot more than it can handle on a long-term basis, but I don't think it'll give us any short-term problems. If all get through we'll outnumber the natives almost two to one—and the survivors will be the prototype souls for the reseeding. We'll give them part of the bargain—a chance at building their own Paradise."

Gypsy, who so far had made no sound, said quietly, "The natives aren't stupid, I wouldn't think."

Brazil's eyebrows rose. "Huh?"

"Well, suppose you were a Well World potentate and you got the story and were suddenly knee-deep in fanatical converts. I don't know what *you'd* do, but if these folks are as nasty and scared as you say, I'd set up my own army or whatever in Zone, wherever they come in—and I'd kill 'em as fast as they came through."

Brazil leaned back, lit a cigarette, and considered his point. "I guess I'm just getting soft. That never occurred to me. Of course you're right. But there's little we can do about it. The thing in our favor is that the only people they'll trust less than us are each other. It'll take a while for them to catch on, longer to get together and decide on a logical course of action, and they'll need a majority of Zone races to break the rules and keep an armed force there. That'll take some time. They'll probably be inundated with Entries before they take effective action, and it might be too late to stop us. Still, we have to face facts. The nastiest of them will start pogroms, killing all Entries as soon as they appear in their own lands. Don't need a vote for that." He sighed. "I didn't say this enterprise would be easy. We could well fail. The only thing I can say is that we either call the whole thing off now, or we try for it now. You're the council for this operation. On your heads will be most of the responsibility for the operation. What do you say? Yua?"

"Do it," she responded instantly.

"Gypsy?"

"I'd rather die fighting than be wiped out of existence by some crazy crack in space."

"Marquoz?"

"This is beginning to look interesting, a true challenge," the little dragon responded. "I wouldn't miss it for the world."

"Mavra?"

She sighed. "Let's get it over with. At least I won't have to finish life as a Rhone."

"All right, then. You four will go in *first*. Obie indicated that he had some way of influencing the Well's choice, so I can assume that all four of you will somehow be placed to do me and yourselves maximum good. I don't know whether he'll be a hundred percent successful in this but I expect you to be rallying your Entry armies around you by the time I get there. After giving you sufficient time to become adapted to your new forms and environments, I'll start sending in the hordes. The hue and cry will be enormous and immediate. There'll be a new body in every back yard. You'll know when. Time your actions properly—don't move too soon or the locals will be on to you before you have sufficient strength to tell them where to go. Then, and only then, rise up, announce yourself, rally the newcomers around you. Later Entries will carry a more sophisticated timetable. That's what I'm going to use my nonhuman friends for. More likely even after they've begun to shoot all the Amazonian women they see, they'll let others pass. Rally and move to consolidate your forces as quickly as possible. Move on Ambreza, which is where everybody knows I'll appear."

"But Ambreza is the hex of the big beavers," Mavra objected. "I remember that much."

"But you forget that they had a war with the humans that the humans lost and they swapped hexes," Brazil responded. "So as a human I'll show up in modern-day Ambreza."

"Sounds a little odd to me," Gypsy remarked. "Seems to me that as we sweep down we'll tell everybody when and where you're coming."

Brazil grinned. "Seems like it, doesn't it? But, you see, you won't have any idea where I am or when I'm coming through. If I need you I'll contact you, but otherwise you'll not know. I could arrive early, in the middle, or at the end. All your marching and fighting and all the rest of that will be the big show, the window dressing. In the meantime I'll be sneaking up toward the Avenue."

"In other words, we might not even know if you've succeeded—at least until the newcomers start vanishing around us?" Mavra said, incredulously.

He chuckled. "Oh, everybody will know before that. I wish it would go that smoothly, but it won't. I'll need firepower before the end—I just hope it isn't until we're almost there. And I'll have to let everybody know—it isn't so simple to reseed a Universe, particularly when you have so few races to work with. I'll give the Northerners the option of losing half their people or being left out—that may be enough, with some of them. But you'll know." He turned and looked straight at Mavra Chang. "You in particular will know. If you're still alive, if you survive, you'll be there with me, inside the Well, and *you* will give me the order to turn off the juice. If you fail, Mavra, then it'll be one other of you four. And one of you had better survive—because I will not turn the Well off except on somebody else's orders. The responsibility will not be mine."

He looked around at them. "All straight? Well, let's get started, then. We've got a lot of groundwork to lay, a whole population to brief, and that'll take time and sweat. Let's move!"

Serachnus

THE SHUTTLE LANDED WITH NO FANFARE. THERE wasn't anyone present; no marching bands; no good-luck parties; nothing. It was a dead world of barren rock pitted by countless meteor strikes.

It was a ghost world, too; they could see that as the landscape, slowly rolling past their screens now as Nathan Brazil put on the brakes, showed areas blasted eons ago through high mountains and vague traces of roadways. Occasionally they would pass over a dead city, strange-looking places with hexagonal central squares, and strange, twisted buildings and spires. All dead now, all dead for ten billion years or more.

"Once this was a green place," Brazil noted, sounding almost nostalgic. "The air was sweet, the climate warm and comfortable, and several million people lived in those cities."

"Markovians, you mean," Mavra remarked. "Not people."

He nodded vigorously. "People. Shaped like big leathery hearts with six suckered tentacles and all sorts of yucky attributes, yes, but people all the same. Not too different, deep down, from us, I suspect, considering how similar our wildly varying alien civilizations have developed. We're their children, remember. Down there they lived and laughed and played and worked and thought just as people have been doing for ages, and down there they worried and decided and left. They left to go to the Well World, to give up their mortality for our kind of existence."

"You seem pretty certain that we can get there the

same way," Marquoz noted. "There is some sort of transportation system, you said?"

Brazil nodded. "A Well Gate. It'll open if you want it to open and it'll take you one place if you really want to go there. The Markovians built their machines too well; the computer that once sustained a civilization in a materialist utopia is still alive, still waiting for instructions. If somebody orders the Well Gate to open, it will respond and do so—and send you to the Well World. You've been well briefed; you remember the facts."

"Just hard to believe," the Chugach replied. "I mean, all these computers and nobody's ever been able to make 'em do anything—and, heaven knows, enough time, trouble, and money's been spent trying to make them do something. Not even discover the Well Gate, as you call it."

"People *have* discovered the Well Gate," Brazil told him. "People who wanted to find it found it—and it swallowed them, took them to the Well World. Others, well, there are gates all over, even on asteroids where Markovian worlds used to be, that snare the bored, the fantasizers, the would-be suicides—the people who are sick of their own lives and earnestly wish for a new start. The computers see that as a reflection of the Markovian attitudes. That's how people like Ortega got to the Well World. That's how Mavra's grandparents returned not once but twice."

"Do you think either may still be alive?" Mavra asked him.

He shook his head. "I doubt it very strongly. It's been too long. Some Well World lifeforms live an awfully long time, but none lives that long."

"Ortega," she pointed out.

"A special case," he replied. "Still, your name should also be known to a lot of the Well World from your part in the wars; if any of your relatives who got through are still alive, I'm pretty sure you'll have no trouble finding them. They'll find you."

He set the boat down on a barren plain. "Far as I go," he told them. "I can't just fly into it or past it; it'd probably snatch me, too, and I can't go just yet. I can hear it screaming for me now, though. So into your pressure suits and out you go."

They dressed quickly, almost in silence. Tension, already high, was practically visible now. Finally they were all set, all on internal air and power, and Brazil threw the switch that isolated the scout pilot's cabin from the rest of the ship.

He leaned over and flicked his communications switch. "Mavra, use your own judgment with Ortega. The rest of you—you don't even know each other."

"Don't worry," Marquoz grumbled. "And don't keep repeating the obvious so much. If you didn't trust us with this thing then you shouldn't have sent us."

He smiled, knowing what was going on inside all of them. They were saying good-bye to their pasts, their worlds, their Universe. The ones who'd never been on the Well World before were at the biggest disadvantage, but for Mavra, too, it was highly traumatic. He understood that. She loved freedom most of all, and freedom to her was a fast ship crossing the starfields.

Not for the first time did he worry about Obie. Could the computer really influence what they'd become? And had he done the best job in that regard? If they all wound up immobile, or mass-minds, or water-breathers they'd be of precious little help to him when it counted.

He checked his screens. "There. It's open. See it ahead of you on your right?"

They were out of the ship now, four white-suited figures against the dull-gray rock, walking single-file with Mavra's Rhone body leading.

They stopped and looked. It was there, on the plain—a huge hole, it seemed, with infinite blackness filling it. If they had been airborne they would have seen its hexagonal shape.

"Just walk into it," he urged. "And—good luck to all of you. I hope to see you all one midnight at the Well of Souls."

There was no response. He sat back, sighed, switched off the transmitter although he left the receiver on, and lifted off. In the airless void they hadn't heard or noticed his slow departure, but he wanted to remove any possibilities of second thoughts now that they were so close. Alone, with a day's air or less and no food, they had little choice but to walk into the hole no matter what.

They were at the edge now. He knew it even though he was too far up to see them clearly. Just their breathing and their noise—or sudden lack of it—told him.

"Well? Who's first?" he heard Mavra ask, nervousness creeping into her voice. Up until this time the plan had just been theoretical; now this one act was one of irrevocable and possibly fatal commitment.

"I'll go," Gypsy's voice responded. Brazil heard some shuffling, then the strange man's voice say, "Not too bad. It's not a hole at all. Still solid. I guess—"

And that was it for Gypsy. Brazil knew that on the ground he had simply winked out. He could hear from the slight decrease in static that the man was no longer anywhere nearby.

"We've followed each other over fifty worlds," Marquoz said dryly. "Here goes."

"Yua? Shall we go together?" Mavra asked.

The Olympian swallowed hard. "Yes, I—I'd like that," she responded. "I—oh! It sort of tingles, doesn't it?"

"No different from Obie, I don't think," Mavra replied.

"It's—it's so *dark* . . ."

They were all gone now.

Brazil sighed, lit a cigarette, and punched in the codes to return to his main ship and from there to the *Nautilus*. It's done, he thought. It's started. Damn! I wish I could know what's going on at the other end!

South Zone

"MAVRA? HELP ME UP, WILL YOU? I FEEL A LITTLE dizzy," Yua muttered.

Mavra knelt down on her forelegs and reached out, helping the Olympian to her feet.

"That was a *decidedly* uncomfortable ride," Marquoz grumbled. He looked a little unsteady himself.

Mavra looked around, suddenly puzzled. "Where's Gypsy?"

The other two suddenly realized that they were only three and peered around. The chamber was huge; they stood on a flat, smooth, glassy black surface of unknown composition. The slab was six-sided, but so large was the hall it was difficult to tell. Illumination was from a massive six-sided panel on the ceiling. A rail concealing what appeared to be a walkway circled the chamber, and steps led to gaps in the rail.

"We might as well get going," Mavra said, making for the nearest steps, which appeared to be made of stone. The walkway was a series of moving belts, they saw—but still now.

"You've been here before. How do we start the walkway?" Marquoz asked Mavra.

She chuckled. "I was never here. Here is where everybody else arrived who wasn't born here. I arrived by ship. I crashed. The only time I was ever in Zone was a brief stay as a prisoner in an embassy. I'm afraid this experience is as new to me as it is to you. Just remember, though I've been on this planet before, I haven't been through the Well. I'm as raw as the rest of you about what to expect."

Suddenly they heard a whirring sound from far off in the chamber and felt a vibration through the rail. "Looks like our welcoming committee is coming," Mavra remarked.

Marquoz looked back out at the glassy floor. "But where is Gypsy? I know he came here. He went first."

Mavra sighed. "I don't know. There's been something eerie about him since the moment I met him. He's *your* friend. I can't think of any reason why he wouldn't be here no matter who or what he was, though."

Marquoz shrugged. "I've known him for years yet I don't really know him at all. Perhaps what we all saw was some sort of disguise. Perhaps he was a noncarbon-based lifeform that fooled us into seeing him as a man and he's in North Zone. Who knows? Obie did, I think. I think it's best not to mention him at all right now, though. There may be more afoot than we know."

Mavra nodded. "I agree—but I don't like it. I don't like puzzles at all."

Suddenly Marquoz pointed.

Approaching them was a huge creature. It had a deep-brown torso shaped like a man's, but plated. Six arms, extended from the sides of the torso four of them rotating on ball joints, yet terminating in fingered hands. All six looked hard and muscular. The head was ovoid and had no ears. Deep, black human eyes flanked a flat nose below which grew a massive white moustache. Below, the torso ended in long, serpentine coils.

The creature approached them without fear—which was natural, since he was obviously master here. He slapped the wall sharply as he drew within a few meters of them and the walkway stopped. Bushy white eyebrows rose.

"A human, sort of, a Dillian and a Ghlmonese? What is this?" He seemed genuinely perplexed. "Do you understand what I am saying?"

Mavra nodded. "Ah—yes, perfectly," she said, only partly feigning nervousness. She had never met such a creature as this before on or off the Well. "We are from the Com."

Amazement spread all over the creature's face. "The Com! And not one of you true human! Oh, my! How things must have changed since I was last there!"

Yua gasped. "*You* were once in the Com?"

He smiled a very human smile beneath his bushy moustache. "Oh, yes. Once I was human like you—well, I didn't have a tail like that, and I was a man, and women sure didn't look as good as you—but you know what I mean." The voice was deep, thick, and rich but had no trace of an accent. Only Mavra understood immediately that a translator, a small surgical implant made by a Northern race, was really doing the talking. She would need one soon; they all would. She'd had one, once.

"The Com has many races now," she told the creature. "All living in peace. That is, with each other. Together we just fought a war with a no-compromise nonhuman race."

The creature was still wondering at it all. "Multiracial cooperation in the Com! Who'd have thought it! You mean the brotherhood boys were right all along about improving the human race?" It was more a question directed at himself than one to them but Marquoz answered anyway.

"If you mean their petty little social philosophies, no," he told the alien. "That's mostly breaking down now. And having spent the last several years in the human worlds I can tell you that I was tolerated more than embraced."

The six-limbed creature shrugged all his limbs. "So? In my day it would have been war and intolerance all around. Death and destruction." He grew a little more serious. "But you said there'd been a war? Is that why you're here?"

Mavra jumped in quickly. "I don't know why we're here—and I'm not sure where 'here' is. No, it wasn't the war, though. We won that. We won it, but tore a hole in space–time to do it. It is eating the Com now. You might say we were refugees, although how we wound up here I don't know. We set down on an old world to take a vote on just where to go and the lights went out. We woke up here."

The creature nodded. The explanation was about

what he expected to hear—which is why the cover story had been invented in the first place.

The creature slithered back, allowing room for all of them on his section of belt. "You can take off the spacesuits, by the way. The Well pressurizes before it brings you through so right now it's set to be comfortable for you. Or keep 'em on until we get to my office, as you will."

He slapped the wall with his lower left hand, swiveled without really turning, so he was facing the other way, and the belt whirred to life.

"What are your names?" the creature called back to them as they traveled.

"I am Tourifreet, a Rhone," Mavra told him. "The human is Yua, an Olympian, and the Chugach is Marquoz."

"Pleased to meet you," the creature responded amiably. "It's been a long, long time since anybody from my old stamping grounds has been through here. People fall into those holes all the time, like I did—maybe a hundred a year, give or take. But no humans in the last century or two. Been a while. I, by the way, am Serge Ortega."

Mavra's head snapped up and there was a sudden, odd gleam in her eyes. Ortega, his back to her, saw nothing. "Easy, girl," Marquoz whispered.

Ortega! She thought. After all this time! After all this . . . Ortega, still alive, still in charge. The man who imprisoned her so many years ago, coldly, cruelly, for so very long.

The one man for whom she still felt a smouldering hatred.

And here he was, leading them calmly into the depths of Zone, back to her. How easy to plunge a knife in that broad, leathery back—if only she had a knife. To kill this man who treated people as playthings, and had been doing so for over a thousand years.

They left the big chamber now and headed down an oval tunnel, a large corridor whose junctions were curved and smooth. It seemed to be made of some heavy, grainy stone that had been painted a dull yellow.

They passed chambers as their tunnel twisted and turned; it wasn't a single corridor but a labyrinth. Each chamber, Ortega told them, contained a mini-biosphere for one of the Well World's fifteen hundred and sixty races. The ones in this section were the embassies of the seven hundred and eighty Southerners.

When they reached his office and began to relax, Ortega sent for food and drink. He told them what they already knew, about the Well World and its foundings, about the hexes, zones, and gates. They listened as if they had never heard any of it before, asking all the right questions; but it was Ortega's political map of the Well World that held their interest. Brazil had done a rough one from memory and it had been all they had; now they could see the true complexity of the Well World and the enormity of their task. In particular, they saw, for the first time, the vast oceans of the Well World and the topography of the landscape. Mavra located the areas she'd been in, and spotted Glathriel, which, Ortega explained needlessly, was where the human race now resided in tribal primitivism.

That hex held a different interest for them, for next to it was Ambreza, the original home of humanity and the point at which Nathan Brazil must emerge once he arrived. That was their initial goal.

Mavra knew the place well. Glathriel had been her prison so many years before, and she doubted the Ambreza had let it change much. Her eyes drifted northward, to Lata and Agitar and other exotic names from the Wars of the Well, and to Olborn, where she'd been half-turned into a beast, and to cold, mountainous Gedemondas, whose strange inhabitants had destroyed the rocket engines for which the war had been fought. They had also predicted her future. She wondered what the Gedemondas were predicting now.

Ortega replaced the map, seemingly oblivious to their real interests. "Enough politics," he told them. "After you arrive at your home hexes you will have opportunities for more relaxed studies."

Yua could hardly contain her fright at those words, but it only lent verisimilitude to her staged question. "What—what do you mean, our home hexes?"

Ortega smiled. "From here, you will shortly be taken to another gate. It is the Well Gate. It removes you from the Universe you have always known and makes you a part of the Well. Once inside, the Well analyzes you according to criteria we've never been able to understand and chooses a form for you. You will wake up, as if from a sleep, as one of the seven hundred and eighty Southern races—just as I did, long ago. The Well helps in that it makes you comfortable with your new form and conditions, so you won't feel totally alien, but it does not toy with your memories—you will still be you and you'll remember all that has been. From that point you're on your own. Don't fight it. Whatever you wake up as you will be for the rest of your natural lives."

It was a sobering thought. The rest of their lives as something—else. Something alien. To some it might have had a romantic ring, but to these comrades who were not on the Well World out of desperation but on a mission, the words had a particularly forbidding sound.

But Ortega wasn't through with them quite yet. He pumped them about conditions in the Com. They were pretty honest about it—they told him of the Dreel, and the Zinder Nullifiers, and the widening hole in space. They did not tell him about Obie or about Nathan Brazil. It was Ortega who brought up the latter's name.

"I wouldn't worry about it," he consoled them. "The Well will repair it. If it didn't there's a surviving Markovian around to make the repairs and he'd have been here by now if it were necessary."

"How do you know he hasn't?" Marquoz asked pointedly.

Ortega smiled. "I know him. He's human—looks like a skinny little runt, goes by the name of Nathan Brazil. If he'd passed through here I'd have heard of it." He scratched under his chin with his upper right arm and stared at them. "You know, it's funny. I been looking at you two women and feeling I know you—or should know you. Funny, isn't it? It isn't possible, of course."

Mavra coughed slightly. "No, hardly."

He shrugged. "I guess in your case," he decided, looking at Yua, "one or two of your fellow Olympians musta come through a long time ago. There's been so many and it's so long . . ." He seemed to be wandering, then looked back at Mavra. "And you—seems even further back. Damn if I can think why, though. You just look a little like somebody I used to know, way back—ah, well. No matter. Ready for the Well?"

"No," Marquoz told him. "But what choice do I have other than to move in with you or the—what was it?—Ghlmonese ambassador?"

Ortega laughed. "All right, then. Come along." The door opened and he slithered out. They followed as close as they dared, trying not to come too close to his lower coils.

They entered a normal room, a rectangle except for the rounded corners, barren of furniture. The door closed behind them.

Walls, floor, ceiling were of the same grainy yellowish material as the corridors except the far wall, which was another dose of total darkness.

"The Well Gate," he told them. "You have no choice at all now. The door behind me will not open from the inside. The only way out is through the gate—and the Well."

That was a lie, and Mavra knew it. Still, she could see that it would be useful in his line of work.

They had shed their spacesuits in Ortega's office and were all naked now. Marquoz had salvaged his cigar case and he and Mavra puffed on the last of them. Both wondered idly if they'd ever do it again.

Mavra looked at Ortega. She still hated the man, but he seemed less an ogre in person than as an untouchable she'd never even seen. He'd been quite pleasant with them, even a little charming, and that in itself was unsettling. Brazil had called him a total scoundrel yet liked him all the same, and they'd had long debates on whether to trust the snake-man with the advance secret. And after all these years, he was still here, still in charge, never leaving Zone, never getting a day older thanks to Well magic and a liberal dose of blackmail—Mavra knew he'd had just about every embassy in Zone—and possibly a lot more places—bugged.

"Who first?" she asked the others, feeling as if it were a replay of the scene back on that dead Markovian world. Then Gypsy had stepped forward and vanished—Gypsy, who had vanished utterly, it seemed.

Whatever you wake up as you will be for the rest of your natural lives.

The sentence haunted them all.

"Oh, the hell with it." Marquoz mumbled and stepped on the butt of his cigar. "I'm out of cigars, anyway." He walked up to the black wall and through. It swallowed him utterly.

Yua turned and looked at Mavra, and there was fear in her eyes. Not for the first time Mavra wondered why Obie had chosen this one from those he could have selected for this mission. Only Obie knew, and Obie was far, far away.

"We'll meet again," the Olympian said quietly to her, taking and squeezing her hand. Then, unhesitatingly, she turned and walked the route Marquoz had walked, stepping boldly into the engulfing blackness.

"And then there was one," said Serge Ortega behind her.

She smiled to herself. He was so cocksure, so rock steady. She took a step toward the darkness, then stopped, her mind, unbidding making the choice Brazil had left to her.

"Wait a minute, Ortega," she said coolly, and turning to face him. "I am going to need your help."

He was taken aback. "Huh?"

"The other two—they are meaningless to you or to anybody else. Window dressing. I'm not. I've been standing around debating this moment since I arrived at the entrance gate and had just about decided not to say anything, but I think I'm taking a reasonable risk."

He coiled his serpentine body tightly and rocked his torso atop the heap, all six arms folded. "Go on. I'm listening," he said, curious.

"The Well *is* broken. It's shorted out," she told him. "Slowly by cosmic standards but actually pretty quickly the whole damn Universe is being snuffed out.

In a while the rift will grow so big it'll damage the Well beyond repair. Shortly—very shortly—you're going to be inundated with refugees, mostly Olympians, from the destruction of the Com."

"Go on," he said, not changing position or expression. "I'm listening."

"They're to be the seed for new races," she continued. "They are the ones who'll provide the souls or whatever once the Well is fixed."

"But if the Well is fixed all will be as before," he pointed out.

"No, it has to be turned off first. The whole experiment of the Markovians is over, and it failed. Time to press *reset* and start again. You *must* help. Those people must be allowed to do what we are doing, go through the Well, come out as something else. You know better than I the reaction that that many people coming through is going to cause. We need your help."

Ortega remained impassive, saying nothing, betraying no emotion, for over a minute. Finally he said, "What you're telling me is that not only is Nathan Brazil coming back but this time he's going to really do something serious."

She nodded apprehensively.

"And how do you know all this?"

She considered how to tell him, had thought about this moment a long, long time. "Because this centaur body isn't the real me. Because it was made by Obie. Because I'm Mavra Chang."

Serge Ortega almost fell over backward. Then he chuckled, then he laughed, and continued laughing until he couldn't stop for a bit. Finally he said, "How is such a thing possible? Obie was destroyed. Mavra Chang was still on Obie, so she was destroyed with the computer. We had witnesses to this return."

"We faked it," Mavra told him. "We had to. Otherwise Obie, totally in control of himself and beyond any override—and a miniature Well of Souls—would have been hated, feared, perhaps eventually destroyed in spite of his powers. And me—if you'll remember, I was in the worst shape of anybody to face rejoining the human race. I had no desire to come back as a circus freak, didn't know that Obie was still alive, so to speak, and decided to die with him. I didn't. We went to a far galaxy and had a lot of fun together."

He swayed back and forth a little but Mavra couldn't tell what he was thinking. The reptilian part of him was in command now, a solid mask.

"And Obie? Where is he?"

She sighed. "Dead—or good as." Quickly she told the past history of Obie and Brazil as truthfully as she could.

"And Brazil? When is he coming through?" the snake-man pressed.

She shrugged. "I don't know. Nobody but he does—and I'm not sure if he isn't just waiting for the right moment."

"And he told you to tell me all this?" Ortega asked skeptically.

She smiled. "He left the decision to me. He said you'd be essential as an ally, but if you weren't to remind you that he beat you once when he didn't know who he was fighting and he could do it again with his eyes open if he had to."

Ortega rocked with laughter again. "Yes, yes! That is Brazil! Ah, this is marvelous!"

Then all the mirth seemed to drain from him. He suddenly looked very ancient, as ancient as he actually was, then his eyes seemed to soften. "You are really Mavra Chang?"

She nodded.

"Well, I'll be damned. God is good even to the fallen," he muttered to himself. He looked up at her. "You know, in all the time I lived I killed an awful lot of people, almost all of whom were either trying to kill me or who deserved killing, anyway. I screwed a lot of people who deserved to be screwed and, you know, if I had it to do all over again, I would. There's only one blot on my conscience, one person who has haunted me through the years—even though I had no choice, which made it all the more maddening. What you're saying is that I have achieved absolution. That one person lives, and has lived a full life, lived longer than any except maybe Brazil and myself. You're telling me I did the right thing, that I'm forgiven now."

She peered at him, a little uncomfortable with his

reaction. It was not what she'd expected from the man at all. She could almost swear that there were tears welling up in his eyes.

"I haven't forgiven you, Ortega," she said evenly. "You are the one man I could still cheerfully kill—if I didn't need you."

He chuckled. "You really are Mavra Chang?" He seemed to need the reassurance, as if he couldn't accept the truth. "I'll be damned." Suddenly he hardened. "Listen. If you *are* Mavra Chang, then you owe me."

It was her turn to be surprised. *"I* owe *you?"*

He nodded. "If I hadn't done what I did back then you'd be out there someplace, right now, dead these seven hundred years, dead and buried. Dead never having gotten off this stinkin' world, never having seen the stars again. I saved you and you owe me that much. I saved you and that means everything to me." His eyes were burning now. "How I envy you. Seven hundred years out there. I haven't seen the stars in much longer than that. I haven't been out of this stinkin' *hole* since long before you were born. Do you know what that means? I was a captain too, you know."

She *did* know what that meant, although it was unnerving, somehow, to find it still in Ortega as well. She tried to imagine it. All this time Ortega had been built up as a Machiavellian mastermind, the true ruler of the Well World—and, in fact, he really had tremendous power, more power than anyone had ever had here. People lived or died, governments rose and fell, trade was or was not accomplished according to his will and whims. And yet . . .

He nodded and smiled slightly. "I see that you understand me. I am a prisoner, more than you ever were. All this power is meaningless. A diversion for an old man in an artificially lit prison cell who hasn't seen a star or a blade of grass except in pictures in almost a thousand years." He sighed. "You know, old memories keep popping up here and there. I remember the last time Nate was here. He said the only thing he wanted to do was die—he was sick of living. He'd done everything, been everything, lived too long.

I thought he was nuts. The only difference between Brazil then and me now is that he took longer. So will you, although you probably won't live that long. You were probably just reaching the first stages of boredom, I think. You lasted longer than me because you could move, see the stars and trees and bright desert colors and blue skies. Even in Glathriel you had that. Imagine your last seven centuries locked in *here*."

She shook her head in wonder. "If you feel that strongly, why not just walk through that gate with me? Go home to Ulik and see the deserts and the stars?"

He chuckled dryly. "You want to know why? You think I haven't thought about it, over and over again, every spare hour? Every time I feel the walls close in, or I see my distinguished colleagues return, rested, from trips home? You want to know? I'm scared. Me, Serge Ortega. I'll match swords or guns or anything else—including wits—with anybody. I'll charge into Hell itself—but I will not go there invited."

She stood there, listening to him, and discovered to her surprise that much of the hate and resentment she had felt for him was gone now, replaced by a slight but no less genuine pity for a man who had built his own prison and had been suffering in it.

"You don't have to worry about Hell, Ortega," she said softly. "*This* is Hell. You made it. You created it out of your own fears and guilts. You live in it constantly, forever, all the more Hell because you know you can leave. I feel sorry for you, Ortega. I really do."

She turned, faced the blackness. "I think I'm ready to go now. Take this trip I was due to take seven hundred years ago but for your own efforts. Full circle, Ortega. Will you help us? You don't owe these people anything. Not now. Please help—if only for my sake."

He smiled. "I'll do what I can. But what's interesting for me will be hell for the rest of the races here. You realize that. I might not be able to stop things."

"Do what you can, then," she responded. "If you do not, then we have a date, you and I, here, in Zone; this I swear."

"I certainly hope the day never comes when I have to choose you or me," he murmured, sounding sincere. "I—I just don't know which I'd choose."

"I'll be back, Ortega, one way or the other I'll be back. Bet on it!" she snapped and started off at a gallop, vanishing quickly into the darkness of the Well Gate.

Serge Ortega just sat, rocking back and forth on his serpent's coils, for a long, long time, staring into the blackness.

Hakazit

MARQUOZ AWOKE.

He groaned, stretched, and looked about curiously at his new land. It was not a cheering sight; he was on a high plateau and had a good view of the lay of the land for many kilometers. The land was rugged, almost ringed, it seemed, by towering volcanic peaks some of which were venting smoke. Below stretched a great plain, but a plain strewn with black rocks and boulders and thick layers of volcanic ash broken occasionally by tiny cinder cones that did not look reassuringly old or extinct.

There was grass, yes; a sickly yellow grass that grew tall and wild and waved in the wind that swirled around the volcanic bowl, and off in the distance he could see a huge body of blue-green water that had to be an ocean. Only near this great sea were there splotches of deep green indicating cultivation.

It was an active landscape. There were rivers, many of them, all in perpetual youth thanks to the obviously continuous volcanism. The source of the water was obvious; the prevailing winds blew in from the sea, were captured and forced up against the high volcanoes, many with snowcaps, and cooled, producing rains that flowed down here in the back country.

He marveled at the extent of his eyesight; everything was incredibly sharp and clear, and he could pick out individual trees farther away than he could have seen anything at all in his old body. His hearing seemed normal; he could hear the rush of wind and the sound of dripping water, neither anything he would expect to have heard differently—before.

Before what? he wondered suddenly. There were roads down there, nice-looking ones, but little sign of habitation. Were all the people in hibernation except him, or did they simply all live near the sea? Animal, vegetable, or mineral?

Well, he was one of them himself now, whatever. He knew that, felt strange and massive. He knew, too, that he could get some idea of his new race by simple self-examination, yet he hesitated, a little afraid at what he might find.

Some big, majestic black birds swooped nearby; for a second he was afraid that they were his new form—but, no, he had no wings, of that he was sure.

Slowly, acting as if the mere sight of his own body would turn him to stone, he looked down at himself.

His new body *was* massive; that was the only word to describe it. No, not huge—although far larger than his old form—but thick, dense. His skin was a metallic blue and seemed thick enough to stop arrow or, perhaps, bullet, and terminated in two very thick legs that rested on large, wide, wickedly clawed feet.

Those claws, he thought idly, look as if they are made of the strongest steel.

His old arms were short and stubby; they now matched the legs, perfectly proportioned to the body and so thick and powerful looking that he would not have been surprised to bend steel bars with them. As he'd seen but four toes he wasn't surprised to find three long, thick fingers faced by an abnormally long opposable thumb.

He raised his hands to his face. The neck was thick and apparently bone plated, but it was difficult to tell anything about his head except that it was more ovoid and flatter than his had been, more like a human's—although it felt hard, thick. It's almost as if I am a huge insect, he thought, with leathery skin over my exoskeleton. He wasn't sure—maybe his guess was close to the mark.

There was some room to move on the plateau so he took a hesitant step forward and immediately realized that, as before, he still had a thick supporting tail, this one longer than his old one. He looked over his shoulder while bringing the tail around, dislodging rocks in the latter operation, and stared. The tail, too, was thick and plated, but there were bony ridges running in pairs from his back down to the tip, and the tip terminated flatly, not pointed, and out of it rose two incredibly wicked-looking spikes, perhaps a meter each. He tested the tail as he would a weapon, and knew that it was exactly that. His old tail was strictly for sitting and balance; this one could be used like a thick tentacle, and those sharp points would close in on just about anything at great speed. He was certain that those of his new race practiced the wielding of it as some human cultures and his own Chugach practiced with swords.

I'm a creature built like a war machine, he told himself. He looked back again at the bleak and violent landscape. If each hex on the Well World was designed to test a lifeform, then that land down there must be very dangerous indeed.

He studied his hands again, flexing the fingers, and discovered that his first impression was correct—the nails were long, nasty sword-points that were retractable with a flick of internal muscles.

Still, he could see the logic of it. He had been assured by Obie that the computer had in some way influenced what each would become, and this form, for all its nasty toughness and bulk, was not so terribly alien to what he'd been. He was not, after all, to live in this place but to make war from it. This was a form built for war.

He tried to reach back into his throat, to the sacs where internal wastes produced the flammable gases of the Chugach, and tried to blow some fire. There was nothing; that ability was gone, and he would miss it. A pity, though, he reflected. Such an ability would be appropriate here, in a land of volcanoes.

The sun was already behind the mountains; dark shadows closed in on the landscape as he watched. Soon it would be very dark, he knew, and he was in the middle of nowhere with no sign of his new people, no sign of huge settlements or even tiny villages, and no weapon with which to defend himself against whatever might be laying in wait for him out there on that darkening plain. He wished for a club, something with which to arm himself against the hidden foes he knew must be waiting, but there weren't even trees from which clubs might be improvised.

He considered staying on the little plateau until morning; it was tempting, but he was ravenously hungry and wasn't even sure what the hell he ate.

He was still pondering this problem in the gathering gloom when the one thing he absolutely least expected occurred.

Down below, in orderly succession, the street lights came on.

It was amazing how the barren landscape was transformed by the tiny lights—thousands, no, tens of thousands of them, stretching out from just below him all the way to where he knew the sea to be. Tremendously variable in color, too; intelligently arranged in geometric patterns of greens, blues, reds, yellows—all the colors. It was beautiful, even if the landscape did now seem to look like a massive aircraft landing field.

Still, the sight puzzled him as much as it fascinated him; there had been roads, yes, but no sign of such an array of electronics that he'd been able to see, nor any sign of where the energy was coming from.

Almost in reply to his thoughts, he felt a slight rumble in the ground, and nearby, dislodged rock fell crashing to the plain below. He knew the answer in an instant—geothermal power. These people had learned to make such a violent land work for them.

There was a pathway down to his right, he saw, but he hesitated before using it. Those lights were electrical; that meant that this was a high-technology hex, a land where machines obeyed the same rules he'd been born and bred to take for granted. That meant communications networks, computers, perhaps, and—guns. He felt confident that he could stop most projectiles, but this skin and bone would be little protection against a laser pistol, for example—particularly one designed by a people to be used on their own kind.

He felt certain there was more danger from his own new race than from any hidden menaces. The civilization had proved out long ago, millions of years perhaps. It had proved itself by conquering whatever horrors his new body was designed to combat, and it had built a technologically sophisticated civilization on that result. There would be no hidden enemies down there, only new ones he would make.

He sighed and started carefully down the path. It wasn't hard, although he had to remind himself now and then that his tail was longer and thinner and solidly weighted, and had to be watched lest it start a landslide of its own.

Vision wasn't much of a problem, he noted with interest. The Chugach had terrible night vision, since they lived beneath the sands and used senses other than sight much of the time. This new form saw extremely well in the daylight and even better at night. Though it distinguished virtually no color the night vision was precise where it needed to be. As he had seen the greens and blues and yellows quite clearly earlier, Marquoz surmised that his night vision emphasized contrast and depth perception at the expense of color. It probably got in the way, he thought—but, no, the color sense *was* still there; he'd seen the differences in the mass of lights.

Tradeoffs, he decided. You had the senses you needed when you needed them. That was convenient.

He hadn't expected much activity so close to the volcano slopes and he wasn't disappointed; these giant volcanos were *active*. Anyone building at the base would be buried in stone and ash, probably. Only a nut would take the risk.

Still, there was some traffic; he heard it as he reached the bottom and started off on the plain. The sounds of trucks and heavy machinery all over. This was a busy place, anyway. He wondered what the hell they did.

It was not long before he reached a road. The lights outlined it in ghostly pale orange; small ball-shaped ones set into the ground, apparently to show the left and right limits of the road.

As he stood alongside the road a vehicle approached. He quickly saw why they needed the limit markers. Not only was the thing gigantic but it was bearing down on him at a tremendously high rate of speed. In only seconds it had approached and roared past him.

He saw the driver, although the maniac never took his eyes off the road markers. The vehicle itself had been a great mechanical shovel built to scoop huge amounts of earth and deposit it elsewhere. It didn't look that different from those of several other races. The driver, though, had afforded him his first real look at his new people.

Centauroid, yes, but two-legged, his face a bony, demonic mask flanked by sharp horns, his eyes seemed to be seas of deep fiery red without pupils. He resembled the demons of Chugach mythology, the kinds of creature his people had used in their darker legends to scare the hell out of children and gullible adults.

He heard a rustling sound nearby. Startled, he whirled on it, only to discover a tiny lizard staring nervously back at him. At his movement it froze, then saw it was spotted and looked up into his face with a hopeful expression.

"Cherk?" it piped in a high, squeaky voice.

"Your guess is as good as mine," he told it, and it seemed to accept that and suddenly scampered off. Nothing nasty from *that* native.

He turned back to the road, trying to decide what to do. He would like merely to be noticed and picked up, he decided, but that was no sure thing along here, not at the speeds the natives drove—and that single-minded, straight-ahead stare on the driver didn't inspire confidence. It would not do, he decided, to get run over by a truck before he'd even said hello.

He started walking alongside the road, choosing the direction leading away from the mountains. That might be a mistake, he knew, as that driver had definitely been going somewhere. Still, there was little sign as to where these people kept themselves in the daytime, or why they were nocturnal despite having keen day vision. There were some interesting puzzles here he'd love to start solving.

A second vehicle roared by him, this time from the opposite direction, not a shovel but an enormous truck filled with gravel or sand or ash or something. The driver didn't see him, either.

He stopped short. Ash! Of course! These huge volcanos probably popped off pretty regularly but the slow, chunky aa lava he'd seen indicated that they were probably not dangerous to people on the plains. It would be the ash that would be the problem—layers of it, meters thick, perhaps, at times. Even if the eruptions only occurred every year or two it would mean frequent rebuilding. After a while the natives would have stopped bothering; they'd have built permanent structures underground, in the most solid bedrock they could find. With a high technology that would be easy. Just as his own Chugach had learned to live with the thick desert sand by building and living below it, so must these people have found refuge from the constant threat of eruption by an underground civilization. Only near the sea, farthest from the volcanos and probably with a good, irregular volcanic coastline that made for deep water harbors, would they exist aboveground.

Idly, he wondered how they coped with seismic quakes but decided that they had had an awfully long time to learn to cope with that. There might well have just been an eruption—they would be hauling away the ash, clearing, and rebuilding. It might well be their chief export, as volcanic ash made the best mineral-rich soil known. Mineral-poor and overworked hexes would pay through the nose for a steady supply.

He began to feel better. Even before he had met or talked with one of these people, he felt he knew them.

He was still deep in such thoughts when five small sledlike hovercraft sped up to him. Each bore a single rider, a demon prince of Chugach legend, and each stopped close to him. They nearly surrounded him. He looked up into their faces and felt childhood fears surface. He pushed them back as best he could and summoned up his courage.

All five wore official-looking leather-like jackets, plus holsters. Empty holsters. The pistols were all out, all pointed at him.

Oddly, he felt better at this. He'd been noticed—probably by one of the truck drivers—and he was now face to face with the local constabulary.

Brazil had told him he would automatically be able to speak their language, so he didn't hesitate. He held up his hands, slowly, palms out, to show that he was carrying no weapons.

"All right, you got me," he said lightly. "I'm an Entry, I think you call it. The new boy here. Take me to your leader or my leader or something like that."

They just sat on their funny little sleds for a moment, staring at him with expressionless, demonic faces, pistols drawn. Finally one with some extra buttons on his jacket hissed in a low and nasty voice, "All right. Move. Start walking."

"Anything you want," Marquoz responded agreeably and started forward. They followed, pistols still drawn, not saying another word.

They walked for several kilometers. Marquoz was thirsty and hungry, but his captors supplied neither rest nor food nor conversation. He was no longer as sure about this culture as he had been, but he knew he didn't like these five.

His first guess had been right as to where the people were, though. They came to a junction and he could see cross-shaped plates where the two roads met. As they approached, one of the plates lowered, forming a downward ramp below the other road. He wondered where the controller was. The way these people drove he fervently hoped that it was efficiently automated.

The surface roads were duplicated below, although he had a fair downhill walk before they reached the living levels. Alongside each cavernous route, though, were moving walkways. He took the walk while his escort kept to the road, although he knew that eyes and weapons were upon him. Still, this was easier; he stood and machines did the work, as he was always sure the gods meant it to be.

Suddenly the walls dropped away and he found himself on a bridge overlooking an enormous cavern, one of the largest he'd ever seen. A city was below him, a stunningly beautiful city aglow in colorful lights. Thousands of people rode the intricate network of moving walkways that passed below him. Occasionally Marquoz and his escort would reach a platform and siding where a truck was loading or unloading what looked like great freight elevators. There were no shafts; the great cubes just seemed to float up and down. He guessed it was somehow done with magnetism.

He'd stopped, absently looking over the view, and that irritated his captors. "Keep moving!" the leader hissed at him.

He stepped back onto the walk and let it carry him. "Sorry," he said, "it was just very beautiful—and very unexpected." That seemed to mollify and please them; after that they didn't seem quite so nasty. They weren't too bright, he reflected. When he'd stepped off the walk to look they'd gone several meters past before they realized he'd stopped. If he had a little more experience being whatever these people were and if he hadn't *wanted* to be a captive, he could have escaped them easily or knocked them all off.

There were uniforms and uniforms, though. Loads of uniforms and symbols of what he took to be rank. It was funny, really. The place looked to be a parody of a military state, an almost perfect place for someone of his talents, background, and experience.

They finally reached the place they wanted, a large elevator or whatever with siding, empty now. "You get in," the leader ordered. "You will be met at the bottom."

He nodded absently and entered, making sure he cleared his spiked tail before the door rumbled closed.

The descent was quick; more, it was fascinating, since the rear of the cube was transparent and afforded him a nice view of the city. He noted absently the little device in one corner of the ceiling that had to be a camera of some kind. He had seen them all over. A dictatorship for sure, he decided. He wondered what the hell they were so scared of.

The view was suddenly masked as the cube settled in its berth and he turned to the door. He felt a bump as the car settled, then the door slid open to reveal a single creature staring at him with those eerie burning eyes. The reception committee's jacket had slightly more decoration; Marquoz had been passed on to a higher-up, although one not very high, he decided. He saw no squads of nervous guards, no hidden cops or nasties. He was disappointed; he was beginning to like being considered an important enemy of the republic or whatever.

"I am Commander Zhart, two hundred ninety-first District," the creature told him, his voice a hissing echo of the man above.

Marquoz bowed slightly and walked slowly from the elevator. "I'm Marquoz, formerly of Chugach, a new Entry to this land and this world," he responded. "Glad to meet someone who'll at least talk to me," he added.

"Just come with me," the commander chided and started off. He followed, noting that the ability to avoid stepping on the spikes of the next person's tail was an art.

"Just where am I?" he asked casually.

"You are in Hakazit," Zhart told him. "Specifically, in Harmony City."

"Hakazit," he repeated. That was how his mind saw it; actually the sounds they were using to converse would have been impossible for human or Chugach. "Well, this is a most fascinating and beautiful land you have here, Commander. I look forward to a new life here."

The commander was pleased. "I must say," he noted, "that you are remarkably calm and relaxed for an Entry. Our last Entry—about thirty years ago—was a frightened wreck."

"Oh, it comes naturally," Marquoz responded casually. "I've spent a good part of my life in strange cultures among alien people. The new and the strange fascinate more."

"A commendable, if surprising, attitude," Zhart approved. "You are a most unusual individual, Marquoz. Tell me, what brought you to such other worlds and creatures? What did you do formerly? A salesman, perhaps?"

Marquoz chuckled. "Oh, my, no! Dear me, no!" He continued chuckling. "I was a spy."

Commander Zhart stopped short, almost causing Marquoz to step on his tail. He looked back gravely at the new Hakazit and tried to decide if he was being put on.

Marquoz was still chuckling. "A salesman indeed!" he snorted.

South Zone

"THERE ARE *HOW* MANY ENTRIES IN THE GATE?"

"Between three and four hundred, Ambassador" came the reply on the intercom.

Serge Ortega settled back on his coiled tail. "All Type Forty-one, you say?"

"That's correct, sir. What do you want done with them? We hardly have facilities for so many."

He thought for a moment. "Keep them there," he instructed. "I'll be down shortly. We'll just have to do a mass introduction right there and shove 'em through the Well in shifts. Get any personnel you might need from the dry-land embassy staffs. And find me a public address amplifier."

"At once, sir."

He did not move at once; they would need some time to set up anyway. He flicked on a televisor screen, one of a number recessed in his curved control console. The screen showed him the great chamber where all those who happened on Markovian gates found themselves. The sight of so many Entries was stunning, even though the chamber was so large that they were still but a small dot in the middle of it. He adjusted some of the controls and zoomed in on them. The other embassies' officials wouldn't be able to tell, of course, but it was clear enough to him. They were all stunning human females and all looked just about exactly alike except for hairstyle and some body decorations. Like that woman, Yua, but without the tail. Olympians.

"So it's begun." He sighed. Slowly, still considering

all the steps he might take, he slithered out the door and down the long corridor to the entry chamber.

It took very little time to brief them, a lot longer to organize the multiracial staff that would escort them in groups of ten or so to the Well Gate. The Olympians all knew what they were about; Brazil and his agents had briefed them ahead of time. But even this early, the pretense was gone—except one, of course. They all claimed that their planet was being destroyed and that a strange little man named Brazil had offered to save them.

That was bad enough. The other staff members would be rushing back to their bosses with the news that Brazil was alive, that he was actively shoving an entire planetary civilization through—and who knew what else?

It took several hours to handle the whole operation. Still uncertain as to his immediate course of action, Ortega called the Czillian Embassy, explained the situation, and advised that race of scholarly plant creatures to activate the Crisis Center at their computer-laden central research complex. The others would have to be briefed, and soon, before they started jumping to the wrong conclusions and taking even worse action unilaterally than they would collectively. A Council meeting, a great conference call of all the seven hundred and one ambassadors, who currently kept embassies at Zone, would have to be called. Ortega was about to order it when his intercom buzzed.

"Yes?" he snapped, annoyed. He needed time to set this all up, time to get everything together, and, most of all, he needed time just to think.

"Sir! It's incredible! No sooner did we clear the last group than an identical group appeared! At least as many as before! Sir! What do we do now?"

Ortega sighed. No time, damn it all. No time at all. "I wish I knew," he told the panicked aide. "I really wish I knew."

Awbri

She awoke with a start. The last thing she remembered was stepping into that blackness, and now, as if waking from a long sleep, here she was—where?

On a damned tree branch, she realized suddenly, and pretty precariously balanced. All around her an enormous forest grew, a jungle, really, stretching out on all sides as well as above and below her. No sunlight seemed to penetrate the dense growth, although some must, she knew, in order for there to be so much green.

She knew immediately that her body had changed. The fact that she was grasping the thick branch with clawed hands and with feet that felt very much like hands told her as much.

She had never been particularly fond of great heights, but this was somehow different. She felt no vertigo and had a fair sense of confidence; the limb seemed almost a natural place to be.

Almost without thinking about it she let loose the branch and looked at one hand. Very long, thin fingers of tough skin covered with light reddish-brown fur. Moving the hand up and over generated other movement, and she felt a slight drag on her right side. She twisted her head and saw that there were tremendous folds of skin starting at her wrist and down the length of her body. She couldn't imagine what the skin was for, but some flexing showed that it was tough and also covered in the reddish-brown fur yet stretchable, almost like rubber.

She risked movement on the branch and realized

almost immediately that she had a tail. Trying to keep a good hold on the branch she twisted around to see it. Broad, flat, and squared off at the end, it was not one tail but a series of bones that, fanlike, she could open or close, to widen or narrow the tail. Between was the same rubbery membranous skin.

She was still staring, trying to figure out what to do next, when she heard a sudden tremendous noise and the tree shook. Frightened, she tightened her grip with all four hands.

"You there! Just what the hell do you think you're doing in my tree?" snapped an odd, high nasal voice just above her.

She started and looked up to see who was speaking. It was easy to see him—but a shock as well, for she knew instantly that she now looked much like the creature who stared at her angrily.

His head was small and flat, almost like a dog's except for the mouth, which resembled the bill of a duck. A long neck led to a rodent's body, soft and lithe, looking as if it were capable of bending in any several directions all at once. He too had the flat fanlike tail and the long, thin, powerful-looking arms and legs. The thing was also almost a quarter larger than she, and its fur was a mottled gray.

"I'm sorry, but I'm new here. I came in at Zone and was sent through the Gate and woke up here as this. I'm afraid I don't know where I am or what I am. I don't even know how to get down from here."

The creature's feline eyes widened slightly in surprise. "So you're an Entry, huh? You must be, otherwise you'd never make crazy statements like that. Get *down?* Why in the world would you want to get *down?*"

"Well, I have to get *somewhere,*" she responded, a little irritated at the man.

"You can't stay here, that's for sure," the creature snorted. "Hell, I have too many mouths to feed now."

"But I don't know where to go," she said. "I just woke up here on this branch. If you'll just tell me *something.*"

He seemed to be considering things. "Don't have

time to dawdle over your problems," he told her. "Right now you just get off my tree and that'll be the end of *my* problem."

"I don't think you're being very friendly at all," she huffed. "And, besides, I'd love to get off this diseased old tree if only I knew how."

"Diseased! I'll have you know that this tree is one of the best in all Awbri! Why, alone, all year it supports twenty-two people! Now what do you think of *that?"*

"To be honest," she said truthfully, "I couldn't care less. I'm sorry I called your tree diseased, but I would very much like to know how to get off it and where to go from there. Don't you have some sort of government here, some kind of authority?"

He cocked his head slightly, as if thinking about something. "Well, I suppose you can go to the local Council. We don't need much here in Awbri; no big government or things like that. The Council's the biggest thing about here, so that's where you should go. The cowbrey bush in the center of the glade yonder, maybe half a kilometer that way." He pointed with a foot, idly, index finger outstretched. Truly there were no differences between hands and feet on these people.

She looked in the indicated direction but could see nothing but trees and undergrowth.

"How do I get there?" she asked him. "Walk along the branches from tree to tree?"

He gave a sound that sounded like spitting. "If you want to, sure. But you can fly through a lot easier. The way's been cut, as you can see."

She stared. It was true. Openings had been cut, trimmed through the lush growth like roadways in the air. But—fly?

"I—I don't know how to fly," she told him.

He made that sound again. "Damn! Well, I don't have time to teach you. Crawl along, then; you'll get there sooner or later."

And suddenly he was off, before she could say another word, shaking the tree again as he leaped into the air, spreading hands and feet and opening his fan tail, sailing off down one of those avenues.

She sighed and started to make her way along the

branches in the direction he'd indicated. She couldn't say much for the manners of these people but there were some possibilities here that were exciting. Never had she felt so keen a sense of balance nor fantastic depth perception! To fly, like that—man?—had flown!

She would learn, she told herself. She would soar effortlessly through space with confidence someday. She could hardly wait.

The journey was not without its problems. The branches were often several meters apart and she was a long time getting the confidence to jump from one to another over such a wide gap. She always made it, though, with unerring accuracy.

She met other—people—too. Most ignored her or looked at her strangely but none bothered to stop and talk. They jumped from every limb of every tree and they flew all over the place, mostly going to and fro on errands that were unclear to her. A few were more obvious; they scampered up and down thick trunks and off onto limbs great and small, spraying and cutting and pruning their trees. Clearly these trees were life in them, they ate their leaves and fruit, they lived symbiotically.

Here and there she came across spots clear to the sun above or to the forest floor below. She immediately understood why the man had wondered at her request to go down; it was an ugly swamp down there, covered with sticky mud, stagnant water, and the occasional growth. Occasionally she spotted great, nasty-looking reptiles, all teeth, lying in mud holes or sliding through the bogs. Not the kind of creatures she really wanted to meet on their own ground. Fortunately, none looked capable of climbing trees.

She finally reached the glade, a nobby knoll of high ground atop which grew the largest tree she'd ever seen, a great green ball that towered above the other trees and masked the sky that should have been visible. It was a good hundred meters or more from the end of her tree to the beginning of the great one.

The muddy swamp was still below her, then the knoll rose, covered with sharp grass stalks leading up to the tree. A large number of Awbrians flitted back and forth effortlessly above the swamp, but she was hesitant. A hundred meters was a long way and she couldn't possibly manage that kind of jump.

She called out to passing Awbrians but they ignored her pleas and went on about their business, only an occasional passing glance showing that she was being ignored, not overlooked.

She sighed. The light was growing dim; darkness was something she would not like to face here without some kind of refuge. She cursed Obie if he had indeed made her this, and she cursed the Awbrians who ignored her. She was a High Priestess, damn it all! She was used to making an utterance and having it instantly carried out. Never before had she felt so ignored and helpless.

Never before had she felt so alone.

She heard a rustle and an Awbrian landed near her, vibrating the tree. She was used to it by now.

"You look like you're in trouble," the creature remarked. "Are you hurt?"

She turned anxiously, relieved to find a friendly voice, relieved that somebody had acknowledged her existence.

"No, I'm not hurt, thanks," she responded. "I'm just new. I'm—well, I was a different kind of creature until I woke up here a few hours ago. I'm confused and alone and scared."

The Awbrian, a female, clicked her bill in sympathy. "An Entry, huh? And I guess somebody sent you to the Elders."

She nodded. "I guess so. These—Elders. They're the same as the village Council?"

The other made a head motion that also seemed to be a nod. "Yes, sort of. I guess they are the ones to handle you." She turned, facing the tree. "There's only one way to get there. It's easy."

"You mean—fly?" Yua was more than hesitant.

"Sure. Oh, it won't quite be flying here. Just get an idea of the breeze, go with it, jump off like you were aiming at a nearby branch, spread out your arms, legs, and tail, and look straight at the cowbrey bush there. You'll get there. You won't fall. Trust me and don't panic. When I jump off, you follow right away." She poised for the leap.

"Wait!" Yua cried. "Let me get my courage up for this. Tell me—this land is called Awbri?"

"That's right," the other agreed. "Well, come on. It's getting dark and I don't like to be away from my tree at night." With that she launched herself.

Steeling herself, Yua, too, jumped off and spread her tail and the folds of skin. She was amazed at how the air seemed to push against her, keeping her aloft as if in a long leap, although she was falling, very slowly, and the whole thing felt like descending in an elevator.

It was actually only thirty seconds or so until she reached the tree, but it seemed an eternity, and she feared she wasn't going to make it. She didn't dare look down, though; she kept her eyes on the tree and on the friendly woman nearby.

And now she was there, in the branches. She grabbed and hung on for all she was worth. That she had done it did nothing to calm her down, so she clung tightly to the limb until the shakes had subsided somewhat.

Her friend had already scampered off deep into the interior of the tree but Yua was in no condition to follow.

Several minutes later the woman was back, looking slightly amused at Yua's still trembling perch. "Oh, come on! You did the worst of it! Follow me. I've told the Elder's Secretary that you are an Entry and here and they want to see you immediately. Hurry along now! I have to be getting home. It's almost too late." And with that she was off.

Yua followed her with her eyes until the woman was out of sight. I never even knew her name, she thought. Taking a few deep breaths she relaxed and headed into the interior of the cowbrey bush.

The entrance was easy to spot as she approached the great trunk, for there was a large door in the tree, decorated with unfamiliar carved symbols. Yua opened the door hesitantly and entered.

Oil lanterns lit the interior; it was bright, cheery,

and absolutely hollow. For a plant that appeared so healthy outside it was a nothing in its base.

A large male was seated behind a carved wooden desk writing with what appeared to be a quill pen. He looked something like a great duck-billed squirrel wearing large horn-rimmed bifocals.

He stopped writing and looked up at her. "You are the Entry?" he asked crisply.

She nodded. "I am Yua, formerly of Olympus," she told him.

He sat back, relaxed. "We don't get many Entries," he told her. "You're the first I've ever met. Had a devil of a time going through the manuals of procedure to see what is to be done with you." He gestured at a large bookcase filled with impressive-looking red-bound volumes.

"However, the first thing I'm supposed to do is welcome you to Awbri. Welcome. The second is to give you this little speech."

She sighed and relaxed. The Awbrians were a tough people to like.

"First of all, we don't know who or what you were before you came here," he continued, "nor do we care. That is irrelevant. You are on the Well World to stay and the sooner you forget your former life and adjust to your new one the better off you'll be. You are now an Awbrian. This, too, will not change. You come to us from an alien form, but, more important, you come from an alien culture. Adjusting to your new physical form will be relatively easy; the cultural adjustment, however, is very difficult. You must accept the culture that has existed here for tens of thousands of years before you were born. You will probably not like it at first, will find it uncomfortable or hard to accept. The important thing to remember is that it *is* the culture here, it *is* the product of millennia of social evolution, and it works for us. We will do what we can to help you in that adjustment. Any questions?"

"Hundreds," she replied. "But—tell me of this culture. I have seen some of it and guessed some, but I would like to know it all."

"You'll learn it in the days to come," the secretary

assured her. "However, some basics. We are divided into family groups, each group having a tree. It is their tree and no other's. You can use another family's tree to pass through, but for no other purpose. Almost all the trees are hollow, as is this one, and those are used for living quarters. If a tree is carefully managed it can support a reasonable population, since the rain-forest climate here allows phenomenal growth. For every five thousand population there is a village Council on which the wisest men called Elders, sit. Age is revered here. There is also, off in Gaudoi, around the Well Gate, a Maintenance Administration that makes sure the paths and airways are kept clear, administers what little trade there is between the various villages, and settles intervillage disputes."

"I notice you say wisest *men*," she said carefully. "Then it is the men who run things here?"

The secretary's bill opened slightly in surprise. He was not ready for the question and thought a moment.

"There is a division of responsibility, culturally," he replied. "Exterior maintenance of the tree, cultivation of leaves and fruits and the careful management of the harvest, are the responsibility of the males, who also assume the role of protector of the tree and family against anything. They also represent the family group to the outside. Females have the responsibility for internal maintenance, including cleaning, furnishing, and decorating, as well as food preparation and distribution and the bearing and rearing of the young."

It didn't sound like such a logical deal to Yua, but she let it go for now.

"What about professions?" she asked. "Surely not everyone is a tree farmer."

"There are some," the secretary told her. "I am of the professions. There are, after all, a large number of excess males for whom there is nothing in family life to offer support. Doctors, lawyers, traders, and maintenance personnel are needed. Those books had to be written by someone and printed and bound and distributed by others, for example."

She frowned. "Excess males? No females?"

He cleared his throat lightly. "I know that there are some cultures where the females have a different role, but not here. I mean, after all, one male can, ah, service a number of females but not the other way around. It is only logical, you see."

She didn't see the logic of it at all. It was more than a slight shock to come from a culture where males were almost nonexistent and used for only one purpose, anyway, to such a culture as this.

"So what is my place in such a culture?" she asked warily.

"Tonight you'll sleep here as the guest of the Elders," he responded casually. "Tomorrow you'll be interviewed by them, then placed with a family willing to accept you."

She didn't like that. "And suppose I don't want to go with that family—or any other?"

He actually chuckled. "Oh, there is no choice. After all, what would you eat? And where? Where would you sleep at night? You see? Here you must have a family and a tree or you starve and die. Don't worry, though. There are potions, things like that, to help you adjust, forget your former cultural patterns and fit in."

The fact was that it *did* worry her. She didn't want to be drugged and passed on to some oppressive, nasty male to whom she was only a bearer of babies. She couldn't afford to be. She had been sent to the Well World not as a refugee but as a soldier. She had things to do, and this sort of life was not part of it, would *never* be a part of her existence.

But—she had no really clear idea of what it was she was supposed to do once here. Obie had said that things would work out so that she'd know when the time was ripe, but when would that be? What if he was wrong? What if Awbri wasn't where and what she was supposed to be?

She didn't know what to do, and, worse, she had only one night to figure something out.

She only knew that this wasn't what she expected, not at all . . .

South Zone

"THEY'VE BEEN COMING THROUGH STEADILY," ORTEGA said to the Southern ambassadors and the representative from the North. "So far we're processing about one hundred an hour and there's no sign of stoppage. In fact, the number continues to grow. Already we've called upon some of you to supply extra manpower, even army units, to keep everything orderly—but that won't last. We're literally being flooded with people!"

"What about simply leaving them in the chamber?" an ambassador asked. "Won't that block the arrival of newcomers?"

"For a time," Ortega acknowledged. "But the place isn't set up as a living area. We have no way to feed them or eliminate their wastes."

"You say it's an entire planetary population?" another voice chimed in. "Good heavens, man! That could mean billions! Do you realize what that will do to us? The world can't support such a population! It'll be chaos, social, political, and economic. It could destroy us! Something *must* be done!"

The massing of mutterings indicated that this ambassador had a lot of support.

"In all the history of the Well World," one said, "there has never been such an event. An entire planetary population! It's like the Markovians all over again, but the planet is already populated. Many of our ecosystems are in a very delicate balance, which this influx will tip. I say we have no choice. For our own well-being, we must kill these newcomers as they arrive."

His conclusion shocked a lot of them. Silence

reigned for a moment, although Ortega knew that many of the ambassadors would overcome their shock and start thinking just that way.

"This isn't a random occurrence," Ortega suddenly announced. "It is deliberate. You all know that there is a surviving Markovian technician, Nathan Brazil. He is behind this. I think for a particular reason."

There was quiet on the other end. They were listening.

"You all know the standing rule if Brazil were to appear today. His mental state wasn't all that great the last time. I know—I was there. Even then he was claiming to be God, the one creator of the Universe, Markovians, and all. We don't know what another thousand years have done to his mind. Should he get into the Well of Souls again he might take a different course. Suppose his god complex has grown? Suppose he decides to play god for real next time? You know the fear is a real one. You know that once inside he could do anything he wants. Procedures have long been established to stop him and keep him captive should he arrive.

"Well, colleagues, I believe the time has come. Brazil is going to appear again, this time deliberately, and all this confusion is but a smokescreen. He may be mad, but he's not stupid. He knows we're laying for him. What better way to mask his coming and increase his chances of success than by camouflaging his actions in this way? By finding a planet in trouble, dying, and running its population through. He knows what chaos the overcrowding will cause. And while we're coping with total disruption, he'll try to sneak past us. Kill them? No, I don't think that's the solution. What would we do with the bodies? Better we cope with the mob, for the moment putting up the newcomers in our home hexes as local conditions allow. The genocide option is open to us at any time as long as we keep track of these Entries. Right now let's just concentrate on orderly processing—but send in some really good troops to guard the Well Gate. He must go through it. Once he's through I'll wager the flood of new Entries will slack off. But he must not pass!"

All present murmured agreement to that.

"For now I'll set up what procedures I can," Ortega told them. "I hope all you air-breathers will cooperate by sending whatever personnel in whatever quantities are necessary. Troops will be posted with adequate weapons. If Brazil tries to sneak through, they will be instructed to shoot to kill."

Dillia

MAVRA CHANG AWOKE. IT WAS SLIGHTLY CHILLY but not unpleasant; a peaceful forest with the sound of a running stream nearby. She was relieved; going through the Well hadn't been any trouble at all.

She began to move forward and instantly stopped. She turned to examine her body, then she started cursing.

Damn Obie! she thought angrily. She was still a centaur! He had known it—that had been why he'd insisted she keep the Rhone form. He was getting her used to it.

She walked down to the water. There was a waterfall, small but pleasant-looking, churning the water below but it ran off into a broad pool and almost slowed to a start. Just downstream a bit it was almost a mirror-like lake and she quickly took advantage of it.

She was not the same centaur she'd been, she saw that reflected in the pool. She was larger, stronger, more powerful-looking. Her head and the equine part of her body were covered with a yellowish hair, blonde and majestic. Her body, amply-built but strong and sturdy, was light-skinned and her face retained no trace of its Oriental cast. It was a strong, attractive face with, of all things, blue eyes staring back at her from the reflection.

And yet there was something oddly familiar in the visage, as if it reminded her of someone she'd known long ago. She couldn't think of who it might be; she'd never seen anyone so fair of skin nor with blue eyes—except—who?

A memory stirred, struggled, then came forth, a

memory so long buried that she could never have recalled it on her own. Obie had been at work; his reach extended past his own demise.

A tall, handsome, muscular man with deep-blue eyes and a smaller, stunningly beautiful dark-haired woman with very fair skin.

Her parents.

Somehow she knew now, understood what the Well had done. Mavra Chang had been the creation of back-alley surgeons, a shape and form so different that none would ever recognize her as the refugee child from a doomed planet.

This was what she would have looked like if she'd been allowed to grow up normally, to be the true child of her parents.

Despite the centaur's form, for the first time in her life she was seeing herself as she might have existed in human form. It startled her, even scared her a little. She shivered, only partly because of the slight chill.

She looked around her. High mountains off in the distance, not very far, really. She was essentially up in them even now. She knew where she was, where she must be. She'd come out of those mountains once before, the strange, quiet peaks of the hex named Gedemondas. This was Dillia, the land of peaceful, centaurs, uplake—at the head of a massive glacial body of water. There was a village down there, she knew. Filled with friendly centaurs who drank and smoked and told great stories. And up there, in those mountains, was the strange mountain race who had powers and senses beyond understanding.

She seemed to understand Obie's intent, but she was still alone, in a chilly forest, without even a coat to keep out the chill.

All right, Mavra, she told herself. Here you are the would-be warrior queen with no followers and no army. Here you are, a long, long way from Glathriel and Ambreza, naked and alone and you're supposed to start a revolution.

All right, superwoman, she told herself, you're on your own now. No Brazil, no Obie, nobody. Just the way you wanted it to be. Now how are you going to do the job you have to do?

She sighed and turned, walking slowly from the stream toward the village she knew was there. First warm clothing, some food and drink, then conquer the world, she told herself.

Yeah. Conquer the world. You and what army? the darker part of her whispered. She had no reply.

Durbis, on the Coast of Flotish

HE WALKED ALONG THE DOCK IN THE GATHERING twilight, slowly, confidently. He reached into a pocket and pulled out a pack of cigarettes, removing one and lighting it with a custom-made lighter. The sound of his boots clumped hollowly on the boardwalk as he approached a particular dock and looked at the ship anchored there.

"Hello, aboard!" he called out.

The ship, a sleek two-masted schooner, seemed deserted.

"Hello, there!" he yelled again. "Anybody aboard?"

A scaly horror of a face peered over the rail at him, fish eyes, unblinking, staring at him suspiciously. "Hello, yourself," the creature croaked. "Who the hell are you and what do you want?"

"I contacted your agency in Zone," he called back. "I understand you are for charter."

"Come aboard," the creature said sharply.

He walked confidently up the gangplank and onto the ship. The creature turned to meet him, both round eyes still fixed on the stranger.

The creature was a Flotish; humanoid in that it had head, arms, and legs in the right places, but otherwise totally alien. It was a sea creature, of that there was no doubt; its thick, scaly body looked somewhat armorplated, like scales atop an exoskeleton; its hands and feet were webbed and clawed and oversize for the body, and its face was a horror with unblinking large yellow eyes. It had fins in several places and a dorsal fin on its back. It had no business here, not in the upper air, and in fact it normally breathed through gills although it could exist in air for several hours before it would finally suffocate. It solved its breathing problem simply, with a small apparatus worn helmet-like around its gills and resting above the dorsal on its back. Not good for long periods, it nonetheless allowed the creature a measure of comfort in the atmosphere.

"Come into the main cabin," the Flotish invited. "I have a tank there that makes things easier on me."

He followed and saw that it was so; the tank allowed the creature to relax in sea water while keeping its head out in the air. There was no furniture that fit his form, which was natural, so he sat on the edge of a table and faced the strange sea creature.

"It's not often that I see water-breathers with surface ships," he remarked.

"They go down in our waters, we get them, fix them up, refloat them, and sell them for a profit," the Flotish replied. "It's a good business, salvage, particularly good when you're bordered by land on four sides."

He nodded. "I wish to buy this one," he told the creature.

"Medium?"

He smiled. "Gold, if you want, or diamonds. Even if you don't use the medium yourself they're useful in exchange."

"Either is acceptable," the Flotish replied agreeably. "We'll deal in gold. This ship has been completely refitted. It's in tip-top shape, was down because it was swamped by an incompetent captain in a storm. No structural damage; we had it refloated within two days. Good hardwood, solid."

He nodded. "I like the looks of it. There's an auxiliary engine?"

"Steam," the sea creature said. "Brand new, not salvage. You can see the small stack aft. Useful only in emergencies, though. You wouldn't make two knots with it. It's when you let out the sail in a fair breeze that this thing really moves. Eighteen, twenty knots. A fantastic ship. As is, forty-seven kilos."

The man laughed. "You've got to be kidding. Forty-seven kilos of gold? You could buy a dreadnaught for that."

"But dreadnaughts require records," the Flotish responded. "This does not. No records, no bills of sale, yet all legal and aboveboard. Not traceable, since it's a salvage refit."

"I could buy a new one for half that amount," the man retorted.

"Less," the creature agreed. "But you wouldn't be here if that were your first criterion. I don't know what you're planning—smuggling, piracy, or what. But we wouldn't be meeting in this way if it was anything honest and you know it. You get what you pay for and what you're paying for is a great ship and total anonymity."

The visitor chuckled again. "It's not as bad as that," he told the creature. "It's convenience. Flotish is near where I have to be, and timing is more important than hidden registry. Twenty kilos and I'm being robbed at that."

The creature chuckled evilly. "Twenty won't get you a lifeboat. Forty."

They went back and forth for a while, each giving a little, until finally they were haggling over grams and not kilograms.

"Thirty-one, my final offer," the man told the Flotish. "That's it. Any more and I'll gamble on a little extra time and go up to Vergutz."

The creature spit. "They'll sell you trash. But—all right! Thirty-one it is. You'll make the transfer through Zone?"

He nodded. "You'll know the name. Nobody else is likely to use anything remotely like it. Now I'll need a crew. Versatile, good sailors, experienced on this type of craft. Men who stay bought if overpaid."

The Flotish looked thoughtful. "I think something might be arranged."

"I'm sure it can," Gypsy replied.

South Zone

THEY WERE COMING IN BY THE THOUSANDS. IT WAS unbelievable, Ortega thought. He wondered how the hell Brazil had managed it. The Well was coping, sending Entries evenly to the Southern hexes, but so far the impact had been small. If this kept up, though, it would soon tax their entire resources. Already he was getting reports of killings in some of the hexes and a panic mentality setting in. People had been killed because they were *thought* to be Entries.

They trooped down the hall in a steady stream, halting only every once in a while so that an ambassador from a water hex could flood the chamber and move to a gate himself to report home.

The Entries moved under the watchful eyes of hardened troops of dozens of races, all armed with wicked crossbows and similar weapons. Although all technology worked here, sophisticated weapons would not keep the peace. It didn't matter what killed you, though; a bolt of searing fire or a spring-propelled arrow.

It was more than a week before something new happened. He heard it, heard the shouts and yells and screams and tramping of feet, and was immediately out into the corridor. Frightened Olympians pressed back against the walls to avoid being trampled by the formidable serpentine ambassador as he moved with amazing speed toward the source of the commotion.

There were a number of soldiers there, all standing around something, some great insects with nasty-looking projectile weapons, were all staring down at a body on the floor.

He pushed his way through the mob and came up to the body, still bleeding profusely. No less than sixteen arrows penetrated all parts of the body, including the skull which was crushed from the back.

The figure was a man, lying face down in a pool of blood. He leaned over and examined the body carefully. There was no question; it was dead beyond any hope of magical resurrection or reconstruction. This was no trick. Slowly, carefully, Ortega turned the body over. The look of stunned surprise was still on the dead face, eyes staring wide but no longer seeing the missiles which killed him.

He felt odd, not relieved one bit but almost unbelieving at that face.

"So it was a crock of shit all along," he sighed, talking to the dead body. "And your luck finally ran out." He looked up at the insectile soldiers who had done the deed. "You can relax a little now. You've just done the impossible. There's no doubt in my mind. Nathan Brazil is dead at last."

*

This adventure will conclude in
TWILIGHT AT THE WELL OF SOULS:
The Legacy of Nathan Brazil,
Volume 5 of The Saga of The Well World.
(To be published Fall, 1980)

About the Author

JACK L. CHALKER was born in Norfolk, Virginia, on December 17, 1944, but was raised and has spent most of his life in Baltimore, Maryland. He learned to read almost from the moment of entering school, and by working odd jobs had amassed a large book collection by the time he was in junior high school, a collection now too large for containment in his quarters. Science fiction, history, and geography all fascinated him early on, interests that continue.

Chalker joined the Washington Science Fiction Association in 1958 and began publishing an amateur SF journal, *Mirage,* in 1960. After high school he decided to be a trial lawyer, but money problems and the lack of a firm caused him to switch to teaching. He holds bachelor degrees in history and English, and an M.L.A. from the Johns Hopkins University. He taught history and geography in the Baltimore public schools between 1966 and 1978, and now makes his living as a freelance writer. Additionally, out of the amateur journals he founded a publishing house, The Mirage Press, Ltd., devoted to nonfiction and bibliographic works on science fiction and fantasy. This company has produced more than twenty books in the last nine years. His hobbies include esoteric audio, travel, working on science-fiction convention committees, and guest lecturing on SF to institutions such as the Smithsonian. He is an active conservationist and National Parks supporter, and he has an intensive love of ferryboats, with the avowed goal of riding every ferry in the world. In fact, in 1978, he was married to Eva Whitley on an ancient ferryboat in midriver. They live in the Catoctin Mountain region of western Maryland.